PROXY

GARY GIBSON

Brain in a Jar
BOOKS

First Published by Brain in a Jar Books 2022

First Edition.

Cover art by Ben Baldwin.

❀ Created with Vellum

CONTENTS

AUTHOR'S NOTE

The final draft of this novel was completed in late September 2019. The first reported outbreak of coronavirus in the Wuhan Province of mainland China occurred three months later, on 31 December 2019.

CHAPTER
ONE

STACY

As soon as the train pulled into St. Pancreas, passengers started pushing open overhead bins, squeezing past each other, or dragging heavy luggage on their way to the doors. Stacy Cotter, however, remained in her seat, staring fixedly out at the grey expanse of the station platform, gripped by a familiar panic.

Was it too late now, she wondered, to turn back? To return to the life she had made for herself in Paris? A small and quiet life, certainly, with small pleasures and a minor administrative role in an academic publishing house. But one that was, nonetheless, pleasingly anonymous.

Then she reminded herself for the thousandth time why she had come all this way and finally forced herself to stand.

Pulling a single, small bag over one shoulder, Stacy joined the flow of bodies out of the train and onto the platform. Nobody looked at her: indeed, nobody had paid her the slightest bit of attention from the moment she had first boarded the train back at Gare du Nord.

Yet there remained that same lingering fear that she was

being watched—that her every movement was on the verge of being splashed across social media.

How many times, back in the bad old days, had she glanced over her shoulder only to find someone with their phone or bracelet up, its lens pointed straight at her, a cruel smirk twisting their mouths out of shape?

Too many by far.

So when she glanced around the concourse, it was not entirely a shock to discover a man about the same age as her —twenty-four or twenty-five, give or take—staring at her from a neighbouring platform with a puzzled expression, as if she might be someone he knew but couldn't quite place.

She ducked her head down and picked up her pace, tugging her hoodie up until it partly concealed her face. Her bobbed hair was the very opposite of the style she'd worn when she had fled the British Isles, but clearly that wasn't enough to conceal her identity from those with long enough memories.

The station was filled with a cacophony of voices, synthe-sised and otherwise, announcing departures or delays as she followed in the wake of the other train passengers. The station, she saw, was dotted with even more cameras than she remembered, whether hidden within dark mirrored domes or nakedly visible. She hunched her shoulders and kept her head down, all too aware that English paparazzi were in the habit of secreting illegal lenses in train stations and airports in the hope of catching the great and the good unawares.

Or maybe, she thought as she hurried along the platform towards the main concourse, she was fretting over nothing: when she had last spoken with Wilber via an encrypted app, he had repeatedly assured her that both the press and the public had long since forgotten about her. It had been years, he had reminded her, since the scandal that once made her briefly notorious.

Even so, her heart beat faster when she passed her data

bracelet above the security gate and it chimed to let her pass into the security zone of St. Pancreas. Medical border staff stood at tables, wearing surgical masks and latex gloves, waiting to process the new arrivals from the European mainland.

When her turn finally came, Stacy handed over both of her passports—her regular passport and her medical one. A government information film, demonstrating how to detect signs of pandemic and whom to report them to, ran on a wall-mounted screen nearby.

Then, at last, Stacy found herself alone in the centre of the station's main concourse and realized she no longer remembered which way to go. Everything looked dustier and more decrepit than she remembered, and most of the shop windows were boarded over. Then again, only a few people could afford to travel abroad these days, so perhaps this wasn't so surprising.

Just for a moment, Stacy's gaze met that of another man, clad in a green bomber jacket and standing at a kiosk close by one of the station exits. He quickly glanced away, focusing a little too intently on an interactive station guide next to the kiosk. He had dark hair cropped close to his skull and a slight overbite. After another moment he tapped his data bracelet and walked out through the exit and out of sight.

She had the sudden nagging sensation she'd seen him somewhere before. Had he been on the same train from Paris?

No, she decided: she was imagining things. He was just another random passerby, like the man she'd caught staring at her from a neighbouring platform. Perhaps he, too, had been trying to place her, and perhaps days from now he might remember something about a girl who looked just like her, and who had been all over the news a few short years before.

At worst, he could be a journalist, staking out the station.

But it didn't matter: he was gone now, disappeared into the bustle of the London streets.

Stacy forced herself to relax and breathe more evenly. Tapping at her own bracelet, she spoke her destination, and the bracelet vibrated against her wrist to indicate which way she should go.

Turning, she at last saw the sign for the subway and made her way down the broad stone steps leading to the underground platform.

———

DISEMBARKING AT ANGEL STATION, Stacy made her way back up broad steps leading to a wide boulevard. She tasted the warm, muggy air of a city she hadn't set foot in for the better part of a decade. Everything looked different after so many years in Paris; or perhaps, she mused, it was she who had undergone the greater change.

Making her way across the street, she felt some of the tension that had been building up inside her ever since she had decided to return home from Paris finally begin to dissipate. Those men she had caught looking her way had no idea who she was. Few had reason to remember Stacy Cotter— except perhaps for Martin Wilber, the man who had agreed to tell her story.

The *true* story.

You're just yesterday's news, Stacy reminded herself. The thought was curiously comforting. It wasn't like there was a lack of fresh scandals to keep people entertained on their morning commute.

Finding her way blocked by unexpected building works, Stacy tapped once again at her bracelet until it provided her with a new route. Then, as she turned to retrace her steps, she saw the same man she had seen back in the station, recognisable by his green bomber jacket, turn the corner towards her.

His gaze remained fixed on the pavement, but some instinct made her certain beyond all doubt that he had followed her here, all the way from St. Pancreas.

At last, his gaze flicked up and their eyes met. His expression didn't change, but he immediately came to a halt and began tapping at his bracelet, as if consulting it for directions. At no point did he appear to acknowledge he even knew she was there before at last turning to walk back the way he'd come with an unhurried pace.

Now she was sure she'd seen him somewhere before. Feeling a tightness in her lungs, Stacy forced herself to breathe out. But where had—?

And just like that, Stacy remembered exactly where.

She had seen him not once, but several times, in a coffee shop she frequented close by her flat in Paris's twentieth arrondissement.

What was he doing here in London, and seemingly following her, when the medical visas necessary to cross most international borders could cost a small fortune?

Stacy lifted her data bracelet to her mouth and called Wilber. She heard the slight tremble in her voice as she spoke his name. He picked up immediately.

"Miss Cotter?" Wilber asked. "You're on your way?"

"Someone's following me," she said, crossing to the other side of the street and turning right to join the flow of pedestrians down St John's Street. "I saw him in Paris, and now he's here."

There was a slight pause before Wilber replied. "You're quite certain he's following you?"

"Very."

"Another journalist, perhaps? Or—?"

He paused, and she finished his sentence for him. "Or sent by Raphael?" she said breathlessly, picking up her pace. "It's possible."

"Where are you right now?" he asked.

"St John's Street."

Another pause. "So you must be walking towards Friend Street?"

Glancing ahead, she saw a street sign confirming what the journalist had said. "I am."

"Excellent," said Wilber. She heard a slight strain in his voice and guessed he was climbing the steps from the basement café where they had arranged to meet. "There's a pub down the other end of Friend Street called the—"

"The Black Friar," she said, suddenly remembering it from years before. "Yes, I know it."

"It's much closer to where you are than the café," he said. "I think it's best we get you off the street as soon as possible. We'll meet at the Friar instead." His voice huffed slightly as if he were hurrying. "I'll be there in a minute or two. All right?"

"Sounds good," she agreed, cutting the connection and picking up her pace even more. A moment before she turned into Friend Street, she glanced back over her shoulder: to her endless relief, there was no sign of anyone in a bomber jacket.

Friend Street was quiet and residential, with hardly any foot traffic. She could see the warm and welcoming lights of the Black Friar pub up ahead at the next corner. Her footsteps echoed loudly on the concrete, and she slowed a little to catch her breath.

A taxi passed her, its batteries emitting a soft hum. It pulled up sharply just a few metres in front of Stacy. She faltered, afraid of who might emerge, but the man who disembarked from the taxi wasn't anyone she'd seen before; he quickly ascended the steps of a house, touching his bracelet to the lock of the front door and stepping through as it swung open without once glancing her way.

The taxi, a flimsy-looking plastic bubble with two empty couches facing each other, drove itself off into the distance.

You're overreacting, Stacy chided herself, and resumed walking.

Stacy had hardly taken more than a few steps before someone slammed into her from behind, hard enough to knock her off her feet. Fingers wrapped themselves around her face, pressing a soft cloth over her nose and mouth. She kicked wildly and tried to prise the hand free, but something sweet and cloying filled her lungs when she drew breath to shout for help.

All of a sudden it became infinitely easier not to struggle and to let herself go limp. There was somewhere she had to be, but she somehow couldn't quite remember where or for what purpose. Her limbs felt pleasantly heavy, and as she slipped into darkness, she heard a taxi door being opened.

The last thing she remembered before she passed out was a flash of green fabric close against her face.

———

THE PAIN WOKE her more than anything else.

Opening her eyes, Stacy saw dusty concrete beneath her sprawled legs, her spine pressed against something hard and narrow and vertical. She was slumped forward, both arms twisted painfully behind her back and joined together by something sharp and tight that dug into her skin.

She tried to pull her hands free and yelped at the feeling of something cutting deep into her skin. She leaned back immediately to relieve the pressure, feeling beads of sweat pop out on her forehead.

Tendrils of panic were by now worming their way deep inside her, her heartbeat loud and rapid in her ears. The room she was in was small, not much larger than a cupboard. It had flaking plaster walls, bare floorboards, a single closed door and no windows. The only light came from a single lightbulb overhead.

Sucking in a breath to try to steady her nerves, Stacy felt around with her fingertips. Her wrists felt like they were bound to something set almost flush with the wall behind her and with only a narrow gap between.

Tilting her head back, Stacy saw a metal pipe, orange with rust, rising vertically from immediately behind her before passing through the ceiling and out of sight.

Her mouth and throat felt desert-dry. Maybe it was something to do with whatever had been used to knock her out. And as to who had kidnapped her, well... that wasn't hard to guess.

Further tentative exploration suggested her kidnapper had used zip ties to bind her wrists. And judging by what else her fingers were telling her, he'd looped a tie around each of her wrists, with a third joining them together around the back of the pipe.

Then Stacy looked down at her legs and realized there was something wrong with them.

Her jeans were a different colour than the ones she'd been wearing, and instead of sneakers, she was now wearing heavy black boots identical to those worn by the green-jacket man.

They weren't, in fact, *her* legs.

The realization of what must have happened—that, rather than being the victim of an ordinary kidnapping, she had been body-jacked—washed over Stacy in a tide of horror.

And that meant her kidnapper was running around somewhere out there, beyond this room, inside *her* stolen body. And he could do anything he wanted to with it.

Stacy fought back a rush of nausea, her breathing hard and shallow. Then she screamed, because it was the most obvious, practical thing to do: someone, somewhere, might hear her. But when the sound emerged from her borrowed throat, it sounded closer to a bellow, frightening in its maleness.

She screamed and yelled again, then listened, chest heaving, hoping someone might have heard her.

She heard no response: no sound of movement or voices making startled queries. Worse, the plaster walls appeared to be doing an excellent job of absorbing all the noise.

She knew then, with a rush of dreadful certainty, that no one was coming.

Only then did Stacy become aware of a faint throbbing sensation between the shoulder blades of her involuntarily borrowed body. It could only, she realized, be the proxy bead her kidnapper had used on her.

Usually, proxy beads were injected into the skin at the back of the neck over the spine, so why, she wondered, had the body-jacker instead injected it between his shoulder blades?

The answer came almost as soon as she had asked herself the question: it would be just about impossible for her to dig the bead back out, should she get her hands free and find something sharp enough to cut the bead out of her flesh.

Think. It wasn't like she was the first woman to be body-jacked against her will.

It had been the one constant danger of the bad old days, that a proxy session with a client might end up with her tied up helpless while some stranger ran amok with her flesh and blood. It was the kind of thing the other girls like her had all talked about; how to get free, how to get the proxy bead back out, how to get help if you found yourself trapped in that one shared nightmare scenario.

She could figure a way out of this somehow. She just had to not let herself give in to panic.

She forced herself again to breathe more shallowly and take care to more closely study the room around her, in the hope of finding something—*anything*—that might tell her where she was or offer a way to get herself free.

It struck her then that the room looked unfinished, with bags of cement piled in one corner, and the door appearing to be little more than a sheet of plywood mounted on cheap hinges.

Wherever she was, she knew, it would be someplace her kidnapper didn't expect her to be found anytime soon. And so long as he had complete control of her body, he could pump it full of deadly drugs or poison, or drown it in the sea, or walk it in front of a bus or a train.

She could die at any second, and the only thing that would happen to him was that he would suddenly find himself back here, inside his own body.

Stacy swore under her breath. That was the wrong thing to think about.

Proxy links, everyone knew, typically lasted anywhere from three to eight hours—although some of the new hopscotch beads she had heard about reputedly lasted far longer.

Whatever her kidnapper had planned for her, as soon as their proxy session ran out, her kidnapper would be back in his own skin. And that brought to mind another question: just how long she had been unconscious? Minutes? Or hours?

There was no way for her to know. She might have hours to live, or seconds.

And there was always a chance he had an accomplice. Tying oneself up was certainly possible, but far from easy. And he might have needed help to inject his proxy bead into his spine.

But if he'd acted alone, she thought, then he surely must have a way of getting himself free again once he was back in his own skin…

Use your brain, Stacy. Figure it out.

Stacy found she had just enough wiggle room to move her wrists from side to side, and slide them up and down the length of the pipe. There was nothing to prevent her standing upright, if she could get her feet under herself.

With some considerable effort and no small amount of

cursing, Stacy scrunched her borrowed feet under her borrowed butt and pushed herself up into a half-crouch, carefully sliding her bound wrists along the length of the vertical pipe behind her.

Pins and needles erupted in her shoulders and legs. She swallowed back despair when something—perhaps a bracket holding the pipe to the wall—prevented her from standing fully upright. Her borrowed body, at least, was flexible and strong, and for that much she felt grateful. She wasn't sure she could have managed even this much in her own body.

This is all your own damn fault, Stacy chided herself. She'd been the one who insisted on meeting Martin Wilber in the flesh, rather than safely proxying from Paris through a legally rented skin.

But she'd had other reasons for wanting to return to England in person, reasons to do with her father and the things she'd learned from him—secrets she wanted to share face-to-face with the journalist rather than risk an encrypted link which, given his nearly limitless technological resources, Raphael could surely hack with ease.

All of which made it depressingly easy for Stacy to guess why she'd been kidnapped. Clearly, Raphael would stop at nothing to silence her or anyone else who might discover the truth about him.

And if she didn't find a way to free herself, he'd get away with it.

That thought filled her with a burst of determination sufficient to overcome, however briefly, the growing agony in her borrowed arms.

Still in a half-crouch, Stacy leaned forward, tugging hard in a desperate effort to yank the half-rusted pipe loose of the wall. The pain in her wrists was indescribable, and a thin, high wail found its way out from between her gritted teeth.

Strong her kidnapper might be, but the pipe didn't budge. Worse, it felt like she was yanking her—*his*—arms out by their sockets, and the more pressure she applied, the more numb her hands became as the zip ties dug more deeply into the flesh.

She half-expected someone to come bursting in through the door to see what was going on, but no one did. Perhaps, she thought, he didn't have an accomplice after all.

Stacy leaned back against the pipe, dizzy and exhausted from her efforts. Then she used her fingertips to further explore the pipe up and down the whole of its length.

What else could she do? Sitting and waiting wasn't an option, and the fear of what might happen to her felt tangible and alive, like something that lurked in her belly, poisoning her thoughts with nightmare scenarios that all ended with her dead.

Then she felt the zip-ties catch on something.

She froze. Whatever it was, it was just beneath the bracket holding the pipe to the wall, and which in turn prevented her from standing fully upright.

She slowly pushed her wrists back up the pipe, exploring with her fingertips until they came into contact with something sharp around the back of the pipe. She yelped, feeling something into the skin.

Easy, she warned herself, her kidnapper's heart hammering in his chest. *Go slow*.

Whatever it was poked out of something with a substantially different texture to the rest of the pipe, like thick tape wrapped around the bracket. She found herself picturing a piece of broken glass, perhaps, or a razor, duct-taped to the pipe just beneath the bracket.

Once he'd finished whatever he had planned for her, and once he was back in his own body, he could seesaw the zip ties back and forth across the blade, or whatever it was, and cut himself loose.

Working feverishly, Stacy scraped the plastic zip-ties back and forth across the sharpened edge to try and do just that.

It took concentration, and lots of it, to keep from missing the edge altogether. She was already breathing hard from standing in such an awkward and unnatural position.

The pipe soon felt slick with what she strongly suspected was blood. And even though she knew it wasn't her own blood, but that of her kidnapper, a part of her was nonetheless convinced she was doing terrible damage to her own body.

She kept working, the pipe vibrating hollowly as she worked the zip ties back and forth, back and forth, back and forth. The numbness in her wrists faded, giving way to a different and altogether worse kind of pain.

Still she worked, picturing her kidnapper walking her body into the sea, or stepping off an underground platform just as a train pulled in.

The pain grew yet worse, to the point she wasn't sure she could bear it any more. She let out another scream, this one born more of pain and frustration than terror, echoing flatly from the bare walls around her—

Something gave.

Stacy stumbled forward, sprawling face-first onto the dusty concrete. She swallowed and coughed, her body wracked with a thousand aches. Then, with an almighty effort, she brought her borrowed wrists and hands around in front of her and saw the terrible damage she had done to them.

She saw plastic zip ties tightly cinched around each of her kidnapper's wrists, while the jagged edges of a third poked out from each. It must, she thought, have been loose around the back of the pipe.

Stacy laughed, the sound half-hysterical and freighted with terrible pain—the pain of a body that was not hers.

She was free, but that wasn't enough. To save her life, she now had to break the proxy link connecting her to her kidnapper, breaking his hold over her body.

She didn't even try to dig the proxy bead out of the small of her back because she knew she couldn't do it, at least not without help and not with her wrists so bloodied and ruined. And even if she did eventually find someone who could help remove it, it would be much too late.

That left her with two options: first, to call the police.

They were, after all, well-equipped to deal with most proxy crimes. But she'd have to find a bracelet in order to make that call.

She started to search through her kidnapper's pockets. He didn't have his jacket with him, and she—*he*—wore only jeans and a t-shirt.

She found nothing, certainly not a bracelet. Not that he'd have been dumb enough to make it quite so easy for her.

Which left her with a second, rather less pleasant choice: to kill her kidnapper first.

The moment his body died, the proxy link would be severed, and she'd be back in her own skin.

Either he died, or she did. It was a matter of simple survival.

Staggering upright, Stacy quickly found that the door was locked. However, a dozen or so adrenaline-fuelled kicks soon broke the flimsy lock and sent the door slamming open.

Murderous asshole or not, Stacy was grateful her body-jacker had spent as much time in the gym as he clearly had.

Past the door, Stacy found herself in an abandoned and empty flat. A quick search through a half-ruined kitchen with mould running up one wall turned up nothing she could use to kill the body she currently occupied—not even so much as a blunt dinner knife.

Then she found herself inside an equally decrepit bathroom, with an intact mirror above the sink. Stacy stared at her kidnapper's reflection for a moment, then formed his right hand into a fist and punched the mirror as hard as she could.

The glass starred on the first impact and shattered on the second.

The pain was horrendous, certainly enough to make her let out another animal bellow. She clutched at her borrowed fingers, hissing through her teeth. Then she reached into the basin and carefully picked up the longest shard she could find and held its razor-sharp edge against her kidnapper's throat.

The man's reflection was clearly visible in the few fragments of mirror that remained attached to the wall. His skin was deathly pale, the hand clutching the shard trembling visibly.

Die, you miserable fucker.

But the hand remained where it was, the mouth twisting up in disgust until, with a howl of frustration, Stacy threw the shard back down.

I can't do it.

Stacy fell onto her haunches, her balled hands pressed against her temples. She couldn't do it. That it wasn't her own throat she wanted to cut made no difference to her unconscious mind.

Then another idea occurred to her.

Peering out of the bathroom's one tiny window, Stacy saw an empty moonlit street a few storeys below. The surrounding buildings, all of which prominently displayed demolition notices, were a uniform six storeys in height.

The front door of the flat was missing. Stacy hurried out of the flat and made her way along a corridor with stairwells at either end. She ran upwards, her kidnapper's strong limbs carrying her with ease.

When she burst through a door and onto the rooftop, she saw London's silver towers in the distance, and the warning lights of transport blimps blinking on and off far to the North. The edge of the roof—and a six-storey drop—was only a few steps away.

Nothing could be quicker or easier.

Borrowed blood thundered through borrowed ears.

Do it, she screamed inside her head. *Do it now, before he—*

Running forward with a yell, and still struggling to ignore the part of her mind convinced she was about to kill herself, Stacy very nearly faltered at the last moment.

Then she pushed off the edge of the roof with one foot, arms cartwheeling as she plummeted. A fresh scream ripped from her borrowed lungs in the last instant before the ground came rushing up and—

—she was somewhere else, suspended high above a chasm of air.

————

FOR ONE TERRIBLE MOMENT, Stacy thought she had somehow returned to the rooftop of the same building from which she had leapt. But the place where she now crouched with her back to a concrete wall, a street visible far beneath her feet, was much, *much* higher than the six-storey block in which she had been trapped.

Cold wind whipped at her face—her *real* face, Stacy realized, with a mixture of terror and joy. She looked at one of her wrists and let out a sob when she saw the unblemished skin there.

It didn't take too much work to piece together what had happened. Her kidnapper, it seems, had meant to kill her in precisely the same way she had in fact killed him—by throwing himself, inside her body, from a very great height.

And by the looks of it, she'd beat him by mere seconds. His body had hit the ground first, killing him and severing the proxy link between them.

It could so easily have been the other way around, in which case she'd most likely have been written off by the police as the unwitting victim of some anonymous suicide junkie—people who got a kick out of proxying with unwitting strangers and then killing them for the sheer rush of experiencing death without themselves dying.

People would have shrugged or shaken their heads and said it was inevitable, given her reputation as a rich kid who'd gone off the rails. That Stacy had left proxy-hooking far in her past would make little difference to them or anyone else.

Looking up and behind her, Stacy saw a domed roof with irregularly shaped edges rising high above the ledge on which she crouched. A freezing wind cut deep into her skin.

Her bracelet was long gone, so there'd be no help coming that way. The concrete beneath her fingers felt damp from recent rain.

She made the mistake of looking down again, and swallowed back a rush of sour vomit. The street looked impossibly far away from so far up.

Glancing to one side, Stacy caught sight of a scaffolding platform a little further along the ledge she was crouching on. This, she guessed, must be how her kidnapper had got up here. Which meant she could get back down by the same route.

Easiest thing in the world.

It took another minute for Stacy to even begin to summon up the necessary courage to slowly shuffle along the ledge towards the platform. The breath caught in her lungs with every gust of wind. The ledge seemed to sway beneath her, as if trying deliberately to tip her into oblivion.

Somehow she made it, sobbing with relief when she at last reached out to cling to the scaffolding. Rain touched her skin, but was immediately carried away by the wind.

A ladder led down through the scaffolding platform and terminated ten meters further down at a narrow balcony. She could see there was some kind of service door there, one that presumably led inside the building. Descending the ladder proved to be easy enough: within seconds she found herself standing on the balcony.

The door, however, was locked.

She kicked and punched it, but it remained steadfastly secure. Neither did yelling for someone to come help her bring any response.

Finally, Stacy slid down until she had her back against the door. She was alive, at least, while her kidnapper was very much dead. She could end up waiting all night before someone found her. Maybe even longer.

And maybe nobody would come. Some of the scaffolding looked rusted, like it had been there for a long time.

A sudden thought sent her searching through her pockets for a key, but that hope soon vanished. Even if her kidnapper had had a key for the door, he might well have tossed it away the moment he was outside on the roof in her body.

Leaning over the railing, Stacy caught sight of a second, much larger balcony directly below the one on which she now stood. Much of it was taken up by a carefully tended garden.

She realized, then, that the building on which she was stranded must be one of the new, self-contained arcologies that now dotted the capital, their floors arranged atop one another like untidy stacks of dishes. More balconies could be glimpsed further down, each one equally dense with carbon-absorbing greenery.

Decorative brickwork to one side of the balcony on which Stacy stood formed a kind of ladder leading down towards the uppermost garden balcony. And, judging by the light spilling across those bushes and wildflowers, someone was home.

Her guts roiled at the thought of trying to work her way down the brickwork like some freestyle mountaineer, but it was the only way she could see to ensure her survival. And there was still a risk her kidnapper had an accomplice, even now on his way to finish the job.

Plus, she had to contact Wilber and warn him things had become even more dangerous than she had thought they might.

Swallowing her terror as best she could, Stacy swung one leg over the railing, took a grip on part of the brickwork and soon found herself clinging to the side of the building high above the garden balcony.

Stacy took another glance downwards and immediately regretted it. Was it fifteen metres down to that garden balcony? Or twenty?

Or even more?

Either way, she'd surely die if she slipped and fell now.

She began working her way down, her eyes fixed on the brickwork just inches from her face. Her arms and legs soon ached from tension. Then she glanced down again and, to her shock, discovered she was nearly halfway there.

I'm going to make it, she thought, feeling something like hope almost for the first time since she had disembarked from the train.

Just then, light flickered from somewhere above her. Startled, Stacy glanced up, seeing the light of a torch shining down from the tiny maintenance balcony she had just departed.

She thought immediately of the kidnapper's accomplice. *They've found me.*

"Hello?" a voice called down. "Who's there?"

No, she realized—it was a maintenance worker, or a janitor. But she had allowed herself to be distracted too long; her fingers slipped on the rain-dampened brickwork, and she tumbled away from the side of the building.

She landed amidst bushes, hard enough it felt like the hammer of some angry war-god slamming into her chest. But she was alive, alive, *alive*, and she held on to that thought, that knowledge, even as she heard alarmed voices calling to one another, and the sound of a door close by slamming open.

CHAPTER
TWO

RAY

"Marky," said Harry, his tone good-humoured, "for someone who's supposed to be an expert at this stuff, you're taking so long I'm getting worried."

The garage smelled of machine oil and leather cleaner. Stacks of battery units covered most of one wall while half a dozen petroleum engines sat along another. The murmur of voices came down a stairwell from the floor above.

"Depends on the car." The man whom Harry thought was Marky, but was, in fact, an entirely different man named Ray Thomas, tapped his way through a series of diagnostic menu items on the dashboard of a vintage cream-coloured Volkswagen. A laptop loaded with software purchased over the darknet for the precise purpose of circumventing encrypted automobile management routines sat on the seat next to him, connected to the dashboard by a cable.

Marky might be a real wizard when it came to making all kinds of illegal software modifications, but Ray definitely wasn't. He felt an unreasonable degree of relief when the dashboard—really a single giant touchscreen—flashed orange, showing that it had accepted his software modifications.

"Okay," he said, climbing back out of the car and pushing the door closed, "that's the GPS reprogrammed."

Harry, who had been leaning against the bumper of a half-gutted Audi, watching while he worked, nodded with apparent satisfaction. "Finally," he said, standing up and stretching his spine, the heel of one hand pressed to his lower back. "I remember when you used to be able to take care of a job like that in half an hour, but that took you most of half a day. Losing your touch?"

Ray stepped around to the Volkswagen's engine compartment, its five-cylinder petrol engine long since replaced by a single large battery unit, and closed the hatch. Even the batteries had been hacked to remove embedded software that could track the vehicle's movements.

"The firmware's a lot harder to get around these days," Ray explained. "You have to take extra precautions to be sure they won't be identified as stolen." He glanced towards Harry. "I could do it faster if you like, but if I did, I couldn't guarantee whoever ended up buying it wouldn't get nicked. And that risks leading the police back here."

"Fair enough," said Harry. He nodded up at the ceiling. "I think such blatant disregard for the law of the land deserves a beer, don't you?"

"Seconded." Ray unplugged the laptop and powered it down, hearing laughter from upstairs. His palms were still dirty from rooting around inside the Volkswagen's engine compartment to try and find a port he could plug the laptop into. "Just let me wash my hands first."

"That's the problem with a job like this," said Harry. "Can't help but get your hands dirty." He grinned broadly, as if they were sharing a private joke. "Know what I mean?"

"Sure." Ray smiled back uncertainly. Something in the way Harry had said it gave him a moment's pause.

"By the way," said Harry, his tone casual, "Al dropped in for a visit. Figured you might want to say hello, seeing you used to be cellmates and all."

"Al Stokes?" Ray didn't need to pretend he was pleased, if for entirely different reasons than Harry might have suspected. "Long time no see. Did he say anything about...?"

Harry clapped him on the shoulder. "He did. I put in a good word for you, but you know Al. Wouldn't trust his own mother. I think he just wants to talk to you first."

At last, thought Ray. *I'm finally getting somewhere.*

————

RAY HEADED through to the back of the body shop, passing by cars raised high on hydraulic jacks, and washed his hands in the tiny washroom. The garage made most of its money converting ancient petrol-guzzlers to electric to keep them straight with the law, but hacking the onboard computer systems that otherwise allowed stolen vehicles to be traced brought Harry a brisk under-the-counter trade.

Once he had finished washing his hands, Ray studied the face that looked back at him from the mirror above the sink: Marky Stevenson, car thief and hacker extraordinaire. Marky's face was freckled and round, with blond-ginger hair and a nose that had been broken more than once. To say he and Ray bore little resemblance to one another was something of an understatement.

Ray dried Marky's hands and checked his watch. He'd been proxying with the carjacker for just over three hours now. That left him another three to four hours at the very most before the proxy beads in both his and Marky's necks dissolved and they each found themselves back in their own bodies.

He thought about the way Harry had looked at him and felt a stab of worry. Pretending to be the person you were proxying with required a certain degree of acting skill. You had as much as possible to mimic their habits, body language and speech patterns, but Ray knew from bitter experience that there were a thousand ways to slip up or otherwise reveal oneself.

It was possible Harry had figured out someone was proxying with Marky, but there was no way to be sure.

And even if things went wrong, well, one way or another he'd be back in his own body before long.

And it wasn't like you could just stop proxying any time you wanted. Short of digging a bead out of your neck, you had to ride a proxy session out to the bitter end.

"You don't have to do this," Ray said in a low voice to the face in the mirror.

But if you weren't doing this, said a small voice in the back of his mind, *what else would you be doing? Working night shifts as a security guard for some supermarket chain?*

At least now he'd hit bottom, there was nowhere else to fall.

———

Returning from the washroom, Ray headed upstairs to a storeroom that also functioned as a break room. There, he found Harry Cutts sitting on a stool before a scarred coffee table. Across the table from him, and squeezed together on a crumbling couch, were Jayden Cutts, Al Stokes, and Harry's nephew Dylan Wicks, with whom Harry owned the garage.

Stokes had long, dark hair that spilled across his shoulders in greasy waves. Ferret-like eyes gleamed from beneath a side-parting, while a cigarette poked out from between scarred knuckles.

The murmur of conversation abated when Ray entered.

"We were just talking about you," said Jayden, pulling the top off a beer bottle and passing it to Ray as he approached.

Ray took a slug of beer and felt it wash the dust from his throat. "Good things, I hope."

He studied the men around the table to try to get some sense of what was on their minds. Something definitely felt off. None of them quite met his eyes, and their smiles looked less than genuine.

Regardless, Ray extended a hand to Stokes, and they shook. "Good to see you again, Al," said Ray.

"I was telling them about when we shared a cell," said Al, taking a long drag on his cigarette. "There are too many stories to count, yet these arseholes seem to want to hear every one of them."

Everything Ray knew about Al Stokes came from a police interrogation of Mark Stevenson that had taken place two weeks before. He'd been nicked driving a stolen vehicle, and his connection with Stokes had attracted the attention of the CID.

A raid subsequently carried out on Stevenson's home had produced enough evidence to put him away for a long, long time—unless, as the police had explained to him, he was willing to aid them in their ongoing pursuit of Stokes.

The way Ray heard it, the carjacker had been almost embarrassingly eager to tell his interrogating officer all about his two years as Al Stokes' cellmate.

But reading a police report and being face-to-face with Stokes himself were two very different things.

Ray produced what he hoped was a convincing smile. "Like the one about that bloke they caught fucking a teddy-bear?"

Jayden's eyes grew wide, and he half-choked on his beer. Harry, by contrast, laughed uproariously.

"All true," Stokes said to Jayden. "He even had it smuggled into prison because he couldn't bear to be without it." He took another drag on his cigarette. "No," he said, looking back over at Ray, "I was thinking about the time they searched us for drugs, forced you to strip and discovered you were wearing nappies."

"Fuck off," said Jayden, staring at Ray in horrified amazement.

Ray's hand tightened around his beer bottle. Marky had mentioned nothing about that.

"He's having you on," said Ray, sweat beading his borrowed skin.

"Maybe you're right," said Stokes. "Was it someone else?" He tapped the fingers of one hand on the side of his head. "Wait. Was it whatsisname? Do you remember his name, Marky?"

"Fucked if I remember," said Ray, his fingers tight around the bottle.

He'd have preferred almost anywhere else for this meeting. There was one window, but it was covered over by an advertising hoarding, and that meant the only way out was down the stairs.

"But you remember when it was, don't you?" Stokes asked, something feral in his gaze. "Last time I saw you, in fact."

Ray made a helpless gesture. "I can't remember what I had for breakfast this morning let alone what happened years ago," he said. "I guess maybe it was."

Stokes made a noise in the back of his throat and nodded to himself as if coming to a conclusion. Then he stood and walked over to where several chairs were pushed into a corner. He picked one up, placed it by his own chair, and gestured to Ray to sit next to him.

Ray sat by Stokes' side and they clinked beers. "You've been asking about me, right?" Stokes asked, his expression suddenly sombre. "And not just because we used to be cellmates."

Ray drank more beer. The alcohol would affect Marky's brain, but not his, and so he could remain fully alert. But he couldn't drink too much, either, because the alcohol would slow down his skin's ability to react if things went south.

The act of drinking, however, at least gave him time to think.

"Well," Ray replied, "I'd heard you were in a certain line of business and it sounded, you know, interesting."

"And what line of business would that be, exactly?" asked Stokes.

"I heard you were running a proxy factory down in Shoreham. And I just thought, well…maybe I could help."

"Because you've heard there's a lot of money to be made manufacturing proxy, right?"

"It's getting harder to crack cars by the day," Ray explained. "And I've got Marjorie and two kids to look after."

"All good points," said Al, putting his beer down and stubbing out his cigarette before lighting another. "But here's the thing."

Stokes put his left arm around Ray's shoulders in what at first appeared to be a friendly embrace. Then, before Ray quite knew what was happening, Stokes took hold of Marky's head in a vice-like grip and jammed the glowing tip of his cigarette into one of the carjacker's eyes.

Ray smelled burning flesh. The shock of the heat and pain felt like an icepick driven into his skull. It hurt just as much as if it had been Ray's own eye, rather than Marky's.

Ray tore himself loose of the other man's grip and let out a bellow of pain and anguish. He pushed himself upright, his chair tumbling to one side.

"Jesus!" Ray screamed, pressing his hands against Marky's injured eye. "What the fuck did you do that for?"

Too late, Ray became aware that the rest of them had stood as well. He looked towards the stairs and freedom, but before he could take a single step in that direction, Jayden and Harry had grabbed him by the shoulders, twisting his arms behind his back. Stokes, meanwhile, lurched upright and began raining punches into Marky's belly.

Ray felt every blow. His legs gave way beneath him and, if not for the two men holding him upright, he would have slumped to the floor.

The blows kept coming, and coming. Ray tried to twist out of the way of Stokes' fists, but it was useless; he tasted the copper scent of blood, mixed with the sordid stench of his own fear.

If he just stuck to his role—if he could still somehow convince them he really was who he said he was—maybe there was still a chance he could get out of this without having to live through whatever they had planned for Marky.

At last the blows ceased. "Al," Ray rasped, his bruised lungs snatching at the air, "why are you doing this?"

"Don't you fucking 'Al' me," Stokes screamed. Then came more punches and, finally, Ray was allowed to crumple to the floor.

"It wasn't Marky who wore the nappy," Stokes snarled, his chest heaving from his exertions, "that much you got right. It was Sharpton. Marky and him hated each other's guts. Marky couldn't shut up when they caught Sharpton wearing nappies and you—I mean, he—said he'd remember that day for the rest of his life. I should know. I was stuck in that fucking cell listening to him rabbit on and on about it for fucking *years*."

Stokes lit another cigarette, his hands trembling with adrenaline or perhaps from fury. "This lot have been onto you for days, mate," he said, pointing the lit cigarette at Ray, "whoever you really fucking are. They noticed the way you kept slipping away at odd hours, I'm guessing so you could put a new bead in Marky's neck and keep the link going. Jayden," he said, snapping a look at the other man. "Go get us a bucket of water and some of those rags from downstairs. Make sure it's full right to the top."

Jayden nodded with clear excitement and dashed downstairs.

"How about dropping the bullshit, lad?" Stokes asked Ray, who still crouched on the floor surrounded by his tormentors. "Who have we really been talking to? And how long have you been proxying with Marky?"

Ray considered keeping up the pretence, then discarded it. Instead, he responded to Stokes' question with a tight shake of the head.

Stokes half-kneeled before Ray and opened a pocket knife, its serrated edge gleaming dully beneath a bare overhead light-bulb. "Proxy's a wonderful thing, innit?" said Stokes. "Just like magic, you stick a little bead under your skin and all of a sudden you can walk around in someone else's body. You can feel everything they can, and vice versa. Even pain." He held the blade close to Ray's—Marky's—cheek. "If I cut you right now, you'll feel it just as much as if it was your own skin."

"You wouldn't do that," said Ray, his voice tight with pain.

"Why not?"

"You'd be hurting Marky, not me. I'll be fine when the proxy link breaks."

"On the contrary," said Stokes, his eyes gleaming, "it'll hurt you in the short term, and Marky very much in the long term. Because there's no way you'd be here, proxying through the miserable little turd, unless he'd already told you something he shouldn't have. So tell me—what was it you were sent you to find out? It was summat to do with me, right?"

Jayden returned just then, a bucket of water in one hand and a pile of dirty rags in the other. Water slopped over the sides of the bucket as he placed it next to the coffee table.

Stokes grabbed Ray by the chin, digging the tip of his knife into the skin behind the carjacker's ear.

Ray howled from the pain.

"Now tell me," Stokes growled, "why the fuck you're here?"

"Fuck you," Ray grunted between panicked gasps.

"Think," said Stokes. "What kind of a miserable life is this, stealing people's skins and spying on their friends and family?" Stokes sneered. "I've met blokes like you. The police won't use proxy themselves because they think it's beneath them, so they hire idiots like you to do it on their behalf." Stokes shook his head. "I'm betting this isn't the first time you've been caught out, is it?"

Ray saw no point in denying it. "No, it isn't."

"Fine then," said Stokes. "Now, I figure you've been at this game long enough that your pain threshold must be pretty high by now." His expression became almost sympathetic. "You know, you could save yourself an awful lot of bother if you just told me what I want to know. You know that, don't you?"

Ray knew, but he still didn't tell Stokes anything. At least, not at first.

When he didn't immediately receive an answer, Stokes's expression became contemptuous. He stepped over to the coffee table, sweeping the empty beer bottles and ashtrays onto the floor. Then he had Jayden and the others lift Ray up and onto the table, laying him out like a corpse on a slab.

Harry punched Ray in the belly a couple more times when he tried to struggle upright. By then, he was too weak to resist when Stokes pressed the oily rags down over his mouth, nose and eyes.

Then came a rush of water as one of Stokes' cronies upended the bucket over Ray's face. The water tasted as cold and pure as death, his lungs struggling to suck in air that suddenly wasn't there. He coughed and spluttered and gagged as the water filled his nostrils.

They waterboarded him twice more, just to be sure. Ray

struggled and kicked and screamed the whole time, Jayden running back downstairs whenever they needed a fresh bucket filled.

After the third waterboarding, Ray told the assembled faces anything they wanted to hear. He told them he worked as a licensed body jacker for a private investigator and that Marky had been promised leniency if Stokes, a wanted man, was finally cornered.

In the middle of his confession, a sensation of falling away into darkness came over Ray. Within moments the stink of the rags was gone, along with Stokes, Cutts and the whole garage crew.

———

RAY'S LUNGS seized at the air. His hands—*his* hands, not Marky's—gripped the armchair in which he found himself sitting. Around him was a sparsely furnished office with stained blinds part-drawn over unwashed windows dark with grime.

Ray twisted to one side and vomited noisily onto green linoleum.

When he looked back up, Ray saw a man had entered the office with a large mug gripped in one hand. A tiny kitchenette was visible through a door behind him. The man had a wool balaclava pulled down over his face so that all Ray could see were his eyes and mouth.

"Christ on a pogo stick," said the man in the balaclava, staring at the puddle of vomit. "Am I going to have to clean that up?"

"Tip," Ray gasped. "It's me."

The other man's eyes narrowed with suspicion. "What's the code phrase, then?"

Ray coughed and cleared his throat, his tongue still sour

with the taste of vomit. "'I have CCTV evidence that you once fucked a badger'," he rasped.

Tip's eyes grew wide, and he yanked the balaclava off, revealing a man in his early sixties with a shock of untidy steel-grey hair and a chin scarred by childhood acne. "Shit, Ray. Throwing up after a proxy session is a bit amateur, innit?"

"I talked to Stokes," said Ray, wiping his mouth with a sleeve. His hands were shaking. "But he was onto me. They all were. Call it in, but I'll be surprised if Stokes is within thirty miles of the garage by the time the Met gets there."

Tip looked pained on receiving this news. Ray knew what he was thinking: Stokes' capture meant a fat reward, and both of them needed the cash.

"I'll call it in anyway," said Tip. He let out a sigh of disappointment and raised his data bracelet to his mouth. "Maybe there's still a chance."

Tip turned and disappeared back into the office kitchen. Ray watched through the door as the private investigator pulled open one kitchen cupboard after the other at the same time that he spoke to his contact at the Metropolitan police.

He ended the call and came back through, grasping a roll of paper towels which he tossed underhand onto Ray's lap.

"Get that mess cleaned up," he said, his mouth twisted up in disgust, "then I'll make you a cup of tea and you can tell me all about it."

Ray ripped a fistful of paper from the roll and cleaned up as best he could before carrying the sodden mess through to the toilet and flushing it away. He rinsed his face and mouth at the sink and resisted the urge to check for bruises that he could still feel, even if they weren't on his own body.

By the time he re-emerged from the toilet, Tip had prepared a bucket of soapy water. He handed it to Ray along with a scrubbing brush.

Ray just stared back at him.

"Come on Ray," said Tip, looking aggrieved. "You've met the landlord. Just imagine how much more of a total pain in the arse he'll be if that linoleum gets stained."

Ray glowered and snatched the brush out of Tip's hand. Then he got to work scrubbing and mopping with more paper towels.

At least it kept him from thinking too much about what he'd just been through. Once he'd finished, he collapsed into a chair next to a scarred metal desk and watched as Tip took a seat across from him.

"There you go," said Tip, handing him a fresh mug of tea.

Ray took a sip. The tea was lukewarm and had enough sugar in it to stun a horse.

"I could tell Harry was onto me," said Ray, putting the mug back down with a grimace, "even before I got face-to-face with Stokes."

"Ah." Tip eyed him speculatively and not without a hint of sympathy. "So how did you wind up vomiting all over my nice clean office?"

"They waterboarded me."

Tip's eyes widened slightly. "Could have been worse," he said. "At least they didn't go after your—well, Marky's—nuts with a pair of pliers." He licked his lips. "Did you…tell them anything?"

"I told them my real name," Ray admitted.

Tip stared back at him with a mixture of fury and aston-ishment. "For fuck's sake, Ray!"

"You ever proxy with someone, Tip?"

The other man visibly shuddered. "Christ, no. You know I haven't. That's what you're here for."

"Being tortured under proxy feels exactly the same as if they were doing it to my own body. Stokes knew exactly what he was doing. He knew I'd tell him anything to make him stop."

Tip gnawed at the knuckles of one hand. "And did you tell them anything about me?"

"No," Ray said with all sincerity. Although in truth, if Stokes had expressed an interest in that information, he wouldn't have hesitated to provide it. "The proxy session ended before he could ask anything more."

"Just your name?"

"That, and some details you told me about the case and what the Met has on file about Stokes."

"Shit." Tip balled one hand into a fist and pressed it against his mouth. "That's on me, I think. It'd have been smarter not to tell you anything." He sat back in his chair, thinking as he stared at the ceiling. "Let's just see if they corner Stokes or not, then figure our way forward from there."

And if they don't? Ray wanted to ask. Instead, he stood, feeling wobbly on his legs.

"I'm going home," he said. As he turned towards the door, he paused and looked back at the private investigator. "You'll try not to be late with my fee this time, yeah?"

Tip gave him a look as if the very idea he might be less than prompt in such matters was inconceivable. "Of course it won't be late," Tip huffed, pulling a pair of spectacles out of a pocket and sliding them onto his nose. He tapped a small button on the side of the spectacles and reached out to touch a screen visible only to him. "Good work, Ray," he added distractedly, then paused and looked over at him. "I mean it. I couldn't do what you do in a month of Sundays."

Ray did his best to ignore the implied suggestion that this only proved how much smarter Tip was. He stepped out through the front door of the P.I.'s office and into a narrow corridor with a stairwell at one end and a window at the other.

Walking over to the window, he pressed his forehead against the cold glass and closed his eyes for a moment.

Stories abounded of proxy investigators winding up with severe psychological damage. The number of suicides wasn't exactly cheering either.

Long ago, Ray had promised himself he'd never become one of those stories; but today had been worse than most.

Once he'd made his way back outside and onto the London streets, Ray touched his bracelet and called a cab. One pulled up to the kerb just moments later; it looked surprisingly intact for this part of London, or at least, none of its windows were broken. Then again, the graffiti that covered nearly the whole of the vehicle's exterior, including the windows, made it just about impossible to see what horrors might lie within.

As it turned out, however, the interior was in perfectly fine condition. Ray collapsed into the rear of the taxi, his bracelet emitting a faint chime as the cab deducted his fare. There was a bottle of Glenlivet waiting for him at home—one he'd been keeping especially for a day like this.

Maybe if he could drink himself to sleep, there'd be less chance of him waking up screaming in the middle of the night.

———

IT DIDN'T WORK.

Later that night, Ray jerked upright in bed, each breath coming fast and hard. He'd dreamed he was drowning, trapped, at the bottom of a deep well, his lungs cold and heavy, invisible hands reaching up to drag him down into ink-dark depths.

His bracelet, lying on its charging point on the bedside table, buzzed again. Good news, he knew from long experience, never arrived in the middle of the night.

Even so, he mumbled a voice command, and the bracelet changed from red to green.

"Hello?" Ray said, slipping the bracelet onto his wrist.

"Mr Thomas?"

Ray had expected to hear Tip's voice. Instead it was that of a woman. A glance at the screen of his bracelet showed him that the call was anonymous and encrypted.

"Who is this?" Ray demanded, his voice sharp.

The woman took so long to reply he started to think she might have hung up.

"My name is Cotter," she said at last. "Amy Cotter."

Christ, thought Ray. *It can't be her.*

Ray forgot all about the pain and trauma of the day before and sat up, suddenly alert. "Do you usually call people in the middle of the night, Miss Cotter?"

"My apologies," she said, her voice trembling slightly. "But I wouldn't be calling unless it was an emergency."

An emergency? What kind of emergency had the ex-wife of Raphael Markov calling him in the middle of the night?

"Tell me what it is, Miss Cotter."

"It's about Stacy, Mr Thomas." He heard a catch in her voice, like she was struggling to keep from crying. "It's about my daughter."

CHAPTER
THREE

ISAAC

"Mr Sizemore?"

Isaac squinted into the light from a lamp placed in the middle of the desk between him and the man addressing him. The light was blinding—intentionally so, since the lamp had been angled to shine directly into Isaac's eyes. The rest of the room was layered in shadows.

A name floated up from the depths of Isaac's memory: *Finch.*

Yes, he remembered now—the man addressing him was called Finch.

Why, he wondered, was it so hard to remember anything? Why did his every thought feel as if it were shrouded in thick, grey fog?

"Isaac," Finch asked again, leaning forward and into the light. He had thinning brown hair, his narrow features twisted in a contemptuous scowl. "Answer the question."

Yes, thought Isaac; he was beginning to remember Finch now. They had met before like this, hadn't they? And they had known each other before as well, a long time ago.

Finch glanced at a sheet of smart-paper on the desk separating them, reading something scrawled there. "Lewis," he asked, looking up and past Isaac's shoulder with a frown, "how much did you give him?"

"Exactly what you told me to," said a voice from behind Isaac.

Isaac felt his eyelids grow heavy, his head tipping forward on his shoulders.

"Isaac," Finch barked. "Please stay awake."

Isaac forced his eyes back open with reluctance. He tried to raise a hand to keep the light from shining in his eyes, but found he couldn't. Glancing down, he saw that his wrists were bound with leather straps to the armrests of a wheelchair.

That seemed strange. Or did it? He had been strapped into this wheelchair before, hadn't he? How many days had he been here…wherever *here* was?

He looked back up in time to see Finch eyeing him with a look akin to hunger. Finch leaned back again, his face fading to a barely perceptible silhouette behind the desk lamp.

"Our last talk together didn't go so well, did it, Isaac?"

Gripped by inexplicable panic, Isaac twisted his wrists inside their restraints, desperate to get free. But the straps were tight—excessively so—and it hurt. A lot.

But the more he twisted them, and the more it hurt, the more clearly he seemed able to think.

"That's not my name," he said. His tongue felt thick and unwieldy in his mouth.

Finch made a clucking sound in the back of his throat. "We're back to that, I see."

"My name is…"

Isaac tried to focus. But his name *was* Isaac, wasn't it?

Confusion flooded him.

Or was his name Dominic Fiori?

Suddenly he wasn't sure what to think.

Rows of lights flickered behind Finch's head, drawing

Isaac's attention. He squinted into the shadows and the lights resolved into a mobile medical monitor. It sat against the wall behind Finch. Graphs flickered and shifted on its screen.

Isaac could always think more clearly when it came to machines. They were, he had found, so much simpler than people. Judging by what he could see, the machine was measuring someone's heart-rate and skin conductivity. His, presumably; Finch must be using the monitor as a crude lie detector.

He twisted his wrists a little more, trying not to look obvious about it. The leather tore his skin and he bit back a sharp hiss of pain.

The clouds fogging his mind parted a little.

"Were you about to say Dominic Fiori?" Finch asked him.

Isaac nodded. "Yes."

"You have a driving licence in that name," Finch replied. "And a birth certificate. But they're fake. Your real name is Isaac Sizemore. You were one of Telop's star researchers until you disappeared."

Another twist of his hands inside their restraints, and Isaac stifled a grunt. He felt warm blood trickle down one wrist, invisible in the shadows.

Yes, he remembered Finch more clearly now; a jumped-up research assistant always waiting for a chance to get in tight with both Raphael Markov and his father, David Markov.

Waiting, Isaac had always suspected, for him to slip up.

Another memory came flooding back, from what must have been only days before. He'd blown a tyre on a lonely midnight road somewhere in the Scottish Highlands. Halfway through changing it, an unmarked van had pulled up next to him. Two men wearing plastic Halloween masks had got out and grabbed him before he could so much as stand up. One had pushed something into his shoulder and then—

And then he was here.

"I want," Finch continued, "to know why you left your job at Telop so abruptly all those years ago." He paused. "And why you did what you did."

"Did what?"

"I'm talking about proxy, Isaac. Stop playing games. We were colleagues once. Equals. I'd like us to be again."

"You were never my equal," Isaac snarled. "I remember you. You never had one original idea in your life."

Isaac could still only half-see Finch's expression in the shadows, but he nonetheless caught the glint of barely repressed fury on his interrogator's face.

"Raphael," Finch continued, his tone carefully neutral, "has invested heavily in the attempt to track you down. You did valuable work for him and his father, and then you threw it all away for nothing. He wants to know why." He glanced back down at his notes. "He also wants to know why you arranged to meet with some journalist."

Isaac's mind seemed much clearer now—and not just, he sensed, because of his self-inflicted wounds. He twisted his head around to try to see the orderly still standing behind him. Had the man given him a lower dosage of amobarbital than he had overheard Finch instructing him to?

Yes, Isaac decided. He must have. And if so…why?

In that same moment, and while Finch was distracted by whatever was on the sheet of smart paper, the orderly stepped forward until he was standing next to Isaac's wheel-chair. When Isaac glanced up at him, the man gave Isaac the faintest conspiratorial nod.

Isaac stared back up at the orderly, dumbfounded, then felt an electric shock of realisation pass through him.

My God, he thought, quickly looking back down at the desk before Finch could see his expression: had Zero found a way to proxy with the orderly?

"Isaac?" Finch asked, clearly noticing something in his expression. "What is it?"

Isaac brought his chin back up, regarding Finch through narrowed eyes. "I would rather die," he said carefully, "than do anything for the Markov's ever again."

The muscles around Finch's jaw tensed. "That's unfortunate," he said. "Especially since we found it necessary to waylay Stacy on her way to meet the very journalist she'd arranged for you to talk to."

Isaac felt himself grow rigid. "What are you talking about?"

"Let's just say that an...associate of Raphael's intercepted Stacy. What happens to her next depends largely on your cooperation, Isaac."

"She..." Isaac swallowed with difficulty, his lips and throat bone dry. "Where is she?" He demanded, straining against the cuffs.

A greasy smile spread across Finch's lips. "I think that's enough for now. I'm sure the next time we meet you'll be much more open to talking." He glanced at the orderly. "Lewis, take him back to his room. Then I need you back here."

"Sir," said Lewis.

Isaac heard a door open behind him, then hands took hold of the wheelchair's handles, spinning it around before pushing it through the door.

"Zero?" Isaac whispered once they were out in the corridor.

"Not yet," the orderly warned him in a low voice. "I'll come and speak to you later."

Joy flooded Isaac's chest and his cheeks grew damp from his tears. "I'm so glad to see you," he said. "How did you—?"

"Later," Zero promised him.

———

LATER THAT NIGHT, Isaac woke to darkness and sensed he wasn't alone. He sat up on his cot and saw a silhouette standing at the open door of his room, a collection of keys hanging from one meaty hand.

The man stepped further into the room and Isaac saw it was indeed Lewis.

But was Zero still proxying with the orderly? It had been hours since their brief snatch of conversation following Finch's interrogation. Surely by now, Zero's proxy link with the man would have run out?

"Zero?" Isaac asked regardless, his throat dry and scratchy.

"It's me, Doctor Sizemore," the orderly whispered in response. "I need to get you out of here as soon as possible."

"Not yet," said Isaac, levering himself up from the cot. "Close the door so we aren't overheard. How did you even find me here?"

Zero did as he was told and shut the door before turning on the light. The room contained five other cots, all empty.

"After you disappeared," Zero explained, "I hacked into several security databases and tracked down the licence plate of the van that took you. The van is registered to this institute, the Abbey Rush Treatment Centre."

"And how did you manage to proxy with Lewis Finnegan?"

"I accessed this facility's security network and ran an analysis going back six months that strongly suggested Mr Finnegan had been availing himself of medical supplies from secure storage cupboards and selling them for a profit," Zero explained. "I emailed him anonymously and told him I wouldn't go to the police so long as he agreed to proxy with me at certain prearranged times and places. He agreed. I contacted a local proxy dealer via the darknet, and had a proxy bead delivered to his home with instructions for when and how to inject it."

Isaac couldn't figure out whether to be appalled or amazed at Zero's ingenuity and ability to improvise a solution to his kidnapping. "That's…that's very good, Zero," he said with sincere appreciation. "Even so, it's important to me that no one is hurt as a result of our actions. Not even someone as unpleasant as Lewis Finnegan."

"Of course not," Zero replied. "I would never deliberately injure a human being or, through inaction, allow a human being to come to—"

"You don't need to explain to me, of all people," Isaac reassured him. "Now tell me what you know about Stacy. Is she safe? What has Raphael done with her?"

"I know very little on that front, Doctor Sizemore. And I can't ask Doctor Finch too many questions without arousing his suspicions. But I believe an attempt to kidnap or otherwise harm Stacy was made shortly after she arrived in London. However, that's largely conjecture on my part."

"And the source of your conjecture?"

"An overheard phone conversation between Doctor Finch and someone I assume to have been Raphael Markov. From that I deduced they had paid someone to kidnap Stacy. The tone of the conversation and Finch's wording suggested this attempt hadn't gone to plan, but again I lack any details beyond that."

Isaac stepped over to the orderly and gripped him by the shoulders. "And where is she now?"

"I don't know, Doctor Sizemore. But I'm working on finding out. All of this only occurred in the last few hours."

Isaac stepped away from the orderly and pushed his hands across his scalp. "I can't allow them to harm her. There must be some way to find out where she is!"

"Whatever has happened to her, they can't use her to threaten or control you if you're not here," Zero reminded him. "We need to go. I've disabled all the security cameras, but a new shift starts in fifteen minutes. We have to be gone before then to avoid risking detection."

Isaac regarded the beefy orderly with sudden curiosity. "You've changed," he said, remembering how Zero had fooled Finch into thinking he was Lewis. "I believe you've learned to lie."

"I am incapable of lying," Zero replied.

Isaac wanted to ask him if that was a lie too, but Zero was right about one thing—they were running out of time.

"There is one other detail of which you should be aware," Zero added.

"Which is?"

"After I removed you from Doctor Finch's office following your interrogation, I was asked to return there. Doctor Finch instructed me to fill a syringe with a lethal dosage of haloperidol and place it in a drawer in the room where he's been interrogating you. He didn't say why, but the only reasonable conclusion I can draw is that he's prepared to kill you if either he or Raphael aren't satisfied with whatever information you supply them with."

Isaac stared at him, stunned, then looked down at the over-sized pyjamas he had been given to wear. "I need clothes," he said. "I can't go wandering around outside looking like an escaped mental patient."

"I can get a change of clothes for you," said Zero. "But first you have to meet me outside."

At first Isaac thought he had misheard him. "You're standing right there, Zero. What do you mean meet—?"

Just then, a second orderly appeared in the doorway behind Zero. The blood nearly froze in Isaac's veins. This one was even more of a hulking brute than Lewis.

"There isn't time to explain," said the new arrival, his tone oddly similar to Zero's. Isaac gaped at the new arrival in mute astonishment. "The hospital rules say a patient has to be accompanied by two orderlies at all times outside hospital grounds."

The second orderly stepped past Lewis to take one of Isaac's arms. "I know this must seem confusing to you, Isaac," this second orderly said, "but we have to hurry. I'm waiting in a van outside. I'll be able to tell you everything once we're under way."

"But…" Isaac's gaze darted between the two men. "I know who you are," he said to Lewis. He turned back to the second man. "But what do you have to do with any of this?"

"Doctor Sizemore," the second orderly said with seemingly infinite patience, "I'm Zero too. We both are."

"You're…?"

Isaac swallowed, unable to make sense of what they were telling him.

"Let's go," said the first Zero, taking Isaac's other arm. They escorted him down a corridor, then through a kitchen area and finally out through a back door.

Someone else Isaac had never seen before stood next to a van with the logo of a local pizza delivery service on the side.

"Hurry, Isaac," said this latest stranger, stepping around the back of the van and pulling the rear doors open. Lewis and the second orderly helped Isaac up and inside.

"Wait," said Isaac, turning to stare at the three men. "I don't understand." He looked imploringly at Lewis. "For God's sake, Zero, they can't all be you! It's impossible. It's…!"

"We're all me, Doctor," said Lewis, his tone not unsympathetic. "But right now we need to be on our way."

And with that, he swung the van doors shut.

CHAPTER
FOUR

RAY

The morning after he'd failed to catch Stokes, Ray caught the underground into Piccadilly and headed for the small, upmarket coffee shop where he had agreed to meet Amy Cotter. Every step took an effort of will; every step filled him with the urge to turn back, to go home and hope he would never see or hear from her again.

There were too many bad memories associated with the woman. Memories he'd worked hard to forget.

His feet, however, had other ideas. Long-dormant feelings of anger and frustration had kept him awake until dawn following her unexpected call, and consequently he'd slept very little. His hands clenched and unclenched into fists as he walked, and more than one person on the rattling subway train had glanced nervously at him.

Keep it cool, Ray chided himself, seeing someone look hurriedly away when they happened to glance in his direction.

He took a deep breath and tried to keep from scowling, pushing his hands deep into the pockets of his overcoat. He was already in danger of turning into a bitter old man as it was. And Raphael Markov wouldn't be losing any sleep thinking about him, that was for sure; the bastard probably slept deep and well every night of his life.

And given how things had worked out the last time he'd gone up against Markov, meeting up with his ex-wife probably wasn't the wisest idea Ray had ever had. But by God, was he curious to find out what on Earth she wanted from him.

————

HE ARRIVED a few minutes before their agreed meeting time and peered in through the window of the coffee shop. Amy Cotter had already arrived, and was seated beneath an animated reproduction of the Mona Lisa whose gaze shifted around the room and who also, very occasionally, lifted a coffee cup to her lips.

Amy Cotter still looked as elegant and composed as she had during the television interviews she'd given following her daughter's arrest all those years ago. Back then she'd been straight-backed, with a dancer's poise, but with the shocked expression of a celebrity caught shoplifting. This time her expression was more pensive, her mouth pinched into a thin and worried line.

Her gaze flicked towards Ray as he entered the coffee shop and she stood automatically, undoubtedly recognizing him from the news. It was, he realized, the first time they had actually met in person.

"Miss Cotter," said Ray.

They shook hands. Her clasp was warm and dry.

They sat across from each other and some moments passed before she realized he wasn't going to speak first.

"You look a little tense, if you don't mind my saying, Mr

Thomas," she said with the faintest trace of a smile. Her eyes didn't quite meet his as she spoke.

"Given who your ex-husband is," said Ray, shifting uncomfortably on the narrow wooden stool that passed for the coffee shop's idea of a seat, "I have every reason to be tense."

Amy Cotter drew in a breath in the manner of a doctor about to deliver bad news. "I...suppose you've heard the news about Stacy?"

Ray shook his head, baffled. "I've been out of circulation the past couple of days. Why? What happened?"

She blinked in surprise. "So you're not at all aware that some lunatic tried to murder her?"

Ray stared at her, then touched the tabletop display, bringing up the menu and ordering a black coffee with no sugar. It gave him time to think.

"Perhaps," he said at last, "you should tell me about it."

Amy nodded, then filled Ray in on the basic details. "The way the police have it," she explained, "the only way my daughter could have wound up on the roof of that building is by illegally proxying with someone who hired her through a darknet agency. From what I've heard it was sheer luck she recovered control of her body in time to save herself. But not soon enough to keep from getting quite badly hurt."

In other words, thought Ray, the Met had assumed Stacy Cotter was up to her old tricks and had been unlucky enough to proxy with a suicide junkie. Certainly that would have been his own assumption.

Ray tried not to make his next question sound like an accusation. "You sound like you don't believe she was proxying with a client."

Anger flashed in Amy's eyes, her knuckles whitening where they gripped her coffee cup. "I know for a fact she hasn't been involved in all that sordid business for years," she replied, her voice piano-wire taut. "However she came to be proxying with this...*person* can't possibly be connected to any of that."

Ray kept his expression blank, far from sure he shared her conviction. "Have they found or identified the—" Ray caught himself before he said *suicide junkie* "—whomever she was proxying with?"

Amy's expression became steely, as if she knew precisely what Ray was thinking. "Before I say anything more, Mr Thomas, I need you to understand that everything I know about what happened to my daughter I got from a reporter who woke me very late at night looking for a statement."

Ray nodded. "I see." That, at least, explained why she'd called him so late at night.

"I've heard nothing from Raphael," she continued, referring to Stacy Cotter's father, "and if not for that guttersnipe reporter the first I'd have known about any of this would have been from this morning's news." She swallowed a gulp of air, her mouth twisting as if she'd eaten something sour. "If the police or anyone else knows the identity of the person responsible," she continued with growing indignation, "they're not saying. And they're certainly not prepared to tell me."

As she spoke, Ray tapped at his data bracelet to bring up a news summary. Stacy Cotter had indeed made the headlines, but a spate of recent government scandals had already pushed her far down the list of trending items.

Even if she was news at the moment, she wouldn't be for much longer.

A waiter finally arrived with Ray's coffee and he gulped half of it down in one go. "The last I heard," he said, "Stacy had gone abroad to make a new life for herself. What's she doing back here? A family visit, or something else?"

"I'm afraid I had no idea she was even back in the country," Amy replied sadly. "Let me assure you, however, that everything the police are saying about her is wrong."

The coffee tasted sour and bitter, but at least it chased away some of Ray's memories of the night before. "You know," he said, choosing his words carefully, "it's always hard to see these things clearly when it's your own flesh and blood that's involved."

"Except the police's story doesn't add up," Amy responded with sudden vehemence. "This 'theory' they have —" she spat the word *theory* out like a bullet "—that Stacy was proxy hooking, or whatever in God's name they call it these days, is just that: a theory that's both unsubstantiated and, I assure you, untrue. That revolting period of my daughter's life is far in the past. Stacy had her life back on track, despite her father's continued refusal to acknowledge her existence." She sat back and stared hard out of the window. "It's like they're not even trying to find out why that man wanted to kill her!"

"Well, what's Stacy's take on the whole thing?" asked Ray. "And to be frank, Miss Cotter, what do I have to do with all this?"

At these words, Amy Cotter seemed to fold in on herself, her anger and bitterness now replaced by a kind of melancholy.

"I have no idea what her 'take' is," she replied in a low voice, her gaze fixed on the table between them. "I've been prevented from speaking to her."

"I don't understand," said Ray. "Prevented by whom?"

"By her father," Amy replied. She lifted her gaze to meet his. "He has her locked up in a private clinic he owns in Kensal Green. He's paying for her treatment."

"So when you say, 'locked up' you mean…?"

"He won't let me visit her," she explained. "I tried earlier this morning to see her and the hospital security turned me away and refused to tell me when I might be able to see her.

Can you imagine?" she spat. "Her own mother. And it's not just me—they're saying she's too badly hurt to speak to anyone, including the press. That sounds to me a lot like she's being held prisoner. Otherwise, why keep everyone away like this?"

Ray found himself recalling having seen Amy Cotter speaking at a hastily-organized press conference the same night the scandal over Stacy had broken. She had sat rigidly before a microphone, flanked on either side by Raphael Markov's lawyers, her face a mask of fear, anger, outraged pain and not a little disbelief at the sight of so many journalists arrayed before her.

"Well," he suggested, "from what you've told me she had a pretty nasty fall. She might not be up to visitors just yet."

"Even so," she insisted, "I should at least be able to find out what her condition is." She leaned towards him, her expression intent. "Don't you see that this makes no sense? Mr Thomas, both myself and my daughter were effectively disowned by her father when he and I divorced. So why, after all these years, is he only now concerned with her well-being?"

The divorce, Ray recalled, had been spectacularly acrimonious. Gossip columnists had piled onto the whole thing like an army of ants fighting over a mound of sugar. "Perhaps he's had a change of heart," he said with a shrug. "It's been a long time, and she is his daughter, after all. Perhaps he's finally starting to think about his legacy."

"Mr Thomas," Amy said with sudden icy calm, "let me be clear. When I say Raphael cut us out of his life, I mean *completely*. After his lawyers were done with me, I had almost nothing. Stacy's despised her father ever since, and he, in turn, has never expressed the remotest interest in either communicating with her or having anything to do with her whatsoever."

She pursed her lips and stared hard out of the café

window. "To be honest, I don't care about that. The further he is from me and my daughter, the better. But now Raphael has her locked away in that hospital of his and I've no idea why. I can't ask her if that's what she wants, although I don't imagine it is." Her gaze shifted back to Ray. "I know her well enough to know she can't possibly be there out of choice."

"Miss Cotter—"

"All I want, Mr Thomas, is to talk to her long enough to find out if she's all right and if she even wants to be in that clinic."

Ray drained the last of his coffee. "I entirely understand why you're so upset, but I still don't see what I have to do with any of this or what I could do to help."

"There are things about Raphael you don't—" She caught herself mid-sentence and looked away from him.

Ray lifted his eyebrows. She was hiding something. But what?

"I don't what, Miss Cotter?" he asked, feigning merely casual interest.

"Nothing." She swallowed, her hands twisting around her coffee cup, even though it was by now quite empty. "I called you because you're the only person I can think of who might listen to me. I know that you have feelings of antipathy towards my ex-husband, and I thought that might make you more sympathetic. Just help me talk to her, or even just pass a message to her." She hesitated, her pale skin flushing red. "And despite what I said about Raphael leaving us with nothing, I can afford to pay you. I've done not badly for myself over the intervening years."

Judging by her designer jeans and cashmere sweater, Ray didn't doubt it.

"This just sounds like history repeating itself to me, Miss Cotter." He turned one hand palm upwards, as if weighing the options before him. "Say I got involved. Eventually the police would find out about my involvement, and then

Raphael Markov would find out, and then he'd set his attack lawyers on me." He dropped his hand back down. "And then it'd go very, very badly for me."

"But—!"

"Do I really need to explain this?" Ray said, interrupting her. A vein throbbed deep in one of his temples. He leaned towards her, tapping a finger on the table. "Any contact I've had with your family, Miss Cotter, has been—and I choose my words carefully—fucking disastrous for me. Raphael Markov framed me," he continued, his voice growing hard and tight. "I can't prove it, but I know he did it. And he did it because *I'm* the one who arrested and charged your daughter."

Amy stared back at him, her lips drawn tight and her eyes bright with shock. "If it's any help," she said, sounding flustered, "I can well believe Raphael would be capable of such a thing."

The memories felt as raw and painful as an open wound, even after so long. The evidence against him had been damning, but Ray hadn't been lying when he told a Metropolitan disciplinary committee he had no idea how so much money could have wound up in his account. Worse was the corroborating evidence that seemingly proved the money came directly from proxy dealers—backhanders supposedly paid to him so he wouldn't raid their factories.

It was bullshit, all of it.

The throbbing in his temple grew worse, and Ray once again felt his hands form into fists beneath the table where Miss Cotter couldn't see.

He drew in a breath and stood, suddenly wanting nothing more than to be out of there. "I'd like to wish you the best," he said, "but I can't help you. Raphael Markov destroyed my life once. I can't take the chance of him doing it a second time."

"Please," said Amy, "if you change your mind—"

"I won't," he said abruptly. "Goodbye, Miss Cotter."

He turned and left before she could say anything else that might dissuade him. She called after him, but whatever she'd said was lost in the blare of traffic as he stepped back onto the street, his mind still full of the events that had brought his life to a crashing halt.

CHAPTER
FIVE

ISAAC

Isaac woke to a knock on the door of the hotel room. He had been dreaming about Amy again. It ended the same way the dreams always ended, with a door bursting open and masked men in black taking hold of her.

It must, he decided, be his subconscious mind's way of reminding him not to involve her for fear of placing her in danger.

"Doctor Sizemore?"

The muffled voice coming from the other side of the door sounded unfamiliar. Sitting up, Isaac licked dry lips, his body filled with a sudden nervous tension.

It could be Zero in yet another body. Or it could be someone else entirely. Someone sent by Doctor Finch…or, worse, Raphael.

Glancing around the cramped hotel room, which still retained the lingering odour of its previous occupant, Isaac decided that if Finch's men had tracked him down yet again, there was little he could do about it.

"Who is it?" he asked warily.

"Zero."

The door opened and a heavily overweight man entirely unfamiliar to Isaac entered, bearing two paper bags above a broad white belly partly exposed by a too-small T-shirt. Isaac studied the man with a pang of distress, wondering with whom he had been proxying when Zero had, by some mechanism that still defied his understanding, taken control of this stranger's body.

Isaac was still coming to terms with the revelation that Zero could not only hijack control of people's bodies, at least so long as they were actively proxying with others, but also—incredible as it seemed—occupy *more than one body at the same time*.

In the process of the first few hours of his escape from Finch's sanatorium Isaac had encountered four different individuals, all different from each other, but all responding to the name 'Zero'.

Some of these borrowed bodies almost certainly belonged to proxy addicts—people whose self-loathing spurred them to spend as much of their lives as possible inside someone else's skin, even for just a few hours. And there was no lack of people willing to rent their bodies out for cash, universal credit chips or untraceable crypt-coin.

When Isaac had asked Zero how many bodies he could control simultaneously, he was both astounded and horrified to learn that Zero couldn't give him a definite answer. Meaning, potentially, there was no limit.

With that understanding, Isaac had foreseen a terrible future for humanity, should Zero ever fall into the wrong hands.

"I brought you breakfast," said this particular iteration of Zero, putting one of the paper bags on the bed next to Isaac.

"Thank you," said Isaac, reaching into the bag and lifting out a coffee and fresh bagels, both contained within edible takeaway boxes. He ate a bagel with one hand and searched around on the floor with his other for the pyjamas he'd worn during his escape from the sanatorium.

"There's no need to put those back on, Doctor Sizemore." Zero handed him the other paper bag. "I bought you new clothes."

Isaac peered inside the proffered bag and found it contained jeans, fresh underwear, several T-shirts and a pair of sneakers, all freshly printed by the smell of them.

"Thank you," he said, pulling the clothes on. Then he paused, one leg halfway into the jeans, and frowned at the big man. "How did you get all these things?"

"I bought them, Doctor," the fat skin wheezed.

Isaac's eyes narrowed. "With what?"

The fat man whose body Zero occupied wheezed again, as if the journey up the steps to the third floor of the motel had been the challenge of a lifetime. "With money."

Isaac stared at him for a moment, then pulled the jeans the rest of the way on and sat back down. "You don't have a bank account." His eyes widened. "Do you? Have a bank account, I mean?"

"No, Doctor. Or at least, not one I can access that wouldn't draw unwanted attention were I to spend it on such things." The fat man pressed two fleshy hands against his chest. "I borrowed the money from this man."

"Oh, Zero." Isaac pressed one hand against his brow. "You stole from him. You can't do that!"

The fat skin's face twisted up in surprise and hurt. "I'm sorry, Doctor Sizemore," he wheezed, and reached out for the paper bag still sitting on Isaac's lap. "I'll take them back. I'm sure they'll agree to refund me if I—"

"No, wait," said Isaac, putting a hand out to stop him.

He needed a coffee—several, really—in order to think clearly. He had needed clothes, and Zero had brought them to him in the fastest, easiest, most efficient and—unfortunately—most immoral way possible.

Zero gazed back at him with an expression like a hurt child and Isaac felt a stab of pity. "Does he have any identification? The skin you're wearing right now? A wallet, perhaps, or anything else?"

"Yes." The fat skin dug around inside his pockets and produced a chip-phone. Isaac took it from him: it was probably voice- or retina-locked which, given Zero was already occupying its owner's body, wouldn't have presented any challenge to an entity such as he.

"All right," said Isaac, passing the phone back. "Here's what you're going to do. You're going to write a note—" he paused and studied the fat man as a sudden thought occurred to him. "I know this might sound stupid, but you do know how to write? I mean, using a pen?"

"I can write by hand, yes," Zero agreed. "I don't find it easy, however." He flexed the fat man's hands. "It never looks quite the same from proxy to proxy."

It hardly surprised Isaac. Handwriting was one of the surest ways of detecting whether the person you were talking to was in fact the owner of that body, and not someone controlling it remotely via proxy.

"Write a note," Isaac instructed him, "explaining that you borrowed the money in an emergency and that we will pay it back. Don't sign it or provide any other form of identification, but place it in one of the proxy's pockets. Include an apology for taking control of his body, however temporarily, without his permission. Then search the rest of his pockets for any other signs of identification. If you find them, make a second note for ourselves, so we know where to send him the money."

"Yes, Doctor Sizemore," Zero agreed. "What about the others?"

"Other what? Other bodies you borrowed?" He hadn't thought of that. "How many of them are there?"

"Approximately forty-three at this moment, Doctor Sizemore."

"Oh, for…" At least the AI was of the benevolent child-like variety. If Zero had been anything like the ones that featured in the violent action films of Isaac's long-distant youth, God only knew what horrors he might have perpetrated by now. Not that Isaac would have allowed any such artificial intelligence to come into existence.

"There's something else, Doctor Sizemore. I discovered Stacy's whereabouts, but I'm afraid she's been hurt."

Isaac stared at the fat man with a mixture of fear and hope. He'd been stuck in this shitty little hotel room for the best part of two days, his terror growing exponentially for every second that passed without word from Stacy.

"How bad?" he asked, his voice betraying a slight tremble.

Zero stepped towards a wall-panel TV and turned it on. He selected a news channel and Isaac saw a scrolling summary running along the bottom of the screen with Stacy's name: WOMAN INJURED DURING POSSIBLE PROXY SUICIDE ATTEMPT IN NORTH LONDON IDENTIFIED AS ESTRANGED DAUGHTER OF BILLIONAIRE RAPHAEL MARKOV.

Other scrolling headlines replaced the words and Isaac felt something lurch deep inside his chest.

"She's in a hospital," Zero explained. "One owned by a Telop Industries subsidiary."

"How did it happen?" Isaac croaked, staring at the screen in horror.

"The initial reports said she tried to commit suicide by jumping from the roof of an arcology, Doctor Sizemore, but only fell a short distance before landing on a balcony and injuring herself. Some news feeds are speculating about whether she'd gone back to proxying illegally, only to have one of her clients try to kill her."

A suicide junkie, in the current parlance: the very words

sent a chill deep into Isaac's bones. There were people out there who got a sadistic kick out of murdering anyone foolish enough to proxy with them, so they could experience the thrill of violent death without actually dying.

"Well," said Isaac, "we know now that's not true." Finch had even known they were meeting with a journalist. "Where is this hospital?"

"Kensal Green," Zero replied.

Isaac nodded with determination. "I don't know what Raphael has planned for her, but we have to get her out of there somehow."

"Of course, Doctor Sizemore."

"Zero?"

"Yes, Doctor Sizemore?"

"Remember to call me Isaac, won't you?"

The fat man hesitated, then complied. "Yes, Isaac."

Isaac stood. "You understand what I'm saying, don't you? If I know Raphael, whatever intentions he has towards her, they won't be good. He'll have her under tight security. We're going to have to figure out some way to get her out of there. And do it without harming anyone."

Long seconds ticked by before Zero finally responded. "That could be difficult, Isaac. People might get hurt regardless."

"You're the supercomputer, Zero. Make sure they don't."

"Even so, it will be difficult."

"But not impossible?"

The fat man shook his head. "No."

CHAPTER
SIX

RAPHAEL

Far below where Raphael Markov stood looking down from his office window, traffic and pedestrians moved through the city of London like cells in some vast living network.

He stepped back from the floor-to-ceiling window and in response it became semi-opaque, filtering the exterior light. An icon blinked in one corner of his vision and he lightly tapped a silver ring clipped to his right ear, catching sight of his reflection in the window as he did so. The ring, he thought not for the first time, gave him a certain piratical edge.

"Sir?" said a voice in his right ear. "I'm afraid there was another security breach this morning—a journalist. He got as far as the nurse's station on the second floor of the Peartree before one of our security teams intercepted him."

"Thank you, Goulding. I'll handle it from here."

"Sir." Goulding cleared his throat. "Should I advise your gym staff regarding whether you'll be needing them today…?"

"Tell them I'll be on schedule," Markov replied. "Send Lovatt through."

He tapped the ring again, breaking the connection before

stepping over to his desk. Holograms of water-lilies span in a slow current beneath its glass surface. He touched the glass and an icon blinked in the simulated depths.

Thirty seconds later the door to his office slid noiselessly open. "Sir," said the man who entered, his expensive suit doing little to conceal his musculature.

"Lovatt," said Markov, looking over at him. "I just learned some journalist managed to get inside the Peartree and came very close to speaking with my daughter. Do I need to emphasize how very, very unhappy that makes me?"

Lovatt nodded. "My apologies, sir. We've tightened security, but there's only so much we can do without attracting more press attention. The hospital staff have been complaining about having to present identification every time they leave or enter the building. Plus, they've been asking a lot of questions about why so much security is required when—"

"I don't give a fuck about your excuses!" Markov bellowed. "Make sure nobody gets in or out unless I say otherwise, whoever the hell they are, or you can hand in your resignation here and now. And if they complain, tell them the same thing I just told you. They work for me."

Lovatt inclined his head once more, betraying no outward sign of emotion. "Understood, sir. Is there anything else?"

Markov fell into the seat behind his desk and smoothed his hands over his face. "My apologies for shouting at you," he said after another moment. "Circumstances have made me…somewhat tense."

"That's understandable, sir."

Damn Finch! Raphael's gaze alighted on a framed photograph that sat on a shelf close by his desk. It showed a man in late middle-age clinging to a sheer rock face somewhere in the Ardennes, a seemingly bottomless gulf of air beneath his feet. The man grinned up at whomever had been holding the camera. Raphael's own features, reflected in the frame's glass, were nearly identical to the older man's.

"Any news about Isaac Sizemore?" he asked Lovatt, without shifting his gaze from the photograph.

"We still haven't been able to track him down. Someone disabled all the security cameras in the Abbey Rush Centre just minutes before he disappeared."

Raphael nodded, thinking. "In other words, he had outside help."

Lovatt inclined his head slightly. "We did, however, source CCTV footage from a hotel around the corner from Abbey Rush. It shows a van departing the Centre in the early hours of the morning. A few hours before that, the same van was reported stolen."

Even if Finch hadn't drugged him into a stupor, there was no conceivable way Isaac could have organized an escape without someone's help. But who?

Raphael started at a sudden, terrible thought: was it possible Isaac had offered his services to someone else? Could there be other players in this game apart from Telop Industries, perhaps another corporation or even a government?

No, he decided; if that was the case, Lovatt and his men would never have been able to track Isaac down in the first place while travelling south through Scotland. Isaac would have long since disappeared into some secure lab, most likely with yet another new identity to further obfuscate his trail.

And yet, someone had helped him escape...so who?

"Keep at it," Raphael told Lovatt. "Report to me the instant you hear anything."

Lovatt nodded curtly and departed.

Raphael stayed where he was, hands steepled together and his gaze fixed on the virtual water lilies. He'd often wondered over the years whether he was wasting his time, hiring a private security firm to monitor Stacy in the increasingly dim hope Isaac might get in touch with her...until, at last, he had.

After that, it had been a simple matter to uncover Stacy's plans to travel back home to England in order to meet an investigative journalist named Martin Wilber. When Isaac had suddenly shown up at almost the same time, travelling by ferry and train from Norway to Aberdeen, it was easy to conclude he was on his way to meet both Stacy and Wilber.

And that was something that could never be allowed to happen.

Subsequently, Raphael had ordered that Isaac be captured at the soonest opportunity. The scientist might still have valuable information buried in his demented skull.

The girl, however, was valueless, so he had hired a specialist to take care of her in such a way that her death would draw few questions. Isaac, locked in a ward as he was, would have been none the wiser.

All had seemed to go well until the specialist hired to kill Stacy fucked up spectacularly, leaving him with no choice but to put on a very public show of taking care of her instead.

Maybe, thought Raphael, his gaze still fixed on the water-lilies, some good could come out of this; maybe the girl could be used as leverage to make Isaac come to *him*.

CHAPTER
SEVEN

ELIJAH

Elijah saw the bunched fist swinging towards him at the last second.

Twisting to one side, he slammed himself up against the wall of the prison workroom. Stobbs let out a guttural snarl and swung at him again, his scarred and battered face twisted up in fury.

Only then did Elijah see the shiv, clenched in the other man's calloused hand.

Stobbs was the big and muscular type, and brute force was pretty much all he had going for him. Elijah, by contrast, was lighter and faster, and as Stobbs came lumbering forward Elijah brought up one knee, feeling it crunch satisfyingly into the other man's balls.

A rush of air escaped Stobb's lungs and the shiv slid from his grasp, clattering to the workroom floor. Pressing his advantage, Elijah wrapped both arms around his attacker's head and slammed it repeatedly against the side of a machine press.

Then Elijah turned and ran out of the workroom and down a corridor past the laundry rooms, wondering all the while just where the fuck the guards had all disappeared to. They'd been everywhere a moment before, and now it was like they'd all vanished into some nether dimension.

He'd never crossed Stobbs—indeed, he'd barely exchanged a word with the man since starting his sentence. There was no reason, no rhyme to the attack.

But then again, Stobbs was an enforcer for the Cullen firm. And the only reason for Stobbs to try and kill him was that someone, somewhere had ordered a hit.

Well, balls to that.

He crashed past two other inmates, not looking back to see if Stobbs was coming after him, and burst into the kitchens. A fat blob of a man with a shaven head crossed his path, carrying a huge pot of something that bubbled and steamed.

Hearing the commotion, he turned to look Elijah's way. His eyes grew round as saucers, his gaze focused on something behind Elijah.

Elijah squeezed past the fat man, then turned and shoved him hard in the small of his back. The man stumbled, sloshing boiling water onto the kitchen floor—and onto Stobbs, who'd been in close pursuit.

Stobbs screamed and stumbled backwards, slipping on the wet tiles and hitting the floor with a thud. Knives and pans came clattering down around him, and Elijah could see that his pursuer's neck and forearms were already turning beet-root-red.

"Tosser," Elijah muttered, panting hard.

The screws finally put in an appearance, four of them bursting into the kitchens with their batons drawn. When Elijah saw the look on their faces, he knew immediately it wasn't Stobbs they'd been expecting to have to scrape off the floor.

Elijah stepped up close to the fat kitchen worker, who looked as perplexed as he did terrified.

"It was an accident, right?" Elijah said to him in a low voice, fixing him with a hard stare. "You didn't see nothing suggesting otherwise."

"Yeah. Sure." The fat man's head jerked up and down. "Accident."

Elijah breathed hard through his nose and flexed his fists, but didn't resist when the prison guards grabbed him and cuffed him.

There was more than enough time for Elijah to figure out who was gunning for him. And then they'd wish they'd never heard of him.

———

"LISTEN," Lorenz told Elijah the next day, waving a roll-up in his face, "nobody does a fucking hit in this establishment unless it comes through me first." Lorenz leaned back, folding one tattooed arm under an armpit and regarding him through the smoke. "Sure you didn't tickle Stobbs' balls for a laugh?"

"Very sure," said Elijah.

They were sitting in Lorenz's cell in the early evening, an hour during which the Scrubs allowed prisoners to mix with relatively minimal supervision. It had only confirmed Elijah's worst fears when he wasn't charged for assault; nor was there any mention of Stobb's shiv. Instead, they treated the whole thing like it had been an accident and let Elijah go before loading Stobbs into an ambulance.

It took a lot of money to make that many screws look the other way and avoid any chance of an official enquiry.

Davie, Lorenz's second-in-command, stood by the open cell door, his unwavering gaze fixed on Elijah.

Lorenz took another drag on his cigarette. "And the screws just vanished, you say?"

Elijah nodded. "Like smoke."

"Not much chance of asking Stobbs who paid him to have

a go at you now he's in intensive care." One corner of Lorenz's mouth creased into a grin. "You upset anyone before they tossed you in here?"

Elijah shrugged. "Lots of people."

Lorenz made a noncommittal sound. "You're in for proxy dealing, right?"

"Ah heard it wis murder," said Davie, in a booming Glaswegian accent.

Elijah stared at Davie. "Sure, yeah, that too. But it was a stitch-up," he quickly added.

"Oh?" Lorenz said. "How so?"

"I got body-jacked," Elijah explained. "Somebody clubbed me in the back of my head when I stepped out of the building where me and my mate had our proxy factory and the next thing I knew, I was handcuffed to a desk in a trailer. The walls were all covered in circus posters in some language that wasn't English. And the skin I found myself in was dressed up like a circus acrobat."

"A—?" Lorenz coughed out smoke and stared at Elijah in disbelief. "A what?"

"Point is, I was stuck in that bastard's skin for six solid hours with no idea what the hell he was doing with my own body. When I finally found myself back in my own skin, I was inside my proxy factory, covered head to foot in blood, with a hammer in one hand and my best mate's corpse lying at my feet with his skull smashed in."

"In fairness," said Lorenz, looking amused, "there's hardly a murder trial these days where the defendant doesn't claim they were forcibly proxied. It's not the most original defence."

"Yes, I know that," said Elijah, "but in my case it's true. It happens, you know. Someone tipped the cops off. They turned up in force barely a minute after I woke up back in my own skin. They knew exactly where to find the factory."

"Kind of ironic, though," said Lorenz, picking at an ear.

"You running a proxy factory, then getting set up by someone using proxy. Any idea who might have wanted to take you out of the picture?"

Elijah shrugged. "Most likely someone wanted to take over my business. After they locked me up, I paid someone to try and track down the guy who'd used my body to murder Rob, but the best they could figure out was that they had been proxying with me from somewhere in Eastern Europe. Dead end, basically."

Few proxy factories lasted as much as six months. Either their owners got nicked, or they got taken over by some other crew. It was quite possible someone had set Elijah up precisely so they could take over his and Rob's factory, secreted as it was in a disused building in a run-down industrial estate on the outskirts of Croydon.

Plus, word had been getting around about just how much money he and Rob had been making, manufacturing the new, longer-lasting proxy technology known as hopscotch. There was no lack of willing buyers, and that kind of attention could either get you nicked or killed.

But Elijah had had questions about hopscotch. Questions he'd been warned never to ask by the mysterious benefactor who supplied them with the recipe.

Rob, however, hadn't cared where this new, more powerful form of proxy came from nearly so much as he cared about the money they were making from it. Rob had even talked about getting a licence to set up a legal proxy business, once the proposed changes to the law came about.

Until then, the only legally allowed use of proxy had been by the police and by disability charities. But things had been getting more relaxed, especially after Pandemic Three scared almost everyone off international travel.

Just like that, proxy had gone from being perceived as sleazy, immoral and potentially lethal to just about the safest way to travel abroad without risking a potentially deadly infection since, after all, it didn't require either user to actually go anywhere.

And proxy, relying as it did on quantum entanglement to create its unique bond between a pair of human minds, could work across any distance. Not that Elijah could have taken advantage of those changing laws, being banged up in the Scrubs by that time.

If he'd just listened to Rob, stopped asking so many questions and been happy to just take the money, he might still be a free man...

...and Rob might still be alive.

But that was his curse, wasn't it? Elijah thought miserably. He was naturally inquisitive, always asking questions even if nobody wanted to give him the answers. Whatever people didn't want him to know, he tried to find out. Even if it got him into trouble.

Their unnamed benefactor had been the first person Elijah thought of, when he found himself standing over Rob's corpse with a hammer in one hand: the weirdest thing was that the man had insisted he didn't want a share of their profits from selling hopscotch.

And statements like that were just guaranteed to raise Elijah's curiosity to epic levels.

"So what exactly is it you want from me then, Elijah?" Lorenz asked him.

"I need a skin," said Elijah, his thoughts returning to the present. "Someone on the outside, so I can try to find out who's got it in for me."

Davie sniggered. "You couldn't afford something like that."

"Shut it, you daft twat," Lorenz said over his shoulder without once taking his eyes off Elijah. "Proxy dealing is as good as printing your own money." He focused on Elijah with renewed and greedy interest. "That's right, isn't it?"

"We did all right," Elijah said guardedly.

"Because," said Lorenz, "as Davie so rightly points out, it's going to cost you. Want to know how much?"

Elijah shrugged like that was the last thing he cared about, but his blood cooled a couple of degrees when Lorenz named a figure.

He could afford it, but only just.

"It's a lot, I know." Lorenz tried to look sympathetic, but he was clearly struggling to keep a feral grin off his face. "But it's not like you've got much of a choice, is it?"

CHAPTER
EIGHT

STACY

"Miss Cotter?" The doctor closed the door of the private ward behind him. He glanced at a wall-monitor above her bed and then returned his attention to Stacy. "How are you feeling today?"

The doctor looked the young and bright-eyed type, thought Stacy, like a college girl's wet dream of perfect husband material. His name tag read Doctor Taft.

She groaned and moved her one arm that wasn't immobilised by heavy bandaging. Even the simple act of breathing created a sensation like razor-edged daggers sliding beneath her ribs.

Bright and unwelcome sunlight streamed through broad windows, and someone had arranged cut flowers in a vase on a table next to the window while she had still been asleep. A shelving unit filled with unread paperbacks stood next to a leather couch in the far corner. Apart from the bed, it looked more like someone's lounge than a hospital room.

She had relived the long tumble onto the balcony of the arcology over and over again in her dreams. Landing on bushes and freshly turned soil rather than hard concrete had saved her life, but the awful, racking pain she'd endured waiting for an ambulance crew to arrive—far beyond anything she might have believed possible—would remain with her forever.

"I want more morphine," Tracy croaked, the words finding their way past shards of diamond glass that had taken up residence inside her ribcage.

Doctor Taft glanced again at the wall-monitor above her bed and put on a professional, if not entirely convincing, smile. "You're about ready to get out of that bed and start walking around again, Miss Cotter," he said. "More morphine would be a bad idea. Frankly, you've been extraordinarily lucky not to have suffered far worse injuries. Anyway," he added, "I thought you'd like to know that we've been keeping your father up to date on your progress."

Stacy coughed weakly. "I'm sorry, did you say my father?"

"Mr Markov, yes." The doctor frowned, wondering, perhaps, if she had suffered more than just a bad concussion from her fall. "We had this conversation just yesterday, Miss Cotter."

She blinked at the doctor. "We did?"

"You weren't so lucid at the time, admittedly." Doctor Taft touched a stylus to an electronic tablet he grasped in one hand. "A physical therapist will be along to see you in a few hours. The good news," he added, looking back up, "is that he's coming to visit you tomorrow morning."

Stacy's heart began to pound so loudly she wondered how the doctor couldn't hear it. "Who is?"

The doctor gave her an odd look. "Your father, Miss Cotter." He turned back towards the door. "I'll ask the nurse to come and take your lunch order," he added over his shoulder.

"There's someone I'd like to call," Stacy said in a rush. She did a bad job of hiding her panic. "Can I have my bracelet, please?"

The doctor, when he turned back around, had an evasive look on his face. "We really can't allow the use of bracelets on the premises, I'm afraid, Miss Cotter. They interfere with the equipment."

This was bullshit. She knew it, he knew it. "Then might you perhaps get me a chip-phone?" Stacy asked, keeping her voice just on the right side of hysteria. "Just a cheap one is all I need. You could allow that, couldn't you?"

Taft hesitated a moment far too long for her comfort. "Of course," Taft said at last. "I'll ask one of the nurses to do just that."

Liar, thought Stacy as Doctor Taft departed, closing the door behind him.

She tried to remember anything else between falling onto the balcony, being scraped up out of the dirt and put into the back of an ambulance, and…and waking up here. She couldn't.

Instead, it occurred to Stacy that it was surprisingly quiet for a hospital. One might even think unusually quiet.

She could wait and see if someone would bring her some kind of phone she could use, but once Raphael's name had been mentioned she'd felt sure beyond a flicker of doubt that they would not.

Nor would they allow her to leave, at least not alive, not if Raphael Markov had anything to do with it.

The silence of the room quickly became oppressive. Then she glanced at the TV mounted to the wall opposite her bed and wondered if she could use it to access the net. If she could, perhaps she could send Isaac a warning.

Fat chance. But she tried anyway, voicing commands.

The screen came to life, but she was hardly surprised when it turned out she couldn't use it to access the net. The best she could make it do was change channels.

She let her head sink back against the pillows and thought bleak thoughts. The window didn't have bars, but it might as

well have; all the professional manner and lounge-like deco-
ration didn't make her feel any less of a prisoner.

Could she walk out of here, she wondered? She tried
sitting up and felt a sharp pain in her chest. Grimacing, she
eased herself back down. And even if she could, what would
they do? Keep her under sedation around the clock?

Just how thoroughly were the staff in this hospital, or, or…
clinic or whatever it was, under Raphael's thumb?

She needed to think.

Just then, she glanced back at the television, which had
defaulted to a 24 hour news channel, and saw her own face
from a few years before displayed slightly above and to one
side of the news anchor.

Stacy sat up again, ignoring the fresh stab of pain this
brought. She increased the TV's volume and quickly discovered the story was—unsurprisingly—about her near-death
experience.

They weren't openly speculating about how she had come
to be stranded atop the arcology, but neither were they reticent about pulling up old news stories regarding her past
misdemeanours.

Stacy fought back the bitter taste in the back of her throat
when they displayed pictures of her slumming it in London's
nightclubs when she'd still only been a teenager. These were
followed, inevitably, by a recap of how her mother had come
to be divorced by Raphael Markov, one of the world's richest
and most influential tech entrepreneurs.

It got worse. Her guts roiled with shame and horror when
the next image that flashed up showed her being escorted in
cuffs to a police car on charges of proxy-hooking.

None of it would have happened if it hadn't been for Gabe.

Gabe had been Stacy's boyfriend, but also her business
partner—or so he had liked to tell her. She first met him in a
Camden squat she'd crashed in on the night of her sixteenth

birthday, desperate to get as far away from her mother and home as possible.

She couldn't remember who exactly had introduced her to Gabe. Everyone seemed to know him, although it wasn't until later she learned this was only because he was a proxy dealer. Gabe was popular because he made some people... well, not rich, but better off enough they didn't have to stay in a squat any more.

All they had to do was rent their bodies out to Gabe's clients.

In those first few days of their fumbling courtship, it had felt inevitable to Stacy that she and Gabe would become lovers. It was only now, with the perspective of adulthood, that she could see the ease with which he had manipulated her. He'd only been in his early twenties at the time, but to a sixteen-year old runaway, he had seemed impossibly mature and mysterious.

Gabe talked about proxy like using it represented an act of supreme charity and sacrifice. Many disabled people, he explained—paraplegics, the paralysed or the terminally ill— were hungry to proxy with anyone who had a healthy body, even if only for a few hours. They got to run or swim or go outdoors and, yes, he admitted with a sly grin, make love.

And then there were the elderly couples who wanted to experience each other the way they had when they first started courting, with long, smooth-skinned limbs and bodies that responded immediately and fully to every touch and sensation.

And then there were those who were perfectly able-bodied and young, but felt an intense desire to experience each other in the bodies of strangers.

And some of these people were prepared to pay a very great deal of money for the experience.

He'd waited a couple of weeks to make his pitch to her,

and after they had more or less moved in together. They could, he explained, make a lot of money from such people.

And it wasn't like hooking in the old sense, he'd explained —Stacy would never have to sleep with anyone other than him. Instead, they would each proxy with one half of a couple, and let them do what they would inside their own, more youthful bodies. Stacy and Gabriel, meanwhile, would wait out the proxy session in the bodies of those who had paid them for the privilege.

And yes, there were dangers—which was why it was illegal. Clients might literally murder you while they were in your bodies, or inject you full of dangerous drugs or go on a rampage.

But such things, Gabe had assured her, were rare. Very, very rare.

And it had been fun, too, for a while anyway. But there had been another reason Stacy agreed to the arrangement— one she had never told her new lover.

When she had still been very young, Stacy had managed to convince herself that her mother, Amy, had done something to cause her father to push them both out of his life. If she could only speak face to face with her father, Stacy had come to believe, she could find out why he'd gone to such lengths to reject his own daughter when she had been hardly more than a baby.

Not that she hadn't already tried asking him. She had even written letters to Raphael Markov following her parent's separation, without her mother ever knowing. She never received an answer.

Barely a year before she first met Gabe, Stacy had travelled to the London offices of Telop hoping to find Raphael there, only to be gently rebuffed by the security staff. They had called her mother, and Amy had been forced to come and pick Stacy up, warning her the whole way back home to never try such a thing again.

Most of the people Gabe arranged for them to proxy with were rich. They had to be, to afford the prices he charged. And a very few of them, she quickly realized, moved in the same circles as her father.

When she and Gabe proxied with their clients, they most often found themselves occupying their client's bodies in a locked hotel room that had been rented for that specific purpose. Most often, the door was locked to prevent them going walkabout in their borrowed rich person's skins.

But on one particular occasion, Stacy had discovered her father was speaking at a conference held within the very same hotel she and Gabe found themselves in while waiting out a proxy session.

Picking the hotel room's electronic lock was easy, once Gabe showed her how. Still wearing the skin of a woman twenty years her senior, Stacy went in search of Raphael, but it still proved impossible to get anywhere near him. Security was tight and ever-present, and the skin was no one her father would recognize.

But if she could find the right client in the right place, perhaps she could finally get close enough to him to ask the question that had filled her dreams and nightmares ever since she was a little girl.

It was a ridiculous, childish fantasy, and the images on the television screen brought every last awful memory of that time flooding back.

Not that he would ever have told her the truth, she knew now. The same truth that had brought her back across the English Channel for the sole purpose of meeting with an investigative journalist, and which had nearly ended in her death.

Ordering the TV back off, Stacy felt the first real stirrings of anger. The implication of the news report was clear: she was nothing more than a messed-up rich kid who'd turned to proxy hooking for a cheap thrill. They had reduced her to a two-dimensional sound bite entirely lacking in agency, some-thing for worried parents and the narrow-minded to tut over.

And now here she was, waiting for her estranged father to finally come and meet her...and it was the last thing she wanted.

Moving carefully, Stacy drew back the sheets covering her. Tugging up her nightdress, she winced at the yellow and blue bruises that dotted her legs, stomach, arms and chest.

She had to get as far away as possible from the hospital before Raphael arrived. Most likely, he was coming with the intention of pumping her for information about both Martin Wilber and Isaac. And after that...well, he'd have no further reason to keep her alive.

Stacy pulled the sheets aside and gently placed her feet on the floor, but even that simple motion was enough to make her head swim.

Christ, she thought. *I'll be lucky to make it to the door.*

She forced herself to breathe evenly and tried hard to ignore the pain in her back and shoulders. After another minute, she tugged loose a monitoring cuff that had been placed around her wrist and tried to stand.

She was a little wobbly at first, but managed to stay upright.

Okay. Stacy shuffled slowly over to the door, seizing its handle like it was a lifebuoy thrown from a sinking ship.

To her surprise, it wasn't locked, as she'd fully expected it to be. She eased it open, then peered down the corridor outside.

She found herself looking at the broad shoulders and back of a large and very muscular man wearing a dark suit and talking quietly into his data bracelet. He had to be security, placed there to keep her from leaving.

Closing the door again with care so as not to make any noise, Stacy tottered back across the room and over to the window. Rolling the blinds up, she found herself looking at part of a metal fire escape. The opposite side of the street was taken up by a windowless brick wall, and when she pressed her nose against the glass and looked down, she could just about make out a row of open-topped industrial-sized waste bins set beneath the fire escape.

When she reached for the window latch, Stacy was relieved to find that this, too, was unlocked.

She hobbled back across the room, wincing with every step, and took hold of a cheap aluminium folding chair sitting under the TV. She dragged the chair next to the open window and carefully stood on it, then eased one leg over the windowsill and onto the fire escape.

She rested for a moment, one hand braced against the jamb, then swung her other leg over the sill.

It took time, but she managed to descend most of the way to the ground before running into an unanticipated problem: the fire escape came to an end a dozen feet short of the ground and just above the row of bins she had seen earlier. There was a drop-down ladder, but it was padlocked into place.

She sat down to catch her breath, already feeling winded. At least, so far as she could tell, no one had seen her or noticed her absence.

But someone would come to check on her before too long, and she needed to be far away from here before that happened.

Somehow, she found the willpower to lever herself over the fire escape railing and drop, gracelessly, onto a mound of hospital refuse bags stacked in one of the bins.

"Ow," she said, fighting her way upright amidst the bags of stinking refuse. Something unpleasantly slimy and cold pressed against the back one of her legs. "Bloody fucking *ow*."

Placing both hands on the outside edge of the bin, and ignoring the throbbing pains in her arms, belly, back and shoulders, Stacy looked up and down the narrow street that ran along this side of the hospital. No one had seen her escape. The hiss and roar of passing traffic came from a neighbouring road.

With one arm still bandaged, it took longer to climb out of the bin and drop down onto the pavement than it had taken her to climb down the fire escape. Worse, she stood out somewhat in the cheap hospital gown she was wearing.

Moving slowly, Stacy limped towards the sound of traffic. The end of the street formed a T-junction with another road along which a number of cars passed.

She thought of hailing a cab, then remembered she didn't have her bracelet. Self-driving cabs all had inbuilt protocols that meant they had to respond to an emergency request, meaning she could still use one, but it would deliver her straight to the police and then, most likely, the police would deliver her straight back to her father.

It was still a chance, she told herself. If she could make even one person listen, or persuade someone to loan her their bracelet long enough to call Martin Wilber and tell him where she was, she might still be able to get out of this mess.

Up ahead, she saw the entrance to a small park opposite the hospital. When she got to the end of the street, her heart spasmed with joy when she saw a cab sitting waiting at the lights a block or two away and apparently unoccupied.

She stepped towards the edge of the road to hail it, then glanced over her shoulder in the direction of what she could now see was the front entrance of the hospital. Another man who looked like he spent a lot of time in the gym stood outside the entrance, a cigarette halfway to his mouth, his eyes wide as he stared back at her.

The cigarette slipped from his fingers as he raised his bracelet to his lips, speaking rapidly into it even as he broke into a run towards her.

CHAPTER
NINE

ELIJAH

The four days after Elijah spoke with Lorenz felt like the longest four days of his life.

If there was a bright side, nobody tried to murder him. It didn't make Elijah any less certain it was just a matter of time before someone else made the attempt.

On the second day, Davie, Lorenz's second-in-command, asked Elijah a series of questions. The fastest way for a screw to work out if an inmate was proxying his way out of prison was to ask him his birthday, so Elijah supplied Davie not only with his date of birth, but his mother's name, her maiden name, and a bunch of details about where he'd lived and gone to school, along with the details of his arrest and trial: details which could be used by whomever he wound up proxying with to convince a suspicious screw he really was speaking to Elijah Waits.

On the morning of the fourth day, Sloane, another of Lorenz's helpers, pressed something into Elijah's hand as they passed by each other in the prison canteen.

Elijah folded his fingers around the paper-wrapped package without so much as glancing at Sloane. He pushed the package deep inside a pocket and tried to make it look like he was scratching his thigh. After all, you never knew who might be watching.

After that he worked in the laundry for a couple of hours before returning to his cell and pulling out the package. Unwrapping the brown paper, he found a 3D-printed proxy applicator and a slip with '3 A.M.' scrawled on it. The applicator came preloaded, as Elijah had expected, with a single proxy bead.

After lights out, Elijah stared up at the underside of the bunk above his without sleeping. His cellmate snored noisily. From time to time Elijah glanced towards a radio-alarm sitting on a shelf beneath the window.

The minutes and hours dragged past as slow as continents forming and reforming over geological ages.

The instant the clock read 3 A.M., Elijah sat upright, placed the applicator against the back of his neck above the spine and pressed the trigger.

The applicator hissed faintly, firing the bead it contained deep beneath his skin.

He winced at the sharp pain. A better-quality applicator would have numbed it, but this had felt like jabbing a knitting needle into his neck.

Lying down again, Elijah pulled the applicator apart with his fingers, then tore it into strips and chewed them down. The applicator was made of a non-toxic edible material, a necessary step to reduce the risk of discovery.

Cheap or not, the proxy link kicked in within seconds. Elijah experienced a fleeting moment of vertigo before—

—finding himself looking up at a pale grey ceiling, neon light washing through half-drawn blinds.

The world span drunkenly. Everything looked too small, somehow, as if he'd suddenly grown bigger and taller. When he sat up, unfamiliar muscles shifted beneath his borrowed skin.

Still disoriented, he got himself upright without crashing into anything and staggered through to a tiny bathroom where he vomited noisily into the toilet bowl. Then he went to wash his face and stared at the unfamiliar reflection in the mirror.

He couldn't help but laugh out loud. After all, it wasn't as if he'd specified his proxy had to be black.

"Hello there," said Elijah, testing out the proxy's vocal cords. The voice sounded deep and resonant—and very, very Glaswegian. Elijah grunted out another laugh. Most likely, the proxy was someone Davie knew.

The proxy looked fifteen or twenty years older than Elijah. A scar, mostly faded, ran down one pale-skinned cheek. Another, much deeper scar, ran from one corner of the mouth most of the way to the right ear. The hands were large and spade-like with calloused, blunt fingers.

He looked, thought Elijah, like a gang enforcer on his night off—which he might well be.

"Well," said Elijah, in as soft a voice as his proxy was capable of producing, "I'll give you this, Lorenz. You fucking delivered."

When he stepped back out of the bathroom, Elijah saw that he was in a hotel room barely larger than his cell. The furniture looked cheap and a strong chemical smell emanated from the carpet. A glance at the bed revealed something he'd missed: an envelope, with his initials scrawled on it.

Inside the envelope he found a pre-paid disposable bracelet. Slipping it onto his left wrist, Elijah activated it, finding it came with a linked account containing enough cash to hire a car or rent a room for another night—not that he expected the proxy session to last more than four or five hours before it wore off.

Which meant there was no time to waste.

A search of the proxy's pockets brought up some loose

change, a business card for a betting agency, and a screw-driver with a sharpened point.

Lovely. Elijah grimaced, but didn't throw the screwdriver away.

Pulling on a heavy woollen overcoat that lay draped over a chair by the door, Elijah made his way down a cramped stairwell and past a self-service check-in desk. Stepping outside, he found himself on a quiet side-street somewhere in London.

He got moving. His proxy's stride was much longer than his own, and his eyes a good foot further from the ground than Elijah was used to, and so he walked a little awkwardly at first. But he knew from experience he'd get used to it soon enough.

The pre-paid bracelet guided Elijah towards a row of parked cars. A few people passed him on the street, and he observed—not for the first time—how different it felt to walk around in a white, rather than a black, skin. Even a huge, ugly fucker like his proxy didn't draw the nervous, darting glances he had too often endured as a black man.

The first time Elijah had walked inside a white man's skin, years before, it had been a revelation. He had to suppress a grin when he passed some coppers and they didn't so much as blink, let alone look his way.

Imagine what the world would be like if more white people got to walk around inside my skin, he thought, not for the first time. *Then they'd see things differently.*

Yes, some few still thought of proxy as nothing more than a cheap route to sexual kicks, but it was much more than that: it was the future, or so he fervently believed. He was convinced it was how people would live all the time in a hundred years, swapping themselves in and out of each other's bodies all around the world, all the time, instead of furtively and in the shadows.

Upon a time, Elijah had been downright evangelical about

the possibilities. It was the reason why he'd asked so many questions after their mysterious benefactor supplied him and Rob with a new, more powerful recipe for proxy. Powerful enough to make Elijah think the future he had imagined might be closer than he had at first believed.

His first taste of proxy came just a few months after his return from the total shit storm that had been the war in Korea. Back then, proxy was brand-new—so new, in fact, it wasn't yet illegal.

That had come soon enough. First, three South Korean military pilots had been forcibly proxied in a carefully coordinated attack that ended with them crashing their jets into Seoul's National Assembly Hall. Then a white supremacist organization nobody had heard of before forcibly proxied a dozen carefully selected targets, packed them with explosives and walked them into offices and bus terminals around Washington before detonating themselves.

Those responsible, of course, simply woke up back in their own bodies and entirely unharmed.

The Second Korean War had lasted just long enough to kill a couple of hundred UN Peacekeepers sent to monitor the situation, untold thousands of troops on either side and, according to some estimates, up to a hundred thousand civilians over the space of five years.

But what didn't get talked about nearly as much in the post-conflict analyses, documentaries and special UN hearings were the veterans who had been too close to the 38th Parallel when the nuke was dropped, or who were struck down by nerve gas once the NK government realized they were losing.

Elijah had seen it all, and been lucky to come home considerably more intact than many of his fellow troops. Too many of those who survived spent the rest of their lives dealing with the after-effects of nerve gas and radiation, and Elijah had watched, appalled, as they were effectively abandoned, as if by sweeping them under the carpet the Western nations who had supported South Korea in the conflict could somehow make the whole fucking mess just go away.

Proxy, while far from a solution, had at least been enough to help salve the pain suffered by those affected. That it had helped start the war hardly mattered; Elijah proxied with friends and former colleagues, many of them rendered invalid and nearly all in near constant pain; for a few hours they got to walk around inside his skin and remember what it felt like to run and jump and shout and just breathe without their every nerve end screaming in protest, without worrying if their dwindling support payments might stop or be reassessed…without wondering if they might actually be better off dead.

Moving into manufacturing proxy himself had seemed like a smart move, financially as much as anything else. And it had been good for a while, until the world's terrorists and murderers invented yet more new and innovative ways in which proxy could be used to slaughter the innocent.

Still, Elijah was committed by then, and the money he was making was good enough that he'd kept right at it until the day of his first arrest.

They'd put him inside for three years. By the time he got back out, most of his veteran friends had either succumbed to their post-war illnesses or killed themselves. He tried going straight, using some of the cash he'd squirrelled away to invest in a chain of nightclubs, but proxy was too alluring, too easy, too *profitable* for it not to pull him back in.

This time around, he partnered with a fellow veteran, Robin Almuth, and they set up a brand new proxy factory in the basement of a disused print shop.

And now Rob was dead, and Elijah was back inside the Scrubs serving a much, *much* longer sentence. Long enough, it was questionable whether he'd die of old age before he saw the outside world again with his own two eyes.

The bracelet buzzed against Elijah's wrist, on and off again like morse code, shaking him out of his reverie and bringing him to a halt at the end of a quiet side-street. His transport turned out to be a white van. When he placed the bracelet next to the van's door, it slid open automatically.

Once inside, a programmed voice emanating from the dashboard asked him where he wanted to go. Elijah thought for a moment, then gave it a destination, putting his seatbelt on as the van backed out of its parking spot.

Time, he decided, to find out who wanted him dead.

CHAPTER
TEN

RAY

Ray woke to the insistent buzzing of his bracelet against his wrist and saw it was still dark outside his bedroom's one tiny window. Half-remembered dreams chased each other across the walls, fading as he found the switch on his bedside lamp. A glance at his bracelet told him it was just after eight in the morning.

Touching a finger to his bracelet, Ray heard a beep, followed by a voice that crackled with faint static.

"Ray? You up yet?"

Tip. "Of course I'm not fucking up," Ray grunted. "Do you know what time it is?"

"Time you bloody got up," said Tip. "Look, Ray..." He sighed. "It might be better if you don't come to see me for a few days."

Ray sat up, still groggy. "Why?"

"There's a problem," said Tip, sounding oddly evasive. "It has to do with Stokes."

Stokes? Ray's grogginess vanished, replaced by sudden alertness.

"I thought you said that was taken care of," he grunted,

cold acid pooling in his stomach. "What about your friend in Scotland Yard? What did he say?"

Tip's voice sounded strained when he next spoke. "Well, it seems they caught up with Stokes, thanks to all your efforts, but in the end they...well, they decided to turn him loose, Ray."

Ray's nerves shifted into cold anger. Stokes had connections—the kind that could make your life short and brutal if you crossed him. And thanks to the debacle at the garage, Stokes now knew exactly who Ray was.

"According to you," Ray hissed into his bracelet, "there was more than enough evidence to lock him up until the end of fucking time!"

"Well," Tip said with an embarrassed chuckle, "turns out the old bill wanted to cut a deal with Stokes. My friend wouldn't go into the details, but he gave me enough to read between the lines."

Ray listened to the sound of the other man's breathing and fought down the urge to vomit. "What kind of deal?"

"Seems like the police have bigger fish to fry, and Stokes is their route to them."

Ray leaned back and closed his eyes. "You mean they turned him into an informer."

"So I gather," said Tip, sounding regretful. "It means Stokes stays free—no charges or nothing."

"And in the meantime, Stokes can do what he likes. Is that it?"

"Pretty much," said Tip. "I mean, obviously if he went out and murdered someone in broad daylight, they'd have to do something about it. Assuming he didn't just get someone else to commit a murder on his behalf, should he have reason. But my feeling is you're going to have to lie low for a while."

Great, thought Ray. *Just absolutely, totally, fucking great.*

"How much of a while?"

"Couple of months." Tip paused for several long seconds. "Or six."

Ray groaned inwardly and climbed out of bed, going over to the window and pressing his forehead against the glass, half afraid he might see Stokes glaring back up at him. "For God's sake, Tip! I have rent to pay."

"Yeah…about that. Might be an idea not to stay where you are, if you follow me. Take yourself on holiday. Maybe get your medical visa up to date and go abroad for a while."

Like he could afford such luxuries, even if he wanted to. "You fucking owe me, Tip," said Ray, his voice trembling with fury. "I put my neck on the line for you."

"I wish I could help, but I'd be risking both our necks, not just yours. Take care of yourself, all right?"

"Tip?"

It took Ray a moment to realize the old bastard had ended the call. He stared down at the street below. Nobody was watching for him, but he had a feeling it was only a matter of time.

It took an effort of will not to punch the glass until it shattered. Things had already been tight, or he wouldn't have been proxying for Tip in the first place.

Water from the tap in the kitchen tasted sour and flat on his tongue. On went the kettle, and Ray reached for the jar of instant coffee that sat perpetually next to it. His hand froze mid-reach, and a groan escaped his lips.

There was a solution to his dilemma, but not one he liked.

Before he could change his mind, Ray sank into a chair next to his kitchen table and spoke a command into his bracelet. Barely a second passed before someone picked up on the other end of the line.

"Hello?"

"Miss Cotter? It's Ray Thomas." Ray closed his eyes and waited a beat before continuing. "I'm sorry to call you so early, but I've reconsidered your offer."

———

TWO AND A HALF HOURS LATER, and with a confirmed transaction that placed enough money in his account to cover his rent for the next six months, Ray sat in a hired car across the road from the Peartree Medical Institute watching people come and go from its main entrance.

Somewhere inside that building was Stacy Cotter, and all he had to do was talk to her on behalf of her mother and find out if she genuinely wanted to be there.

According to the research he'd carried out en route, Amy Cotter had been correct in saying that the Institute belonged to a subsidiary of Telop Industries. And that made it the property of Stacy Cotter's father and Amy's ex-husband, Raphael Markov.

The clinic had apparently begun life in the last century as an upmarket housing development, before being repurposed as a private hospital for London's wealthy elite. The complex sprawled across several adjacent buildings linked by covered walkways.

In the hour he'd been sitting there watching the front entrance of the Institute, Ray had noted the presence of half a dozen private security guards patrolling the surrounding streets. Either that, or a number of large, broad-shouldered men who clearly spent a lot of time in the gym and all liked to wear black bomber jackets and jeans had randomly decided to stand around the private hospital and its neighbouring gardens with tight, watchful expressions for no other reason than it was a sunny morning.

One of them, loitering at the corner of the building nearest to Ray, glanced towards his hire car, perhaps noticing it had been sitting there for a while.

Afraid of arousing suspicions, Ray told the car to drive three blocks, then pull over. Once it had parked, a few minutes later, he got out and walked back the way he had come, entering a café directly opposite the Institute's main entrance.

The café proved to be surprisingly busy. Ray bought a coffee from a woman with a peculiarly tight-lipped and nervous expression. He sat near the window and pretended to read the news on the cheap tablet bolted to the table-top.

It didn't Ray long to sense that something felt off. Despite being full, and despite the tight clusters of customers gathered around its tables, no-one in the café had uttered a single word to each other since he'd stepped inside.

Instead, they were all quietly staring past Ray and at the Institute's front entrance with what struck him as singular collective focus.

A prickle of unease edged its way down Ray's spine. Among the café's clientele he noted several pensioners, a greater number of people in their twenties, and a smattering of ages and types all across the social spectrum.

Ray's sense of discomfort only grew when he noticed that every single one of them had the exact same order on the table before them: an untouched egg and mayonnaise sandwich and a glass of water.

No wonder the café proprietor looked so freaked out. Perhaps, thought Ray, it was some kind of performance. Or perhaps they were members of some odd religious group who'd taken a collective vow of silence.

Ray tried not to let the weirdness of the whole situation get to him and stuck it out for another half hour, keeping his attention focused on the Peartree Institute across the road. Apart from the obvious security guards, the only other people he saw coming or going were a couple of nurses presumably on their lunch break. There was little sign of anyone who might either be a patient, or coming to visit one.

All of which was very odd.

It had occurred to Ray to wonder whether Amy Cotter might have been demonstrating excessive levels of paranoia

by claiming her ex-husband had for unknown reasons impris-
oned their daughter, but perhaps, given what he could see, he
had misjudged her. The security might only be there to keep
people from bothering Stacy—which was entirely possible,
given her prior notoriety—or they might equally be there to
keep her in.

Despite an initial flurry of reports and frantic speculation
about her near-fatal dive from the top of a building, the press
already seemed largely to have forgotten about Stacy Cotter.
Or at least, the security didn't appear to be fighting off hordes
of invading paparazzi.

A quick glance back over his shoulder revealed that the
café's clientele still sat in uncanny silence. Nor had he seen
sight or sound of the café's owner in what felt like quite a
while. If she'd done a runner, he didn't blame her in the
slightest.

As it was, things were getting just a little too creepy even
for Ray. Those few other passers-by who had stepped through
the door of the café had taken one look at the silent, staring
crowd within and ducked straight back out.

Tired of waiting for something to happen while being
stuck in a room full of people who exhibited all the self-
awareness of a cabbage, Ray exited the café, and shivered
despite the midday heat. Some mysteries, he decided, might
best be left unsolved.

In the meantime, he needed to stop waiting and take
action.

Ray walked across the road, past a parked ambulance and
straight towards the Institute's front entrance. One of the
guards moved to intercept him, sunlight gleaming from his
shaven head.

"I'm sorry, sir." The hired goon put out a hand. "The
Peartree's closed for the day."

"Closed?" Ray acted as if he hadn't heard him right. He
caught a whiff of aftershave—*eau de thug*, perhaps. "My son is

in there," Ray blustered, stabbing one finger towards the entrance of the Peartree like an enraged father used to getting his way. "Are you taking the piss?"

As he spoke, Ray glanced past the man's shoulder and inside the front entrance to where he could see an unmanned reception desk within a tiled foyer. A nurse, hands pushed deep into her pockets, hurried past him and up the steps. The look she gave the guard blocking Ray's path gave him a pretty good idea what she thought of all the security. Further inside, a second goon ran a hand-scanner over some kind of electronic tag she had clipped to her uniform.

"All the patients have been temporarily moved to another hospital," the goon explained, sounding like he was reading from a script that tested the limits of his intellect. "An infection spread through the air ventilation. If you call the Institute help desk, they'll explain everything."

Best to leave it at that, Ray decided. Playing an outraged relative was one thing, but getting into a fight with a serial steroid abuser would not help him get any genuinely useful information.

With a parting scowl, Ray went back across the road, continuing past the café and around a corner. He stopped and took another peek back at the Institute's entrance. A youngish-looking doctor came hurrying down the steps, pausing only to have his tag scanned by a security guard.

Without one of those security passes, Ray knew, there was no way he was getting inside the Institute short of shimmying up a pipe and breaking in. And somebody would definitely notice if he did that.

He watched as the doctor crossed the street and out of his direct line of sight. Ray leaned around the corner and saw the doctor enter the same café where he'd spent part of his morning.

Ray hurried after him, re-entering the café. The doctor had

stopped just inside the door. Ray couldn't see his face, but he could guess at his expression.

The doctor turned around, either having noticed no one was actually manning the counter or too freaked out by the silent, glassy-eyed crowd within to want to remain there a moment later. Ray started forward immediately, colliding with him.

"Christ!" the doctor spluttered, putting his hands up. "What's the hurry?"

"Sorry, mate," Ray said as apologetically as he could, putting his hands on the doctor's chest as if to steady him. He nodded around the café. "What's going on here?" he asked in a loud whisper. "Do you know?"

"No idea," said the doctor with evident irritation. His expression shifted to unease when he again scanned the crowd around them. "Excuse me, will you?" he said, brushing past Ray. "And watch where you're going," he added. "You nearly sent me flying."

"Sorry about that," Ray called after him. Then he reached into a pocket and folded his fingers around the plastic ID tag he'd pulled from the doctor's shirt.

Ray left the café again and returned to his hire car. He got in and unzipped a duffel bag tucked under one seat, pulling out a set of hospital scrubs.

Ray changed quickly before anyone noticed him undressing inside the car. Those few people who did hurry past appeared too caught up in their own thoughts to notice.

Once he had the scrubs on, Ray shoved his own clothes back inside the duffel bag, then ordered the car to drive to a service entrance in another part of the Peartree complex he'd scouted out earlier.

He found another goon standing guard there. Ray got out with his stolen ID pinned to his chest and headed for the door.

The trick to getting inside places you weren't supposed to

be, he'd long since learned, was to act like you belonged. Get that right, and you were as good as invisible.

The guard, who had the glassy-eyed stare of the terminally bored, hardly looked at him as he ran a hand-scanner over Ray's tag.

And just like that, he was in, and hoofing his way up the first flight of stairs he saw. His scrubs weren't quite right—the ones the clinic used were an entirely different shade of blue—but the guard either didn't notice or didn't care.

The steps led up to a first-floor corridor. Ray quickly made his way along it, seeing nothing but deserted wards. Once he was sure Stacy wasn't anywhere on that floor, he continued on up to the next floor, finding more of the same.

He was already starting to feel worn out by the time he reached the top floor, but he still kept going. Once he was sure this particular building was entirely empty, he hurried along an elevated walkway to the next building and resumed his search there.

Working hospital or not, it was soon clear that the Peartree Institute was now entirely devoid of patients. And, judging by how few doctors, nurses or cleaning staff he saw, maintained by a skeleton staff.

Yet as far as he had been able to ascertain, the Peartree was a busy working hospital, with dozens, if not hundreds, of patients.

How much effort and money had it taken to empty the entire place so quickly? And why so much effort, to isolate a daughter Raphael Markov had, as his ex-wife made clear, long ago disowned?

At one point Ray grabbed a clipboard from an unmanned nurse's station and carried it under an arm for extra camouflage. Then he turned a corner on the third floor of the second building and saw two more goons standing on opposite sides of a door as if they were the guardians to some dead king's tomb.

This *had* to be where they were keeping Stacy, Ray decided, briskly walking straight past the guards and up to the door, reaching out to push it open.

They swung open, revealing a private hospital room with a single bed. Ray caught a glimpse of a frail-looking figure in the bed with long, brown hair splayed untidily across the pillows. One of her arms was wrapped in thick bandaging.

One of the goons took a hold of Ray's upper arm before he could take another step.

"Badge," said the goon, and Ray pinched his blues so that the guard could run his hand-scanner over the stolen ID a second time.

Ray's heart beat loud and hard inside his chest. How long did he have before the doctor whose ID he'd stolen either returned to the Peartree or noticed it was gone?

Not long at all, he suspected.

The goon stared at the screen of his hand-scanner and frowned. Any second now, thought Ray, they were going to drag him down to a basement and beat the living shit out of him.

Instead, the goon put his scanner away and nodded to Ray.

Ray let out a slow breath and entered the room. ID or not, he didn't fail to notice that the guards had left the door open, presumably so they could keep an eye on him.

Which was going to make talking to Stacy just about impossible. Unless he could find some way to distract them, he'd gone to all this effort for precisely nothing.

Looking around, and working hard to look like he knew what he was doing, Ray stepped towards a wall-mounted screen displaying medical information of some kind.

He peered at the girl from out of the corner of his eyes. Stacy looked older than he recalled, and somewhat thinner. She had changed her hair, which was longer and less stylised than it had once been. There were bruises on her neck and arms, presumably sustained during her fall.

Her eyes opened just then, and she gazed, slack-mouthed, up at the ceiling, her pupils round and huge. She showed no awareness he was there, even though he was standing right next to her bed.

Drugged to the eyeballs, Ray concluded with a sinking feeling. Fat chance he'd get anything comprehensible out of her, let alone something that might satisfy her mother.

Still, he had to try.

Stepping up next to the bed, Ray placed a hand on top of a wheeled machine that had been placed there and wondered what the hell to do next.

He took another quick glance at a wall monitor. From out of the corner of one eye, he saw with relief that the two goons had finally turned away. One was conferring quietly with someone via his bracelet while his colleague listened in with a concerned expression.

That's it, thought Ray. *I've been rumbled.*

He tensed for a fight.

Instead, they continued to pay him no attention. He couldn't make out most of what the guard speaking into his bracelet was saying, although he did catch something about a mob.

A mob?

The first guard lowered his arm and said something to his colleague, then hurried away as if on some vital errand. The sole remaining guard stared after his colleague with a look of perplexed worry.

Ray didn't waste his chance. He leaned in close to the half-comatose girl and shook her shoulder.

"Stacy?" he whispered.

Stacy blinked, her eyes opening a little wider. Another moment passed before she appeared to focus on him.

"My name's Ray," he continued in a loud whisper. "Your mum sent me."

Stacy mumbled something incomprehensible.

Ray stiffened, hearing footsteps come up behind him. He turned to find the remaining goon scowling at him.

"You're not supposed to be talking to her," he snapped. "Them's the rules. We made that clear, right?"

Ray tried to look distracted and annoyed, like a busy doctor who had better things to do. "I forgot."

The goon's expression darkened further. "I want to see your ID again."

Just then, Ray heard a burst of frantic shouting coming from the street outside. The goon stepped past Ray, pushing aside the window blinds and peering down.

Just then, the remaining guard's data bracelet emitted a tinny jingle. He stepped back from the window and tapped at his bracelet, studying some message that had appeared on its screen.

The sound of shouting and scuffling escalated, as if a large crowd had gathered outside.

"Excuse me," asked Ray, gesturing to the window. "What's going on out there?"

The goon ignored Ray, instead heading back out through the door at a brisk trot. Ray followed after him in time to see him running towards a bank of elevators.

This, thought Ray, was definitely turning out to be one of the weirdest days of his career.

He looked back in at Stacy. She had tilted her head to one side, regarding him with a groggy expression.

"I don't suppose you've any idea what's going on?" Ray asked her.

A slurry of incomprehensible vowels emerged from deep within the girl's throat. Her eyelids flickered shut and her head fell back against her pillow.

She began snoring loudly.

Ray went back over to the window to see for himself what was going on. All he saw at first was a brick wall and some bins lining an empty street. Whoever had been out there was gone. He could still hear shouting, but it was further away now, coming from the other side of the building.

Crossing to the other side of the corridor, Ray looked out of the window in an adjacent room and down to the café across the road. Its silent occupants had finally ended their strange vigil, and were now streaming out of it *en masse* and towards the Institute's entrance.

Ray reached for the latch and swung the window open so he could lean out and get a better view. At least a dozen cars had come to a halt all across the street in front of the Institute's main building, blocking the traffic in the process. He watched with slack-jawed amazement as yet more people came streaming out of adjacent streets or emerged from newly arrived cars. Far more of them than had been in the café, and all headed towards the Peartree.

A phrase floated up from the earliest years of Ray's youth: flash mobs, crowds of people who organised online before carrying out spontaneous group actions or protests at a prearranged time and place.

But what, Ray wondered, were they protesting about? Assuming they were protesting about anything?

As Ray continued to watch, a private-hire bus came around a corner and pulled to a halt in the middle of the road, adding yet further to the chaos. Yet more people came pouring out of it. They were of all types, ages, genders and backgrounds: he saw old men and young women, some in suits and others in overalls or uniforms or even in their pyjamas. Some looked like down-and-outs, while others wore expensive jackets or had artfully arranged hair like they'd come straight from a fashion shoot.

They acted as one, swarming towards the Institute's front entrance as if they all shared the same clear sense of purpose.

He leaned a little further out, seeing now that the entrance was crammed with dozens, if not hundreds, of people all pushing to get inside.

He could see no sign of Markov's private security. Either they'd been pushed back inside the building, or they had fled.

Unease stirred deep in Ray's chest. He stepped back through to Stacy's room—so far as he could tell, the Institute's one and only patient—and regarded her speculatively.

It wasn't possible, was it, that all of this chaos and bustle had something to do with her…?

The idea was ridiculous, to put it mildly. Even so, Ray made a further attempt to try and wake Raphael Markov's daughter from her drugged stupor. Perhaps his only recourse, if she was in danger, was to try and get her out of the building himself.

Stacy's eyes flickered back open, her gaze still vacant.

"Your mother sent me," said Ray, more loudly now they were alone. "Amy Cotter. Do you understand?"

"Mhm," Stacy slurred.

This time he heard shouting that sounded like it came from inside the building, echoing up the stairwell next to the bank of elevators.

A trickle of cold ice found its way down Ray's spine. He darted over to the window in Stacy's room and pressed his face against the glass. Now the street below was crowded with yet more new arrivals; several bicycles lay abandoned next to the bins, and he saw a woman in bare feet and wearing a nightie hurry out of sight and undoubtedly headed to join all the rest.

Ray heard shuffling feet from down the corridor. The trickle of ice turned into frigid fingers around his heart.

Just as he was about to lift her out of the bed to try and carry her out of the Peartree, a kid in ripped jeans appeared at the door of the private room, followed by a woman in her forties wearing running gear.

Then more came flooding in, cramming themselves into the room and cutting off any potential avenue of escape. Ray found himself surrounded by a tide of human flesh, and he let out a bellow of fear, afraid of what they might do to him.

Instead, they were surprisingly gentle. Hands peeled Stacy out of Ray's grasp, while others held him back from interfering. Ray recognized one of them from the café. Two of them slid a pair of shoes onto Stacy's feet while a third, a man, took off his heavy coat and worked her arms inside its sleeves.

Stacy, clearly still drugged to the eyeballs, offered no resistance.

"Hey!" Ray shouted ineffectually, as angry as he was terrified. "Put her down!"

None of them showed any indication they even knew he was there.

It's like I'm a ghost, he thought, trying to push past the people separating him from Stacy.

Despite all his efforts, Ray was gently but firmly repulsed. More people crammed inside the room until he was nearly crushed against a wall.

He had one brief glimpse of the top of Stacy's head as the mob bustled her into the corridor, several holding onto her arms and shoulders to keep her from sliding to the floor.

Ray grabbed hold of a skinny student-type with a backpack and a thin fuzz of beard and demanded to know who he was and who had sent him.

The kid just stared blankly back at him like a sleepwalker. A second attempt to communicate with another member of the mob got Ray no further.

Not one of them had said so much as a single word.

The room began to empty once more as the mob exited into the corridor. Ray followed behind, standing on tiptoe to try and see Stacy, and caught a glimpse of her being guided down the stairs.

Rather than keep fighting his way through the mob, Ray headed for the elevators. If he could get downstairs ahead of them, perhaps he still had a chance to grab Stacy and get her to safety, or at least figure out where they were taking her.

By the time he emerged on the ground floor, however, the entrance and vestibule were so flooded with milling bodies it was impossible to push past them. No matter how hard he tried to force his way through, the crowd pushed back with equal or greater force in perfect, unspoken unison.

Helpless and frustrated and more than a little horrified, Ray had no choice but to watch as Stacy Cotter was rapidly led out of the Peartree Medical Institute and into the sunlit street beyond.

The crowd surged out of the building in her wake, as if she exerted some magnetic force that drew them to her. Ray followed as close behind as he could, seeing several of Markov's goons standing in stunned silence further down the road at what they presumably considered a safe distance. One had a bloodied nose, and the arm had been ripped from the jacket of another.

The mob rapidly began to dissipate. Ray ran among them, shouting Stacy's name, but she'd as good as vanished amidst the chaos. The same people who'd carried her off had already slipped down side-streets or boarded cars and buses already pulling away into neighbouring streets.

But she had to be somewhere close by. If only he could find her...!

After another minute, most of the mob had entirely dispersed. It was enough to make Ray wonder if he'd imagined the whole thing.

Then he heard the wail of police sirens, drawing closer.

CHAPTER
ELEVEN

ELIJAH

Light hadn't yet dawned above the London rooftops by the time Elijah, still wearing the skin he'd used to proxy out of Wormwood Scrubs, pulled up in the van outside his old mate Dom's place.

To his surprise, he saw Dom standing outside the door of his mum's house. He wore a courier's uniform, and a bicycle leaned against a railing next to him.

When Elijah got out of the van and walked towards him, Dom, who had been in the act of pulling on a pair of finger-less gloves, regarded him with apprehension. Clearly, he was wondering why an enormous, scarred thug was headed straight for him. He swallowed visibly, but remained where he was.

Elijah stepped right up to Dom and pulled at the lapel of his courier uniform. "What's this shit?" he demanded. "You legit now?"

Dom stumbled back, his eyes wide and frightened. "Do I, uh… do I know you?"

Elijah couldn't keep a broad grin from spreading across his borrowed face. "It's me, Elijah," he said, pointing at the back of his own neck and making a trigger-pulling motion. "Long time no see, Dom."

Dom blinked rapidly, his mouth opening and closing again. In the next moment a mixture of horror and fascination replaced his fear. "Elijah? Elijah Waits?"

Elijah nodded.

"Prove it," said Dom, his eyes narrowing with suspicion. "What was the name of that bird you were dating whose brother nicked my wallet that time we met at the Infirmary?"

"Julie," Elijah replied without hesitation. "It's good to see you, Dom."

Dom's shoulders sagged, and he glanced at the house behind him. "Look, I'd invite you in for a cuppa before I went to work, but Mum might think you was a bailiff after her ex or something."

Elijah chuckled. "I don't have enough time, anyway. I've got maybe a couple of hours at most before the proxy runs out."

Dom nodded. "Just to be clear, you're still inside the Scrubs? As in, right this second?"

Elijah nodded. "Afraid so."

Dom sucked air through his teeth. "Risky. They're coming down hard on prison proxying, I hear."

"Risky, but necessary. You still got that key I left with you?"

Dom thought for a moment. "The one for the storage unit?"

Elijah nodded. "Get me that key," he told Dom, "and I'll be out of your hair in two minutes."

———

IT TOOK five minutes rather than two, but soon Elijah was back in the van. The sky had turned a smoky orange by the time he pulled up outside a self-storage warehouse in

Walthamstow. The whole place was automatic—not a human being in sight—and had the added advantage of requiring neither fingerprint nor retinal ID to get inside.

Elijah headed straight for Unit 155 and unlocked it, then got to work digging through piles of old furniture that had belonged to his gran. It wasn't long before he found the filing cabinet right where he'd left it. The bracelet he'd come for was still duct-taped to the underside of a drawer.

Turning the bracelet on, Elijah accessed its settings and changed its colour from black to green so he could more easily distinguish it from the one he already wore, and which had been supplied to him along with his thuggish proxy. After slipping it onto his wrist, he looked around some more until he located a hunting knife he'd stashed at the bottom of a box of mouldering paperbacks.

Next, he went looking for Stan, all too aware as he departed the warehouse that his time was already running out.

———

BY THE TIME Elijah parked in a lane near Tower Hamlets, the streets were busy with morning traffic. He'd been half afraid The Saracen's Head might finally have been demolished, but it was still there, and still open, even at this godforsaken hour of the morning.

Stepping inside the pub felt like stepping a hundred years into the past. The interior walls were still painted black, and Ernest was still working the early, early morning shift behind the bar as if the intervening years had never happened.

The only customer at this time of the morning, however, was Stan. Even hardened alcoholics needed to sleep some-times, Elijah assumed. Elijah knew it was Stan only because Ernest allowed no-one else to sit at the table closest to the men's toilets.

Today, Stan wore the body of a forty-something down-and-out—most likely one of his regular crew of proxy partners. Nobody knew what Stan himself really looked like. He sat on a three-seater lounge sofa that looked like it had been rescued from a demolition site.

"Eli," said the down-and-out as Elijah approached the table. "Thought you might come to visit."

Elijah stopped and stared at him. "Stan. How did you know—?"

"I heard on the grapevine you were out and looking for information. Who else were you going to talk to, if not me?"

Elijah realized his mouth was hanging open and quickly closed it. Ernest took a seat on a stool behind the bar, reading a tablet and pretending not to be listening to everything they said.

Elijah wrinkled his nose. "No offence meant," he said, "but your proxy stinks something awful."

Stan smiled, revealing several cracked and yellowed teeth. "And you're fucking ugly." He gave Elijah an up-and-down look. "Is that really the proxy Lorenz gave you?"

"He's big and he's strong," said Elijah. "Better than that pile of rags you're wearing."

"Ex-paratrooper," said Stan, one grimy hand patting layers of clothes laid over the proxy's chest. "Fucker can move fast when he wants to." He glanced towards the bar and nodded to Ernest. "Let's get down to business, shall we?"

In response, Ernest folded his tablet up, tossed it onto the counter and disappeared into the back office, closing the door after him.

Elijah waited another moment, then stepped around the table and dropped onto the sofa next to Stan. This close, the smell of urine and cheap alcohol was particularly overpowering. At the same time, he let the hunting knife slip from out of the sleeve of his skin's jacket and pressed its tip against the proxy's inside thigh.

Stan looked down at the blade and back up at Elijah. "Am I supposed to be scared of that? You know this is why I always wear a skin when I do business, right?"

"Last I heard," said Elijah, his voice low and even, "you got a couple of your regular skins killed and now you're finding it harder to persuade anyone to proxy with you, however much you pay them." He nodded at the proxy's ragged clothes and sneered. "Your standards have dropped since the last time I saw you, Stan. The way I see it, one more dead proxy and you're as good as out of business."

Stan shrugged. "One makes do with what one can."

"The night I got nailed for Rob's murder I had arranged to come here straight from the factory to see you," Elijah continued. "Someone grabbed me from behind and forcibly proxied me with someone else. When I got back inside my own skin, I was standing over Rob's corpse with a hammer in one hand, wondering what the fuck was going on even as the boys in blue were pulling up outside." He leaned in closer to Stan's proxy, ignoring its foul odour. "Apart from Rob, you were the only one who knew where I'd be, and when."

"That doesn't mean I had anything to do with it." Stan gazed back at him, seemingly unperturbed. "Do you know the most important thing in my line of business, Elijah? It's trust. People come to me because they trust me with information. If I started sharing that information with people who shouldn't have it, that trust would be gone and I'd be out of business." The proxy reached out and placed one finger against the top of the blade, gently angling it away from his groin. "I didn't tell anyone anything about you that could possibly have led to your friend's murder. If I did things like that, I'd be long out of business."

"Yeah, but—!"

"Elijah," Stan said a little more firmly. "Have you ever heard any suggestion I was anything but completely reliable?"

Elijah let out a disgusted snort and leaned back. He kept the knife in his hand, though, laying it flat across his lap. "Fine, then. So who could have set me up?"

"Manufacturing and selling proxy is a dangerous business," Stan replied. "I shouldn't have to tell you that. As I recall, you and Rob were doing great business selling hopscotch at a time absolutely no one else even knew such an advanced form of proxy existed."

"So?"

"So that's the kind of thing that makes people jealous," said Stan. "Some bigger dealers wanted you to sell the hopscotch recipe to them, didn't they?"

"Yeah, they did," Elijah admitted. "Except we weren't selling."

"Which threatened to hurt *their* business," said Stan. "Is it really so surprising somebody decided to put you out of commission and steal the recipe?" Stan leaned closer, enough so that Elijah found himself holding his breath rather than inhale the putrid stench emanating from the proxy's diseased mouth. "Nowadays hopscotch is everywhere, innit?" He touched one grimy hand to his chest. "Even I use it. Makes my job a lot easier, I'll tell you. Wouldn't have taken much to set someone to keep an eye on you, then take you and your friend out when the opportunity arose."

Elijah stared back at him. "The cops impounded our 3D printers and equipment. I always figured one of them must have taken the hopscotch recipe from the backups and sold it on."

Stan nodded. "Now, if you'd only done a deal with those people when they were willing to ask nicely, you'd be sitting here in person."

Elijah ignored the jibe. "Except someone just tried to have me killed inside the Scrubs. That's why I'm here: to find out who."

"I see," said Stan. "Any idea why they'd want to do that?

It can't be business rivalry, not after this long. And half the planet has hopscotch now."

Because I still want to know where hopscotch came from, thought Elijah. *Because I'm still asking questions.*

"All I care about," he said by way of an answer, "is finding out who's after me. So can you help or not?"

Stan shrugged. "Maybe." He leered at Elijah. "But it'll cost you."

Elijah felt himself tense. If this kept up, he wouldn't have any money left. "How much?"

"First," said Stan, his eyes flicking down towards the knife in Elijah's lap and then back up, "you put the fucking pig sticker away. Then we talk."

They stared at each other for a long moment, then Elijah tucked the knife inside his proxy's jacket.

"Better," said Stan. "But before we talk about who's trying to kill you, I want to talk about hopscotch. You and Rob were the first to get hold of it. So how did it wind up in your hands?"

Elijah regarded him through narrowed eyes. "Why do you want to know?"

"Because," said Stan, "no one ever improved on the original recipe for proxy until you turned up. You want my help? Fine. But first, I want to know how you did it. How you created hopscotch."

Elijah thought about lying. It had been fun, after a fashion, to pretend that he and Rob had come up with an improvement on the original proxy recipe all by themselves. It had lent them both a certain glamour, for a while at least.

But it had also raised difficult questions, like how they could possibly have improved on proxy when nobody else could even figure out how proxy worked in the first place.

"The truth is," Elijah admitted, "we didn't. Someone gave it to us."

Stan's expression twisted into a frown. "Who?"

Who was an easy enough question to answer on one level: Elijah could still picture the man who had supplied them with the recipe.

For a while, he and Rob had speculated that their mysterious and anonymous donor might even be the same equally anonymous genius who had created proxy in the first place.

Proxy had first appeared as a downloadable recipe on a website dedicated to home-brew open-source recipes for high-end 3D medical printers. Back then, in the early 2030s, such devices had been the only things sophisticated enough to produce proxy, being capable of printing not just organs but even customized DNA.

Once some few brave souls had printed the first p beads and followed the instructions, the technology, infinitely replicable, spread like wildfire. Most people who proxied inevitably used it for sex, swapping bodies with people known and unknown to them. Websites appeared that offered couples the opportunity to anonymously swap skins with other likeminded adults without risking meeting in the flesh, something that became especially important at a time when the world was enduring a second wave of global pandemics.

For a time, sex by proxy became all the rage, with special courier services delivering quantum-entangled beads and applicators to those seeking to proxy with each other.

There had been other benefits to the technology. Those with severe disabilities could proxy into healthy volunteers for a few hours at a time, much as Elijah had done for his fellow veterans. For a few brief months, it had been permissible for witnesses to violent crimes to proxy through court-appointed skins to protect their identities.

Then had come Korea, and the Washington attacks, and proxy had been outlawed almost overnight.

But even that wasn't nearly enough to make it go away.

Instead, it went underground, its popularity only growing, spurred by the development of ever more sophisticated

3D printers. Before long the price of such devices had dropped low enough—and the profits high enough—that any black marketeer with enough capital and the right contacts could start churning out proxy beads to almost inexhaustible demand.

"I don't know who," Elijah replied. "This... man approached us and offered me and Rob samples of hopscotch. He never gave us his name. Refused when we asked. But he was posh, you know? Wore a nice suit. He said he'd printed the beads himself and they were superior to regular proxy."

"And you believed him?"

Elijah shrugged. "He talked a good talk. And paid us a couple thousand quid just to let him make his pitch." He shrugged. "What did we have to lose? We listened to him, then took some paired beads from him and gave them free to some of our regulars to check out. When they came back, they said they'd stayed linked with their proxy partners for most of a week instead of just a few hours." Elijah allowed himself a small smile. "We thought they were lying until we tried it for ourselves."

"And what did this unnamed man want in return?" asked Stan, his face drawn into a tight frown.

"Nothing."

Stan's frown grew yet deeper. "Nothing?"

"I know we should have asked more questions," said Elijah, "but it felt like looking a gift horse in the mouth, you know? He said he'd give us the recipe free and clear, and he was true to his word." He shrugged. "Neither of us could make any more sense of it than you can."

"What the fuck did he get out of this arrangement?"

Elijah shook his head. "Search me."

Stan was quiet for a long moment. "I think you're having me on," he said at last.

"Yeah, I know it sounds like I am," Elijah agreed. "It made

little sense, just giving it to us for free. Which is why I tried to find out more about it."

"What do you mean?"

"I asked questions," said Elijah. "I wanted to know who he was and why he was giving us something so incredible for nothing. Questions he'd made it very clear he wanted neither of us to ask."

"Maybe you shouldn't have asked, then," said Stan.

"Maybe not," Elijah agreed, "and I think maybe my asking those questions is what got Rob killed. My theory is, framing me for Rob's death was a way to keep me from nosing about."

"And you think this same man is the one who put out a hit on you? Why would he wait until now? You've been inside a few years now, haven't you?"

Elijah sighed. "This past year I've been talking to a lawyer and also a private investigator. There was CCTV footage of me being mugged right before Rob's murder. It was supposed to be part of my defence, except the video files disappeared from police custody before the case even opened. We still had the case the hopscotch beads came in, and they could have had his fingerprints on it, except that disappeared too." Elijah slowly shook his head. "I don't think that's any accident."

Stan nodded with clear understanding. "So let me get this clear. You think asking questions about hopscotch got Rob killed, and you framed. And now that you're asking more questions from behind bars, someone, maybe the same man who supplied you with the recipe for hopscotch, is gunning for you a second time?"

"It can't be anyone else," said Elijah. "And I need you to help me figure out who he is."

Stan blew air out from between pursed lips. "You're asking me to find someone who never gave you his real name, told you nothing about his background, whom you haven't seen in years and has enough resources to set you up and then send someone after you in prison? However you look at it, it's going to be a tough job."

"I know it's a long shot," Elijah admitted.

"All right." Stan said brightly, slapping one knee and settling back against the couch. "I like a challenge. You remember what he looks like?"

"Perfectly," said Elijah.

"Then I want you to describe him to me in detail," said Stan, reaching into a pocket and producing a notepad and pencil. "How you met him, how tall he was, what kind of accent he had, the clothes he wore and the car he arrived in, if any. Anything and everything that comes to mind."

The way he talked made Elijah wonder about some of the whispers he'd heard that Stan was really a cop. What better way of keeping tabs on the criminal underground than by selling them the information they sometimes needed?

It took Elijah more than an hour to answer all of Stan's questions. At one point, Ernest stuck his head out of the door at the back of the pub and, seeing them deep in discussion, locked the front door before disappearing back where he'd come from.

To Elijah's surprise, Stan proved to be a skilled artist, sketching out a pretty decent image of the man who had supplied him and Rob with hopscotch. Elijah described their first meeting with their benefactor in much greater detail, and how he had initially posed as a potential bulk customer before making an offer that left both his and Rob's heads spinning.

"All right," said Stan, studying the detailed drawing he had made, "I'm going away for a little while. You stay here. Ernest's in back, but he'll keep an eye on you and the place."

"Just remember," Elijah reminded him, "I'm using regular proxy. I've got maybe an hour or two left at the most before I'm back in prison."

Stan nodded and stood. "I should have what you need before then."

Elijah nodded. Stan walked into the same office Ernest had disappeared into.

Elijah passed the time by scrolling through the headlines on his bracelet. Occasionally he'd hear the front door of the pub rattle as someone tried and failed to open it.

Stan reappeared most of an hour later. "That took a while," said Stan, resuming his former seat.

Elijah regarded him in disbelief. "You're not seriously telling me you figured out the man's identity already?"

"Unfortunately, no." Stan reached out with one grimy hand and placed a scrap of paper on the table in front of Elijah. "But I do have an address," he explained, keeping his hand on the scrap, "where someone very closely matching his description made a habit of coming and going at all hours." He leered. "I'll be frank with you, Elijah. This is going to cost you."

Elijah licked suddenly dry lips. "How much?"

Stan named a figure with enough noughts in it to make Elijah's—or rather, his proxy's—heart clench.

"I know you can afford this," Stan said softly.

"It's most of what I have," said Elijah, his voice on the verge of trembling.

Stan shrugged. "Take it or leave it."

Elijah swore under his breath, knowing he had no choice. He tapped at his bracelet, set up the transfer and put his left hand palm-down on the table.

A smile curled up the corner of Stan's mouth. He placed his own hand next to Elijah's, revealing a total of four bracelets arrayed on his wrist. One bracelet on Elijah's wrist and one on Stan's briefly flashed yellow.

And with that, the transfer was complete.

———

FIVE MINUTES LATER ELIJAH, considerably poorer than when he entered The Saracen's Head, walked back out with a scrap of paper in one hand. He'd gained little more than an address in North London.

He got back in the van and headed there as fast as it could take him.

On the way, he checked the time and realized his proxy session could run out at any moment. If he found anything at all in what little time remained to him, it'd be sheer luck.

When the van pulled up outside a decrepit-looking office block, Elijah just about ran inside its dimly lit foyer.

No one manned the front desk. After quickly checking the scrap of paper again, Elijah took the elevator up to the eleventh floor, making his way along a row of identical doors until he found the one he was looking for. A plaque on the door read Čapek International Imports.

A curse escaped his lips when he found the door was locked. The next door along, however, was unlocked, the room within empty. A quick glance at several other doors revealed that they, too, were unlocked and empty. Most if not all of the building was deserted.

Fuck it. Bracing himself against the wall opposite the door of Čapek Industries, Elijah gave the door seven or eight good, hard kicks until the lock came apart and the door slammed open.

One more benefit, he thought, of wearing a skin built like a tank.

Stepping inside, Elijah saw an office space as unfurnished as all the others, except for a battered-looking desk with missing drawers. The air smelled dry and dusty. Further investigation revealed a toilet barely large enough for a midget and an equally tiny kitchen unit.

Walking over to the window, Elijah pushed aside blinds grey with dust and stared out and down at a scrapyard. A sour feeling gathered in his belly at the thought of just how much money he'd spent for so little apparent gain.

However much it had cost, though, Stan's information was nearly always good. There had to be something here.

Peering in and around the desk proved fruitless, as did prying at the power sockets. He'd held out a faint hope one of them might prove to be a fake, perhaps hiding a safe or concealing a memory stick. A cardboard box in a kitchen cupboard proved to contain nothing more tantalizing than an electric kettle.

It wasn't until he dug around inside a waste bin beneath the sink that he found a business card. It read:

ZACHARY FINCH, DR.

CONSULTANT PSYCHIATRIST

USBORNE HEALTH & CARE

The card's other side had an address and phone number printed on it. He tried the number, but it proved to be out of service. The address was for some place near Southampton.

Next, he ran a search on Finch. The top hit revealed a round-faced man with gold-rimmed spectacles and receding brown hair cut close to his scalp.

A grin of pure joy split Elijah's face nearly in half. It was him, all right: the same anonymous individual who had supplied him and Rob with the recipe for hopscotch.

After memorizing every detail of the business card, Elijah tore it up and threw the remains back into the wastebasket. Then he drove back to the storage facility, half-expecting the session to end before he got there.

Instead, he got back with just enough time to spare to return his bracelet to where he'd found it and lock up again. He'd spotted a same-day delivery business on a neighbouring block, and he hurriedly packaged up the key for the storage locker and mailed it back to Dom for safekeeping.

Dwindling funds or not, it was clear he'd need at least one

more proxy session to track Finch down—perhaps several more, if the money stretched that far.

Stepping back out onto the street outside the delivery company's shopfront, Elijah saw that it was turning out to be a sunny morning. He closed his eyes, enjoying the warmth, then opened them seconds later to find he was back in his own body, sitting across from Davie in the prison canteen.

He blinked rapidly, swallowing down a familiar rush of nausea.

"Welcome home, lad," said Davie with a lopsided leer.

CHAPTER
TWELVE

RAPHAEL

After the meet and greet with some minor celebrities lending their public support to the Cardiff Wildlife Rescue Centre, Raphael Markov made his way up onto a temporary stage erected next to the park's front gates. From there, he could look out past the visitor centre to newly fenced-off acres designed to shelter species otherwise threatened with extinction in their natural environments.

Taking his position behind a podium, Raphael took a moment to scan the audience of journalists, minor celebrities and environmental activists, noting as he did so that television vans from most, if not all, of the major TV and streaming platforms were present. Camera drones darted here and there like so many robot insects.

"First," he said into the microphone, "I want to say thank you to everyone who's helped to make this Research and Rescue Centre possible."

This produced a smattering of applause. "Like most of you," he continued, "I grew up in a world from which innumerable species vanished forever with almost every day that passed. That, unfortunately, is still a reality midway through the 21st century."

He paused briefly, savouring the drama. "Slowly but surely, however, we're turning the tide—not only rescuing and preserving endangered species in order to one day return them to their natural habitats, but even resurrecting some of those we've lost this century through the use of advanced gene manipulation techniques developed in Telop Industries' own research labs."

He looked around, gauging his audience and seeing heads nod in agreement. "In a moment, I'll hand you over to Nat Dorsey. Thanks to her diligent and tireless work in preserving our world's genetic inheritance, more than three hundred species of animal, bird and fish have been rescued from the brink of extinction over the last decade. To rescue just one would be the work of a lifetime for most people."

That got more scattered applause, and even a couple of whoops as Alice Wong, the park's head keeper, came up onto the stage to hand Raphael a pair of oversized scissors.

As he took hold of the scissors, Raphael became aware that a number of journalists and TV presenters had begun staring down at their bracelets or speaking with their cameramen and colleagues in hushed, rapid tones rather than paying any attention to him.

One of the journalists looked up from his bracelet and straight at him. "Mr Markov!" he shouted. "Can you tell us anything about the abduction of your daughter from a private hospital?"

Raphael stared at the journalist for a moment, then glanced down at his own bracelet. More than a dozen unnoticed text messages and emails had arrived in just the last few minutes. He looked around for his security chief, Lovatt, and saw him standing by the side of the stage, studying the screen of his own bracelet with a look of deep consternation.

With an effort, Raphael forced a smile onto his face even

as he felt a tight knot of panic forming in his belly. "As soon as we have a clearer idea of just what happened, I promise there'll be an official comment," he improvised. He at least managed to keep his voice even.

More shouted questions followed. Raphael stared back at his audience, suddenly aware of how flustered he must look. Then, remembering the oversized scissors, he took a firm grasp on them and made his way down from the stage and towards the front gates.

Earlier that morning, one of the Centre's animal-keepers had strung a red ribbon across the gates. The gathered journalists immediately swarmed after him, filling the air with a cacophony of questions about Stacy.

Raphael quickly cut the ribbon and tossed the scissors to one side. "I'd like to declare this Research Centre open," he shouted over the noise, then headed for the main reception building, pushing past journalists even as they swarmed around him with their microphones.

Lovatt, who looked no less flustered than Raphael, hurried to his side. "Sir," he shouted over the hubbub, "I still don't quite have a handle on what happened, but it appears a mob broke into the Peartree and—"

"Not now," Raphael snapped at him. "First, get these people out of here, then find out what the hell's going on."

"Yes, sir," Lovatt replied promptly.

"Tell them I'm not answering questions or speaking to anyone from the press until I have a better idea of what happened. Refer any further questions to our public relations department. Got that?"

Lovatt nodded. They reached the entrance of the main building, which was currently empty, and Raphael dived inside, quickly locking the door. Lovatt remained outside, turning to face the onslaught of journalists, his arms spread wide as he called for their attention.

Raphael stepped into a vacant side-office and caught his

breath. He could hear Nat Dorsey's amplified voice from the direction of the stage; she was making a valiant effort to explain the Centre's importance to an audience that had lost all interest in anything she had to say.

Dorsey had fought long and hard to have this Centre built, and as Raphael listened, he almost felt a twinge of regret for the price he'd extracted from her in return for Telop's support.

Almost.

———

LATER, after the television crews and journalists had finally departed and Raphael had been fully apprised of that morning's events by Lovatt, he spoke to Doctor Dorsey alone in a laboratory filled with new and still shrink-wrapped equipment.

"The animals," he asked. "Do you have them ready?"

Whenever Dorsey spoke to her television audience, which numbered in the millions, she did so with overwhelming confidence. Her strong and craggy features bore evidence of a life lived mostly outdoors and in a variety of inhospitable and often remote environments. Now, however, much of that aura of confidence had fled, and as he spoke her gaze remained fixed on a point somewhere past his shoulder.

Raphael turned to see that her attention was directed at a window behind him. Through the window, past high wire fencing, he saw a dark shape silhouetted by the fading light of the afternoon sitting high in the branches of a tree.

"I'm not happy about this," said Dorsey when he turned back to face her. This time she met his gaze with eyes that were full of defiance. "I want to save these animals, not... *exploit* them." Her lips curled in disgust. "Especially not like this."

Raphael raised an eyebrow. "They are being saved, Doctor

Dorsey, as well as being protected. That's why the Centre is here."

"Yes, but…" She paused as if summoning inner strength. "But what you're asking of me goes against the grain." Her words took on a beseeching quality. "It's not what I spent a lifetime working in Africa and South America for. Can't you at least tell me why you're doing this to them?"

"I don't recall you complaining when I offered to help save you from bankruptcy," Raphael replied. "As to why, I have my reasons."

Dorsey's mouth formed into a flat, thin line. "I could talk to the press," she said. "Tell them about the…the experiments you've been doing."

"Yes, you could," said Raphael. "And it might make things difficult for me, for a few days. But your career would be over the moment the world learned of your complicity in those same experiments."

Dorsey's head ducked down in a signal of defeat. Raphael tried not to let his satisfaction show. "Now tell me if you've done what I asked."

"I've injected the gorillas with the hopscotch beads you gave me, just as you asked." Her voice was low and bitter. "But I very much want to know why."

"That's my business," Raphael reminded her firmly. "But if you must know," he said, "it's my intention to proxy with them personally."

Her eyes widened in horror and she took a step back from him, bumping into one of the long tables that filled the laboratory. "You can't be serious!" she cried, clearly appalled. "Think of the damage you could do to yourself, let alone the gorillas. Assuming it's even possible to proxy across species. Nobody's ever managed to—!"

"If you don't do precisely what you're told without questioning me further," Raphael said as evenly as his growing temper would allow, "I'll have you escorted from the premises and make sure you never set foot in here again."

That shut her up. Crimson flowed up her neck and into her cheeks, her anger blossoming into barely suppressed fury.

For a moment, Raphael wondered if perhaps he had pushed her too far to be sure she would keep her silence. He could arrange for her to have an accident, of course. But the death—accidental or otherwise—of someone with so high a public profile carried with it the risk of a major investigation.

And that was something he couldn't afford. Not when he was so close to achieving everything he had been working towards for so long.

Even the simple act of trying to keep Stacy from speaking to a journalist had triggered a whole hornet's nest of complications just when his attention needed to be focused on his long-term survival. Somehow, and by some means that defied his comprehension, she had slipped from his grasp. Not that she should have survived the encounter with her intended assassin…

No, he decided, from now on he would take care of such matters himself. There would be no more hiring of third parties.

Raphael's bracelet buzzed at that same moment.

"Excuse me," he said to Dorsey, stepping away from her.

"Sir?" Raphael recognized Lovatt's voice. "I thought you ought to know that the police intend to launch their own enquiry into your daughter's disappearance from the Peartree."

Raphael swore under his breath. "Get onto Peterson at the law firm," he ordered Lovatt. "I want the police as far from this as possible. Emphasize that this is a private matter. We can make up some story for them—say she wasn't kidnapped, but that she voluntarily left with those people. Have Peterson send me hourly updates. And I want the same from you—is that understood?"

"Sir."

Raphael ended the call, feeling his hand tremble slightly as he lowered his arm. It was a ridiculous suggestion he'd made to Lovatt, but he could try and come up with a better explanation for Stacy's disappearance later.

He returned his attention to Dorsey, who regarded him with a mixture of sour distaste and something that might be cunning. Perhaps, he thought, she was hoping the act of proxying with her animals would cause him irreversible brain damage or even kill him.

To his surprise Raphael felt a sudden, unexpected desire to tell her of his plans, of how he was not only fighting for his life, but that the very experiments that aroused her ire might help him—and by extension, the whole human race—achieve something very like immortality.

"The enclosure," he said to Dorsey. "I want you to take me there now."

At least Dorsey's anger appeared to have abated. She complied without another word, her manner listless as she led him towards the locked gates of the gorilla enclosure.

The enclosure occupied several acres of woodland bordered by stainless-steel mesh. A steel-framed door led inside the enclosure, while near-indestructible netting slung over the treetops kept the animals from escaping their new home.

"The keys," said Raphael, his voice betraying his excitement.

Dorsey placed the enclosure's keys in his outstretched hand. "I suppose," she said, "I should remind you there's a decent chance they'll rip you limb from limb."

Her tone made it clear she'd be perfectly fine with that outcome.

"You can go now," he replied curtly.

Dorsey turned and walked away, her gait stiff-legged.

Raphael waited several minutes until he saw the lights of

her car come on from far across the park, then move along the road leading away from the Centre. Once she was gone from sight, he unlocked the gate to the animal enclosure, almost dropping the keys in his haste.

Once he was inside, the gate closed behind him. Heart beating thunderously in his chest, he stared into the darkness between the trees, hearing the rustle of leaves in a passing breeze.

As he waited, he thought of Isaac. Was it possible *he* might have something to do with the events at the Peartree? But if so, how could he possibly have organized so many people to come to Stacy's rescue?

Not unless he, too, could somehow…

No. No, that wasn't, couldn't be possible. There had to be another explanation.

Raphael took a deep breath, then let the air seep slowly from his lungs as he listened for sounds of movement. When they'd reached the enclosure, Raphael had felt another impulse, to ask Dorsey to wait by the enclosure gate long enough to bear witness to the impossible thing he was about to do.

But would she have understood? Would she have shared his sense of triumph, or have been just as short-sighted as all the rest?

The latter, most likely, he decided. And even if he had let her stay, he couldn't possibly have allowed her to live, not so long as there was a chance she might tell others what she had seen.

Just then, Raphael heard a rustle of leaves and looked up, seeing a silhouetted shape moving amidst the branches high overhead. The shape, black against black, dropped onto the grass a few meters in front of him.

The gorilla raised itself up on two legs, its huge barrel chest making Raphael think of old monster movies. Only now that he was so close to the beast could he see how enormous it was—and how utterly terrifying.

Moonlight glinted from its fangs, the pale whites of its eyes showing as it peered at him with little more than passing curiosity.

Then he felt the shift happen, and just like that, Raphael was looking back at himself through the creature's own eyes.

Yet rather than being under the control of the gorilla, his own, human body remained his to command. He was in complete control of both, simultaneously, while the gorilla's own consciousness had been reduced to a dormant state not unlike deep sleep.

Something that, so far as anyone else knew, should be impossible.

Then more dark shapes came lumbering out from amidst the trees, curious to see what threat this intruder might represent. One of the gorillas was even bigger than the first, and looked like it could rip him limb from limb as easily as Raphael himself could tear a sheet of paper.

This larger beast sniffed at the air, then bared its teeth as if to challenge him.

In the next instant a second connection was established. Raphael's human body fell to its knees, overwhelmed by the experience. Now he was in control of three bodies: two gorillas, and one human.

Then another of the gorillas came under his control, and the number increased to four.

Then five.

Raphael had feared the experience would overwhelm him. Instead, the shift to multiple simultaneous perspectives and consciousnesses was ecstatic, bordering on holy.

One might even say godlike.

CHAPTER
THIRTEEN

STACY

Stacy became sufficiently aware of her surroundings to register that she sat facing an old woman, close enough that their knees brushed against each other. Looking to her right, she saw buildings and streets flashing by through a windscreen.

Was she still on her way to London from Paris? But hadn't that been aboard a train? And hadn't she already arrived...?

Blinking, she struggled to clear the fog from her thoughts. Her body was a mass of dull aches, and her right elbow itched badly beneath its bandaging.

Then came a screech of tires, and the old woman reached out to Stacy, steadying her with a hand on one shoulder.

They were both sent lurching to one side with enough force that Stacy would have slid from her slender perch if not for the older woman's steadying grip.

She was, Stacy at last realized, in the back of a van. The van's rear doors, to her left, were hidden behind roll-down blinds.

But where were they going?

The old woman gave Stacy an encouraging nod, then sat

back again. She had tangled grey hair and wore a heavy parka that must have been stifling in the warm weather. Beneath it, she appeared to be wearing little more than fluffy pyjamas.

The old woman opened a plastic box on her lap and took out a hypodermic syringe. The van veered around another corner, and once more the old woman grabbed Stacy's shoulder with her free hand to keep her from sliding to the floor.

It was more than just a van, Stacy realized, studying her surroundings more closely. It was old, possibly even from the previous century, at least judging by how dilapidated it looked.

Looking down, she saw that she was perched on the edge of a tiny bed, while the old woman directly opposite her sat balanced on a wooden stool. Shelves and a cooking area had been built into the van's interior, while the blinds over the back windows provided some semblance of privacy.

Curious, Stacy reached out with her un-bandaged arm, pushing the blinds to one side so she could look outside. She saw startled pigeons rising in great flapping clouds from a tree outside a church.

Something stung the back of Stacy's right hand. Gasping in surprise, she looked down to see that the old woman had injected her with something just where her skin emerged from the bandaging.

Within seconds everything seemed brighter and sharper, as if she'd emerged from a dense fog into brilliant daylight. The constant ache in her ribs and right arm began to fade almost immediately.

Someone—a man—sat in the front of the van, driving it manually. Even though she could only see the back of his head, he seemed oddly familiar.

"She's awake, Isaac," the old woman said to the man.

"Pull over at the next corner. It's time to switch to the next car."

Isaac?

Then she looked more closely and realized it really was him. She felt a sudden rush of joy, and something else welling up from deep within her chest that might have been relief or equally despair.

She opened her mouth to ask what had happened to him, or if he had talked to the journalist. But before she could, the van came to a halt with such force it made Stacy gasp. This time, she was able to catch herself one-handed before she slipped off the edge of the bed.

The old woman gave her a reassuring smile. "The shot I gave you should clear things up a bit," she said. "But we're not home-free yet."

"I don't understand," said Stacy.

Hearing a thump, she looked up front and saw Isaac had got out and stepped around in front of the van. He'd hardly looked at her; indeed, he seemed entirely occupied with something, his expression taut with worry. She could hear him muttering to himself, even if she couldn't make out the actual words.

The old woman stood, pushing past Stacy to open the rear doors before climbing out.

"Who are you?" Stacy asked, looking out at the old woman.

"My name is Zero," the old woman replied, then beckoned to Stacy to disembark. "If you don't mind, we really are in a bit of a hurry, Miss Cotter."

Moving unsteadily, her senses still weaving despite whatever had been pumped into her veins, Stacy soon found herself standing on a residential side-street that could have been anywhere from London to Brighton. She had a vague recollection of crowds of strangers guiding her down the steps of a hospital, but it felt more like a dream than anything real.

Somewhere between then and now she had acquired a T-shirt and jeans to replace her flimsy hospital gown. Stained leather boots clad her previously bare feet.

She found she could stand unaided without too much effort. Whatever they'd been treating her with at the Peartree appeared to have set her well on the road to recovery. Or maybe it was something to do with whatever the weird old woman with the even weirder name had injected her with.

Zero shrugged off her heavy parka and held it out to Stacy. "Here," she said. "Put this on."

"I don't need it," said Stacy. "It's too warm."

"That's not why I want you to put it on," said the old woman. "Hurry. Someone might be watching us right now."

A thousand questions crowded Stacy's lips, but she said nothing and put the parka on as instructed. Zero tugged the parka's hood down until Stacy's face was almost entirely concealed. She had a sudden memory of doing the same thing with her hoodie when she had arrived in London.

"Keep your head down," Zero told her in an urgent whisper. "And don't look up. Cameras are everywhere."

Close by the van stood a vintage four-door Jaguar that itself had to be most of a century old. A man in his nineties or early hundreds, dressed in an expensive pinstriped suit and scarlet tie, stood by its open door, clearly waiting for them.

Stacy watched, befuddled, as Zero got back into her van and drove away. She looked around and saw Isaac talking to the man in pinstripes in a low and confidential tone.

"Isaac?" Stacy asked, stepping up to him. Her heart had started to beat so rapidly she could hear it thudding in her chest. "Is it really you? Who are these people?"

Isaac turned to look at Stacy, then immediately wrapped her up in a bear hug.

"Questions later," he said, pulling back so he could see her face. His cheeks were damp with tears as he contemplated her. "I promise I'll have answers. But for now we have to hurry."

He turned back to the man standing by the Jaguar. "Let's go."

––––––

"Who is he?" Stacy asked as Isaac guided her into the rear of the Jaguar. The car's owner got in front and after a moment she heard the soft hum of its batteries.

"Zero," Isaac replied as the car picked up speed.

"I don't mean the old woman," said Stacy, motioning her head at the man who had taken manual control of the Jaguar. "I mean him."

"I know who you mean," said Isaac, a whisper of a smile playing on his lips. "They're both Zero."

She stared at him. "Don't be ridiculous."

"It's confusing, I know," he said. "And I did say I'd explain everything, but I'd still rather wait until we're out of harm's way."

There were four more stops after that. The first took them inside a garage down a side-street. The Jaguar's driver led them inside the garage, down a flight of steps and along a subterranean corridor. Stacy stumbled along after them, baffled and unsure what on Earth was going on.

They emerged in the rear of a charity shop. Walking out through the front entrance, they found yet another car waiting outside with yet another driver.

Isaac guided Stacy into the rear of this new car and, to her increasing consternation, also addressed its driver as Zero.

He did the same with the driver of the next car as well, finding it inside a multi-storey car park.

By then, she was almost too afraid to ask Isaac what was really going on. Fear sank long, sharp claws deep beneath her skin; something was going on she didn't understand, yet she was clearly at the centre of it.

By the time they finally exited the city, Stacy and Isaac were ensconced within a sleek silver bullet of a car, the hum of its batteries barely audible, if at all. It seemed to glide over the road, as if it couldn't bear the thought of coming into contact with crude tarmac. The windows were tinted and entirely opaque to anyone trying to see in.

They passed through farmland and small towns. This time, Zero—whoever or whatever the Zeros were—took the form of a young man barely a few years older than Stacy. Expensively if casually dressed, he looked to Stacy like some young hotshot lawyer or financial consultant on his day off.

The regular hum of the batteries sent Stacy into a deep and, for the first time in days, entirely natural sleep. When she next woke, the sun had moved a long way across the sky and they were rumbling down a long driveway lined on either side by trees.

A mansion or perhaps a hotel became intermittently visible through branches and they soon pulled up outside the front entrance of a huge, rambling edifice of a house. Most of its windows were boarded up.

'Zero' stepped out of the car and opened the door for her. From the way the light slanted through the trees, Stacy guessed it was early evening. The lawns surrounding the mansion were unkempt and overgrown.

"Where are we?" she asked Isaac, getting out and looking around.

"Somewhere safe." He frowned, then turned to their driver. "It is safe, isn't it?"

The latest Zero nodded. "I can't guarantee it's one hundred percent secure," he replied, "since that would be statistically impossible. However, it is very remote."

"Remote or not, if Raphael wants to find us, he can," Isaac warned the younger man. "Remember, he found me."

Zero nodded. "Which is why I recommend that we get you both inside and out of sight straight away." He nodded towards tall wooden doors that stood partway open, a darkened vestibule visible beyond. Figures, concealed by shadows, moved within. "I've made some preparations in advance of our arrival," he added.

Isaac stared at the mansion and then back at the younger man. "For God's sake, how many people are you using now? And where did you find all of them?"

"There are a dozen either in or near the house under my control," Zero replied. "Far less than I used in the Peartree."

"And the ones here came from where, exactly?" Isaac demanded.

"There are several villages within a twenty-mile radius," Zero replied. "Unemployment is high in this part of the country, and so I had little trouble locating a number of habitual users of hopscotch whom I could hire directly without having to co-opt any live proxy sessions they were engaged in. I assure you, Isaac, I'm making use of them only out of necessity. They're being well compensated for their time."

Isaac didn't answer at first, his expression flat and hard. "Compensated how?" he asked. "Where is the money coming from?"

The younger man blinked at him. "I'm drawing on certain discretionary funds within Telop. The money should be untraceable."

"We will not make a habit of this kind of thing," Isaac informed the younger man. "Is that understood?"

"Of course."

Stacy listened, utterly baffled. There was something curiously childlike about the younger man. The way he spoke and the way he looked at Isaac gave her the distinct sense he was determined to win Isaac's approval.

It had been much the same with all the others whom they

had encountered following her escape from the hospital. They all spoke the same way, as well as sharing the same name.

Stacy shivered without knowing why.

Isaac turned to her and gestured towards the house. "Come on. Let's get inside."

The smell of mildew made her nose wrinkle as she followed the two men inside the mansion, which was clearly derelict. From inside a doorway came the sound of shuffling feet. A broad staircase set at the centre of the hall led up into darkness.

The building was most likely another casualty of the post-pandemic years. Empty and abandoned buildings that belonged to those who had succumbed littered the country-side up and down the British Isles.

"Where did you find this place?" asked Isaac, gazing around.

"It belongs to a Telop subsidiary," Zero replied. "Or rather, the land does. They intended it for some research project or other, but the plans fell through years ago."

Isaac frowned. "Why Telop? Isn't that risky?"

"It's more a matter of hiding in plain sight," Zero replied. "Telop own thousands of such properties all across the country, many unused and many acquired in the years following Pandemic Two. My hope is they won't expect us to be hiding in one of their own properties."

Isaac nodded, his manner distracted. "It'll do for now."

————

STACY STEPPED AWAY from the conversation and towards a door through which she could hear movement. Past the door, she saw a kitchen with an old-style log-burning stove, now silent and cold. Cardboard boxes and bundles of discarded shrink-wrap lay scattered about the floor, and two men and a woman were busily opening yet more boxes. They had placed a kettle and a portable battery unit on the floor, along with various pieces of camping equipment and a pair of new-looking rucksacks that still had their sales tags on them.

There was a kitchen table that looked new, and four wooden chairs, also new. Assembly instructions lay on the floor near them.

One man was barely more than a boy, with a pencil-thin neck and a prominent Adam's apple. The second man was large and burly with tattoos beneath his rolled-up sleeves. He looked to be in his late forties. The woman, perhaps thirty- or thirty-five, wore a dark- and expensive-looking wool suit.

Once again, Stacy found herself struck by the disparity of the people she had encountered since fleeing the hospital, as if each of them had been selected entirely randomly from out of the general population.

The boy with the prominent Adam's apple saw her standing just outside the open door and stopped working. Then his tattooed companion, and the woman in the business suit, turned to regard her as if alerted to her presence by some unseen signal. All three wore the same supernaturally calm expressions.

Stacy took a step back, then turned to see Isaac's companion regarding her with that same look of calm curiosity.

If not for Isaac's presence, she would have fled the house immediately and taken her chances in the surrounding woods.

"They'll make you some tea if you like," said Isaac's companion. "We'll be able to cook something soon as well."

"I guess it's time we talked about Zero," said Isaac, his expression sympathetic.

———

TOGETHER, Isaac and Stacy explored the mansion, starting with the upper floor. They set up camp in a room that had a single, huge floor-to-ceiling mirror mounted on one wall. The glass was filthy, but intact, but more importantly the room was in better condition than any other.

Gazing at her reflection, Stacy could see how hollow-eyed and exhausted she looked. When they went back downstairs, another of Isaac's seemingly endless supply of silent helpers gave them each cold faux-beef sandwiches that they ate by the light of a kerosene lamp in the kitchen. They drank tea made with the kettle, now wired into the battery unit, with water from a six-gallon canister.

Isaac's helpers shuffled out of the room and closed the door to give them some privacy. The moment they departed, Stacy let out a sigh that rattled against the back of her throat.

Isaac gave her a knowing look. "Giving you the creeps?"

"A lot," Stacy admitted. "Sorry. But who the hell are they? And what's with them all having the same name?"

"Look," said Isaac, "you know I used to work for Telop back in the 2030s."

"Sure," she said. "From before I was born. You told me."

Isaac's expression grew intent. "But I didn't tell you much about what I was doing there. I didn't talk about it because I was afraid our messages to each other, encrypted or not, might be intercepted by algorithms designed to recognize specific keywords."

"Intercepted by who?" asked Stacy. "Raphael?"

"By people working for him, yes. My primary field of research was in artificial intelligence."

"Sure." She nodded. "Automated planes and cars, that kind of thing? I knew that already."

"That wasn't my real work," Isaac explained. "They put me in charge of a blue-sky research team."

The kerosene flame flickered, sending the shadows around Isaac's face briefly dancing. "The aim was to build a true

thinking machine," he continued, taking a sip of tea. "Specifically, I was doing work on synthetic neural networks
designed to mimic the higher-level reasoning skills of a
human being."

"So…a computer?"

A pained look crossed Isaac's face. "To put it crudely, yes.
The machine we created needed a name, an identity. I
intended it to be a prototype for a first generation of higher-
level fully cognitive AIs. So I called it Zero."

It took a moment for what Isaac was saying to sink in.
Stacy's eyes grew round. "But…those people are human.
Aren't they…?"

"Let me finish," said Isaac. "I designed Zero not just to
mimic humans, but to be smarter than them. Smart enough to
look at the problems facing the world and come up with solu-
tions we mere humans couldn't possibly conceive of." He
shrugged. "One of the first tasks I set Zero was to find some
means by which people might see the world through each
other's eyes. Something that could reduce conflicts and
misunderstandings, whether cultural, political or otherwise."
His mouth curled in a gentle smile. "Smart or not, I didn't
expect him to create a solution that so literally matched my
request."

Stacy put down the remains of her sandwich, her hunger
gone. "Wait…are you talking about proxy? You're making it
sound like you're the one who invented it."

Isaac grinned and shook his head. "Not me, no," he
corrected her. "Zero created proxy."

With a shock, she saw that he was entirely serious.

"But according to everything I've ever heard, someone
anonymously uploaded the recipe to some website." She
swallowed, her throat suddenly paper-dry. "Are you saying
that was you?"

"I'm getting to that. Naturally, I was excited Zero had
come up with something so astonishing in response to a

simple request." Isaac's smile grew wan. "Unfortunately, I underestimated David Markov, Raphael's father. He was still in control of Telop at that time, and his only interest in proxy lay in its potential military applications."

"…military applications?"

Isaac's smile faded. "A spy could proxy with an enemy soldier, for instance, then walk his body onto a military base and wreak havoc. Or the same spy could take over the body of the leader of an enemy nation and have him do or say just about anything. Or simply take over one of his advisers and assassinate that same leader. Nobody would know who to trust ever again."

Isaac's mouth twisted up in disgust as he spoke. "I should have seen it coming. But I let myself be blinded by what I'd achieved with Zero."

If not for everything she'd witnessed in just the last few hours, Stacy might have struggled to believe him. Instead, she nodded mutely.

"Anyway," he continued, his voice fractionally brighter, "I threatened to disrupt the research and prevent it from continuing. David reacted by barring me from any work to do with either Zero or with proxy. I swore then that I would do anything to stop him and Telop misusing either Zero or proxy. So I did."

"You did it," said Stacy, her voice a mixture of awe and horror. "You're the one who put it online."

Isaac nodded. "I modified the recipe so it could be reproduced using only the most advanced 3D medical printers available at the time. That way, I thought, rather than being locked away in some mil-tech lab, proxy could enable humanity to see its commonalities rather than its divisions." His expression grew grim. "Instead, it became a tool for exploitation and murder."

"Did David Markov find out what you'd done?"

"It couldn't have been anyone but me. David knew that.

By then, both Zero and proxy had been classified as military secrets, and that made me the subject of a manhunt the moment I released proxy into the public domain. This wasn't a spur-of-the-moment decision, you understand—I did a lot of preparation in advance. When the time came, I went...off-grid, as they say."

"Where did you go?" Stacy asked, rapt.

"First, I went to Mexico, later Chile. They're good places to disappear, if you know how. I'd sequestered money in anonymous accounts and used it to build myself a new identity."

"This is a lot to take in," said Stacy, staring down at her sandwich.

"Of course." Isaac nodded. "I've waited a long time to tell you all this. And there's more." He stifled a yawn and Stacy saw just how exhausted he was. "Much more."

"But these people," she reminded him. "You haven't explained why you call them by the same name as your machine. Unless they're..." She paused a moment, her eyes growing wide. "Oh."

Isaac nodded. "Proxy."

"But...a machine! How could it proxy with people? And so many all at once!"

"Excellent questions," Isaac agreed. "And ones with very technical answers." He yawned openly this time. "All in good time."

"But if Zero's still operating from inside Telop," Stacy pressed, "then why doesn't Raphael know he's talking to you or using it to control all these people?"

Isaac stood and stretched. "More questions! I need to sleep, and so do you."

Stacy shook her head. "Like you expect me to sleep with all this going through my head?"

"Well, all right then," said Isaac. "During my years on the run, Zero was effectively mothballed when he failed to provide the Markov's with any further miracle technologies they could exploit." Despite his fatigue, a grin spread across Isaac's face. "But they never shut him down entirely. I can only imagine what Raphael might think were he to learn what Zero's been up to behind his back all these years— starting with remaining in constant contact with me. I did create it, after all."

CHAPTER
FOURTEEN

RAY

Ray had to navigate his way around half a dozen narrow village roads before he finally found the address he was looking for. The GPS of his hire car appeared to have difficulty believing any such place existed.

After some exploration and asking random people for directions, he at last pulled up outside a cottage on a lane lined with tall ash trees, a nearby motorway rumbling with London-bound traffic. Stepping up to the front door he saw a doorplate that read 'COTTER, A.'.

There was no response when he knocked on the door. After a minute he tried again, and then again.

Just when he was ready to assume Amy Cotter wasn't home, Ray heard movement from around the rear of the cottage. Making his way through a low wooden gate set to one side of the cottage, he spied Amy Cotter kneeling by a row of plants in a small garden to its rear, trowel in hand.

She glanced up, clearly startled to see him. Standing, she brushed dirt from her jeans.

"Mr Thomas." Her voice sounded tight and nervous. "How did you know where to find me?"

"It's probably best you don't know the answer to that question," he replied. "I've got some news for you."

Amy regarded him warily. "Is it anything to do with the mob that kidnapped Stacy?"

Ray nodded.

"I see," said Amy, gripping her trowel as if she expected to have to defend herself with it. "I...saw some of what happened on the news. Naturally I've been very worried."

"I tried to call you several times today, Miss Cotter," said Ray, taking a step closer to her. "I came all the way out here because I felt concerned for your safety with everything that's been going on. Why didn't you answer my calls?"

"I was quite inundated with calls from journalists," said Amy, looking away. "Fortunately, they didn't find it as easy to locate my home as you seem to have. But since you're here, I regret to inform you I no longer require your services."

She said it without once meeting his eyes. Ray saw how flustered she looked, the words coming out tight and clipped.

"Why?" he asked her.

"Does it matter? You're welcome to keep the retainer I paid you, Mr Thomas, so long as you—"

"Ray is fine."

"Please leave," she said, her voice taking on a harder edge. Clearly, she'd recovered from the shock of his unexpected appearance. "You had no right to come to my home without my knowledge or permission."

"I'm here because I don't think you've been honest with me," said Ray, pushing his hands deep into the pockets of his jeans to show he wasn't going anywhere.

"Nonsense," Amy spat back at him. "I've been nothing but entirely straight with you!"

"You weren't there when that mob swarmed the building," said Ray, stepping close enough to her that she flinched back slightly. "I was, and I've seen nothing like it in my life.

They acted with a common purpose, snatching Stacy from out of her bed before…vanishing with her."

"Well, I can't explain that," she said, her shoulders sagging.

"When you first approached me, I thought it was nothing more than some domestic issue. But after what I saw happen inside the Peartree, it's clear there's a great deal more than that going on here." Ray stepped closer again, fixing her with a hard stare. "Then I began to think maybe you hadn't told me everything I needed to know."

Amy's gaze darted away from his and she swallowed, looking defeated.

Jackpot, thought Ray.

"You need to tell me everything," he continued, "or I'll tell the police what I know about this case and they can ask you questions instead."

"You wouldn't—!" she started, her eyes flashing with anger.

"I very much would." She might no longer be married to Raphael Markov, but he was damned if he'd allow himself to be screwed over by yet another member of the same family. "And they wouldn't be nearly so nice about it as me. So tell me whatever it is you've been keeping from me."

Amy sucked in a deep breath, then tossed her trowel down next to a row of plants. "It's a nice day," she said briskly. "Perhaps we should go for a walk."

————

RAY WAITED out in front of the cottage until Amy reappeared a few minutes later wearing Wellington boots. It had been raining the night before, and even though the sun was out and the day increasingly warm, the grass was still dew-damp and the air fresh and moist. He followed her through a cattle gate further down the lane, then along a rutted path that ran by one side of a fallow field.

"I'm sorry I didn't respond to your calls," she said at last, "but what I saw on the news frightened me terribly. It made little sense to me. I thought somehow it might have happened because I'd got you involved." She glanced sideways at him. "I suppose that was silly of me."

"In fairness," said Ray, "the whole thing scared the bejesus out of me."

She nodded. "If you don't mind, do you have any idea about what happened at the Peartree?"

"Nothing. The whole thing is baffling." One of Ray's trainers sank into sticky mud and he pulled it back out with a grimace. "I barely glimpsed your daughter before those people charged in and grabbed her. I tried following after her, but there were dozens, if not hundreds, of them all working together in perfect unison. Once they had her outside, they most likely bundled her into a car. By the time I managed to get back out and onto the street, it was chaos."

"But surely if someone took Stacy in a car, there's some way to trace it?"

Ray nodded. "The police did trace the car. They found it abandoned in a ditch in Surrey. It looks like the kidnappers switched vehicles a number of times and the police lost track of them." He shrugged. "Right now, she could be just about anywhere."

"And how do you know all this about the police?" Amy asked him.

"With the help of an old friend," Ray replied after a short pause.

Amy Cotter stopped briefly to stare at Ray. "The same one that helped you find my address, perhaps?"

Ray's responded with an enigmatic smile. The less Amy knew about Eunice, the better.

They walked in silence for another minute before Amy

spoke again. "What exactly is it you want from me then, Mr Thomas?"

"Everything and anything you can think of," he said, and shot her a look. "And I mean everything, Miss Cotter. I'll know if you're holding back. I'll decide what's important and what isn't."

She let out a sigh that sounded like it came from the depths of her lungs. "Some things aren't easy for me to talk about."

"Some things never are."

"Very well." She licked her lips and swallowed. "I don't know how this can possibly help you, but…if you must know, Raphael Markov isn't Stacy's biological father."

Ray stared at her, unable to hide his surprise. "Go on."

"I need to explain myself," she said, "for this to make sense. I was very young when I met Raphael. I wouldn't call it a whirlwind romance, but we were married less than six months after we met. It was wonderful at first." Her expression darkened, sodden soil squelching beneath her boots as they walked. "But after we were married things were rather different."

"How so?"

"The only time he paid attention to me after I joined him on his family's estate was when he wanted sex, and then only rarely. Except then he…"

"He what, Miss Cotter?"

"As I said," she replied, "some things are hard to talk about."

"If Raphael isn't Stacy's father, then that puts things in a whole different light, surely you can see that? It makes the question of why he would hole her up in his own private hospital even more pertinent—assuming he knows Stacy isn't his daughter. Does he?"

"He does."

Jesus. It was one thing to hold some things back, but this…

this was more than he'd expected. Even so, he could feel his patience wearing thin.

"You're angry with me," she said, glancing sideways at him.

"I'm not angry with you," said Ray, although in reality this was far from the truth. "I just don't understand why you wouldn't tell me any of this in the first place."

"I've already been through a harrowing divorce and then a court case where Stacy is concerned," she said. "The latter carried out in the full view of the public eye. Having reporters dog your every waking second is not an experience I can recommend, nor one I wish ever to repeat."

"Then understand that whatever you say to me, Miss Cotter, is in complete confidentiality. Please," he said, with all the sincerity he could muster, "if you want me to find Stacy, leave nothing out."

Amy stopped walking and turned to face him, her mouth set in a thin line. "You have to understand that being married to Raphael felt like being married to two different men."

"How so?"

"He hit me. Not often, and only on those rare occasions we were in bed together." Anger showed in her eyes and in the set of her mouth. "I often wished I could have seen that side of him before we were married, but the truth is we waited until our wedding day." She laughed under her breath. "Like a fool, I believed him when he said he liked that I was old-fashioned. Fortunately, after we were married, and I'd seen him for who he really was, he spent most of his time away from home. He was always away on some business trip or other, sometimes for weeks or even months." One corner of her mouth turned up. "The longer he was away, Mr Thomas, the happier I was."

She started walking again and Ray moved to follow. "Then why didn't you leave him?"

"I wanted to," she said, "but Raphael threatened me. He

didn't threaten my life, exactly, although by then I very much believed he was capable of such a thing. He intimated that I would be ruined, that his lawyers would first destroy my life, and then my reputation." She paused, as if steeling herself. "Then I met Isaac."

Ray shook his head. "Who?"

"Isaac Sizemore. A scientist. He worked for Raphael's father, David, back when he was still in overall charge of the company. We first met at a garden party held for Telop's main shareholders and I fell pregnant with Stacy while Raphael was away on one of his trips." She smiled to herself, and Ray guessed she was thinking about Sizemore. "Do you know," she added, "I've never told another living soul about any of this?"

"How did Raphael find out the truth about Stacy?"

"Well, under the circumstances it would soon have been rather obvious. I told him as soon as I knew I was pregnant. And…he was fine with it. He even offered to bring Stacy up as his own child."

Ray gaped at her in surprise. "He did?"

She let out a soft chuckle. "I was as surprised as you are. Raphael demanded, however, that I keep all this secret, especially where his own father was concerned. In return, I could live my life effectively separate from his, and without losing the lifestyle I had become used to."

"So you had to pretend you were still a happy couple."

"Precisely—all for the sake of Raphael's father." The last vestiges of her smile faded. "Nobody was more delighted by my pregnancy than David Markov. It seemed like every time I spoke with him he'd ask if he was a grandfather yet. He framed it like a joke, but he clearly expected Raphael to produce an heir."

They passed into another field and followed another rutted path. They were, Ray saw, following a circular route that would lead back to Amy's cottage. "And what about this man Isaac Sizemore?" he asked. "How did he feel about this arrangement?"

"Well," she said, "that's the thing. I wasn't interested in accepting Raphael's offer. In fact, I had every intention of leaving him for Isaac and taking Stacy with me, even if it meant fleeing in the night and suffering my husband's wrath. But Isaac disappeared before I even had a chance to tell him I was pregnant."

She looked sideways at him, her eyes heavy with regret and decades-old pain. "Isaac would never have done such a thing voluntarily. I confronted Raphael, afraid he might have done something to Isaac, and he told me Isaac was a problem that had been taken care of." Her voice trembled as she spoke. "Do you see now why everything to do with the Markov's frightens me so much?"

Ray reached out and touched her elbow to bring her to a halt. "I want to be clear about this," he said, facing her. "Do you have any proof that Raphael Markov murdered Stacy's biological father?"

"No," she admitted, her voice small and so quiet he could barely hear her over the rumble of the nearby motorway and the rush of the wind through trees. "But the way he said it, I was increasingly sure that was what he meant."

Ray shook his head in confusion, unable to quite yet fit all the pieces together in his head. "I thought Raphael as good as disowned Stacy when you and he divorced. Why go to all the trouble of getting rid of Isaac and taking Stacy as his own daughter, only to disown her later on?"

"Raphael's father is a strict Catholic, and a very conservative one, to boot. I quickly learned he had been unwilling to give Raphael any measure of control over the company unless he first married and produced children."

Amy flashed him a tight smile. "In David Markov's eyes, I was little more than a brood mare. But after the old man had a stroke and wound up in a vegetative state, Raphael took control of Telop. With his father out of the way, he no longer needed to keep up the pretence, and got rid of both myself and Stacy in short order."

Ray nodded slowly. "So you can't think of any other reason why Raphael would suddenly be concerned for Stacy's well-being?"

By now they had arrived back at the same gate near the cottage. "None, I'm afraid. Most likely, Mr Thomas, he's keeping up appearances for the sake of Telop's shareholders. As far as the world is concerned, after all, she's still his biological daughter."

"And you've never told anyone any of this?"

She shook her head. "Never."

Her story seemed plausible enough, but Ray couldn't shake the feeling he'd missed something regardless. "There isn't anything else you can tell me?"

"Frankly, Mr Thomas," said Amy, "I feel wrung out after talking about all this. If I could add anything more, I would have."

"You're sure?"

"Entirely."

Ray held her gaze, sure beyond any measure of doubt that she was still hiding something from him. But what?

"I want to remind you why I'm involved in all this," Ray said, not moving. "Your ex-husband ruined me."

Amy swallowed. "I know you had some difficulties with Raphael back when Stacy…when she got herself in trouble."

"To be precise," said Ray, his eyes still locked on hers, "I was carrying out an undercover investigation into an agency offering third-party proxy access to the skins of pretty young girls—including your daughter. When Stacy was caught in a sting, your ex-husband warned me I'd regret it if I didn't alter my statement and help drop the charges against her."

"Mr Thomas…"

"I'm not done," he snapped. "I refused. Except once the

trial ended, backdated payments appeared in my personal accounts that made it look like I'd been taking backhanders from proxy dealers. Now, I can't prove Raphael was behind it, but I can't think of anyone else with the resources to pull off something like that. It's a little more than 'difficulties', Miss Cotter."

"Of course." Amy nodded, clearly embarrassed and perhaps a little overwhelmed. "If I can think of anything else, I'll let you know. Goodbye."

She turned and stepped inside her cottage, pushing the front door shut. Ray stared at the closed door, trying to figure out what it was that kept niggling at him, then gave up and returned to his car.

It didn't hit him until he was halfway back to London.

In sheer frustration, he punched the dashboard with one clenched fist, then told the car to retrace its journey back to Amy Cotter's cottage.

It took the next off-ramp and Ray paid a premium to qualify as priority traffic. The car swung into a reserved lane and by the time he arrived back outside the cottage the sun had already moved a good distance across the sky.

When he shoved at the cottage's front door, he found it unlocked. Stepping inside, he found Amy in her living room next to an open suitcase, folded clothes in her hands and a look of terrified shock on her face.

"Going somewhere?" he asked.

"I... thought it best, in case any journalists found me as easily as you did. A friend has a place by the sea. I have the use of it any time I want."

"When was Stacy born?"

Amy stared at him in confusion. "March 2033. Why?"

"You said Raphael was like a different man when he shared a bed with you."

"Oh." Her eyes grew weary. "I did, didn't I?"

"You were talking about proxy," said Ray, stepping further

into the cottage. "It was Raphael's body, but it wasn't his mind in control, was it? Proxy was brand-new back then, but Raphael's one of the few people who could have had access to the high-end 3D printers needed to manufacture it."

Instead of issuing a denial, Amy sank wearily into a chair next to a small dining table. "I see now I should have picked my words more carefully."

"This is the last time you'll hold out on me," Ray warned her, taking a seat across from her. "Now tell me everything you left out."

"I only found out about it myself when Raphael's blackmailer contacted me," she explained, looking suddenly older than her years.

Ray felt a jolt of surprise. "Blackmailer?"

"A man named Paul Green. He was Raphael's driver, back when people bothered with such things." Reaching into a cabinet next to the table, Amy took out a bottle of sherry and poured a large measure into a tumbler. "I'm glad I saved this. Do you want some?"

"No, thank you. But feel free."

Amy nodded and drank most of it down, her hand trembling slightly. After composing herself, she continued. "I'd only met this man Green a few times and barely spoke with him. They had a lot of staff on the family estate, so I thought nothing of it when a new driver was hired to replace him. When Green contacted me years later, it was to tell me he'd been proxying with Raphael every time he and I made love."

Ray struggled to contain his excitement. All these years he'd been looking for leverage that could hurt Raphael Markov, and with any luck, he'd finally found it.

"When was it that Green approached you?" Ray asked, fighting to keep his voice steady.

"This was a few years after Stacy was born." She poured herself another measure of sherry. "At first I had no idea what he was talking about. Proxy was still very new at that time.

When I understood what he was telling me, well, I felt utterly violated."

"But why would Raphael go to such extraordinary lengths to avoid being intimate with you?"

The look she gave Ray suggested he was an idiot. "Because my ex-husband is gay, Mr Thomas. Not that I knew it before then."

A sudden warmth enveloped Ray's cheeks. "That would explain it, I suppose."

"Indeed," she said archly. "Green went on to tell me he'd also made a point of telling David Markov everything Raphael had done in order to give his father the heir he so badly wanted. By what I suspect is no coincidence at all, that's almost the exact same time David Markov suffered the first of a series of devastating strokes."

It was clear from her tone that Amy felt little sympathy for the old man.

"Did Green say what he wanted from you?" Ray pressed. "Why did he wait so long to contact you?"

"It seems he'd already tried to blackmail Raphael in return for his continued silence, but Raphael, fool that he is, refused to pay up." Amy lifted an eyebrow. "So Green did as he'd promised he would and told me and David Markov every-thing. He told me if I couldn't persuade Raphael to cooperate with his demands, his next stop would be the press."

"What did you do?"

"What he wanted me to, of course," Amy replied, her voice dark and laden with emotion. "And only because I was determined to keep Stacy safe. Raphael was badly shaken when I called him and told him that Green had contacted me and what he had said. He clearly hadn't taken Green's threats seriously. I told Raphael I wanted to meet with him so we could talk about it."

Something occurred to Ray. "Were you actually divorced at this time, or still keeping up the pretence?"

"Technically, we were still married, although at that time I'd hardly seen Raphael in years. I had my own house on the grounds of the estate and a townhouse in the city where I spent nearly all my time. Once Raphael had arranged for the care of his father following the first of his strokes, we met at his London office."

Amy gazed into the depths of her tumbler as if scrying the future. "Raphael was different—colder and more aloof than I remembered him." She shook her head. "I don't know how I could have ever believed I was in love with him. He agreed to pay Green off and I told him I wanted an immediate no-contest divorce in return for my silence. We'd maintain the fiction that Stacy was his daughter." A wry smile crossed her face. "He agreed, of course, and kept his word. But it was difficult going from what I had grown used to, to…a simpler life, you might say." Her expression grew bitter. "I hadn't realized how hard it would be on Stacy, however. She was still very young when all this happened, but I hadn't thought about how it might affect her later on, having such a well-known father whom she never saw. And who showed no interest in seeing her."

Sensing she had little more to add, Ray stood. "Do you have any idea of Paul Green's current whereabouts?"

"None." Her gaze remained fixed on the now-empty glass, which she turned back and forth on the tabletop. "I suppose you want to talk to him too."

"I don't know if he can explain why Raphael's showing a sudden interest in Stacy's welfare, but he might know something." And that, in turn, could reveal some further chink in Raphael's armour that Ray could exploit.

Her gaze flicked up to meet his. "I don't care about my reputation so much nowadays, Mr Thomas. But I do very much care about Stacy. It was hard for me when she left for the continent, although I entirely understand why she did."

"You never told her about her real father, did you?"

"I was afraid if she learned about Isaac, she might try to confront Raphael over his disappearance. Not knowing what else Raphael might be capable of, I couldn't take that risk."

"I understand." Walking over to the still-open door, he looked back at her. "Please don't go anywhere until I say otherwise. I don't want to have to come looking for you again. Because I will, if I have to."

CHAPTER
FIFTEEN

RAY

Eunice's home and place of work occupied most of a block in Hackney, a crumbling brick building that had started life as a Victorian women's prison, then later a textiles factory and, in its most recent incarnation, a call centre. It had subsequently lain derelict for nearly thirty years following the great exodus of international finance to mainland Europe and throughout the pandemic years.

Some enterprising artist had painted the exterior in a faux-Soviet style, heavy on reds and blacks. Ray stepped towards the entrance, noting the two tattooed heavies who stood guard outside it. From within came the powerful aroma of Moroccan kush and the throb of bass-heavy electronic music.

"What do you want?" asked one of the men in a heavy Eastern European accent. His tattoos covered the entirety of his face and shaven scalp.

"Eunice," said Ray. "She's expecting me."

The other guard deigned to give him a look-over. "What's your name?" he growled in the voice of someone who'd spent his formative years in Brixton.

"Ray Thomas."

"Ray…" Brixton's face darkened. "Wait, are you that fucking cop?"

Ray did his best to mask his dismay. "And why would you say that?"

"'Cause my Uncle Harry told me if I ever met someone with that name, I should break his fucking head open."

"I'm thinking there's probably more than one Ray Thomas in London," Ray offered, steeling himself.

"And I'm thinking there's not," the heavy replied with a snarl, bringing his fist back in preparation to drive it into Ray's face.

Before he could do any such thing, the thug's back arched and his eyes widened with shock. A noisy buzzing filled the air, like a robot insect trapped in a microwave. Then, slowly, the guard crumpled to his knees to reveal Eunice standing behind him at the open door, a taser gripped in one wizened hand.

"Fuckin' hell," she said, staring down at the guard where he lay in a foetal position, "you trying to put me out of business or sumthin'?"

"He's a professional snitch!" Brixton grunted through clenched jaws. "My Uncle Harry told me he caught him in his garage trying to—!"

"Shut up, Barry," said Eunice, her voice weary. Her own accent came via the East End, laden with gravel and tarry as the depths of the Thames. Pushing the taser she had used on Barry into a pocket of her knitted cardigan, and leaning heavily on her walking stick, she finally turned her attention to Ray. "Stirring up trouble again, I see."

Ray felt his cheeks grow warm. "Doing my job, more like."

Eunice shrugged. "Whatever." Turning, she hobbled back inside, her long, grey hair tied into a messy bun, bar some strands that flowed down over a faded and very ancient Gary

Numan T-shirt. "Just hand your gear over and get the fuck inside, Ray."

———

FIRST RAY DIVESTED himself of his bracelet, a chip-phone he kept for backup and a crumpled smart-screen, then stood with his arms spread as a third member of Eunice's security team ran a scanner along all four of his limbs.

Once he was declared clean of all electronics, weapons or potential bugging devices, he followed Eunice into an elevator that looked like it dated from the Victorian era. It shuddered and clanked as it carried them up to the fourth floor.

As soon as the doors of the elevator rattled open to reveal Eunice's private quarters, half a dozen cats appeared from different corners. An overpowering odour of cat urine hit Ray. As on previous visits, he made a point to breathe through his mouth.

The old woman's quarters took up most of the fourth floor. Three walls were entirely hidden behind bookshelves crammed with paper books and pieces of ageing computer equipment. A desk large enough to sail, were you to attach rigging to it, supported a variety of computer components—hard drives, backup units, and five huge screens.

Eunice hobbled over to a swivel chair behind the desk and collapsed into it. A cat jumped up onto her lap and she stroked its fur. Ray found another chair and pulled it up next to one side of the desk where he could see her past the cluster of screens.

"So?" he asked. "You got it?"

"The CCTV?" Eunice shrugged as if stealing police evidence from secure databases barely rated a mention. "Easy-peasy. I'm almost insulted that's all you wanted from me. You know most people are saying it's a fake?"

"What is?"

"That stuff on the news." She waved one nicotine-stained hand in the air. "The Markov girl, the mob in the hospital and all the rest of that palaver."

"I was there," Ray said with a frown. "I can assure you it happened."

"Oh, I believe you. Can't actually fake all those separate CCTV feeds, whatever people say, and I got them straight from the source. But it's unnatural, the way all those people acted, which is why, I think, some prefer to think otherwise." Eunice regarded him with unabashed curiosity. "So what are they, a cult or summat?"

"I'm here to find out myself, Eunice. How about you show me what you've got?"

Pulling a keyboard from out of a pile of half a dozen other keyboards, Eunice began to type on it. The screens, which had been either dark or running screensavers, all came to life.

Ray shuffled his chair around to get a better look. The screens showed numerous still images of the interior of the Peartree Institute. One showed Stacy Cotter propped upright against a mound of pillows, her expression blank and her lips slightly parted, as if she were sleeping with her eyes open.

Eunice looked at Ray. "Drugged to the 'effing eyeballs," she offered. "That's the girl they came for, right?"

Ray nodded. Eunice's wizened fingers once again danced across the keyboard.

"I filched a couple of the arrest reports while I was poking around the Met's databases," she added. "Seems a lot of the people who were in that mob all claimed they were proxying with someone else the whole time this was going on. You know anything about that?"

Ray nodded, his mouth set in a thin, taut line. "I heard the same from a friend in the Met."

"Someone you used to work with?"

Ray nodded. According to the same friend, a certain DCI

Edwards, slightly more than two hundred people in all had been identified as being involved in Stacy's kidnapping.

"Apparently," said Ray, "of the people interviewed so far who were in that mob, the person they each claimed to have been proxying with turned out to be part of the same mob. But so far they haven't found any connection between any of those people and either Stacy Cotter or Raphael Markov."

"Huh." Eunice tapped some more, then nodded at another screen. "They don't look like kidnappers, if you know what I mean. They just look like…"

"Like ordinary people," Ray finished for her. "Who decided to get together, walk into a private hospital and snatch one of its patients while acting perfectly in concert."

"Hang on," said Eunice. "What's the point of proxying with someone else if both of you are going to go and do the exact same thing in the exact same place? You might as well just do it in your own body unless you're disabled or into sex-swapping or something."

"Exactly," Ray agreed. "It makes no sense. But it gets weirder. They all claim not to remember anything, like they were asleep the whole time the raid was underway."

Eunice stared at him. "Asleep?" Her expression made it clear she thought he was having her on. "I must have missed that detail."

"Or at least not conscious, according to what I've heard about their statements." Ray gave her a significant look. "The only commonality is that most of their proxy sessions were a long way from ending. A few of them are still linked even now."

"You're talking about hopscotch. Christ." Eunice waved a hand at the screens. "So what the fuck do you need me for if you've got a mate on the inside telling you all this?"

"Because I need more than just CCTV footage," said Ray. "I also want you to track every vehicle that was in close vicinity to the Institute during the raid. You can use the footage to identify them, then track them down."

Eunice was silent for a moment. "That," she said pointedly, "will cost you."

"It's for a client. They're paying."

Which was far from true, although he hoped Amy Cotter might cover at least some costs. And if not...well, he could worry about that sometime in the future. The alternative was giving up before he got his hands on the man who'd ruined him.

"The current theory," Ray continued, "is that the people who took Stacy Cotter switched cars a number of times after they left the Institute. I know that the Met tracked the first few of these vehicles, but after that, whoever took her got her out of sight of any cameras long enough for her to vanish." He gave her a sly grin. "I know you well enough to know you can get ahead of the Met if you want to."

"Sounds like a challenge," said Eunice, a hungry look in her centenarian gaze. "Tomorrow good enough for you?"

"That soon?" Ray couldn't conceal his surprise.

"Why not?" she replied and shrugged. "I can ask around as well. What cameras can't see, people can."

"Great," said Ray. "There's just one more thing."

"Go on."

"They know which car Stacy Cotter was put in once they had her outside the Institute. I want to see who was in the car with her."

"Can't your mate in the Met tell you that?"

"A proxy investigator's the lowest of the low," he reminded her. "There's only so much I can beg from a former colleague."

Eunice shook her head and got to work, presenting Ray with a number of video feeds within a few minutes. One feed showed two people quickly guiding Stacy inside an expensive coupé. They were barely visible amidst a milling crowd who, nonetheless, worked in perfect coordination to keep Markov's hired security from getting anywhere near the girl.

On one side of Stacy stood a tall, skinny man, in late middle-age and with wiry hair. On her other side was a grey-haired woman wearing a knee-length parka over what looked like pyjamas.

The three of them got into the coupé. The moment it started moving, more than a dozen other vehicles scattered up and down the street in front of the Institute also came to life, zooming here and there in different directions. Ray caught a glimpse of himself, searching frantically, his face a mask of almost comic befuddlement.

Within seconds, and just as he remembered, the road was once again almost entirely clear of vehicles. A chill gripped Ray when he saw how the milling crowd shifted out of the path of the cars with such nimble speed that it made the whole thing appear to have been carefully choreographed beforehand. He'd been too busy searching for Stacy at the time to notice.

Eunice rolled the video back again to a point where Stacy stood next to the coupé, then froze the image. Flashing brackets appeared around the faces of the man and woman flanking her. Long lists of information appeared on several other screens.

"The old bird's name is Olga Lubchik," Eunice said, reading from a screen. "She's a refugee from the six-second war and works as a teacher. The bloke with the frizzy hair is Dominic Fiori." She frowned and tapped again. "Not much information on him."

"Why not?"

She shrugged. "Could be all kinds of reasons." A quick glance at another screen elicited a frown. "Fiori's records only go back to the early 2030s. There's a birth certificate from before that which shows him as fifty-four, but there's nothing about which hospital he was born in, or anything else for that matter, which is very odd in this day and age." She peered past the screens at Ray. "If I had to guess, he's under an assumed identity." Amusement showed in the curl of Eunice's lips. "If you can look past the blatant and highly illegal abuse of government databases, I could cross-reference him with national criminal records."

"I won't tell if you don't," said Ray, inwardly marvelling at the things the woman was capable of.

It only took another minute before she was done. "Nothing." Her swivel chair squeaked softly beneath her as she leaned back. "So either he's had plastic surgery, or he's done nothing criminal in his life. I—"

Eunice came to a halt mid-sentence, peering at a screen. "Wait a second."

Ray leaned forward as she tapped at a keyboard for more than a minute. "What?"

"It says here that a man with that same name was reported missing from a privately owned psychiatric hospital a couple of days ago."

A prickling sensation worked its way up Ray's spine. "What was he in for?"

"According to this, he was under observation following a psychotic break."

"Anything else?"

Eunice shook her head. "That's all I can find."

"It's a start." Ray stood, feeling just a touch of disappointment. He'd hoped for something more conclusive and less random than a teacher and a mental patient. "Thanks, Eunice. Give me a copy of what you've got so far and you can let me know when you track those other vehicles down."

"Be nice to hear how all this works out in the end," said Eunice, tapping away. A printer whirred and a blank sheet of faintly reflective material as far beyond paper as paper was beyond stone tablets spat out of its slot. After first giving it a quick shake so it lost its programmed rigidity, Eunice passed the sheet to him.

Rolling it into a tight tube, Ray thrust the sheet inside his jacket. With a last farewell, he departed Eunice's building, and was glad to see Barry was no longer on duty at the entrance.

Stepping across the road and around a corner, Ray darted a quick look around to see if there were any cameras looking his way, then took the sheet back out and unrolled it.

He soon found himself swiping through page after page of biographical information about Lubchik. Fiori's biographical information, by contrast, occupied barely a single page.

Ray's bracelet vibrated. A glance at its screen revealed an update on the Stacy Cotter kidnapping. Lawyers for Raphael Markov had held a press conference claiming Stacy had in fact been bundled into a car by hospital staff seeking to take her to safety at an undisclosed location.

This explanation stank of so much bullshit Ray was astounded that any lawyer had the gall to stand up in front of the press and say such a thing out loud. Yet the police appeared to be going along with it. It spoke volumes about the power Raphael Markov wielded.

After heading home, Ray handed in his notice to his landlord, made some calls to a couple of agencies, packed the few things he needed into a duffel bag along with some other necessities and headed for a new flat he'd rented on a six-month lease and several miles from his old place; staying there was out of the question, now he knew Harry Cutts had goons out looking for him.

And God forbid Stokes should pay him an unexpected visit.

Once he had collected the keys and walked into his new place, Ray found the bedroom, dropped the duffel bag on the floor, collapsed onto a bare mattress and immediately fell into a deep and dreamless sleep.

———

RAY WOKE, immediately alert, to the sound of someone knocking loudly at his door.

Reaching into his duffel-bag, he pulled out a sawn-off shotgun, then walked, still muzzy, through to the living-room of his new place. He peered through the spyhole, afraid he might see Stokes or one of his mates standing outside his front door with a baseball bat.

Instead he saw a woman in her early twenties wearing a courier's uniform.

"Package," said the woman when Ray swung the front door open. He kept the sawn-off shotgun out of sight behind the door.

The courier thrust an envelope towards him. She had long, sharp features that seemed oddly familiar.

"Don't want me to sign anything?" he asked, taking the envelope with his free hand.

"Here." The courier produced a picture postcard and handed it to him.

Ray studied the postcard in puzzlement. Flipping it over, he saw a picture of Hawaii. Try as he might, he couldn't remember the last time he'd seen an actual, physical postcard. Not since he'd been very young, certainly.

"Does anyone even make these things any more?" he asked, holding the card up.

"Write on it that you're having a lovely time." The courier produced a pen and handed it to him. "But don't put your signature. That way Eunice knows you got your stuff."

Feeling strangely foolish, Ray stepped back behind the door, put the shotgun down, wrote a quick note on the back of the postcard then passed both it and the pen back to the courier. "You sure her mental health is all it should be, coming up with schemes like this?"

The courier regarded him oddly. "That's my grandmother

you're talking about." She got back on her electric scooter and was gone within seconds.

Closing the door, Ray went through to the kitchen and switched on the kettle. While he waited for it to boil, he slid a sheet of smart paper out of the envelope. Apart from some scribbled text at the bottom, the sheet was blank.

The mystery deepens, said the scribbled text. *Look at these specific time-stamps. Whoever you're dealing with, they're very, very organized and very, very thorough.*

Be careful.

- E

Tapping one corner of the sheet caused the handwritten text to fade. A grid of squares appeared in its place, each showing either a view of a street or back alley or the interior of a shop. Some streets were clearly upmarket and lined with trees while others were distinctly grubbier and rundown. Each image, as promised, had a time-stamp in one corner.

A tap and flick motion caused one image to reappear, much larger, on a screen mounted on the kitchen wall of Ray's new place. He found himself looking at a street he recognized, close by Tower Hamlets. Keeping half an eye on the screen, Ray pinched the sheet with two fingers. In response, the image burst into sudden motion.

A van pulled into view of the camera lens. Doors opened on both sides and a man and two women got out: Stacy Cotter, Dominic Fiori and an elderly woman he recognized as Olga Lubchik. Cotter looked dazed and unsteady on her feet.

Another, expensive-looking car pulled up next to the van, a pre-century Jaguar. The elderly but wealthy-looking man who got out of it helped Fiori guide Stacy inside the Jaguar. Fiori joined both Stacy and the younger man in the car, leaving Lubchik alone with the van as they drove off.

Lubchik then got back into the van and drove away in a different direction.

Ray checked the timestamp. Lubchik had been apprehended later that day in her van, which had been parked on a side-street several miles from Tower Hamlets. Another one who'd claimed to be proxying with someone else, but with no memory of anything that had happened at the Peartree.

Eunice had confirmed three more changes of transport after that. In each case, Stacy Cotter was guided out of one car and into another; each time the driver responsible for delivering her to her new location stayed behind while she—accompanied, always, by Fiori—got into another vehicle, which they either found waiting for them upon their arrival or arrived soon after.

The final change of vehicles was the one that truly beggared belief. Ray watched it three times in a row, feeling his heart sink with each viewing.

This time, the CCTV Eunice had acquired showed the interior of a multi-storey car park. From a street sign just barely visible on the edge of the camera's field of vision, Ray worked out that it was somewhere in Tottenham.

A sleek, modern Renault pulled briefly into view. Ray freeze-framed it and increased the magnification: Stacy Cotter stared out of a rear window, almost looking directly up at the camera lens.

Fast forwarding to just a few minutes later, Ray saw an explosion of activity. Fully a dozen vehicles of all sizes and types swept past the camera lens at speed in all directions, including the Renault.

This time, however, the Renault was empty—probably a hire car driving itself back to its rental park.

The video clip ended. Ray sat back, feeling a chill work its way up his spine. What in God's name…?

The last video clip Eunice had picked out for his attention showed the car park's exit from the perspective of a roof-mounted camera pointed down at the street below. As Ray watched with ever-increasing consternation, the same dozen or so cars came racing out, screeching and swerving and scattering in all directions.

Stacy Cotter could have been in any, or none of the vehicles. She and Fiori could equally well have slid out of some other exit on foot and out of sight of any watching lenses before disappearing into London's crowded streets.

If Ray had been the one doing the fleeing, that would have been his chosen strategy.

He stared numbly at the sheet in his hand, then collapsed into a chair by the kitchen table. He lowered his head onto the wood and tried to think.

Impossible ideas crowded his thoughts. The one thing everybody knew was that you could only proxy with one other person at a time. One person proxying with a whole mob of other people wasn't just impossible, it was preposterous.

And yet, how else to explain the impeccable coordination of so many people scattered all across London, all of whom claimed after the fact to have been proxying with someone else? And how else to explain the testimonies from the people who'd actually been part of the mob that forced its way into the Institute?

How could they all have been proxying with each other, yet remember nothing of what they had done?

Personally tracking down every one of the people who'd helped to spirit Stacy Cotter away wasn't remotely possible given the resources available to him, and even if they had been, doing so would surely have drawn the unwanted attention of the Met.

But there was one name that stuck in his mind: Dominic Fiori, who'd been by Stacy's side throughout her journey right up to the moment she had vanished completely.

That had to mean something. That, and the fact Fiori appeared not to have a past.

Fiori... he remembered Eunice mentioning that Fiori was a

runaway from a mental hospital. Scanning online news items eventually produced a minor article—and some new information:

———

POLICE HAVE ASKED *that anyone with information on the whereabouts of a man named Dominic Fiori contact the Southampton Police. He was last seen at the Abbey Rush Treatment and Addiction Centre, where he was being held for psychiatric observation. The police ask that you report his whereabouts immediately and do not approach him.*

———

THE ONLY PICTURE he had of Fiori, however, was the one Eunice had given him. A search of social media and other sites brought up plenty of people with the same or similar name, but their pictures made it clear none of them were the same man.

Fiori was a ghost.

Ray sucked his teeth for a moment, then looked up the website for the Abbey Rush Treatment Centre, copying a general contact number prominently displayed there. When he called the number, someone picked up within a few seconds.

"Abbey Rush," said a woman's voice. "Can I help you?"

"Hi," said Ray, thinking on his feet. "I'm looking for work as…as a hospital orderly. Is there anyone I can speak to about open positions?"

"You need to call this number," said the woman, reading out a line of digits.

After he hung up, Ray called the new number, which turned out to be for an employment agency. Ray gave the man on the other end of the line the same spiel.

"I'm looking at the Abbey Rush Centre in particular," he added. "My Gran lives near there and she's a bit infirm these days. I'm moving in with her so I can help around the house, so I'm looking for a job close by."

"Do you have any previous experience?"

"Not really. Is that a problem?"

"Not as far as I know. But the job requires details of any police records, previous arrests, that kind of thing." Ray listened for a moment to the sound of the other man's fingers tapping on a keyboard. "There are no vacancies open just now, I'm afraid."

"I'm desperate," Ray pressed. "Do you know if there's anyone there I could speak to, in case something opened up? Even if it's just to give them a copy of my CV."

All I need, he thought, *is some kind of excuse to get in there and look around.*

He heard the sound of more typing. "You should speak to Saul Cavendish," the man on the other end of the line said at last. "He's the HR manager at Abbey Rush. By the way," he added, "there are openings for sewage workers in that area. No qualifications required. If you fancy it, I could—?"

Ray hung up and checked the time. It was still early enough he could get out to Southampton, near where Abbey Rush was located, before the end of office hours.

He grabbed his coat, then hesitated and picked up his duffel bag before heading out the door. There were a few things in there he might need.

CHAPTER
SIXTEEN

RAY

"Excuse me," Ray said to the woman manning the Abbey Rush Treatment Centre's reception desk later that same afternoon, "can you tell me where I can find a Mr Saul Cavendish? I have an appointment with him about a job."

The woman hardly glanced up, but when she spoke he recognized her voice from the phone. "Second floor," she said. "Room twelve."

Ray headed for the stairs, clutching a plain envelope in one hand that contained an entirely fabricated CV.

On the way there, a glass-fronted noticeboard caught his attention, and he stopped to study it. Displayed within were photographs of staff and one or two of their more famous patients.

He recognized at least one musician and an actor vaguely familiar from his youth. That made sense, given everything he'd read about the place made it clear that its primary focus was on addiction treatment.

But what drew Ray's attention the most was a printout of a news website article featuring a picture of a grinning Raphael Markov. A quick scan of the text revealed that

Markov had made a large donation to the Treatment Centre a few years before.

A familiar warmth worked its way up Ray's spine. One that told him he was on the right track.

As he made his way up the stairs, Ray passed an orderly dressed in a white uniform. Tattoos adorned the man's muscular forearms, and his head glistened as if freshly shaved.

"Sorry to bother you," said Ray, stopping him, "but did you hear anything about a runaway patient from here the other day?"

From the up-and-down look the man gave him, Ray judged the staff-member as someone who actively looked forward to wrestling with uncooperative or violent patients. "What about it?"

"I'm just trying to get a feel for the place," said Ray, holding the envelope up so the other man could see it. "I'm interviewing for a job, but a mate said he'd seen something on the news about an escaped patient." He favoured the man with a conspiratorial grin. "I've worked some places where you get the blame every time some doctor or nurse leaves a door open. I'd just rather make sure first that this isn't one of those places."

The shaven-headed man seemed to mull this over for a few seconds, then glanced back the way he'd come as if to make sure nobody might overhear him. "Between you and me," he said, "I wouldn't bother with this place. The guy who runs it is a creep."

"Who?"

"Bloke named Finch." He nodded at the envelope in Ray's hand. "I guess you're looking to replace Lewis."

"Who?"

"Bloke who worked here until a couple of days ago." The staff-member took another glance up the stairs, then back at Ray, his voice dropping further in volume. "Lewis Finnegan.

He got blamed after that patient you heard about went missing. The way things are around here, I wouldn't be at all surprised to find out one of the idiots in charge around here really did leave a door open."

"Sounds mental," Ray murmured.

"Mental isn't the half of it." The shaven-headed man gave him a nod and continued on down the stairs.

Lewis Finnegan. It wasn't much, but it was something.

After counting to ten, Ray once more descended the stairs. A quick glance to the right showed him the reception desk. The woman running it was busy talking on the phone.

Turning left into a corridor, Ray saw an unmanned nurse's station. Moving quickly, Ray stepped over to the station and behind the counter. He rapidly scanned the paperwork either scattered around the station or pinned to noticeboards, soon discovering a printout of a shift schedule.

Snatching the schedule down, he rapidly flipped through the pages. With any luck, they hadn't had the chance to update it since Fiori had—

Ray spotted a name: Lewis Finnegan. Someone had crossed it out from that evening's late shift.

Hearing voices approach, Ray pushed the schedule into a pocket of his coat and hurried back towards the front entrance.

It would take some work, and he would have to call on Eunice once more, but with any luck he'd know everything he needed to know about Lewis Finnegan, up to and including his dental records, before the day was over.

———

LATER THAT SAME day Eunice sent him the information he'd been waiting for. Ray left the roadside café where he'd had an early dinner and found a hire car, giving it Lewis Finnegan's address.

It took him into Southampton, a few miles from the Abbey Rush Treatment Centre, and pulled up outside a crumbling semi-detached with a long-neglected garden out front. A child's slide, orange with rust, sat amidst patchy, muddy grass. A refuse bag full to the brim with recycling material sat half-toppled next to the front door.

After rapping on Finnegan's door several times, Ray finally heard unsteady feet within making their way along a carpeted hall. A shape revealed itself through the frosted glass of the front door.

A moment later the door creaked open, revealing a man with the stature of an ex-wrestler long since gone to seed. A few inches shorter than Ray, Finnegan had close-cropped hair, a wide, jowly face and, judging by his red-rimmed eyes, a bad hangover.

"Lewis Finnegan?" asked Ray. "I'd like to ask you some questions."

Finnegan regarded him with mild hostility. "Sorry," he asked, "but who the fuck are you?"

Ray waited a beat. "I want to talk to you about Dominic Fiori."

One of Finnegan's eyelids twitched in a rapid tic. "You're the police?"

"Not the police, Lewis. A friend."

Judging by Finnegan's expression, he was mulling over whether or not to slam the door shut in Ray's face. "Finch sent you?"

Finch. The man in charge of the Abbey Rush Treatment Centre.

"Yes," Ray lied on a sudden impulse. "Finch sent me."

Finnegan's face paled. "Right," he said, his voice betraying a slight quaver. "I suppose you'd better come in then."

Finnegan turned and made his way back inside, wooden floorboards squeaking gently underfoot.

Ray followed. Finnegan's living-room was small and boxy and dominated by a single large television screen mounted on one wall. An open takeaway pizza box sat on a windowsill. The whole room stank of sweat.

Lewis dropped into an armchair, his stubby fingers gripping its armrests. Ray sat on a sofa facing him.

"Listen," said Finnegan, "I don't know what to tell you. I wasn't lying when I said I didn't remember anything."

"How about you tell me everything right from the start, Lewis?"

"What's going to happen to me?" Finnegan demanded, a whining edge coming into his voice. His hands wrung together in his lap. "I got kids. They don't get nothing if something happens to me and I can't keep up my payments. I swear I ain't talked to the police. I already told Doctor Finch I wouldn't ever do that."

What the hell kind of operation was Finch running at the Abbey Rush? Finnegan was talking like he was afraid Ray was there to threaten or even kill him.

"I'm not here to hurt you, Lewis," Ray reassured him. "Just to find out more of the…details."

Finnegan swallowed, visibly shaken. "You promise?"

"I promise."

"All right." Finnegan let out a shaky breath. "Okay, here it is. I got an email, telling me I had to use a proxy bead or else."

"Or else what?"

"Or else they'd go to the police."

Ray shook his head, baffled. "Who'd go to the police?"

"I don't know," said Finnegan, sounding increasingly agitated. "Whoever wrote the email didn't say who they was, just that they knew Fiori was someone else and that he wasn't supposed to be there. And that he'd been, you know… kidnapped. They said I had to inject a proxy bead at a certain time so they could be in my skin while I was looking after him. Looking after Fiori, I mean."

Ray tried his best to sort out everything Finnegan had just told him. "And you injected the bead like this…person told you to?"

Finnegan stared hollow-eyed at Ray. "It came by courier within an hour or so." He shrugged. "Sent by some darknet agency, I s'pose."

"So when you switched bodies with whomever had injected the other proxy bead, what do you remember?"

Finnegan shook his broad, stupid head. "Nothing."

Nothing?

"Come on, Lewis. You must remember something. Even a room. Or was the other person's skin blindfolded? Maybe the lights were off?"

"No. It wasn't like that, More like…nothing. Like the next thing I knew hours had passed, just like that." He snapped his fingers for emphasis. "It weren't like no proxy I'd ever used before. Like a blink, and half a day had gone by."

What Finnegan described sounded uncannily to Ray like the testimonies from members of the mob that had invaded the Peartree.

"Tell me more about Fiori," Ray pressed, gripped by an increasing certainty he was on the right path. "What did Finch want with him, and what was his real name?"

Finnegan squinted at him. "I don't understand. You saying you don't know?"

Finnegan was clearly an idiot, but that didn't mean he couldn't figure out Ray was something other than he pretended to be.

"I want to hear the details in your words, Lewis," he quickly extemporized.

Finnegan made an exasperated sound, but complied. "I dunno, but Finch was obsessed with him."

"In what way?"

"Finch had Fiori drugged to the eyeballs from the moment they brought him in," Finnegan explained. "He wouldn't let any of the other staff near him and they all wanted to know why he got a whole ward to himself. I had to spend half the bleeding day standing outside the door of his ward not letting anyone in or out. I just about went mental with boredom." His eyebrows knitted together in an expression of profound stupidity. "Then there was all those questions Finch kept asking him."

"What kind of questions?"

"Don't you know already?" Finnegan demanded, standing now. "In fact, how come I've never heard of you? I've never seen you around the Abbey Rush, and Doctor Finch never mentioned you or anything."

Game over, thought Ray, eyeing a heavy-looking paper-weight sitting on a shelf just within arm's reach.

"We're not finished here," said Ray, trying to put some authority into his voice. "Sit back down, Lewis."

"No." Finnegan's thick, calloused hands flexed at his sides. "I must be a fucking idiot for telling you all this in the first place when I don't even know who you is!"

Finnegan took a step closer. Ray lunged upright and grabbed hold of the paperweight, swinging it around in a wide arc that ended against the side of Finnegan's head.

It made a sound like raw steak dropped onto concrete. Finnegan made a noise in the back of his throat and fell back into his armchair, blood seeping from a wound in the side of his head.

Ray leaned over him, brandishing the paperweight in one fist and breathing heavily.

"Try that again," he warned Finnegan, "and I'll smash your fucking skull in. And given your past record, Lewis, I don't think I'll have too much trouble calling it self-defence if the police got involved. Do we understand each other?"

Finnegan nodded wordlessly and pressed a hand against his head. Ray backed towards the door, still clutching the paperweight.

"If I need to know anything else," he promised, "I'll be back."

Finnegan didn't respond beyond a last, hateful glare. Ray let himself out and walked fast, afraid Finnegan might yet come after him. He walked five or six blocks before he even allowed himself to slow to a more normal pace.

Before long, he came across a café that was pleasingly ordinary and filled with the chatter of couples and pensioners. Taking a seat near the window, he ordered coffee, then waited for his heart to stop pounding inside his chest.

He watched the sky slowly turn grey. It started raining, fat drops darkening the granite facade of the surrounding buildings.

Once he felt calmer, Ray took out and unrolled a sheet of smart paper, smoothing its edges until it stiffened into a slate. He drew shapes with his fingers to help him focus, connecting the shapes with lines and small notes. He wrote down the names of everyone he had met connected with the Amy Cotter case, trying to find the commonalities between them all.

One thing was clear: much the same thing that happened to the people who had unwittingly spirited Stacy Cotter away had also happened to Finnegan.

Meanwhile, Dominic Fiori, who had been part of the proxy mob, had been held for treatment at the Abbey Rush Centre by this Doctor Finch. Although, given Lewis's testimony, that was clearly a case of kidnapping.

There was someone out there responsible both for what had happened at Abbey Rush and at the Peartree Institute. Someone who could somehow jump into other people's proxy sessions and take them over, without either party being aware it had happened until after the fact.

In all the years since its anonymous creator had first posted it online, proxy had been analysed, discussed, studied, obsessed over, been the subject of multiple failed attempts at reverse-engineering it and become the subject of countless conspiracy theories. And yet, after all this time, nobody appeared to understand how the hell it actually worked.

Clearly, however, there was someone out there who *did* know how it worked—and had found a way to make it do something that had never been done before.

————

"I HOPE YOU UNDERSTAND," said DCI Edwards early the next morning, stirring a criminal amount of sugar into his tea, "that the last time we spoke I said I wasn't doing you any more favours."

"You still owe me," Ray reminded him, taking a sip of his own tea.

Outside the greasy spoon in which Ray and Edwards sat, people shuffled along the damp streets of Brixton on their way to work. Edwards dropped his spoon down and noisily slurped his tea before putting it back down. "I owed you, past tense. That little debt got paid off years ago."

"And yet," said Ray, "here you are, eating the breakfast I paid for."

Edwards nodded approvingly and shovelled half of a fried egg into his mouth. "They do a nice cuppa here," he said as he chewed. "Just what kind of mess have you got yourself into, anyway? You didn't tell me even after I gave you all that information about the Peartree break-in." He raised an eyebrow. "That kind of thing hurts my feelings. Worse, you were present at the Peartree when the whole thing with that Cotter girl went down, and I still don't have a statement from you. That might suggest to certain parties that you were involved in her kidnap. *Consciously* involved, I should say, unlike those other people."

"Is that what they're saying in the Met?"

"Not yet," said Edwards. "But give it time."

Ray sighed. "How familiar are you with hopscotch?"

Edwards' fingers tensed around his mug. "Familiar enough to state unreservedly that it's even more trouble than the original proxy. If they ever invent a proxy that lasts forever, we're royally fucked."

"Let's just say I spoke to someone who might have an indirect connection to the Peartree mob," said Ray, remembering Lewis's story. "He told me that while he was proxying with an anonymous partner, he blanked out for the entire session. His anonymous partner, meanwhile, could still make full use of his skin." Ray folded his hands together and leaned back. "Sound familiar?"

Edwards put down his mug, regarding him with a baleful expression. "If you know of someone who could provide important circumstantial evidence in relation to what happened at the Peartree, then you have a legal obligation to share that information with the police."

"I said the person in question *might* be connected. I can't corroborate anything he told me. Not yet."

Edwards' expression became less friendly. "Ray," he said, "you and me go way back, but here's some advice. You are not well spoken of among certain of my fellow officers. They haven't forgotten what happened."

Ray felt a muscle spasm in one of his cheeks. "And you know as well as I do that someone set me up. You said as much yourself."

"I did," said Edwards, taking a glance around the café and lowering his voice slightly. "But the fact remains that I shouldn't even be talking to you about an ongoing investigation. You're not the one whose career will suffer if that got found out."

Like mine didn't? "Just tell me," Ray pushed. "Was there any sign prior to what happened at the Peartree to suggest more than two people could proxy with each other if they used hopscotch beads?"

"How the fuck should I know? I—" Edwards sighed and closed his eyes for a moment, then shovelled more food into his mouth before putting his knife and fork back down. "Look, I'll tell you as much as we know about hopscotch, but only because we know fuck all."

Ray nodded. "Go on."

"What we know are just rumours. Unlike the original recipe, hopscotch didn't turn up on some forum. Instead, the story is someone approached two proxy dealers right here in London and gave them the recipe. Gratis."

Ray stared at him, thunderstruck. "Come again?"

"God's truth," said Edwards. "In fact, I think you were originally on that case. Elijah Waits?"

Ray had to think for a moment before the details came back to him. "Yeah, I remember him. He murdered his business partner. Someone left an anonymous tip about the location of their proxy factory and we caught him red-handed. I helped gather evidence on the scene."

"But you didn't hear the story Waits came up with while he was preparing his defence," said Edwards.

Ray frowned. "I knew Waits and his partner printed proxy beads, but not that they were hopscotch proxy."

"Ray, had you even heard of hopscotch at the time?"

"Well...no," Ray admitted. "Although I'd heard rumours there was some new kind of proxy going around."

"You were off the case by then, but Waits based his defence around his claim that someone came to him and his partner offering them the recipe for hopscotch but asking nothing in return. They just wanted it out there."

"Bullshit," Ray said automatically.

"Probably," Edwards agreed. "But you wanted to know, and that's the entirety of it. Waits might as well have said he got it from his fairy fucking godmother." He shrugged. "But say just for argument's sake that Waits was telling the truth, and someone deliberately used him and his partner to get hopscotch out onto the streets. Why would they do that?"

The answer came suddenly and immediately to Ray, and he felt cool sweat prick the small of his back: because they could remotely take random hopscotch users over without their knowledge or permission. Body-jacking, but on an unprecedented scale.

"Was there any proof to back Waits' story up?" Ray asked, working hard to maintain a semblance of calm.

"None. But there is one thing nobody seems to be able to answer: how do a couple of low-end proxy dealers figure out how to make a new version of proxy when supposedly no one knows how the original proxy works?"

"And the Peartree mob?" asked Ray. "Did you find any discrepancies in their stories?"

"Their stories all match," said Edwards. "We don't know how it was done. And no, I haven't heard any stories from anywhere else about hopscotch being used in that way— except from you, just now." He pointed his fork at Ray, whose own food still sat untouched before him. "Just remember, the only reason I'm even telling you this much is because you proved I was somewhere else when that impounded heroin went missing. But quid pro quo, mate. I deserve at least a little something in return, even just for the sake of my curiosity. What is it you're caught up in?"

"As long as it's just between you and me. Agreed?"

Edwards nodded. "Agreed."

"Amy Cotter hired me," said Ray. "Stacy Cotter's mother."

Edwards blinked in surprise. "Raphael Markov's ex? What did she want you to do?"

"Find Stacy Cotter."

Edwards grunted a laugh. "Good luck finding her before we do. Unless you know something we don't?" Once again he pointed his fork at Ray. "Quid pro quo."

"Well," said Ray, "it turns out Stacy Cotter isn't Raphael Markov's biological daughter. Her mother told me as much. She had an affair with one of Raphael's employees and got pregnant from him."

Edwards' face froze mid-swallow. He coughed and cleared his throat. "Fucking hell," he said. "That *is* news."

"Which also makes it odd Markov locked his supposed, but not actual, daughter up in a hospital and refused to let her own mother see her when, in Amy Cotter's own words, he cut both of them off following the divorce. It makes little sense to Amy, and it makes even less sense to me. So I'm trying to find out what I can."

Edwards chuckled and finished his meal. "Look, if you find out anything else, maybe we can work out a deal. Wash off some of the muck that got stuck to you after you got booted out."

Ray shook his head. "Thanks, but it's not enough. I want that muck to have never been there in the first place. I want everyone to know I did nothing wrong. That's what I care about."

Edwards nodded to show his understanding and stood. "Thanks for the grub, mate. I get why you're so involved in this case now. You're still convinced Markov stitched you up." He shook his head. "But going after someone like that is a fool's game. My advice? Put the whole thing behind you. It's been long enough."

But I can't do that, thought Ray, watching Edwards exit the greasy spoon. He had to prove his innocence, because he was rotting on the inside—and had been for a long time, if he was honest with himself.

But now he had another story about hopscotch—another piece of the puzzle. Which left the question, assuming any of it was true, of who had supplied Waits and his business partner with the recipe.

And might that person have some connection with whomever created the *original* proxy?

Whatever the truth, he was certain Dominic Fiori, wherever or whoever he really was, had many, if not all, of the answers. Fiori had been by Stacy's side from the moment they'd carried her out of the hospital: he might even have been the one orchestrating the whole thing.

As he stared down at his rapidly cooling meal, a sudden realization came to Ray with such force that he jerked suddenly upright, sending the mug he'd been drinking from crashing to the floor and attracting a few curious stares.

It was something Amy Cotter had said, back when they had taken a walk through the fields near her house. He cursed himself for not having worked it out at the time, but he'd been so frazzled by the entire incident at the Peartree Institute he'd hardly been able to think clearly.

Ray left the café, his food still untouched and his bracelet flashing once as he exited to show that the cost had been deducted from his account. Stepping towards the kerb, he lifted his bracelet to his mouth and spoke Amy Cotter's name.

It beeped for several seconds before she picked up.

"Mr Thomas?" she said, sounding guarded.

"It's about Paul Green, Miss Cotter."

"Yes?" She replied, an audible tightness to her voice. "What about him?"

"When exactly did he and your ex-husband begin proxying with each other?" he asked. "I don't know if you know the specific date, but if you had even a rough idea I'd hugely appreciate it. Believe me when I say it's important."

A longer pause this time before she replied. "I'd like to know why you require this information."

"Please, Miss Cotter. Just indulge me. I know it's ancient history and these things aren't always easy to remember long after the fact. But—"

"Remembering dates isn't an issue," she replied. "Paul

Green told me he first slept with me in Raphael's body on March 9th, 2030." There was a change in her voice, as if she had just stepped back into her cottage from outside.

"You're certain of that?" Ray could hear his heart thudding loud and hard in his chest. "Not 2032 or 2033?"

"Mr Thomas," she said, a certain steeliness now creeping into her voice, "it was the night of my wedding. I could hardly fail to recall it. Now please," she said, "will you tell me what this is about?"

Ray stared into the middle distance, feeling as if he stood at a fork in a road. Down one path lay years of bitterness and self-recrimination. Down the other—maybe, just maybe—lay something closer to redemption.

He recalled what he knew: proxy had first come to public attention in January 2032.

Yet if Amy had her dates right, and if Green had been telling her the truth, Raphael Markov had been proxying with Green up to two years before the recipe for proxy first appeared online.

Two years before anyone in the world had ever heard of it.

And given that Telop were a world-leader in both artificial intelligence and biotechnology, then the only conclusion was that the Markov's had created proxy.

"Amy," he asked, "do you know who invented proxy?"

"I have no idea," she responded dismissively. "I've done my best to avoid even thinking about such things ever since that dreadful man came to me. Why?"

A mental picture developed in Ray's mind, of a woman who had little interest or knowledge of her then-husband's work. Not that he imagined Raphael had cared to share any such details.

"Is the name Dominic Fiori familiar to you?"

"Not at all," Amy replied. "Should it be?"

"He was in the crowd involved in your daughter's kidnap."

"I'm sorry," she said. "I don't recognize the name."

On a hunch, he asked: "What did you say the name of Stacy's real father was?"

"Isaac Sizemore."

"Do you have a picture of him you can send me, Miss Cotter?"

"I…yes, I think so. It might take me a little while to find it." Curiosity edged her voice. "Can I send it to you once I've found it?"

"Of course."

————

"I'm always delighted to see you, Raymond," said Eunice, as a large, bald-headed man with tattoos in Cyrillic placed a blue china plate on the table between them. Half a dozen fairy cakes were arranged on the plate. "But I do worry how you're going to pay for all this extra information."

"You don't have to worry about that." Another enormous thug arrived, bearing a teapot and two cups on a tray which he placed next to the cakes.

"That'll be all, Stanislav," Eunice said. "You and your brother can go now."

The two men exited the room. "It's not a problem," said Ray. "I can afford it." Which was at least partly true.

"Are you sure?" Something feral touched the edges of Eunice's smile. "You're getting quite deep into your savings, aren't you? And it's not like you can rely on your police pension after that unfortunate mess you got into."

Ray opened his mouth and closed it again. "How did you…?"

"Oh, Ray." Eunice tutted and picked up the teapot, pouring them each a cup. "The less you know," she said sweetly, "the better off you are."

Ray stared at her, feeling unsettled. "Then why ask if I can afford your services if you already know?"

Eunice gave him a maternal pat on his hand where it rested on the table. "I just want you to know that I'm concerned. You were a very good policeman in your day, but you don't have the resources of the Metropolitan behind you now."

"With the greatest of respect," he muttered, "I'm not sure that's any of your business."

Eunice gave him the kind of look usually reserved for small children who refused to eat their vegetables. "I know you think I'm being a nosy old lady, but it's preferable to taking people at their word and then having to send Stanislav and Gunter round to break their legs when they screw me over, don't you agree?"

Ray swallowed, his throat suddenly dry. "So I guess I won't be getting the information?"

"On Doctor Finch? Of course you will, for old times' sake. Check your bracelet."

Ray did. He found Eunice had sent him Finch's entire employment history, most of which had taken place under the aegis of various subsidiaries of Telop industries. And while the Abbey Rush Centre wasn't technically owned by the Markov's, it had, as he knew from the Centre's own notice board, benefited from Raphael Markov's substantial donations.

Finch worked for Markov.

Then Ray noticed something that caused his brow to crease in a frown: Finch was out of the country—*physically* out of the country, and not just using a legal proxy.

He was at a conference in Seattle and wouldn't be back for a couple of days. Which was unfortunate, because Ray very much wanted to ask Lewis Finnegan's former employer some very hard questions.

"I don't suppose you had a chance to look into Sizemore?" Ray asked with a sigh.

As soon as Amy Cotter had sent Ray a picture of Isaac Sizemore, it was obvious that Sizemore and Fiori were one and the same. Even so, if he was going to track either Sizemore or his daughter down, he needed background information on the scientist that only Eunice could provide.

"There's not much about Sizemore I can find out, I'm afraid," said Eunice. "You told me he used to work for Telop, but disappeared?"

Ray nodded. "And assumed a false identity."

"I'm sorry to disappoint you," said Eunice, sounding genuinely aggrieved. "But he's clearly highly skilled at covering his tracks. When he disappeared, he disappeared good."

"So you haven't been able to find out anything about him? Where he's been living all these years, either as Fiori or Sizemore or under some other name, or anything like that?"

"Not a sausage. Really," Eunice added with a touch of regret, "someone that good should be working for me." She lifted the blue china plate and held it out to him. "Fairy cake to go?"

CHAPTER
SEVENTEEN

ELIJAH

Davie, Lorenz's second-in-command, brushed past Elijah in the prison laundry where they were both working and pushed something into his hand.

Elijah palmed it and immediately dropped it into the pocket of his overalls before continuing his work.

Forty-five minutes later he was back in his cell. His cell-mate wasn't around, so he tucked himself into a corner of his bunk and pulled out whatever it was Davie had slipped him. It proved to be a sheet of e-paper folded into a small, uneven rectangle.

Smoothing the crumpled sheet flat, Elijah tugged at its corners until the shape-memory polymer caused it to turn rigid. A few taps and swipes, and he was linked into the Worldnet via a prepaid secure connection.

A lack of time forced him to work fast. Thanks to the business card he'd discovered in an abandoned office, Elijah now knew that the man who'd supplied him and Rob with the hopscotch recipe was a Doctor Zachary Finch, and that he ran some kind of psychiatric hospital on the outskirts of Southampton. There were only a few other people with the same name in mainland Britain, and a quick glance at their online profiles allowed him to quickly determine that none of them were the man Elijah had encountered years before.

That left another question: was Finch himself responsible for creating hopscotch, or was he, as Elijah suspected, a go-between for someone else?

Elijah ran more searches, desperately hoping to dig up something that might directly connect Finch either to hopscotch or the original proxy, but found nothing.

With a grimace, he tore the sheet into thin strips and flushed them down the cell toilet. He saw a faint glitter of inlaid circuitry as the torn strips swirled down the drain.

He'd hoped—really, really hoped—that he wouldn't have to go back to Lorenz and rent yet another skin. But it appeared he had no choice if he wanted to find out more.

At least no one else in the prison had tried to kill him again. But that, he greatly suspected, was only a matter of time.

Davie strolled past his open cell, walking deliberately slowly, and Elijah stepped up close to him.

"I need to speak to Lorenz again," he said.

Davie responded with a grunt of assent. "What about?"

"I need to get outside again," said Elijah in a half-whisper. "For longer this time."

Davie snorted a laugh as if this were the funniest thing he had ever heard and kept on walking.

CHAPTER EIGHTEEN

RAY

Ray could still remember the days when medical visas weren't required to travel and wanting to go on holiday was sufficient reason to turn up at an airport. No surprise, then, that after a third global pandemic, proxy had found some measure of respectability within the international business community, even if its legal status remained somewhat murky.

It had occurred to Ray it would be worth visiting Stacy Cotter's flat in Paris to see what clues or information he might find there, and that meant proxying with someone who was actually in Paris. Travelling there in person would be beyond his financial means.

Using one of the new, legal proxy clinics was, however, out of the question: not just because of the bureaucracy involved, but because he'd have to state the exact purpose of his trip and take out insurance guaranteeing whomever he proxied with didn't come to harm and that he wouldn't do anything illegal.

Like, say, breaking into someone's flat as part of a private investigation being carried out in an entirely different country.

And since such legal proxies were also often chaperoned because of precisely such concerns, that left Ray with little choice but to pursue less legal avenues.

After making some calls, Ray left his newly rented flat and hailed a passing taxi, Half an hour later it deposited him outside a row of derelict shops that looked like they'd been shuttered for decades—and in most cases, probably had.

One, however, had a new-looking security camera mounted above its shuttered door. Ray banged on the shutter and waved up at the camera.

Another five minutes passed before the shutter rolled up and a craggy-faced man in his late fifties stepped out of the doorway, wearing a greasy-looking car coat over a T-shirt and jeans. The faint lines of spidery tattoos showed on his stubbled scalp. He glanced up and down the street before so much as looking at Ray.

"Hello Archie," said Ray.

Archie gave him a long, piercing look. "Just to be clear," said Archie, "if this is some kind of bust you won't find anything here. What did you call me for?"

Ray glanced up and down the street. "Can I at least come inside, or do you want to talk business out here?"

"In," Archie commanded, stepping aside, and Ray entered the darkened shop.

Archie rolled the shutter back down. For a moment they were in darkness, then a portable lamp sitting on a dusty counter came to life, filling the small space with a pale yellow light. Empty shelves adorned the walls, while rat droppings lay scattered across the floor.

"All right," said Archie, turning to face him, "what is it?"

"Kind of a special request," said Ray. "Like I said when I called. I want to proxy to Paris."

"In case you haven't heard," said Archie, "that's pretty much legal these days."

"What I want to do there isn't," said Ray. "Plus, I don't have the time for all the paperwork involved."

Archie put up both hands. "Don't tell me anything more," he said. "I'm strictly supply and demand." He peered at Ray. "You still working for Tip?"

"This is something of my own I'm working on."

"I want you to understand," said Archie, "that if I were to help you in any way—and I'm not saying yet that I will, or that we even had this conversation—that you and Tip are strictly hands-off where me and my operation are concerned."

On the walk there, Ray had found himself reflecting on the fact that he was about to make a dodgy deal with a proxy dealer, after having once been framed for doing dodgy deals with proxy dealers. He was now, in fact, committing the very crime that had long ago lost him his job.

With bitter irony, he realized he didn't care as much as he thought he would.

"I can't make any promises," said Ray, "since the Met does what the Met does. I don't have any control over their investigations." He thought for a moment. "Tell you what. I hear anything related to you, I'll let you know."

Archie regarded him in silence for long seconds. "I'm charging you extra," he said at last, then named a price high enough that it felt like a physical blow to Ray's belly.

"Fucking hell, Archie. Maybe you'd like to drain some of my blood while you're at it? See if you can get a price for it on the open market?"

Archie raised his eyebrows. "Still a lot cheaper than going there in person. You buying or not?"

Ray gritted his teeth and tapped at his bracelet. "That's half upfront," he said. "Now here's what I want."

———

IT TOOK the rest of the day for Archie to get everything arranged according to Ray's specifications, and while he waited back at his flat, he looked into Paul Green, Raphael Markov's former driver. The man who, according to Stacy's mother, had been secretly proxying with Raphael back when no one had ever heard of either proxy or hopscotch.

Paul Green wasn't exactly an uncommon name, but he'd been Raphael Markov's driver, and that narrowed things down.

Ray soon tracked down two Paul Greens who fit the bill. One had retired home to Jamaica, while the other, a grinning, red-faced man who looked like someone who had found his niche in life, now owned a wine bar in Hackney.

Both were on social media. Ray took screen captures of their photographs and forwarded them to Amy Cotter, who responded within minutes: Paul Green was the owner of the wine bar. Probably, thought Ray, it was more fun and a lot more profitable than driving rich sociopaths around.

Evening arrived by the time Archie sent him a message to let him know everything was set up.

Ray headed back to the disused shop. Archie himself was nowhere to be seen. Instead, he found a kid with a furtive expression hanging around outside the shop, a bicycle leaning against the shutter next to him.

"Archie sent you?" Ray asked the kid.

The kid glanced around, then slapped a small plastic baggie into one of Ray's hands before getting back on his bicycle and cycling away at speed. Ray opened the bag and found it contained a single proxy bead and a disposable applicator.

I really hope this is worth it, he thought, staring after the kid, who had vanished into the evening gloom.

Back home, Ray dropped the bag and its contents onto the kitchen table, then sat and stared at it for several minutes before putting in another call.

"You got it?" Archie's voice sounded thick and breathy down the line.

"Any trouble setting everything up for tonight?"

Archie chuckled under his breath. "A bit short notice and all, but doable in the end. You ever, uh, proxy with a woman?"

Ray stared down at his bracelet. "Why do you ask?"

"Because finding a willing anonymous proxy partner at such short notice isn't exactly easy if you aren't prepared to tell them exactly what their skin's going to be used for. So unless you want to wait a while longer, by which I mean several more days, the best I can do for you is this French bird I found."

Ray groaned inwardly. He wasn't a prude, but it wasn't something he had, in fact, done before. "Several days?"

"At least." Archie coughed and cleared his throat. "Same price, mind. No discount."

"Fine. She'll do." Ray massaged his forehead with the fingers of one hand. He could feel a headache coming on.

"What time do you want it to start?"

"If she's willing, now is as good a time as any."

"I'll let her know," said Archie. "Wait for the go-ahead. It won't be long."

He hung up and Ray settled back, trying to make himself comfortable.

———

THIRTEEN MINUTES LATER, Ray received an encrypted message informing him that his anonymous proxy partner was ready. Fitting the proxy bead into its applicator, he leaned forward with one elbow on the kitchen table and used his other hand to place the applicator's nozzle against the back of his neck over the spine before pulling the trigger.

A sharp, burning sensation quickly gave way to numbness. Then came a familiar rush of vertigo as the proxy bead connected with its entangled twin in the neck of an anonymous French woman in Paris.

Ray dropped the applicator, folded his arms on the table and rested his forehead on top of them, eyes closed.

The vertigo faded. The air felt suddenly cooler against Ray's skin, and tasted subtly different when next he drew a breath. He took a moment to catalogue the sensations flooding into the senses of his borrowed skin.

He opened his eyes.

Rather than sitting at a table, he now found himself in a reclined position on a worn couch and staring up at a peach-coloured ceiling.

He sat up slowly, giving himself time to acclimate to his new and temporary skin. It felt different from what he was used to—hardly surprising, under the circumstances. He felt lighter, somehow, and there were other, harder to define sensations that were deeply unfamiliar to him.

Rather than think about them, he did his best to put them out of his mind.

A crumpled and used proxy applicator lay on a coffee table next to the couch. Babbling French voices came from a tablet propped on a mantelpiece which, he saw, was running a live news program.

Moving carefully, Ray stood, observing as he did so that his rented skin wore loose jeans and a dark, patterned blouse. He caught sight of his skin's breasts beneath the blouse, and a thousand half-remembered comedy sketches from the early days of proxy immediately came to mind.

"Just get it over with, Ray," he muttered under his breath.

The words came out low and throaty and irritatingly seductive.

Following procedure, Ray carried out a mirror check in his skin's tiny bathroom. His proxy was in her mid to late thirties and had dark pouches beneath eyes that looked timeworn.

He didn't fail to notice the yellow bruises that covered one arm and the fading track marks on the other.

It didn't take much to guess why his proxy needed money so badly she'd be willing to proxy with a complete stranger at such short notice.

He found an envelope taped to one corner of the mirror above the sink. Opening it, he found it contained a set of house keys, a car-hire pass with a photograph of his proxy and the name Audrey Bernard, along with an off-the-shelf burner bracelet.

He pocketed the first two and slipped the bracelet onto his proxy's wrist. Tapping on its screen showed that it had been preloaded with sufficient Euros to get him around Paris for at least the next couple of hours.

Less than a minute later, Ray left the flat and went looking for a taxi.

It felt more than a little odd to walk in his borrowed skin. It didn't move in a way that felt at all right. Before long he saw an empty- and battered-looking Renault driving past and raised his arm. His bracelet flashed, and the car pulled up beside him, its door automatically sliding open.

Before long, bleak concrete tenements and high-rises gave way to elegant Parisian neighbourhoods that seemed to come from a different world from his own. At one point he thought he glimpsed the Eiffel tower far off in the distance.

The Renault let him out next to a four-storey tenement of wrought-iron balconies and wood-shuttered windows. A row of buzzers next to an entrance door included one marked with the name COTTER, S.

Ray pressed the buzzer. He didn't expect a response, but better safe than sorry. He waited a minute, then gave the building's door an experimental tug. Locked.

Next he tried pressing another buzzer selected at random. A brusque voice rattled at him in rapid-fire French.

"Excuse me," he said into the buzzer, trying his best to sound helpless, "I've rented a flat here and I can't seem to—"

Ray heard the click of a receiver being hung up.

He tried three other buzzers. No response from any of them.

The fourth proved to be the charm, however. He didn't even get the chance to open his mouth before they buzzed him in. Probably, he thought, stepping into a cold and darkened vestibule, someone was expecting a delivery.

A voice from above echoed down the steep stone steps and he guessed he'd been right. He stayed where he was until he heard a door close again.

He found Stacy's flat on the third floor. To his surprise, when he pushed at it, he found her door to be unlocked.

Taking a deep breath, he eased the door open as quietly as he could. Even though he couldn't himself come to harm, he didn't want his proxy to suffer injury of any kind.

He stood and listened, but heard nothing. Some inner sense born of experience told him the flat was empty. On stepping inside, he found someone had thoroughly trashed Stacy's flat. No surprises there.

In the kitchen, someone had pulled all the drawers out and tossed their contents on the floor. Rotting orange peel and other mouldering rubbish lay heaped next to an upturned bin. It was much the same story in the living-room and the single bedroom; the whole place had been turned over.

Returning to the kitchen, Ray's bracelet beeped to let him know the first hour of his proxy session was already up.

He grimaced and got back to searching through the wreckage. Most likely anything genuinely useful—anything that might serve as a clue to how or why Stacy's true father, Isaac Sizemore, had snatched her out from under Raphael's nose—was long gone.

After he'd finished with the kitchen, Ray next worked his way through the bathroom and then the bedroom.

Pillows as well as the mattress had been slashed open. Clothes had been pulled out of wardrobes and drawers and lay scattered all around. He searched through everything, peering inside drawers and under the bed, looking for any place useful information might have been hidden from immediate view.

It felt like hardly any time had passed at all before his bracelet beeped again to show he'd already used up two hours of his session.

Finally, he turned his attention to the living-room.

The couch had also been slashed open, while paperback books lay scattered across a wool rug. A television had been pulled down from one wall, presumably in the hope of finding something hidden behind it.

More searching through the wreckage turned up precisely nothing. Meanwhile, his proxy session slowly ticked down to its last minutes.

At last, Ray collapsed onto the ruined couch and stared around, trying hard to think if he'd missed anything.

At random, he picked up a few of the books dumped on the carpet and glanced through them. A couple of biographies, a smattering of thrillers and, more interestingly, a couple of non-fiction works about proxy—and one about Telop Industries specifically.

Then he noticed a scrap of torn paper poking out from between the pages of a book lying on the carpet.

Picking the book up, he flipped it around to see the cover: *The New Slave Trade*, by Martin Wilber. The back cover blurb described it as a journalistic exposé of the proxy trade in Asia. A photograph of the author showed a silver-haired man in his late fifties or early sixties.

The scrap tucked between the pages of the book had a London phone number scrawled on it. It looked like it had been torn from a notepad.

Ray accessed his proxies' bracelet and tried calling the number. Someone picked up almost immediately.

"Hello?" said a man with an English accent, sounding wary.

"Who is this?" asked Ray, hearing his proxy's voice form the words with its distinctive Gallic overtones.

A silence stretched out for some moments before a reply came. "Who gave you this number?" the voice asked, somewhat abruptly.

"Stacy," said Ray, thinking fast. The man on the other end of the line would probably assume he was speaking to one of Stacy's girlfriends. "I'm a friend of hers here in Paris," he continued. "I came around to her flat and I found it wrecked." He tried to inject a note of panic into the words. "I can't find her anywhere. She left your number, and I thought you might be able to tell me where she is? Or if she's in trouble of some kind?"

This time, the silence stretched out for so long Ray started to suspect the man listening on the other end of the line had hung up.

"My name's Martin Wilber," the other man said at last, and Ray let out a long, slow breath. He was speaking to the author of the book he had found. "I'm a friend of Stacy's too, Miss...?"

"Bernard," Ray blurted, without really thinking about it. "Audrey Bernard."

Shit. Using his proxy's real name was stupid, but he hadn't had time to think of anything else.

"Can you tell me what happened?" Ray next asked.

Ray could practically feel the suspicion radiating from Wilber. "I'm afraid," the journalist explained, "I've been trying to learn her whereabouts myself. I suppose you've seen the news about her?"

"I haven't," Ray lied in the husky tones of a Parisian drug addict. "Why? Has something happened to her?"

"If you don't mind, Miss Bernard," Wilber responded, "I would like to call you back shortly. Would that be acceptable?"

Ray ended the call. He had a feeling Wilber knew little more than he himself had been able to find out. If they'd talked any longer, they'd have just ended up going in circles, trying to dig information out of each other that they either didn't have, or were unwilling to give up.

But at least, he now knew something he hadn't before: Stacy Cotter had been in touch with an investigative journalist, one with a specific interest in the illegal proxy trade, just days before her disappearance.

Was it possible Raphael or someone in Telop had taken steps to prevent Stacy talking to Wilber? Was that why she'd been locked away from her own mother in a hospital by a man the world thought was her father, but wasn't?

Ray stood up from the couch, filled with a sudden determination. If he couldn't talk to Finch just yet, being abroad as he was, he could at least talk to Paul Green in the meantime. And if he didn't get anything useful from Green, then maybe Wilber would be his next port of call.

But first, he had to wait for his proxy session to end. And that might take some time yet.

He left Stacy's flat and hadn't walked much more than a few blocks before he felt an onrushing wave of dizziness. His proxy session was ending sooner than he had expected.

Moving quickly, he found a public bench and sat on it, hands on knees and with his eyes closed. The dizziness grew and his senses span, and when next he opened his eyes he was somewhere else.

But not, as he had expected, in the kitchen of his new flat.

Instead, he found himself sitting at a table in a quiet restaurant. Disoriented, he used his bracelet to confirm his location: he was half a mile from his new home.

He looked down, seeing the remains of a meal which,

when the bill arrived, turned out to have been one of the most expensive items on the menu.

Well, at least it's inside me and not her, Ray thought belatedly, and ordered himself a coffee.

In truth, he could hardly blame Bernard, given she had absolutely no idea what he'd been up to with her own body. He paid his bill without wincing too much and headed for Hackney to find Paul Green.

CHAPTER
NINETEEN

RAY

By the time Ray arrived at Paul Green's wine bar it was early evening, and judging by the crowds spilling out of its doors and around the tables and chairs set out on the pavement, it was doing excellent business. So busy and crowded, in fact, that it felt like travelling back to an earlier age when several hundred million people hadn't yet died in a series of increasingly brutal global pandemics.

Ray squeezed in through the entrance and looked around. The bar had Victorian styling complete with overstuffed chairs, brass fittings and large, ornate-looking mirrors mounted behind the bar. A waiter wearing a white apron and sporting a waxed moustache like something out of an old silent movie squeezed past him, carrying a tray of empty glasses.

Ray caught the waiter's shoulder. "Excuse me," he shouted over the din, "I'm looking for your boss, Paul Green."

The waiter frowned. "What for?"

"It's a private matter." Ray nodded towards the bar. "Is he here?"

The waiter gave him a look as if he had said something offensive. "He is, but we're a little busy, mate. Try some other time."

The waiter started to move off, but Ray stopped him again. "I need to speak to him now," he said insistently. "Tell him I'm here on Amy Cotter's behalf. Believe me, he'll want to see me when you tell him that name."

The waiter did a bad job of hiding his irritation. "Just wait a minute then," he said, raising a very un-Victorian data bracelet to his lips as he disappeared back into the mob.

A few minutes passed before the waiter returned for him. "The office entrance is around the other side of the building," he told Ray. "Go back outside, around the corner and keep going until you get to number 429. Press the buzzer and he'll let you up."

———

THE DOOR CLICKED open within a second of Ray pressing the buzzer at number 249. He climbed two flights of stairs before arriving at a door marked GREEN MANAGEMENT AND EVENTS.

Green pulled it open before Ray could knock. Green was in his mid-forties, his hair cropped close to the skull to compensate for a large bald patch. He regarded Ray with evident fear, his mouth twisted into a threatening scowl.

"Who the hell are you?" Green demanded. "And why the hell should I talk to you about anything?"

"My name is Ray Thomas. I'm a private investigator working for Miss Cotter, and she's given me a great deal of information about your relationship with Raphael Markov. So how about you start by telling me why you blackmailed him?"

Green's ruddy complexion paled to a deathly white. For the second time in recent days, Ray watched someone struggle to decide whether or not to slam a door shut in his face.

Green swallowed and pulled the door wider open. "You'd better come in," he said, his voice trembling audibly.

Ray stepped inside, seeing a small and somewhat nondescript office with a single desk, computer and a filing cabinet. Green closed the door and stood with his back pressed up against it as Ray took in his surroundings.

"All right," said Green, "what exactly do you want from me?"

Ray leaned back against the edge of the desk and looked over at Green with his arms folded. He took his time, enjoying having the advantage. So far, Green hadn't even tried to deny anything.

"I'm guessing you set up this business of yours using the money you got from blackmailing Markov," Ray said with an unfriendly grin. "And there was me thinking crime doesn't pay."

"There's nothing you nor anyone else can prove," Green spat back, his eyes wide enough Ray could see the whites all around.

"Amy told me all about how you proxied with Raphael Markov," Ray continued. "And it's a matter of public record you worked as a driver for him and his family. That's more than enough to open a private prosecution against you on blackmail and intimidation charges."

A muscle twitched spasmodically in Green's right cheek. "How much do you want?"

Definitely not a man to beat around the bush, thought Ray.

"I'm not looking for money," he said.

Green blinked rapidly, his pale skin glistening with sweat. "You're from Raphael then," he muttered.

"What? No," said Ray. "That's not what I said. I—"

"Did he send you here to kill me?" Green demanded abruptly, pressing his back up against the door behind him as if he could squeeze between its atoms and out of Ray's reach.

"I'm not a fucking hitman," Ray almost shouted. "And I have no interest in extorting money from you. All I want from you is information. Understand?"

Green stared at him in abject confusion. "Information? What information?"

Ray sighed and stood back up from the desk. "To be clear, Mr Green, it's not you I'm interested in. It's Raphael Markov. I want to confirm that he came to you with an offer to proxy with him in order to have sex with his wife without her knowledge." He gave Green a pointed look. "I don't think I need to remind you that's rape, on top of everything else."

"Then…" Green shook his head. "Then you're not here for me?"

"No," Ray admitted, "I'm not." At least, not in the sense Green meant. And not that he wouldn't love to see the sweaty little shit go down for a good long stretch.

Green licked his lips. "And if I ask you to leave?"

"I'll leave soon enough if you answer my questions," said Ray. "How did Raphael get hold of the proxy beads?"

Green again looked confused. "What?"

"The proxy beads," Ray repeated patiently. "The ones you and he used to swap skins with each other."

"What's that got to do with anything?"

"Nobody in the world had heard of proxy before 2032. Except according to Amy, you were proxying with Raphael up to two years before then. How could Raphael have got hold of proxy beads when, as far as anyone at the time knew, no such thing was even possible?"

Green was silent for several seconds. "Who else have you talked to about this?"

Ray briefly considered his response. "Why does it matter?"

Green let out a shaky breath. "I'll tell you the same thing I told Raphael Markov. I wrote down everything that happened between me and him, on paper, along with dates, times, and places, and made duplicate copies. I put it all in sealed envelopes and gave each to a different law firm with strict instructions to mail them to a dozen news organisations if anything…" he swallowed. "If anything were to happen to me."

Green hesitated for a moment before continuing. "And Raphael told me to my face if I ever talked about this to anyone, he'd have me killed and to hell with the consequences."

That, at least in part, explained the man's evident terror. "Nobody but you knows I'm here," Ray reassured him.

"You can't be sure of that."

"I can. Now, how about you answer my question? Or, instead, I can just let the police ask you the same questions."

Green looked like he was about to argue, then visibly deflated as if someone had stuck a pin in him and air had come rushing out.

Stumbling past Ray, he collapsed into a swivel chair behind his desk. Reaching into a drawer, he lifted out a bottle of Glenmorangie and a small glass, pouring himself a shot without offering any to Ray.

"Before I say anything," said Green, "swear to me you were never here."

"I was never here," Ray repeated, feeling faintly ridiculous. He turned to face Green across the desk. "But I'm not leaving until you tell me everything you know."

"The reason Raphael had proxy beads is that he invented them," said Green. "Or someone working for him did, anyway."

Ray stared at him. "You're certain about this? Telop Industries were definitely behind proxy?"

Green nodded. "Raphael told me himself it was something

they'd been developing in secret. After that, it got out some-how. I don't know how."

At last, thought Ray. *It's all coming together*. "When did Raphael first suggest you proxy with him?"

"A few days before he got married," Green replied, draining the rest of his whiskey and immediately pouring himself another. "Honestly, I thought he was out of his mind when he told me what it was. It sounded like science fiction." He drained the second glass as well and chuckled to himself. "I started to change my mind when he told me how much he'd pay me."

"But why wait until years later to blackmail Raphael?" Ray asked. "Why not do it as soon as he stopped proxying with you, or even after he fired you?"

"Fired me?" Green laughed bitterly. "He didn't fire me—I quit. Although to be honest, I'd expected him to fire me one way or the other eventually. I was sick of him. And…well, there were other reasons."

Ray tried not to show his eagerness. "Go on."

"I don't know what Raphael had got himself into, but the last time I ever proxied with him and found myself back in my own body, I was lying in filth in a deserted alley. I'd had the shit beaten out of me. I think someone must have found me and called an ambulance because the next thing I knew I was in a hospital." He shook his head, his expression making it clear he was reliving one of the worst experiences of his life. "I had lost a lot of blood. The doctors told me I had perma-nent damage to my kidneys, and ever since I've had memory issues. I couldn't tell them the truth about what had happened because they'd have thought I was crazy." He shrugged. "Like you said, nobody knew about proxy back then."

Green seemed calmer now that he'd talked to someone about it. Or perhaps the whiskey had just worked its magic.

"So you had no idea what Markov was doing with your own body while you and he were proxying?" Ray asked.

Green laughed sourly. "I can make some guesses." He held up an arm. "They told me in the hospital I'd had a heroin overdose. In fact, that was the least of what he'd been up to in my skin. I didn't believe them until they showed me the results of a toxicology report."

Christ. "He was taking drugs the whole time he was in your skin?"

"Again," said Green with a visible shudder, "that was the least of it. I confronted him about it, but what I didn't under-stand, or hadn't quite realized, was that while I was in control of *his* body, he could do what the hell he wanted while he was in mine. Although I figured it out pretty quickly while I was in that hospital bed." He shuddered. "I told Raphael I'd had enough."

"Did he say why he'd done it?"

"He tried to justify his actions by saying everything he had done with my body was an experiment to test the limita-tions of the proxy link." He made a face full of disgust and self-loathing. "He said he wanted to see if taking drugs while he was in my body could affect him in his own."

Ray shook his head. "That doesn't work. The drugs only affect the brain of the person that takes them, not the brain of whoever's proxying with them."

"Yes, of course, but nobody knew that at the time. Lucky me, I got to be the guinea pig so he could be the first to prove it." Green's expression became savage. "See, what I realized then is that if you work for Raphael, he thinks he owns you, body and soul." He gripped the now-empty whiskey glass as if trying to shatter it.

"Is that when he fired you?"

"No, I already told you I quit. And that was the end of it, at least until I discovered everything else he'd been doing while he'd been proxying with me." He stared hard at Ray. "I couldn't get close enough to him to kill him, so I blackmailed him instead, and took him for a lot more than he'd paid me in the first place."

"Hold on," said Ray. "What do you mean, 'everything else he'd been doing'?"

"After I quit, I drove other people, at least while there was still money in it. Mostly old and rich people who didn't trust AI or self-driving vehicles. One time, I had a client who insisted he knew me even though I'd never set eyes on him before." He looked Ray in the eye. "He kept calling me Raphael."

Green refilled his glass, his expression miserable. "We got talking and I soon figured out he'd been in a sexual relationship with Raphael the whole time he'd been proxying in my body." He gave Ray a tight smile. "Karmic justice after what I did to Amy, right? And it's true. But I was angry. Very, very angry."

Green sat back, looking as breathless as if he'd run a marathon. Ray could find no sympathy for him. "Did you ever meet a man named Isaac Sizemore?"

Green shook his head. "Not that I recall."

"You're sure?"

"Like I said, I have memory issues. But I don't think so, no."

There wasn't anything more to be gained, Ray could see. He stepped towards the door, then paused as something new occurred to him. "Raphael didn't respond immediately to your blackmail attempt, did he? That's why you told Amy and David Markov what he'd been up to."

Green shrugged. "He said I'd be dragging my own name through the mud as well as his if I went through with my threat. I was already angry, but that just made it worse. I didn't hesitate to hurt him any way I could."

"And after you told David and Amy everything, that's when he became cooperative?"

"Sure. Suddenly he was willing to pay any amount of money to keep it out of the press. And I kept my word, let's be clear on that. This is the first I've spoken of it since." Green let out a shuddering sigh. "Later on I heard from a friend who still worked in Telop's offices that they had overheard David Markov in a furious argument with Raphael at the time, demanding he divorce Amy and disown Stacy."

Ray started. "When was this?"

"Right after I'd snitched to Raphael's father," Green replied with evident satisfaction. "In fairness, no way was Raphael that girl's dad."

"How can you be certain?"

"It wasn't like I was having sex with Amy in Raphael's body every night," Green explained. "It was occasionally at best, even right after they got married."

"Amy told me Raphael would hit her. But that was you, wasn't it?"

Green opened and closed his mouth. "I've got no comment on that."

Ray saw the way guilt flushed the other man's face red, and fought down a sudden desire to hit Green as hard as he could.

"Anyway," Green continued, "there were long stretches where I never set eyes on either of them. Usually, that was because Raphael was abroad on business. And he could be away for weeks at a time, sometimes longer."

Ray intuited where the other man was going. "You're saying Stacy was conceived during one of those absences?"

Green nodded sharply. "I was gone by the time they announced the pregnancy, but I did the sums. I guarantee she's not Markov's daughter."

Ray remembered what Amy had told him: that Raphael, on learning she was pregnant with Isaac Sizemore's child, had been perfectly content to present Stacy as his biological daughter purely to satisfy his own father's desire for an heir.

"That you told David Markov you were proxying with his son is one thing," said Ray. "But figuring out Stacy wasn't his granddaughter is another. How'd he find out?"

"Because I told him as much," said Green, regarded Ray with a curled lip. "Maybe my memory's getting better because I remember you now. You got kicked out of the force, didn't you? Something to do with Amy's little girl."

Ray didn't reply.

"Thought so," Green continued with a baleful expression. "Then you know just as much as me what happens to people who get involved with that family. Bad things happen."

———

ONCE RAY HAD LEFT Green's office he walked a short distance, leaned against a wall and took several long, deep breaths.

It was as good as certain: proxy had originated in some Telop research lab. And Raphael had found a way to use it to his own immediate advantage.

Was that a secret worth killing for? Perhaps—but why, then, put Stacy in a hospital in order to save her life?

Maybe that was it, thought Ray, staring into the distance. Raphael tried to have Stacy killed, but something went wrong, and she survived—forcing the man the world believed to be her father to cover his own tracks by immediately, and very publicly, moving her into a Telop-owned hospital where he could control access to her.

In the meantime, Ray knew he still had to locate Finch and find out why he'd been holding Isaac Sizemore against his will. And what had happened to him after he'd disappeared from Amy Cotter's life.

Then, just maybe, he could find a way to understand just what had been going on over the last several days—and who had been responsible for the Peartree mob, if not Sizemore himself.

Everything came back to Isaac Sizemore, the young woman Ray now knew to be Sizemore's daughter, and whatever they had intended to share with the journalist Martin Wilber.

And if he could find a way to get some leverage where Finch was concerned, then perhaps he'd finally have a chance to take Raphael Markov down and clear his name...all at the same time.

CHAPTER
TWENTY

ELIJAH

Lorenz came through with his side of the deal, but it cost Elijah dearly.

"Bit ironic, isn't it?" Davey said to him the morning after Elijah had made his request for more proxy. They sat side-by-side in the prison canteen. "All that money you made dealing proxy, and now you're in the nick, spending every penny you made just to get hold of a couple of beads."

Elijah stared down at his fried egg and chips and resisted the urge to grab Davie by the back of his neck and shove him face-first into his breakfast. "You got them or not?"

"Not quite yet," Davey said under his breath. "We'll have to take a few precautions."

Elijah darted him a sideways look. "What precautions?"

"Last time," said Davey, pushing a chip into his mouth, "you were only outside these walls for a couple of hours, and in the middle of the night. But since you've asked for hopscotch this time, then obviously you're going to be outside the Scrubs for days."

"You're not telling me anything I don't already know."

"The bloke you'll be proxying with," Davey continued

regardless, "isn't exactly familiar with prison life, making it harder for him to fool anyone into thinking he's really you. Plus, the screws are always on the lookout for inexperienced people like him proxying with cons. They make one slip-up, and the screws'll be onto you." He gestured with his fork. "So we need to arrange for you to get put into solitary for at least the next several days, preferably a week. That way, nobody'll be paying you nearly as much attention."

"Who is he?" Elijah demanded, keeping his voice low. "This skin Lorenz found for me. Are you telling me it's some fucking amateur?"

"Don't mouth off," Davey warned, glancing furtively around. "You said you wanted it as soon as possible. That means you take what you get."

Elijah took a long, deep breath. Nothing was ever as simple as it should be. "Fine. Solitary it is. How are you going to arrange it?"

"We're not," Davey replied with a grin. "You are." He nodded towards a man sitting at another table diametrically opposite their own. "You see Mackay over there?"

Mackay, one of Lorenz's other thugs and the owner of a face like a skinned bull, looked up from his own breakfast long enough to give them both a wary nod.

"You and him are going to have a fight," Davey explained while struggling to suppress a grin. "And I mean a real fight, so it looks proper convincing."

Elijah stared at the man beside him. "You fucker," he growled. "You're loving this, aren't you?"

"Better than Christmas," Davey replied. "This isn't the first time anyone's pulled a stunt like this, of course, which is why it has to look as real as possible, understand? Now, Mackay's got a reputation for serious violence, and I mean really, extraordinarily vicious—"

"I get the idea," Elijah muttered tersely.

"The point is, it has to be you who starts it, so you're the one who ends up in solitary. You'd better get a few good licks in at the beginning, because after that Mackay's going to beat you through the fucking floor."

"Fight over what, exactly?"

Davey nudged Elijah's tray with his elbow. "Does it matter? Just walk over there and dump your leftovers in his lap. Once you're in solitary, we'll get your bead to you and you can proxy in privacy."

"Fuck you," said Elijah, standing with his tray.

Davey chuckled to himself, then kept his eyes fixed on his own breakfast as Elijah stepped over to Mackay and upended his tray into the other man's lap.

The effect was immediate. Mackay leaped up with a roar, one huge fist grabbing Elijah by the neck.

Elijah slammed his tray edge-first into Mackay's face. That gave Elijah the opportunity to get a good few licks in before the other man slammed him onto the floor and began kicking him repeatedly in the groin. The look on Mackay's face suggested he was having the time of his life.

Then the screws piled on top of Mackay, and Mackay toppled on top of Elijah, nearly crushing him.

Only then did it occur to Elijah, as he struggled to breathe, to wonder whether Davey had in fact said anything at all to Mackay about their plans.

However things had been, after that things went exactly as Davey said they would. Elijah refused to explain why he'd attacked another prisoner and within the hour he found himself in solitary confinement. He'd eat and sleep alone for at least the next week, and probably a good deal longer.

———

ELIJAH'S PROXY bead and an applicator arrived with his evening meal, pushed through a slot. Clearly, Lorenz had at least one of the screws on his payroll.

Staring down at the tiny pale bead, and a slip of paper specifying at what time he should use it, Elijah couldn't help but think about just how much it had cost him to acquire. He wondered what his proxy partner would think when they found themselves inside Elijah's bruised and battered skin.

At least by the time Elijah found himself back in his own skin, his bruises might have had time to heal.

Before the allotted time arrived he took his time eating his meal, then fitted the bead into its applicator and waited until the digital clock someone had left on the windowsill hit seven.

As soon as he'd fired the bead beneath his skin, he tore the applicator into strips and flushed them, then sat on the edge of the single fold-down cot, waiting with closed eyes.

The next time he opened them he found himself sitting on a park bench, the early evening air cool against his brow.

Looking down, he saw that his skin's hands were even blacker than his own—almost blue-black. Upon standing, it also became immediately clear that his proxy partner was several inches shorter than he was. The skin wore chinos, a tweed jacket and expensive-looking leather shoes.

The world looked out of focus, so Elijah dug around in various pockets until he found a case containing a pair of black-rimmed spectacles. As soon as he put them on, the world regained its familiar clarity.

He quickly determined that his skin had neither a chip-phone nor a data bracelet. Searching through other pockets, however, Ray soon located a wallet containing a slip of paper with the word AMADEUS printed in neat, cramped handwriting.

Only then did Elijah notice the tiny red icon blinking in one corner of his vision, indicating that the skin's spectacles were net-linked. Within the wallet he also found a plastic card identifying his skin as a professor of English literature at Queens University.

When Davey had said the skin was someone unacquainted with prison life, he hadn't been kidding. Elijah couldn't imagine how someone like this had got himself tangled up with Lorenz so badly he'd be willing to spend a week in solitary confinement inside the Scrubs.

Elijah focused on the icon until it grew larger. "Amadeus," he said out loud, and the icon went from red to green, granting him full access.

―――――

THE SKIN—WHOSE name, according to the same plastic card, was Gerard Adebayo—owned a sleek and expensive-looking Audi parked two blocks away. His spectacles guided Elijah to the car and also informed him he was in Cambridge. That meant he had little choice but to waste valuable time driving first to London, and then to Southampton, the location of Finch's hospital.

Then, perhaps, he could find out whether Finch had framed him for his friend's murder—and why.

First, however, he needed a weapon, and he needed money.

―――――

FOUR HOURS LATER, Elijah had Adebayo's car pull up across the road from the Infirmary, a Brixton nightclub. Peering out through the windscreen, he saw that Mick was still working security on the door.

He got out and walked past the snaking queue and right up to Mick, who towered over his diminutive skin. Then again, Mick towered over almost everyone.

"Excuse me," said Elijah. "I'm looking for a mate. Erik, with a K." He nodded towards the club's booming interior. "Know if he's in?"

Mick gave him the full stare. "I don't think he knows you, mate," he replied, putting a particular emphasis on *mate*.

Elijah grinned. "You still got that scar from when that Russian stabbed you?"

Mick's stare became fractionally harder, and he narrowed the gap between himself and Elijah. "Who the fuck are you?" he demanded in low, terse tones.

"It's Elijah, Mick."

"You're not—!"

Realization dawned in Mick's eyes, one corner of his mouth twitching in a repressed grin. "It *is* you, isn't it?"

"As I live and breathe."

Mick searched his eyes for a moment. "Remember how his brother threatened to bring the Russian Mafia down on both our heads?"

Elijah's grin grew wider. "It wasn't his brother," he said. "It's his mum that threatened us."

Mick's whole demeanour changed to become considerably less threatening. "Had to be sure." He pointedly touched a finger to his neck. "How long you got?"

"Long enough," said Elijah. "So, how about Erik then?"

"He's in the office," said Mick. "I'd better call ahead to let him know it's you, and not some random bloke I've let come wandering in."

———

ERIK STARED hard at Elijah when he entered the office wearing Gerald Adebayo's skin.

"Fuck me," he said with a laugh, "Where d'you get that?"

"Lorenz."

Erik gave him an appraising look. "Can't help but wonder how someone like that got mixed up with someone like Lorenz."

"Nice car, too," said Elijah. "More than I'd have thought

someone like him could afford." He looked around. "This place is looking better than the last time I was here. And business must be good, judging by that queue outside."

Erik shrugged. "Couldn't have done it without your investment and all the time you put into building it up when we started."

"There's some things I need," said Elijah. "They're in the safe in my office."

Erik nodded. "Sure."

Elijah followed Erik through to what had once been his own office, although it appeared to have remained largely untouched since his arrest.

The safe was located behind a wall panel. It swung open when Elijah tapped in a long-ago memorized code. Inside were several bracelets, all preloaded with crypt-coin, plus a pair of handguns and several boxes of ammunition.

Slipping one of the bracelets over his wrist, Elijah took one of the guns and shoved a box of ammunition into Adebayo's jacket.

He started to close the safe again and hesitated. Then he took the second handgun as well.

Erik watched, face blank, as Elijah tucked one of the guns into his rear waistband and shoved the other deep inside a jacket pocket.

"You're aware," said Erik, "that they come down hard on people who commit murder by proxy."

"I'm not killing anybody," said Elijah. "I just need to ask somebody some questions."

Erik sighed. "You know, I heard through the grapevine that someone tried to kill you in prison. There were rumours you might be dead."

"Disappointed?" Elijah nodded around his old office with a grim smile. "After all, you'd own this place outright if I had been."

Erik managed to look offended. "Fuck you, Eli. You know it's not like that."

"Sorry," said Elijah. "I didn't mean that. It's been kind of tough, to be honest."

Erik nodded tightly. "Take Mick with you, if you need the backup."

Elijah shook his head. "Not necessary. But thanks."

"I suppose once this is all over, whatever it is, you'll still be stuck in the nick for a few more years."

"I will, unless somebody really does manage to kill me."

"You've got one of the best business minds I know," said Erik. "You were wasted on proxy dealing. You need to be back here, working with me."

"One of these days," said Elijah. "I promise."

He hesitated a moment, then stepped towards Mick, drawing him into a hug. It felt awkward, because Erik was about Elijah's height, and Gerald Adebayo was nearly half a foot shorter than Elijah himself. Elijah had to just about stand on his toes to get his arms around the other man's shoulders.

Stepping back towards the door, Elijah reached around his back to feel the solid and comforting weight of the gun there. "I'll be back," he said to Erik as he departed. "Don't you worry about that."

It took Elijah longer than he had expected to drive to Southampton. A weather report flashed up on the dashboard of Adebayo's car, warning of high winds and torrential rain. Once he was outside of London he encountered endless tail-backs, and every few kilometres he saw road crews working around the clock to repair the crumbling motorway.

A few years in jail had been enough to make him forget how bad the roads were getting. The people who'd first built the motorways hadn't factored in the gradual rise of global temperatures, and as a result they were essentially dissolving, the tar melting like warm toffee without fail every summer.

And he could have sworn the roadside warnings about mosquitoes and malaria hadn't been there the last time he'd been a free man.

Six kilometres outside Basingstoke the car came to a halt. A message flashed up on the dashboard: there'd been an accident. It advised taking the road to Lichfield and finding an alternative route to his destination from there.

Elijah swore under his breath, thinking of the minutes and hours and days ticking away before he had to return to his cell. If he'd been using regular proxy, he'd have already been back in his own skin by now.

He let the car join a long line of hires that looked like toys next to Adebayo's sleek machine. It was already dark and the weather was only getting worse.

At this rate, he wouldn't reach Finch's clinic until nearly midnight. Cursing under his breath, Elijah used the dashboard to call up a list of hotels that would accept crypt-coin and found one with a vacancy just outside Lichfield.

———

THE ABBEY RUSH Treatment Centre sat at the far end of a winding lane lined by manicured trees and looked more like a conference building than the crumbling Victorian pile Elijah had expected to see when he finally got there the next morning. He peered through the windscreen at the building's front entrance, sipping takeaway coffee from a foldable cup he'd purchased at the hotel. A gravel driveway wrapped around two sides of the Centre, and he'd parked as far as he could from the entrance while still being able to see people coming in and out.

But still no sign of Finch. Not unless he'd got there first.

It was just after nine in the morning and Elijah had

already been sitting watching the Treatment Centre for an hour and a half, fantasizing about pushing his gun into Finch's face and demanding answers.

Fuck it, he decided. He was bored sitting around and waiting.

He left one of the two guns in a cheap travel case he'd bought at the same time as the coffee, tucking the other into the rear of his trousers before exiting the car.

Inside, he found a reception desk manned by a single nurse, a chip-phone clipped to one of her earlobes. She looked up and smiled at Elijah as he entered.

"I'll be with you in a minute, sir," she said, then focused her attention on a computer screen, her fingers moving rapidly across a keyboard.

Looking around, Elijah noticed a glass-covered noticeboard along a corridor. He walked towards it and saw that it displayed photographs of the Centre's staff, including Finch. Under Finch's photograph was a label reading DR. ZACHARY FINCH, ASSOCIATE PROFESSOR AND CONSULTANT PSYCHIATRIST, DSc., DM, FRCPsych, FMedSci.

"Sir?"

Thinking he was being addressed, Elijah turned towards the reception desk only to see that the nurse was talking to someone else.

Elijah froze when he saw who she was speaking to. The man's skin was about the same shade as Elijah's. Even dressed casually in faded jeans and tennis shoes, he still carried the indefinable aura of an off-duty cop.

The stranger glanced towards Elijah without interest, then returned his attention to the nurse. Realizing he'd been gawping at this new arrival, Elijah focused intently on the noticeboard.

He swallowed, his throat instantly dry. Now he remembered where he'd seen the man before: his name was Ray

Thomas, part of the Met's special proxy division. He'd been involved in the investigation into Rob's murder and had even given evidence at Elijah's trial.

But why hadn't Thomas recognized him standing there? Why hadn't—?

Idiot. Elijah forced himself to breathe out, and the pounding of his heart lessened slightly.

Of course Thomas hadn't recognized him: the ex-cop had seen Gerard Adebayo, not Elijah Waits. He wouldn't know Adebayo from a month of Sundays.

"It's very important that I speak to Doctor Finch at the soonest possible opportunity," Elijah heard Thomas say to the nurse. He sounded agitated. "I was given to understand he'd be back from his conference by now."

"I'm afraid his flight was delayed," the nurse replied. "We're not expecting him to come in to work until tomorrow morning. Can you tell me what it's about, and I'll take a message?"

Finch? Elijah felt his eyes widen.

What the hell did Ray Thomas want with Finch?

Sensing that the nurse had, for the moment, forgotten about him, Elijah slipped across the corridor to an open-plan waiting area furnished with couches and chairs, from where he could listen more easily while remaining unseen.

"It's regarding a man named Dominic Fiori," Thomas explained to the nurse. "He was one of Doctor Finch's patients until very recently."

"I'm sorry," the nurse interrupted him, sounding startled. "What was that last name again?"

"Fiori," Thomas repeated. "Dominic Fiori. And I'd like to speak with him urgently as well about another man named Isaac Sizemore. And tell him if he doesn't talk to me, I'll talk to the police."

The young nurse sounded confused. "The police…?"

"Just make sure he gets the message the moment his flight

lands," Thomas insisted. "It's important. He'll want to hear it."

"Could I ask you to take a seat for now?" Elijah heard the nurse say. "I'll check in case he's landed already."

"I'll wait," said Thomas. "But if you get hold of him, make it clear I need to speak to him about this in person."

Elijah frowned as he continued to listen in to their conversation. Who the hell were Dominic Fiori and Isaac Sizemore? And what did *they* have to do with Finch?

Thomas stepped towards the waiting area and Elijah fought down a rush of unnecessary panic.

He doesn't know who you really are, he reminded himself, and went to stare out a window while Thomas took a seat close by.

Twenty minutes passed before the nurse asked Thomas to return to the reception area. Thomas got up and Elijah moved back over to where he could listen in once more.

"*How* long?" he heard Thomas exclaim.

"He's landed, but he can't make it in to work before very late tonight," the nurse explained, sounding apologetic. "Perhaps you could give me your name and—?"

"Tell him I'll meet him here, at his clinic, tonight," said Thomas, sounding angry, his words a harsh bark. "I don't care how long it takes him to get here, or how much hassle it is. Did you mention I'll talk to the police if he doesn't?"

"I did, yes," said the nurse, her voice sounding considerably more strained than it had a moment before.

A few seconds passed and Elijah heard the Centre's front door chime as it swung open. He let out a rush of air that came from deep within his lungs.

"Sir?" said the same nurse, coming to find him a moment later. She looked pale, as if she'd had a near-encounter with death. "I'm sorry for keeping you waiting, but there was a...a small emergency. How can I help you?"

"Actually, it's nothing," said Elijah, and he hurried past her and towards the exit.

Stepping outside, Elijah saw Thomas climb into a hire car parked on the gravel driveway next to a line of half a dozen other vehicles. Elijah headed back to Adebayo's Audi, trying to look purposeful and taking care not to look Thomas's way.

Only once he reached his skin's Audi did he glance back and see Thomas had slunk down low in the seat of his car, his gaze fixed on the front entrance of the Abbey Rush.

Elijah realized with a shock he wasn't the only one staking out the Centre. Which meant Elijah had no choice but to sit in Adebayo's car and watch both Thomas *and* the Centre.

Fortunately, Elijah had parked on a part of the driveway outside of Thomas's direct field of vision. Elijah kept himself low in his own seat in case Thomas glanced his way.

The hours passed with infinite slowness. Elijah fell briefly asleep and came to with a snort. Thomas was still right where he had been, watching people and cars come and go.

From the way Thomas's jaws moved, Elijah could see he was eating something. His own stomach growled in response.

He ignored his hunger, only cracking open the door of his car once so he could take a pee on the gravel when he was sure no one would see.

Eventually the sky grew darker, and he watched as most of the staff got in their cars and drove away. Lights within the clinic dimmed.

Just after nightfall, headlights appeared along the lane, and a car that put even Adebayo's to shame pulled up outside the Abbey Rush Treatment Centre.

Finch got out of the car and looked furtively around. His tie was askew and his suit looked rumpled. His gaze darted here and there precisely as if he were expecting someone to leap out at him, his cheeks and forehead pale and shiny and his mouth set in an attitude of dread. He dashed up to the Centre's entrance and touched a keypad.

Elijah watched Thomas emerge from his car, hurrying towards the entrance before the door could swing shut behind Finch.

Elijah cracked open the door of his own car and stood, wanting to see what happened next.

CHAPTER TWENTY-ONE

RAY

Ray grabbed Finch by the elbow, spinning him around until they faced each other outside the entrance of the Abbey Rush Centre. Finch reacted with a look of shocked outrage and terror.

"I'm the one who wanted you here," said Ray, pushing Finch further inside the lobby and letting the door swing shut behind them both. "You and me are going to have a little chat about Isaac Sizemore."

Finch's Adam's apple bobbed up and down. He cast a nervous glance towards the reception desk, where a nurse on night duty regarded them both with clear alarm.

"This isn't the time or place," Finch said tautly. "How dare you accost me—!"

"We can talk right here," said Ray, "or in your office. But I'm guessing you don't want any of the staff to hear what I have to say."

"That…that won't be necessary," said Finch, his face shiny with sweat. "We'll speak in my office. Alice? Please see that I'm not disturbed."

The nurse nodded, her expression wary and confused.

Finch nodded to Ray, who followed him down a corridor to an office. Once they were inside, Finch retreated behind a desk, standing there rigidly and staring back at Ray as he closed the door behind him.

Ray wasn't in the mood to waste words. "How long did you have Isaac Sizemore locked up in here?" he demanded. "And why keep him in here under an assumed name?"

"I don't know what you're talking about," Finch stammered.

"Don't waste my fucking time," Ray shouted. "I know both you and Sizemore used to work for Telop industries, and Sizemore was part of the mob that kidnapped Stacy Cotter straight out of her hospital bed."

Finch's nostrils flared as he sucked in a steadying breath. "I know nothing about any of that," he said, his voice shaking so hard a vigilant Boy Scout could have recognized he was lying.

"Like you don't know about proxy having come out of a Telop research lab, right?"

Finch sank into the seat behind the desk, looking like he might faint. "I'm not saying one more word until you tell me who you are and what you want," he rasped.

"I'm a private investigator," said Ray, stepping up close to the desk and fixing Finch with a hard stare. "Which is all you need to know. Right now the police aren't involved, but it'd take only a word from me to bring them here. I hate to think how people would react if they learned one of the biggest technology companies in the world was so irresponsible that it'd make proxy available to literally anyone with the means to print it." He paused for a beat. "Or the fact that one of Raphael Markov's employees used it to have sex with his boss's wife without her knowledge."

To Ray's surprise, a little fight came into Finch's voice. "If you knew anything about Raphael Markov," he said, "you'd never dare talk to me like this. What do you want—is it money? I can pay you." With one shaking hand, Finch tugged back one sleeve of his suit to reveal an expensive gold-plated bracelet. "I can do it right now in non-traceable crypt-coin—"

Ray stepped forward, putting his hands on Finch's desk and leaning forward until he was almost nose to nose with Finch.

Finch recoiled, falling back into a chair. His hands gripped the chair's armrests like a drowning man clutching at driftwood.

"Tell Raphael that I want to speak to him, in person, and soon," Ray growled. Then he took a pen and a sheet of notepaper from Finch's desk and scribbled down a series of numbers and digits.

"What is this?" Finch asked, looking down at the sheet when Ray scooted it over to him.

"An encrypted address," said Ray. "Markov can contact me via it. Make sure he gets it. And if I don't hear back from either of you in the next forty-eight hours, you can tell your side of the story to the Metropolitan Police instead." Ray made a show of thinking for a moment. "Or the press. Your choice."

Without another word, Ray spun on his heel and left, slamming the door shut behind him.

———

ELIJAH CAME CLOSE to following Finch and Thomas inside the Centre a half dozen times. Each time he took a step towards the front entrance, and each time he retreated. In the end he opted for standing next to his skin's Audi and staring fixedly towards the Centre's entrance.

Barely ten minutes after Ray Thomas had pushed Finch inside, the ex-cop appeared, pushing his way out into the night air.

Elijah slid back inside the Audi, closing the door carefully so as not to draw attention. Thomas, oblivious to Elijah's presence, got back in his own vehicle.

Instead of driving away, Thomas resumed watching the front entrance of the Centre even as Elijah, in turn, continued to watch him.

Goddammit. Elijah punched the Audi's dashboard and wished hellfire upon Thomas. He was tired of waiting!

Then Finch came hurrying out of the Centre, looking even more harried than before.

Clearly, Thomas had put the frighteners on the man. As Elijah watched, Finch got back in his own car and drove away at speed, his headlights flickering past the trees that lined the driveway.

The headlights of Thomas's car flipped on immediately, and Elijah watched as he set off in pursuit of Finch.

At last. His muscles thrumming with nervous tension, Elijah spoke a command. In response, a steering wheel unfolded from a hidden groove within the dashboard, and pedals pushed up against the soles of his feet.

Self-driving vehicles weren't designed to follow other cars except in response to traffic conditions. And that meant he'd need manual control of the Audi if he was going to tail both Finch and Thomas.

He gripped the steering wheel with renewed energy and started the engine.

CHAPTER
TWENTY-TWO

RAPHAEL

"Sir?" asked Carlson, Raphael's PA. "It's a call from Doctor Finch. He says it's urgent."

Raphael looked up from the papers he'd been studying at his desk to see his PA hovering at the entrance to his office. His mind had been elsewhere, thinking about acquisitions he'd been looking to make—mostly tech companies specialising in life extension, a field in which Telop had recently made some major investments.

"Tell him I'm busy," said Raphael, picking up a manila folder and opening it. He crossed his legs and tried to focus once more on his work.

"He's quite insistent, sir. But if you like I could—?"

For God's sake. Raphael dropped the folder back down with a thump.

First Amy, now Finch; he was regretting ever having taken the Doctor into his confidence.

"Fine," he said. "Put him through."

Carlson nodded. "…and if Miss Cotter should call again?"

"The only time I want to speak to my ex-wife," said

Raphael, fixing the PA with a stare, "is when I choose to. Is that understood? I don't want to hear one more word about, or from, her."

"Sir."

Carlson exited the room, closing the door after him, and Raphael breathed a heartfelt sigh of relief. The only reason he hadn't taken out a restraining order against the woman was his fear of attracting yet more media attention. Clearly, nothing he could say or do would satisfy her, now that her daughter was officially missing.

Light shimmered within the smooth glass of Raphael's desk, forming into images and text. Finch's name appeared next to a phone icon.

"Accept call," said Raphael.

"Raphael?" Finch's voice came through without a picture, breathy and ragged.

Something in Finch's tone sent a prickle of concern down Raphael's spine and he sat up straighter.

"Please don't address me by my first name," Raphael snapped. "You're my employee, not my fucking golf partner."

"I'm sorry, sir. There was a man just here," said Finch. "At the Abbey Rush Centre. I don't know what he wanted, but he seemed to know everything about...about us."

Finch sounded on the verge of a breakdown. "What do you mean, 'everything'?"

"About Isaac and proxy," Finch babbled. "That Isaac took Stacy out of the hospital. That...!"

Finch's voice choked off. *Jesus*, thought Raphael, was the idiot *crying*?

"Where are you just now?" Raphael demanded, his unease growing. "Are you still at Abbey Rush?"

"No," Finch replied. "I'm just driving around. I didn't know what else to do." His voice almost became a wail. "He talked about the police!"

"Did you at least get the man's name?"

"He said he was a private investigator. He wouldn't tell me his name. The only thing he gave me was an encrypted address he said to give to you so you could contact him. And...and he said he wanted to meet you in person. Within forty-eight hours, or he'll go to the police."

"Send the address to me," said Raphael, the muscles around his jaw tightening. "I need you to think carefully and tell me every detail of what he said and did. Don't miss out anything."

"He turned up at the Centre this morning and left a message saying he wanted to talk about Isaac."

"This morning?" Raphael stared into the obsidian depths of his desk. "And you didn't think to mention this before?"

"I...no." Raphael listened to the harsh sound of Finch's breathing for several seconds. "I'm sorry. I didn't think."

No, you didn't, thought Raphael.

The problem with men like Zachary Finch was that they were brilliant in their primary fields of research, but in everything else they were like children, demanding of an adult's guidance.

Isaac had been like that, too. Brilliant, but disconnected from the world at large.

"When I finally got to the Centre he was waiting for me," Finch continued. "He knows we kept Isaac there. And that we invented proxy."

That last one Raphael felt like a physical blow to his belly.

"If he really knew anything at all," said Raphael, struggling to sound like he was in control, "he would have gone to the police or the press first. He's trying to force a reaction out of you, Zachary, because he can't prove a thing."

"But what do I do?" Finch whined. "If he knows that much, what else does he know? What about our mind upload research, or what you did to your own—"

"Shut up," Raphael hissed at his desk. "Did you even stop to think he might have bugged your car?"

"I—God, I'm sorry. I know I panicked."

It struck Raphael that it wouldn't take much pressure at all to make Finch sing like a songbird if the police got hold of him. A solution came to him then, and he relaxed slightly.

He'd deal with Finch, and then he'd meet with this detective or blackmailer, whoever or whatever he was. And then he'd deal with him too.

"I can take care of this," said Raphael, doing his best to sound reassuring.

"Thank you, Mr Markov," said Finch with almost childlike gratitude. "Just let me know how I can help."

"Let's meet somewhere private. We shouldn't be discussing this over any kind of phone connection. I'll need your help to fix this."

"Yes," said Finch, clearly desperately relieved. "Thank you, Ra—I mean, sir."

"I'm sending you some directions," said Raphael. "Make sure you speak to no one else until I see you there in a couple of hours."

He swiped two fingers across the desk, sending the details to Finch's bracelet.

"A wildlife park?" Finch asked a moment later.

"I'm a co-founder. It's closed for the night, but you can use your Telop credentials to get in through the front gate. Meet me at the main car park. We won't be disturbed or seen."

Raphael disconnected and sank back in his chair. He counted to thirty, then touched another icon. Carlson entered a few seconds later.

"Prepare an air taxi," said Raphael. "I'll take it from the roof." He stood and picked up his jacket. "I'll be a few hours. When I get back, find one of our trusted engineers and have him delete its route information."

"Sir," said Carlson, seemingly unruffled by this request. "Is there anything else?"

As urgent as meeting with Finch might be, there were other matters Raphael first had to deal with—necessary, unavoidable matters. He should have enough time to stop over briefly at the family estate, then continue on to the wildlife park.

"Call Lovatt in security," said Raphael, stepping towards the door of a private elevator. "I need him to retrieve something for me."

Carlson nodded. "Of course, sir." He turned to leave, then hesitated before turning back. "I believe Lovatt's gone home for the night."

"Then you wake him up," Raphael barked, stepping towards the elevator that would take him to the roof. "Tell him I want all the security footage from the Abbey Rush Treatment Centre for the past forty-eight hours without delay. As soon as he has it, tell him to forward it directly to me."

"Of course."

The elevator doors slid shut and Raphael ascended to the roof of the Telop headquarters. When the doors opened a minute later, a brisk wind scythed across the flat expanse of the rooftop. It felt bracing after the summer heat. An air taxi descended towards him as he stepped towards the helipad.

Raphael's bracelet vibrated as he boarded the taxi and he groaned inwardly. "Carlson?" he said into the bracelet. "Whatever it is, I very much hope it's worth my time."

"It's Amy Cotter, sir. I'm afraid she got inside the building —as far as the twenty-third floor before we apprehended her. She's being taken back down to the lobby as we speak."

Raphael took a deep, steadying breath. "And how did she get in?"

"She used an old security clearance," Carlson explained. "It should have been deactivated years ago, but clearly there's been an oversight. I'll ask Lovatt to conduct a full review of staff clearance first thing in the morning. Sir...should we allow her to wait in the lobby, or ask her to leave?

Raphael sighed, suddenly weary. "Just get rid of her. I don't care if you have to throw her out on the steps. Just get her out of here."

CHAPTER TWENTY-THREE

AMY

The first thing Amy Cotter had noticed earlier that evening, stepping into the front lobby of the Telop headquarters, was how little it had changed since she had last entered it many years before.

From the outside, it remained the same towering fortress of twisted steel and mirrored glass she remembered, like some mutant plant-machine hybrid clawing its way out of the ancient black soil of the London Docklands. Once inside the lobby, however, it felt more like being inside a space station. Everything gleamed, from the marble coffee tables to the cream floor tiles and the ten-meter long reception desk that merged seamlessly with the floor. Even the people who worked there, from the security guards on up, appeared to have been buffed to a polished shine before being allowed within sight of the public.

When she'd stepped up to the desk and asked to speak to Raphael, the elaborately coiffured man standing behind it had stared at her as if she had asked for a personal audience with God. A warmth had crept up her neck as his expression shifted from polite interest to bemusement. Informing him that she was Raphael's ex-wife brought no discernible change in his attitude.

She waited while he went to look for someone else to whom he could pass on the responsibility of dealing with her, and before long another underling a few years older and fractionally higher up Telop's food chain arrived to speak with her.

It made no difference. He had the same carefully worded responses to her request, and the same faint air of condescension, as if she were little more than some random lunatic who had wandered in from the street.

He asked her to wait, and he stepped towards a bank of antique telephone kiosks, speaking into a mouthpiece too quietly for her to make out his words.

Amy fought the urge to turn on her heel and exit the building before she could embarrass herself any further.

But that meant sitting alone in her cottage feeling powerless—and she was tired of feeling powerless.

Despite the detective's request that she remain at home, following his departure Amy had continued to pack her things with every intention of fleeing to her friend's place on the coast.

But she had hesitated on the threshold of her cottage, suitcase in hand, realizing for the first time that her decision to hire Thomas had merely been a way to delay the inevitable: the only way she would ever get the answers she needed was by confronting Raphael directly.

She had convinced herself that, with sufficient tenacity, she could persuade Raphael to grant her an audience. But now she was actually here, in his building, she could feel her conviction faltering beneath a barrage of politely worded, but firm, refusals.

"I'm afraid Mr Markov isn't in the building at the moment," the Telop employee told her after his return from the telephone kiosk. His skin gleamed as if manufactured.

"I know that isn't true," Amy insisted. "If he's not out of the country, he's here—and he never leaves the country these days. Everyone knows that."

The employee pursed his lips. "I'll see what I can do, Miss Cotter." He nodded to some nearby couches, each of which, she recalled Raphael once informing her, cost more than the annual national average wage. "But it might be a little while."

"I can wait," said Amy, her mouth set in a determined line.

And so she did, while people came and went and the day slipped towards evening. She had known even in the early days of their marriage that it was necessary to pester Raphael constantly to get his attention at all.

She returned frequently to the reception desk, seeing the practised smiles grow more strained each time she asked the same questions and got the same answers.

Idly, Amy wondered whether a story about the former wife of a billionaire CEO being thrown out of her ex-husband's place of work might be considered newsworthy. It would be worth it just for the embarrassment it might cause Raphael.

But she had other plans. For the hundredth time that day, Amy felt around inside her shoulder bag until her fingertips touched the rough edge of a plastic card she'd dug out of a shoebox that morning before leaving home.

If they would not let her go to Raphael, she'd just have to go around them.

She couldn't just take an elevator up to Raphael's office, because the reception staff and omnipresent security guards would see her doing so and take steps to prevent her. But neither could their attention be on her continuously, not with so many new arrivals and visitors constantly entering or leaving the building.

Biding her time, Amy waited until a group large enough for her purposes entered the lobby. Her moment came when a gaggle of a dozen or so men and women entered from the plaza outside, talking and laughing among themselves and moving in a loose knot towards a bank of elevators to the left of the reception desk.

If she was going to act, Amy knew, it had to be now.

She drew in a sharp breath and stepped in among the new arrivals as they walked past her, hoping that Raphael's staff wouldn't notice her amidst them, despite the fact that she wore a cardigan and comfortable jeans and they were all dressed in shiny business wear.

Matching pace with them, she followed them inside an elevator and kept to the back.

None of them paid her any attention. They all got off on the tenth floor, and Amy hit the button for the twenty-third. The higher the elevator rose, the more nervous tension tightened the muscles in her shoulders and neck, the plastic card still gripped tightly between her thumb and forefinger.

The elevator doors hissed open and Amy gazed down a long corridor with pale cream walls and soft carpeting. Memory drew her to the third door on the left which, she saw, still had the same retinal scanner and keycard combination she remembered from previous visits many years before.

With one trembling hand, Amy slid the card down a door-mounted slot, then peered into a lens set at about head-height.

Seconds passed, too many for her comfort. At last a light changed from red to green, and the door unlocked with a soft click.

Air rushed out of her lungs. Amy almost sagged with relief. She hadn't thought the card would still work after so many years.

The door swung open on automated hinges, revealing a suite of offices reserved for Raphael's personal staff.

Raphael himself, she knew, would be in here somewhere.

"Miss Cotter?"

The voice came from behind her. At first she froze, but then found the willpower to turn around.

It took her a moment to place the man who had spoken. He'd entered the lobby a number of times while she'd sat waiting through the afternoon, conversing with the reception staff and occasionally with one or other of the security guards. And now that she thought about it, she might also have seen him on television, standing discreetly behind Raphael as he gave a speech at some wildlife park.

The man gestured back towards the elevator. "I'd rather keep this civilized," he said, "but if you don't cooperate, I'm legally entitled to use force if necessary. I need to ask you to leave."

"I just want to speak to Raphael," she babbled. "I have every right to do that. He had my daughter locked up in a hospital against her will and—"

As she spoke, the man sighed and reached into a pocket of his suit, taking out a neatly folded sheet of paper and handing it to her. "Mr Markov is seeking an injunction to prevent you from approaching him or engaging in any further harassment now or in the future. This letter is from his law firm, ordering you to desist or face legal action."

"I'm his ex-wife, for God's sake!" she shouted, appalled. "Surely that counts for something? Why should I of all people have to beg to speak to him?"

Raphael's guard-dog showed no trace of emotion, beyond a slight curl of contempt at the corners of his mouth. "I'm sure you'd prefer me not to call the police," he informed her curtly.

Casting the man a single hateful glance, Amy marched past him and towards the elevator, slamming the button for the ground floor as hot, burning shame turned her cheeks red. The security man stepped in beside her before the doors closed and stood by her with his hands neatly clasped, his gaze fixed on some point in the middle distance.

The trip back down to the lobby lasted about a million years.

When the doors opened, a uniformed guard stood waiting for them. Stepping forward, he took Amy gently but firmly by the elbow and guided her towards the exit and the plaza outside.

If someone had at that moment handed Amy a button that could destroy the building and everyone in it, she would have gladly pressed it.

Amy only remembered to breathe again once she found herself standing on the concrete plaza outside. It was questionable whether she could take any more humiliation. Tears pricked the corners of her eyes and she willed them back, setting her mouth in a firm flat line of determination.

This wasn't over yet.

At that moment she heard a loud drone from above. Glancing up, past the looming expanse of the monument Raphael's father, David Markov, had long ago built to himself, she saw the blinking lights of an air taxi ascending from the roof. It banked south towards the river and quickly vanished amidst towering skyscrapers back-lit by the setting sun.

A bitter, hysterical laugh worked its way up to Amy's throat. Raphael had fled the building rather than confront her.

Well then, she would just have to go to him. That was her plan of last resort—if he steadfastly refused to see her at his place of work, then she would track him down to his home instead.

Filled with a sense of grim determination, Amy Cotter hurried across the concrete plaza and away from the Telop building until she came to a road, issuing rapid commands to her bracelet.

It wasn't long before a vacant hire pulled up next to her.

———

EXHAUSTED from her experiences at the Telop building, Amy soon fell asleep as the boxy little car whisked her out of the city and into the countryside. Dashboard sensors noted her slowed heartbeat and breathing and the interior lights dimmed, the seat beneath her reclining gently. When she woke again, it was to see the moon flickering through trees, their branches overhanging a deserted countryside road.

A quick glance at the dashboard showed she had been asleep for most of an hour. A touch of a button brought her chair to its normal position. The road was familiar, and she realized she had already almost reached the outskirts of the Markov family estate.

Her fingers touched the dashboard and a manual wheel emerged from its groove. It would be easier to find what she was looking for if she had control of the car.

Before long, she came to a familiar turn in the road and pulled over before climbing out. A fine, mist-like rain descended from above the treetops, coating her skin where it was exposed in a veil of moisture. She hardly noticed.

With a touch of her bracelet, she sent the little car on its way. The last thing she wanted was anyone wondering why an empty hire might be sitting untended so close to the Markov estate.

Pines lined the road on either side, appearing as towering black shadows against the night sky. Amy thought of calling the car back, of abandoning this idiotic plan of hers. The Markov estate hardly lacked for security, and the thought of what might happen should she be caught trespassing was not a pleasant one. Not to mention that Raphael's lawyers would have a field day with her in court.

Without quite realizing it, she had started walking into the trees and away from the road, the moon lighting her way. After a quarter of a mile her feet began to hurt enough that she had cause to regret not wearing something more practical than a pair of cheap slip-ons.

Cresting a low hill, Amy looked down and across an expanse of nearly unbroken forest. A few miles distant she saw the lights of the Markov mansion and the various outbuildings surrounding it. If she had stayed in the car and kept to the road, she would eventually have come to the main gates leading into the estate. Cameras would have picked her up long before she got that far, and one of Raphael's security teams would surely have been sent out to prevent her from going any further.

Amy had never been back here once in all the years since Paul Green's revelations.

She kept moving, soon sighting a tall fence that she knew ringed the entire estate. Years ago, while she had still been living here—when she had still been Amy Markov—she had explored the entire estate at her leisure, using it as an opportunity to identify places where the security coverage was less than complete.

Once she knew where those weak spots of coverage were, it had been a simple matter to sneak Isaac into the estate from time to time without Raphael or anyone else being any the wiser.

One such place, she remembered, was only a short walk from where she stood.

Dead branches and leaves crackled under Amy's feet as she stepped up to the chain-link fence, which was supported on metal posts driven deep into the soil. She could see the outline of a security camera on top of a fence post, its lens angled away from her.

Keeping parallel to the fence, Amy walked to her left until she found a wooden gate exactly where she remembered it.

Innocuous as it appeared, the gate was secured with exactly the same kind of security apparatus as Raphael's offices, minus the retinal scanner. Since her keycard had still worked in the Telop building, there was no reason to think it might not work here as well…although she doubted that would still be the case by the time morning arrived.

Swiping the card down through the reader set into the wooden gate, Amy laughed with unbridled delight when it immediately clicked open.

Following an old and rutted path, Amy soon caught sight of a cottage nestled between two forested hills, its windows dark. Stacy, she remembered, had been conceived there during one of Isaac's visits, and while Raphael had been away on one of his interminably long business trips.

She kept moving, letting her feet guide her. Thirty or so minutes passed before she came across another, much larger building silhouetted against the night sky. Unlike the cottage, a number of its windows shone with light.

From far away came the faint buzz of a security drone on its automated patrol.

Amy kept going, slipping past outhouses and a stables until, at last, the Edwardian mansion David Markov had once made the base of his power revealed itself to her. Once the home of a wealthy merchant, it had lain in disrepair for decades before being refurbished at enormous cost while Raphael had still been a boy.

This, now, was Raphael Markov's home—and it had been hers, albeit briefly, until it became her prison.

Self-doubt gripped Amy in its steely talons. *Turn back,* a terrified voice said from somewhere deep inside her. *For God's sake, turn back.*

Birds called to each other through the night. From within the house, nothing stirred.

She reminded herself why she was there. Raphael had spent nearly every minute of their marriage lying to her, and she didn't believe for a second that divorce had made him any more truthful. Even if he didn't know Stacy's current whereabouts, then he at least had to know why Isaac picked this moment to step back into the world of the living—and why some stranger had tried to kill their daughter.

Her doubt faded, replaced by a wave of anger as clear and sharp as if she had dived into a winter lake.

There would be no more dismissing her. This time, there would be answers.

Her feet carried her forward as if of their own volition, towards a door around the rear of the building that led into the kitchens. The door swung open with ease. Moonlight illuminated counter-tops and work tables within the darkened interior.

Amy waited and listened. The house was silent but, she knew, certainly not empty. There were always members of the domestic staff moving around at any hour of the day or night. She crossed the kitchen and stepped through a door, moving with excessive care so as to make as little sound as possible.

Soon, she entered a narrow corridor that ended at the bottom of a short flight of steps leading upwards. Ascending to the next floor, she paused on hearing the creak of a floorboard somewhere ahead.

Moving a few steps back down the stairs to where the shadows would better conceal her, Amy watched as a door on the landing ahead of her creaked open. A member of Raphael's staff emerged, closing the door behind him and walking down to the far end of the corridor before moving out of sight.

Almost there.

Ascending further, Amy came to the third floor, where she remembered Raphael kept his home office. Before her stretched another wood-lined corridor, and this time her ears detected a faint electronic beep from behind a door at the far end.

A plaque mounted on one wall of the corridor read MEDICAL STAFF ONLY BEYOND THIS POINT.

Her brow furrowed. What this meant she couldn't even

begin to imagine. Medical staff? Did Raphael have some condition he'd been concealing from the world?

There was no point speculating. A door to Amy's right stood slightly ajar, and she eased it carefully open, expecting to see the bathroom she remembered had been there. Instead, to her confusion, she found someone had turned it into a storage room filled with racked server units, their status lights blinking from out of the darkness.

The lines of Amy's brow deepened. What could Raphael be doing at home that required so much computer power?

Amy stepped back out into the corridor and looked towards the door of Raphael's office. One trait both Raphael and his father shared was the inability to cease working even when they had returned home. If she would find Raphael anywhere, it was there.

Except...something wasn't right. It wasn't anything she could put a finger on; rather, her skin prickled as if all the angles of the corridor and the surrounding house were subtly wrong.

Voices came from downstairs, and Amy heard someone ascending the same steps she'd climbed only moments before. One voice was recognizably Raphael's.

Gripped by a sudden panic, Amy stepped back into the server room, easing the door most of the way shut. If she were to confront Raphael, she would rather do it when he was alone and away from his security detail.

Moments later, she glimpsed Raphael stepping past the server room and on down the corridor.

He was, she saw with relief, quite alone.

Another second passed, and Amy heard the chime of an electronic lock followed by the sound of a door opening. She waited a beat, then eased the server room door the rest of the way open and slipped back out into the corridor.

The door to Raphael's office, at the far end of the corridor, now stood ajar.

It was now or never.

Steeling herself for a confrontation, Amy stepped quietly towards the half-open door, noting that the light coming from within was dazzlingly bright.

Her sense of wrongness intensified, enough so that she hesitated for a moment before continuing.

Moving soundlessly, Amy stepped around the half-open door and looked into Raphael's office.

Except it wasn't an office any more. Instead, she saw something that more closely resembled a high-tech surgery.

Raphael stood across the room from Amy, his back to her and his attention focused on a large, adjustable hospital bed. The bed had been raised, but Raphael blocked her from seeing if there was anyone in it.

If there was, they were hidden from her sight, beneath a vast tangle of what looked to Amy like thousands of glistening, almost organic-looking tendrils, drooping down from immensely complicated-looking machinery suspended from the ceiling directly overhead.

Amy shuddered inwardly. The machinery looked almost alive, somehow, like some vast, synthetic anemone. The tendrils twitched from time to time, many looking as fine as threads.

The breath caught in her throat when Raphael stepped past the bed and towards a shelving unit. He took down a box and reached into it, taking out what even she recognized as a proxy applicator.

Now that Raphael had moved away from the bed she could now see that it was, in fact, occupied, by a small and frail-looking figure. Much of the upper part of the figure's head was concealed by the tangle of thread-like tendrils, but the face was, she realized with a shudder of horror, quite recognisable beneath its oxygen mask.

It was David Markov...or, judging by what she could see, what remained of him.

CHAPTER
TWENTY-FOUR

AMY

It took Amy another moment to understand what she was seeing.

David Markov's skull lay open, its interior seemingly packed with the thread-like tendrils descending from the apparatus suspended above his bed. As if, thought Amy, someone had wired him directly into the monstrous machinery above him.

Raphael, still unaware he was being watched, turned back towards the bed. Amy automatically moved back from the door, but he still didn't see her, so intently focused he seemed to be on whatever he was doing.

She peered cautiously back around the door and saw her ex-husband lean over the prone, ruined body of his father. With growing consternation, she watched as he placed the proxy applicator against the old man's neck.

Then he stood back up and repeated the operation, this time placing a second bead in the applicator and firing it into his own neck.

As much as she'd tried to avoid thinking about such things over the years, Amy by now understood the basic prin-

ciple by which proxy worked. It had become such a ubiqui-
tous technology that avoiding news about it had become
almost impossible. She also knew that David Markov had
been in a reportedly vegetative state for years now. She had
long presumed David's Catholic faith was the only reason
he'd kept the old man's body in this state of prolonged
misery.

She had also presumed the elder Markov was being kept
in some hospice far from Raphael's sight, but instead he was
right here, in the family mansion.

The revelation came slowly, but with building force as
the disparate parts of the mystery welded together in her
mind.

If Raphael was proxying with his father David...then the
man standing before her wasn't Raphael at all, but David
Markov proxying through his son's body.

How long, she wondered, had the old man been proxying
through his son, her ex-husband? How, given David Markov
had supposedly been reduced to a vacant, mindless shell, was
it even possible?

Even as these thoughts raced through Amy's mind, she
took notice of the look on the old man's face. Rather than
lacking in expression as she might have expected, his lips
moved soundlessly behind his oxygen mask, his face twisted
up in an expression of anguish and horror.

Only then did she fully accept the truth of it, that Raphael
was in there somewhere, trapped in the horrific wreck of his
father's body. And for how long?

Raphael, meanwhile, had moved back around the bed and
towards a computer monitor sitting on a counter.

Somehow Amy found the wherewithal to raise her left
arm and use her bracelet to snatch a brief video of the scene
before her. Then she stepped quietly back from the door into
the corridor, her lungs aching in her chest.

Any desire she'd felt to confront Raphael—no, she

reminded herself; the man she had *thought* was Raphael—fled. Now, she wanted only to warn someone.

Retreating as quietly as she could, Amy slipped back inside the server room and put in a call to Ray Thomas.

As incredible as it seemed, so much that had happened over the years since her divorce made far more sense if David Markov had been in control of Raphael's body for much, if not all of that time. He'd ceased to travel abroad for business, spending most of his time between his home here and his offices in London.

A lot of people had made the exact same decision in the wake of three pandemics, so it was hardly unusual. But perhaps there was another reason Raphael had given up travelling: a proxy session lasted four or five hours at most, which meant David couldn't have risked straying too far from his true body. He'd have had no choice but to renew the proxy link at regular intervals, up to five or six times daily.

The more she thought about it, the more it made sense...and the more it made her skin crawl. David Markov had found a way to keep control of his company, and for the first time in a very long time she felt something approaching sympathy for her ex-husband.

Nobody—not even Raphael—deserved what he was suffering through.

"Miss Cotter?"

Amy nearly let out a gasp when she heard Thomas's voice in her ear. "Raphael isn't Raphael," she blurted in a hurried half-whisper, moving deeper into the server room and turning her back to the door. "He's really David, his father. I think he's been proxying with Raphael all these years."

"What?" Thomas sounded befuddled. "Miss Cotter, you're not making any sense. Can you please repeat that?"

"It's Raphael," Amy repeated, touching her bracelet and sending the video she'd taken to Thomas. "I'm at his estate. He's—"

Behind Amy the door burst open, and a figure moved swiftly towards her, clamping one hand over her mouth and dragging her backwards out into the corridor. Thomas's voice sounded tinnily from her bracelet, demanding to know what was going on.

A fist slammed into Amy's stomach. Rough hands held her upright, even though she wanted to double over from the pain. Then whoever had hold of her let her go, and she collapsed onto the floor of the corridor.

She crouched, coughing and spluttering and trying desperately to suck air into her lungs.

"Good job, Arthur," she heard Raphael say. "You can go now."

"But, sir—?"

"Now," Raphael said, more firmly this time. "And you saw none of this. Understood?"

"Sir," said Arthur, and she heard the sound of boot heels retreating along the wooden floor of the corridor.

She tried to get back up, but a foot slammed her back down. "Stay where you are, Amy."

"You're not Raphael," she said, her voice barely more than a harsh croak.

"I think," said David Markov, "what with Stacy nearly being murdered and kidnapped by unknown assailants, you've been through more mental stress than you can cope with."

"How could you do this to your own son?" she rasped. "How could anyone do that to another human being?"

At last she was able to lift her gaze sufficiently to meet the eyes of the man standing over her. He had something in his hands.

David Markov, as she now knew him to be, leaned down until they were almost face-to-face. "I think," he continued, "that it's quite understandable how all this stress made you want to kill yourself. It's a terrible tragedy."

She tried again to get upright, and once again she was slammed back down. Then Markov kneeled on her back, forcing her flat even as she struggled and twisted and fought.

Then something pressed against the back of her neck, followed by a sudden, sharp sting.

————

"Miss Cotter? Hello?"

Ray stared at his bracelet, perplexed and suddenly, deeply worried. He tried again to call her, but without success.

Ahead of him, through the windscreen, he could see Finch's car. At first Finch had driven aimlessly, but now he appeared to be moving with purpose, heading deeper into the countryside.

Raphael isn't Raphael, Amy had said. *He's David*.

Christ, he thought. It was impossible. Not when the old man had apparently been vegetative for years.

His bracelet blinked, drawing his attention. A glance at his wrist revealed that Amy Cotter had sent him a video file shortly before they'd been cut off. He pushed it onto the hire's dashboard and let it run while he kept one eye on the road and one hand on the manual steering wheel.

He watched with increasing horror as Raphael Markov—or at least, the man he'd always believed to be Raphael Markov—leaned over the still-breathing body of his father and injected it with a proxy bead.

Ray swallowed to try to get some moisture back into his suddenly bone-dry mouth. Lifting his bracelet to his mouth, he called another number.

"Emergency services," said a brisk professional voice. "Which service do you—?"

"I'm concerned for the safety of a woman named Amy Cotter, formerly Amy Markov," he said, cutting the man off. "She's at the country estate of Raphael Markov, the head of

Telop Industries. She's his ex-wife. I have reason to believe her life is in serious and imminent danger."

Ray ended the call and swore in the close, hot confines of the cheap little hire. He'd have to get rid of the bracelet.

What the hell had Amy been thinking, going anywhere near Raphael Markov at a time like this?

Or the man they'd all thought was Raphael, if he could believe what he'd just seen.

Slowly Ray began to realize just how much he had under-estimated Amy Cotter. She'd shown considerable guts and intelligence by getting so close to Markov. And if the police responded in time, David Markov—if it really was him—might think twice about harming her.

For a moment he thought about abandoning his pursuit of Finch and going to her aid. But it would take hours to get to the Markov estate—much too late to be of use.

Up ahead, Finch took a right. Ray turned the wheel to follow, his thoughts a whirl of confusion and revelation.

CHAPTER TWENTY-FIVE

DAVID

Once he'd had Amy dealt with, David Markov boarded an air taxi parked on a broad expanse of lawn next to the Markov family mansion. His consciousness was secure inside Raphael's skin for at least the next six days, thanks to the hopscotch proxy he and Finch had developed.

The taxi rose into the air, banking over the forest and rising high enough for London to become visible on the horizon. As he settled back, David relished, as he had so many times over the years, the strong muscles and taut, smooth skin of his stolen body.

Twenty minutes into his journey, Lovatt squirted a message to him that came with several video attachments. David displayed them on the curving interior of the taxi's windscreen and watched as a dark-skinned man walked in and out of the Abbey Rush Treatment Centre several times over the course of a day, on one occasion accosting Finch as he entered the building.

Lovatt had already identified the man responsible for threatening Zachary Finch, but David recognized him on sight: Ray Thomas, the Metropolitan Detective Inspector who'd refused to take a bribe to keep that little bitch Stacy Cotter from dragging the Markov's name through the mud. The scandal had cost Telop hundreds of millions in plummeting share values.

Was it possible, he wondered, that Thomas had found out about their experiments on patients using hopscotch? Or had something else brought Finch to his attention?

A little while later, another message came through: his technical staff had traced Amy Cotter's call to a bracelet that most likely belonged to Ray Thomas.

Interesting. Perhaps Thomas was the one who had summoned the police to his estate. It had been a minor inconvenience soon tidied up with a few words into the right ears.

Another hour passed before the little aircraft dipped back down towards the ground, landing in a field close by the Wildlife Centre where he'd given a speech only days before. David disembarked and left the craft sitting on an expanse of gravel. He zipped up a leather jacket he wore over black jeans and unlocked a side-gate before stepping into the Centre's grounds.

It took a little while to get everything in place, but once he had, it was only a short walk to the car park where he'd told Finch to meet him. Finding a bench by some trees, he sat down to wait.

He didn't have to wait long. Headlights appeared at the front gates. The timing was perfect, really.

Finch's car pulled into the car park and crunched to a halt. He got out, peering into the surrounding darkness with the expression of a guppy on the wrong end of a fishing line.

David had picked his spot carefully. The trees overhanging the bench on which he sat cast deep shadows, concealing him from sight. He took a moment to prepare himself mentally for what was to come, then stood and stepped forward, raising one hand and calling out to Finch.

Finch turned with a start, then hurried over to Raphael's

side, casting furtive glances around the car park as if afraid they were being observed.

In a way, he wasn't wrong.

"Raphael!" Finch said breathlessly. "I'm sorry for all this trouble, but now you're here, I'm sure we can fix this terrible mess!"

Finch, he could see, was on the verge of a full-blown panic attack. "Calm down, Zachary," said David, putting both hands on the other man's shoulders. "Thomas doesn't know a thing. Not really."

Finch's brow furrowed. "Who?"

"The name of the man who came to see you is Ray Thomas. He was thrown out of the police years ago. I can take care of him, but first I need you to think carefully. Did he say how he came by the information he has?"

All the evidence Raphael's technical staff had so far gleaned strongly suggested that everything Thomas knew had come through Amy Cotter, but there was still an outside possibility the former policeman had some other source of information.

"I—no," Finch stammered. "He didn't. But if he knows about hopscotch, it stands to reason he knows a lot more. I...I think he must have been talking to Isaac."

It was pathetic, really, how quickly Finch fell apart under the slightest pressure. "Don't worry," David reassured him. "I told you, Zachary. I've taken care of everything."

"I see." Finch nodded, his shoulders slumping in relief. "I'm sorry I panicked. It was just such a shock, after everything that happened with—"

From across the car park, in the direction of the animal enclosures, came the sound of a snuffling grunt.

Finch halted mid-sentence and glanced around with a fearful expression. At the same time, David stepped back towards the bench. He couldn't imagine the little man might find the wherewithal to try to attack him, but it still seemed wise to move his primary body out of range.

He could still see, hear and feel through Raphael's body, of course, even with his partially-uploaded consciousness spread across six different organic brains, five of them not human. But he was still learning how to give his full attention to all viewpoints equally. Baby steps were best.

Then came a thudding sound, and a huff of breath. A dark, furred shape stepped out from amidst the trees, leaning forward on heavy black knuckles as it made its ponderous way across the car park towards them. David—

—stood in the gorilla's body, a great black-furred beast, feeling as if he could shred the little cars around him like confetti. Then he—

—ran on all fours between the trees, this time coming from a different direction, air sucking in and out of lungs like giant bellows—

—jumped on top of a car, feeling the paper-thin metal buckle beneath him, and let out a roar that reached back across long aeons of time to a more primal age. Teeth bared, he reached up with fingers designed to grip branches and—

—drew Raphael's skin deeper into the shadows.

David saw Finch gaping around him in horror through six sets of eyes.

"What do you think, Zachary?" David asked, briefly allowing his consciousness to find its focus back in his son's skin. "We talked about delaying the experiment until we were sure it would work, but I just couldn't wait any longer. You're a scientist. I figured you'd understand."

Finch's face was so laden with terror it was almost comical. "David," he said, choosing his words with unnatural calmness, "what are you doing?"

"Evolving," David replied.

Then at last he sent the other bodies rushing towards Finch

with such speed that the man didn't even have time to scream. Killing him felt like snuffing out a match or tearing a sheet of paper. The power in his borrowed muscles was phenomenal.

Raphael's body staggered slightly. The rush of sensory information became almost overwhelming.

Easy, David thought to himself. *Don't rush it.*

He had all the time in the world to learn how to control six bodies, then ten, then a hundred...and then who knew how many? Centuries, perhaps millennia lay ahead of him.

And perhaps even longer. Perhaps—

He stiffened, seeing through the eyes of one gorilla that he —they—were being watched.

The animal's night vision was far better than Raphael's merely human eyes, and so he could discern a lone figure half-hidden behind a tree in the direction of the park gates, a drawn gun held in one hand.

Then he realized who it was: Ray Thomas.

CHAPTER
TWENTY-SIX

RAY

Ray was a long, long way from being entirely sure what he'd just witnessed.

He'd followed at a distance as Finch drove through the gates of some kind of wildlife zoo or nature preserve. Unable to get the gates to open for him, Ray had no choice but to park outside and climb over the railings before proceeding on foot.

First, however, he'd retrieved a sawn-off shotgun from the duffel bag he'd brought with him from home. Somehow, this didn't feel like a situation he wanted to go into without a little insurance.

To his surprise, Raphael—or, if Amy Cotter was right, David Markov in Raphael's body—was already there, presumably waiting for Finch's arrival.

Before Ray could step forward and confront both men, something huge and black-furred dropped from a high wall on one side of the car park, near to where Ray himself crouched. His consternation only grew when he saw it was a gorilla, moving towards the two other men with clear purpose.

Within seconds, yet more of the beasts had appeared and joined the first, surrounding the two men. Ray had considered abandoning his mission and getting the hell out of there, but instead he remained where he was, as fascinated by what he was seeing as he was terrified.

What happened next defied rationality.

The beasts had moved towards Finch while David Markov, in his son's skin, stepped back into the shadows. Within moments the gorillas threw themselves on top of Finch, and he disappeared beneath their black-furred limbs.

Ray held his sawn-off shotgun close by his side, thinking maybe bringing it along was one of his smarter ideas. David Markov, meanwhile, had continued to watch as Finch was torn apart from just a few feet away, so close the animals must surely have been aware he was standing there...

In an instant, Ray's memory flashed back to the café across from the Peartree Institute, and the men and women sitting silently around their tables like human-shaped cells in some vast collective organism.

With a shock, Ray saw that David Markov was now looking directly over at him. Immediately, one of the gorillas came thudding across the car park towards him, the rest turning to follow in its wake.

Ray turned on his heel and fled back the way he'd come, all his plans scattered to the wind. Even if he managed to kill one of the beasts with the sawn-off shotgun, he had a feeling it wouldn't be enough to stop all of them before they had a chance to kill him too.

It wasn't enough. He'd hardly run more than a few metres before one of the gorillas landed next to him and, with a savage roar, batted him against the side of an oak tree.

Ray landed, sprawling, on the grass, white-hot pain flaring in one shoulder. His sawn-off shotgun went spinning into the darkness, lost amidst the tall grass.

The gorilla raised itself to its full height over him, ready to bring both of its enormous fists crashing down on top of his skull.

In that same moment, gunshots echoed through the night, one after the other in rapid succession. The gorilla standing over Ray staggered back, red blooming on one shoulder, and it turned and loped unsteadily off into the darkness.

A second gorilla came rushing towards Ray where he still lay sprawled, but a series of further shots sent it into retreat.

Soon enough, all the gorillas appeared to have fled into the night. Struggling upright, Ray saw someone new come hurrying towards him from out of the gloom: someone human. A well-dressed man with light-brown skin he'd never seen—

Wait. Ray felt a sudden moment of recognition. He'd seen this same man earlier that morning at Finch's clinic. The newcomer held a gun in each hand and, judging from his bug-eyed expression, he'd seen just as much as Ray had. The way he was dressed made him think of a college professor.

"We need to get out of here before they come back," the stranger rasped, pocketing one of his guns before grabbing Ray by the shoulder and helping him stand. "Can you run?"

"I think so," Ray gasped.

The stranger nodded and together they ran towards the main gates. Ray kept up as best he could, glancing back just long enough to catch sight of Markov still staring after them both from across the car park. Finch's body lay, crumpled and torn, at his feet.

Something huffed loudly in the darkness and leaves rustled in the branches above them.

"They're in the trees," Ray shouted, picking up his pace.

"I can see one," said the stranger, coming to a halt and aiming upwards with his gun.

Ray thought of the way Markov had stood as if in a trance, watching as the animals worked together to rip Finch apart…

"Don't shoot the gorillas," Ray shouted, gesturing wildly towards Markov. "Shoot him, for Christ's sake! Shoot *him*!"

At first the stranger stared at Ray with apparent bafflement, then something like understanding dawned on his face. He took the second pistol back out and turned towards Markov, both guns blazing as he fired at him.

They were too far away from Markov for there to be much chance of hitting him. Even so, it got the reaction Ray had been hoping for: Markov stumbled backwards and into the shadows, seeking refuge.

A gorilla dropped out of a tree and almost directly on top of Ray's rescuer, flattening him. The man shrieked as the beast's jaws gaped wide, revealing incisors that looked like they could chew rocks.

As quickly as it had begun its assault, however, the gorilla came to a sudden halt, sniffing the air and looking around as if in confusion. It moved away from the man it had attacked, as if it had forgotten both him and Ray.

Markov, meanwhile, had vanished into the late-night gloom. Ray darted a look towards another of the gorillas, seeing it, too, staring around itself in evident confusion.

The stranger, meanwhile, scrambled back upright, his jacket rumpled and filthy. "Let's get the hell away from here before they change their minds," he said, his voice stiff with pain.

He shoved both guns into the pockets of his jacket and took a single, stumbling step towards the gates before coming to a halt. "Shit. I think I hurt my ankle."

"Get your arm around my shoulder," said Ray, casting a nervous glance towards the nearest of the gorillas.

The stranger nodded stiffly and did as Ray asked. "I saw your car outside the gates," the stranger said. "We'll take mine."

"Why?"

"Because it's faster than your shitty little hire, that's why. And the faster we can get away from here, the better."

Ray nodded. "Fair point."

Together, they limped back over to the gates. The railings weren't high, and Ray had had little trouble scrambling over them earlier that evening. This time, however, he had to ignore a deep ache in his chest long enough to help his rescuer pull himself up and over the railings despite his injured ankle.

Ray followed quickly, pulling himself over the railing and dropping onto the grassy verge on the other side. He saw a large and powerful-looking Audi parked next to his hire. The stranger stumbled awkwardly over to it and yanked its door open.

The stranger turned to look past Ray's shoulder. "Get the fuck in," he said, his eyes growing wide. "They're coming back."

Ray glanced back through the railings and saw one of the gorillas moving towards them with considerably more purpose than it had been showing only moments before. Clearly, Markov had recovered from the shock of getting shot at, and was once again intent on doing to them what he'd already done to Finch.

He threw himself inside the Audi. The stranger was already behind the wheel. As soon as Ray closed the door, gravel spat beneath the wheels, the car fishtailing as it accelerated under manual control.

Something huge dropped onto the roof of the Audi, almost collapsing it on top of their heads. The well-dressed stranger let out a startled yell, twisting the wheel hard enough that the gorilla lost its grip and went thudding onto the road behind them.

"Faster!" Ray screamed.

"What the fuck do you think I'm doing, mate?" The stranger held the wheel in a white-knuckled grip, his teeth bared. Ray glanced back and caught sight of several more gorillas attempting to give chase, but they soon slipped out of sight beneath the darkened sky.

The sound of the two men's breathing filled the confined space of the car. Ray's skin felt cold and drenched with sweat.

"How bad are you hurt?" the stranger asked.

"Not bad enough that I need to go to a hospital, but my ribs hurt like a son of a bitch. You?"

"Apart from a twisted ankle?" He chuckled. "Figure I got off lucky." He took his eyes off the road long enough to glance sideways at Ray. "I saw one of those things pick you up and bounce you off a tree like a football. I'm amazed you got back up at all."

You and me both, thought Ray.

They drove in silence for a while. "Ray Thomas," he said eventually.

"Elijah," the other man replied.

Elijah? Ray stared sideways at the other man. It couldn't possibly be the same man he'd talked about with DCI Edwards, could it? Elijah Waits?

Maybe, maybe not, he mused; there weren't that many men with that name, to be certain.

"How much of all that did you see?" Ray asked him.

"Enough to make me wonder if I hallucinated the whole thing," said Elijah. He let out a long, shuddering sigh and nodded at a road sign that flashed by in the darkness, advertising a garage and all-night café. "I don't know about you, but I really need something to eat." He glanced at Ray. "You?"

"I could do with a couple of whiskeys more than food, but I'm game." He nodded ahead. "But we'd better do something about that ankle of yours first."

CHAPTER TWENTY-SEVEN

RAY

Rather than try to work the pedals with a bad ankle, Elijah switched from manual back to self-drive mode. Before too long they pulled in at another garage which had an automated café on one side and a 24-hour supermarket on the other.

Figuring there was at least a chance the supermarket sold first aid supplies, Ray went to take a look while Elijah waited in the car.

From the way the single shop assistant on duty behind the counter of the supermarket looked at him when he walked in, Ray guessed he must look pretty banged up. He found a compression bandage and a large bottle of Ibuprofen and figured it'd do.

On his way back, Ray stopped in the toilet and winced when he saw himself in the mirror above the sink. His face was as bruised as a cage fighter's, and when he pulled his T-shirt up to inspect the damage he saw several livid red and yellow bruises dotted all across his chest. Twisting the bottle of painkillers open, he dry-swallowed a couple of pills.

He thought about Elijah. If he and Waits really were one

and the same, he looked nothing like the man he remembered. And, as far as he knew, Waits was still in jail.

Which meant if this somehow *was* the same man, then he was using a proxy.

————

WHEN HE GOT BACK to the car, Ray aided Elijah in getting his shoe off, then helped him get the compression bandage around his ankle before handing him the bottle of painkillers.

Ray nodded through the windscreen at the café once they were done. His appetite had, by now, entirely reasserted itself.

"Wait here," he said, "and I'll get us something to eat."

"Like fuck." Elijah manoeuvred himself out of the car and upright, balancing carefully. "I'll walk."

"You need to avoid putting pressure on that ankle," Ray warned him.

"I'm not an invalid," said Elijah. "I'll sit at a damn table if I'm going to eat."

Even so, Elijah didn't complain when Ray helped him to get inside the café. They collapsed into opposite sides of a booth and tapped their orders into a smart-paper menu.

They fell into a mutual, exhausted silence that lasted until their meals arrived, delivered by a robot that looked like an upside-down bucket on wheels. While Ray picked at his egg and chips, Elijah wolfed down a burger developed, according to a card wedged into the condiment holder, from mammoth DNA.

"Have we met before?" Ray asked once Elijah finally sat back.

Elijah met his gaze briefly, then looked out the window. "And if I said we hadn't?"

"You'd be bullshitting me if you did." Ray picked up a

chip and pointed it at Elijah. "You're Elijah Waits. You're proxying with someone."

That got him a hard stare. But after a beat Elijah's expression softened and he picked up his coffee. "And fuck you too," he muttered.

Ray couldn't hide his satisfaction, which got him a sour look from the man across the table from him.

"I remember you too," said Elijah. "A bent ex-copper who got kicked out of the force. I figure that puts us about even, don't you?" He sipped his coffee and regarded Ray from beneath hooded eyelids. "How about you tell me what you were doing, following Finch?"

"I might ask you the same," said Ray. "Did you know what was going to happen back there?"

"With the gorillas and all that shit?" Elijah snorted a laugh. "Christ, no."

"Are you in prison right now, Elijah?"

Elijah stared back at him with a defiant expression, his lip curled.

"Listen," said Ray, "you saved my life back there. So I'm not going to turn you in, if that's what you're wondering. And while we're at it, I might not be a policeman any more, but I'm not fucking bent." He looked thoughtful for a moment. "I saw you hanging around the Abbey Rush Centre this morning, so it must be hopscotch you're using to proxy out of jail. Correct?"

Elijah inclined his head a fraction of a degree.

"One way or the other," Ray continued, "you'll be back inside in a few days. So while we're here, let's just agree to talk candidly and nothing either of us says goes beyond this table. Agreed?"

Elijah pursed his lips. "Fine."

But even as Ray set out the conditions of their conversation, a wall-mounted television visible behind Elijah's shoulder drew his attention. It showed a photograph of a much younger Amy Cotter in an evening gown. It looked like it had been taken at some red-carpet event from years before. A younger-looking Raphael Markov stood by her side. A news ticker beneath the still image announced her death by suicide.

Elijah glanced over his shoulder at the screen, then looked back at Ray with a frown. "Who is she?"

"Amy Cotter," said Ray, his hunger replaced by a trickle of ice water down his spine. "She's Raphael Markov's ex-wife. And I'm pretty sure she didn't die of suicide."

———

SOMEHOW, this development seemed to ease the tension between them. They talked long into the night, and Ray told Elijah about how he'd come to be thrown out of the force, and of how he'd been expertly framed.

Elijah, in turn, spoke of his increasing conviction that Finch was responsible not only for an attempt on his life, but of framing him for his friend's murder.

All of which was yet more evidence that Finch, hopscotch and the Markov family were all intimately linked.

Ray felt little hesitation in telling Elijah everything he knew, since he needed whatever information the proxy dealer could provide him with in return. Plus, Elijah was street-smart enough to be able to tell if Ray was holding anything back.

And the fact was, Ray badly needed an ally. It wasn't long before he got to the part about Amy's frantic phone call, and then he showed Elijah the video she had sent.

Elijah's brows furrowed in confusion as the video ended. "It doesn't make sense. If Raphael is really David Markov proxying in his son's body, how would that even work if Raphael's father's been in a coma all these years?"

"Maybe he wasn't in a coma," said Ray. "We only have his

family's word that his mind was affected. And by family, I mean the man we thought was his son." He thought for a moment. "Let's say for argument's sake it's only his body that's affected, while his mind remains perfectly functional. In that case, he's locked inside his own skull with no way to communicate with the outside world. Except," he added, "through proxy."

Elijah grimaced. "Jesus."

"Let's go back over what we know so far," said Ray, stirring some milk into his tea. "Raphael and David Markov had access to proxy years before anyone else knew it existed. Which means it must have been created by Telop industries."

Elijah nodded. "And David Markov had the first of his strokes just before Raphael and this Cotter woman got divorced?"

"Precisely. So based on what Amy saw in that video I just showed you, here's what I think might have happened. Either someone persuaded Raphael Markov to proxy with his father after he was incapacitated, or he was forced into it. As far as the first option goes, there's precedent. People rendered unable to speak or otherwise communicate are allowed to use proxy to speak with family members or to make or agree to financial or legal arrangements. And Telop are one of the biggest research and development companies around." He shrugged. "It might even have been Raphael's idea, if he needed to smooth the transition of control from father to son."

"And then what?" said Elijah. "Markov Senior just decided to stay permanently in his son's body?" He shook his head. "Either way, he had to have had help of some kind. Even if it was just someone to, I dunno, club Raphael over the head and shoot a bead into him."

"My guess is Finch was David Markov's accomplice in all of this," said Ray. "It might explain why he killed Finch back there, because he was afraid he might talk under pressure. Which he would have."

Elijah massaged his brow and stared past Ray's shoulder. "David Markov would have had to renew the proxy link with his son around the clock. Up to half a dozen times a day, I figure, in case Raphael regained control of his body and escaped the old fuck." His eyes grew round and he looked back at Ray. "Or he would have, until hopscotch came along. Then he'd only have to do it maybe once a week, to be sure."

"You're saying that's why hopscotch was invented?" Ray asked. "So David Markov could proxy with his son for longer stretches?"

"I don't know," said Elijah, his gaze again becoming distant. "Maybe. Or maybe so he could do what he did back there with those animals. Or maybe one or the other was just an unexpected side-benefit. Only way to know is to ask him." His gaze flicked back to Ray. "How do you think all this ties in with what you told me happened at that hospital? The Peartree?"

"You remember I told you about Isaac Sizemore?"

Elijah nodded.

"He worked for the Markov's," Ray continued. "Snatched Stacy Cotter, Amy Cotter's daughter, right out from under Raphael Markov's nose."

"You mean David Markov," Elijah corrected him.

Ray made a dismissive gesture. "You know what I mean. I don't know exactly how this all fits together, but they're all pieces of the same puzzle."

Elijah looked doubtful for some reason.

There's one thing doesn't make sense to me," he said.

"Go on," said Ray.

"You remember that thing," said Elijah, "from when you were a kid? When you try to pat your head and rub your tummy at the same time?" He raised one hand over his head, placing the other over his proxy's belly.

Ray stared at him. "What are you talking about?"

"I mean," said Elijah, "it's hard to do, especially for very long. Because they're two independent actions, right? And it's almost impossible to coordinate both actions effectively, because you have to think about either one, or the other."

He brought his hands back down. "While your attention is on one, you see, you lose coordination with the second."

Ray nodded. "Okay."

"Well," Elijah continued, "if that's hard to do just with your own two hands, how hard can it be for one man to control a bunch of fucking monkeys all at once, so that each of them is carrying out independent actions while they're all supposedly under his direct control?" He tapped one finger on the table. "That's the thing about proxy, isn't it? Even if you could control both your own body and someone else's at once while proxying with them, one of those bodies would just be standing around doing nothing most of the time because you can only focus your attention on one point of view at a time." He shook his head. "The human mind isn't designed to process information in parallel that way."

"Okay," Ray said thoughtfully. "I see what you mean. It should be impossible."

"And those people at the Peartree Institute, the way you describe it, they were all coordinated with each other too, weren't they?" Elijah continued. "The same way those monkeys were." He shook his head. "I don't see how any one human being could control all those people."

He had a point, Ray could see. "Look," he said, draining his mug, "we could debate this until the cows come home, but right now we need to focus on what we *do* know."

Ray rubbed his hands over his unshaven cheeks before continuing. "Right now, my priority is finding Stacy Cotter. Either her or Sizemore, although I have a feeling they're together somewhere. If I can talk to them, I know I can figure out the rest."

"They could be anywhere," Elijah pointed out.

"That reminds me," said Ray, tapping at his bracelet and studying something on its screen.

After a moment the bracelet chimed. "Eunice?" Ray said into it. "Any more updates on what we were talking about earlier?"

A woman's voice with a strong East End accent emerged from the bracelet. "Sending everything through to you now," the person on the other end of the line said. "Check your messages."

"Thanks Eunice," said Ray, tapping again at his bracelet. Elijah could see he was reading something from its screen, a grin slowly spreading across the ex-cop's face.

"Good news?" Elijah asked.

"Like I said, Isaac Sizemore either planned or was involved in the plan to break Stacy Cotter out of the Peartree. And he went to extraordinary lengths to cover his tracks." He allowed himself a small smile. "But there's no such thing as a truly watertight plan."

Elijah lifted his eyebrows. "He cocked up?"

"Turns out," Ray explained, "that one of the vehicles Sizemore and Cotter used to get away was registered to the address of property owned by Telop. No other vehicle there had any kind of link whatsoever to that company." He looked at Elijah with a triumphant expression. "And if you map the routes taken by all the vehicles I've been able to trace, they're like an arrow pointing towards that address, in the North of England."

Elijah nodded. "So you think if we go to that address, we'll find them?"

"It's the only remaining lead I have," said Ray, "apart from the journalist I mentioned. And I'm near as certain he knows a lot less about all this than either of us."

Elijah looked doubtful. "Why would they hide out in

some place that belongs to the very people who mean them harm?"

"Maybe they're hiding in plain sight," said Ray. "Maybe it was the best out of a bunch of not very good options. But unless you can think of something better, I figure that's our next stop."

Elijah gave him a look. "'Our'?"

Ray stood, grinning down at the proxy dealer. "You want to sort this out, don't you? Otherwise, why go to all the trouble of proxying out of a jail cell?"

"Fine," said Elijah. "So where exactly is it we're going?"

"The Kielder Forest," said Ray. "It's up north, like I said. Just a hair's breadth south of the Scottish border." He gave Elijah a speculative look. "How many more days do you have left in that skin?"

"Couple of days, I figure."

Ray glanced out the window at the night sky. "It's a six- or seven-hour drive, but if we start now, we can sleep in your car if need be and be there by morning."

CHAPTER
TWENTY-EIGHT

STACY

The morning after Isaac had brought her to the ancient and crumbling mansion in the north of England, and while Zero was preparing something for them all to eat, Stacy took herself for a walk in the surrounding woods.

She took it slowly at first, her chest still hurting through the numbing haze of painkillers she had been supplied with. She had been given several injections as well, that made it easier to move her injured arm. She wasn't entirely mended, but she was on the way.

She'd got little more than a hundred metres from the house before she saw a middle-aged man wearing a Barbour jacket and a flat cap moving through the trees ahead of her. He had a broken-open shotgun cradled over one elbow, and although he hadn't yet seen her, he looked this way and that, as if searching for something in the surrounding woods.

At first Stacy froze in indecision. Was this Zero, or someone else? Or if this was in fact a local and not a proxy, and he saw her and asked what she was doing there...what should she say?

She took a step back and heard a twig snap under her

heel. The sound resonated through the surrounding trees like a gunshot.

The man in the Barbour jacket turned to see her. He lifted a hand in greeting, coming closer. She saw that he walked a little unsteadily, and he looked, she thought, too thin to be healthy.

"You should get back inside," he said in a Scottish accent. He nodded to the house behind her. "Your father will wonder where you are."

Stacy felt relief flood through her. "For a second there I thought…" She finished with a shrug.

The man—yet another of Zero's many proxies, as she now understood him to be—shook his head. "There's no one around for miles that isn't under my control, Miss Cotter. But you shouldn't stray too far from the house."

Stacy nodded and turned back. It was one thing to accept that the person helping Isaac and her wasn't really a person at all—that he was, instead, some kind of machine Isaac had helped build—but part of her still struggled to accept that the many proxies she'd encountered since escaping the hospital were collectively and simultaneously under that same machine's control.

Even so, she'd become almost used to seeing complete strangers in or around the house, every last one of them identifying him or herself as Zero. They came and went at all times of the night and day, in cars and vans or on motorbikes and even on foot.

It was amazing how something so utterly eerie could so quickly become almost commonplace. And yet, some of them looked like they could barely stand.

Back inside the house, she went through to the kitchen. There, she found Isaac in conversation with Zero who, on this occasion, spoke through the mouth of a distinguished-looking Indian gentleman in his fifties or sixties. He had a whisper-thin moustache on his upper lip and wore a dark blue blazer.

They sat across the kitchen table from each other, deep in discussion regarding some arcane technical aspect of computer technology.

Stacy took the time to study the proxy more closely. His slacks were worn-looking, and some of his teeth were yellowed and broken. A moment's further study revealed that one of his eyes was glass. He had the overall look of a man trying to keep up appearances despite desperately reduced circumstances.

She remembered what Zero had said when they first arrived at this house in the middle of nowhere. The proxies all came from local villages, all long-term unemployed, all users of hopscotch proxy—which in her experience meant they were desperate enough to contract with dark-net proxy agencies.

They might be used as drug mules, or for prostitution, or wind up maimed or dead on the whim of anonymous proxy partners who might be anywhere in the world and completely untraceable.

Nobody did what these people were doing unless they were really, truly desperate.

"I think you should know," said Zero, looking over at her, "that we're working on a plan to get you and your father back out of the country."

She nodded and let out a sigh. "When?"

"Not immediately," said Isaac. "It might take a few days to organise things to be sure we'll be safe. We're considering renting a boat." He peered at her. "Is there something wrong?"

"Nothing," she said, forcing a smile.

———

A FEW EVENINGS LATER, one of Zero's proxies entered the house carrying a smart-paper TV rolled up in a tube. Unrolling it, he hung the screen from a wall in the kitchen.

Such screens, Zero had explained through one of his seemingly infinite supply of rented proxy partners, had the advantage of being effectively untraceable.

As Zero spoke, Stacy recalled that upon arriving at the house, the machine had made a point of collecting her and Isaac's bracelets. Nor did any of the proxies she saw wear a bracelet or carry even so much as a chip-phone that she could see.

Stacy learned of her mother's passing while watching the television over a bowl of porridge early the next morning. Supposedly, she had drowned herself in a lake on the grounds of the Markov estate and the police were treating it as suicide. She had left a suicide note, saying she was sorry for the hurt she'd caused.

Stacy's appetite fled, replaced by a wave of nausea, loss and regret. Amy wouldn't have willingly gone within a hundred miles of the Markov mansion, let alone kill herself and write such an awful, tawdry note.

She thought of how she herself had nearly been murdered and knew, immediately, what must have happened to her mother.

Stacy sat and stared at the television, wondering why the image had become so blurry before realizing she was half-blinded by her own tears.

"I should have told her," she said to herself in a half-whisper.

"Stacy?"

She looked around to see another of Zero's proxies standing by the open door of the kitchen, a cardboard box full of supplies held in its arms. The skin was a straight-backed man in his forties who looked like the type who spent his weekends playing rugby. He was healthier-looking by far than most of the other proxies she'd seen. She wondered what had happened to him that he'd suddenly needed money badly.

She nodded at the television. "Did you know about this?"

"I did," Zero admitted. "They reported it in the very early hours of this morning. Isaac is also aware of what happened to your mother."

"You should have woken me," she said, feeling a sudden rush of anger.

"I'm sorry," said the proxy. "I was concerned with the level of stress you've already had to endure. I thought you might handle the news better if you had first slept well."

Rage rose within her like a blood tide and she fought it back down. Getting angry at Zero made as much sense as getting angry at a toaster. Whatever else it could do, Zero was still at heart a machine.

"Do you have any idea what happened?" Stacy asked, forcing herself to speak levelly.

"Beyond the facts as they're being presented in the media, no." The proxy placed the cardboard box on a kitchen counter and began removing cans of soup and stacking them. "But there's a great deal more going on than meets the eye." Turning towards her with the now-empty cardboard box in one hand, Zero regarded her for a moment. "If you don't mind me asking, what did you mean by what you were saying just as I walked in?"

"You're right," she said. "I do mind you asking."

"Of course." The proxy nodded to her, then stepped towards the door.

"Wait."

The proxy stopped but didn't turn around.

"I meant I should have told my mother I was coming home, and why. Maybe if I had…"

Her words trailed off.

"You're wondering whether she might still be alive if you'd told her of your and Isaac's plans," said the proxy.

A machine, she reminded herself. *Just a machine.* Yet it seemed able to intuit her thoughts as well as any living person.

"Isn't it true?" she asked.

The machine-controlled proxy turned to look at her. "Isaac warned you himself that involving your mother in your plans made the risk to her all the greater. It was better to avoid contact until after you and Isaac had spoken with Martin Wilber."

"Then what was she doing there?" she asked, almost pleading. "Why was she in the Markov's fucking *house*?"

The proxy hesitated. "Your mother didn't lack for motivation to visit Raphael at his home," he said at last. "Especially since she would have already been deeply concerned over your brush with death, and Raphael's sudden and seemingly inexplicable concern for your well-being. As to the exact circumstances leading to your mother's death, I lack sufficient data to come to a clear—"

Something moved inside Stacy, something that brought her up onto her feet and out of the kitchen before the proxy had finished speaking.

She found herself outside, finding her way back into the woods while the light of dawn was still creeping over the horizon.

She stopped when she was too exhausted to continue any further, pain welling up inside her chest. She bent over with her hands on her knees, but the grief didn't come. Instead, there was an emptiness, a void where her mother had been.

After a while she heard someone approaching through the darkness and felt a hand touch her gently on one shoulder. She let the unseen figure guide her back to the house.

———

EARLY THE NEXT morning Stacy woke in her sleeping bag on the floor of an upstairs room to find her father leaning over her, one hand on her shoulder. He was already dressed, a look of worry etched deep into the lines of his face.

"A car is approaching," he said when she sat up, blinking sleep away. "We don't know who it is. You should be ready to move, just in case."

He stood and left the room. Stacy stumbled out of her sleeping bag and pulled some clothes on. She could hear a murmur of voices from the ground floor.

Another of Zero's proxies entered the room before she had finished dressing. This one was a woman in her late twenties with hair gelled into spikes. She wore torn jeans and a T-shirt for some long-ago festival.

"It's probably nothing," said the proxy as Stacy pulled on her boots. "It could be someone lost in the woods, but it's best to be careful. If you follow me, I can take you to a secure location not far from here."

"No," said Stacy, lacing her boots up. "I'm staying right here."

"We're only thinking of your safety," the proxy insisted.

"What about Isaac?" Stacy demanded, rounding on the proxy. "I can hear him downstairs, Zero. Why haven't you spirited him away?"

The proxy hesitated in a very un-Zero-like way. "I must respect your wishes, but there's little for you to do here, anyway. It would be better if—"

"No," Stacy repeated firmly. "Is it just one person? Or a lot of them?"

"Two men."

Just two? Stacy felt herself relax a little. "And you think Raphael sent them?"

"We have no idea. But it's possible."

Stacy stepped towards the door and looked down the stairs, listening. "You have weapons, don't you? Guns? I saw that some of your other proxy bodies were armed. I want something too, so I can defend mys—"

In that same moment she heard the unmistakable sound of a car driving over mud and wet leaves, accompanied by the faint whine of batteries. She hurried back across the room to a window that overlooked the gravelled driveway, the female proxy following close behind.

Looking down, Stacy saw a big and expensive-looking car pull up outside the front of the derelict house. Two dark-skinned men got out, scanning the woods and the house with wary expressions. One looked like a college professor, but his eyes were full of watchful intelligence and his clothes were muddy and torn. The other wore jeans and a leather jacket and had a lithe, dangerous look about him.

A memory tickled the back of Stacy's mind. Suddenly she felt sure she'd seen the second man before. But where?

She noticed then that his companion, the better-dressed one, held a handgun close against one hip. She shrank back from the window, afraid of what he might do were he to look up and see her there.

Maybe it would be better to hide, she thought to herself, her heart fluttering in her chest like a trapped bird.

"I don't think they're from Raphael," the female proxy said at last. She stood to one side of the window, peering down at the car and its occupants.

A number of Zero's other proxies stepped out onto the driveway, including the one wearing a Barbour jacket. He held his rifle loose but ready in both hands.

The two newcomers took a step back towards their car. The professorial one leaned towards his companion and said something inaudible without once taking his eyes off the proxies now standing in a line between them and the house.

The one whom Stacy was increasingly sure she knew from somewhere put up a hand. "We're not here to cause trouble," he said, addressing the proxies. "We're looking for someone who needs our help."

"Looking for who?" replied one of the proxies, an Asian man with scraggly long hair streaked with white.

"Her name's Stacy Cotter," said the man. He darted a look at his companion, then back again. "We're also trying to locate a man by the name of Isaac Sizemore."

The Asian proxy shook his head slowly. "There's nobody by those names here."

"I meant what I said," the man insisted. "We're not looking for trouble. We want to help."

As he spoke, he glanced up at the window where Stacy stood. She automatically took a step back into the shadows.

"Stacy!"

Her body felt like it had turned to ice. He'd seen her.

"Stacy!" he shouted again. "Raphael killed your mother and he's going to try to kill you too. You need protection—both you and Isaac. We can help."

"If you want someone to speak to," Stacy heard a more familiar voice say, "you can speak to me."

Isaac.

Stacy moved back to the window in time to see her father step out of the front of the house and towards the two men. He came to a halt between two of the proxies.

"You're Isaac Sizemore, right?" said the familiar-looking newcomer. "I was at the Peartree the day you snatched Stacy."

"Why do you think I or anyone else needs your help?" Isaac asked him.

"My name's Ray Thomas. Amy Cotter hired me to find your daughter." He nodded at his companion. "This is Elijah. He's…helping me."

Ray Thomas. Suddenly Stacy knew why he had seemed so familiar. He was the same policeman who'd arrested her years before.

But if he had been working for Amy...then maybe he knew what had really happened to her.

Stacy turned and hurried towards the door. The proxy standing by the window reached out to try to stop her, but she tore herself free of the woman's grasp and ran downstairs, taking the steps as fast as she could, ignoring the pain in her ribs and the twinges in her still-plastered arm.

They all turned to look at her as she came running out of the front of the derelict house. "You're looking for me, right?" she asked breathlessly.

"Stacy," said Thomas. He glanced uncertainly at her father, then back. "Are you all right?"

"I'm fine," she said. "You don't need that gun," she added, nodding to the one named Elijah. "I'm here because I want to be."

A light rain began to fall. "Seems to me," said Thomas, glancing up at the sky, "we've got a few things to talk about. How about we do it inside?"

———

ISAAC LED the two men into the kitchen, which was easily large enough to accommodate a dozen people. Most of the windows were still boarded-up: the only light came from a portable lamp set on a shelf.

Several of Zero's proxies followed them inside. Stacy took a seat at the kitchen table along with Isaac and the two newcomers, noting the way Thomas winced as he sat. The one called Elijah walked with a limp.

"What happened to the two of you?" she asked, looking between them. "Were you in an accident?"

"Let's call it that," said Thomas.

One of the proxies put on the kettle while another, an elderly woman who looked like she should be running a community library somewhere, lifted three mismatched mugs and a box of tea-bags out of one of several shopping bags sitting on the counter.

Isaac studied the two men with interest. "If you don't mind," he asked, "how did you find us?"

"With difficulty," Thomas replied. He cast a wary eye at the proxies. "These people…"

"You're quite safe to speak around them," Isaac reassured him.

"Who are they?"

"Proxies," Isaac replied.

"Controlled by who?"

"That," said Isaac, "requires a detailed explanation I'll be happy to give you if you can answer my questions to my fullest satisfaction."

So they talked.

Thomas took the news about Zero being some kind of machine with what struck Stacy as surprising equanimity. He'd also apparently visited her at the Peartree, but she had no memory of that.

Food arrived, the proxies coming and going from the kitchen like silent, shuffling ghosts, opening cans and plugging portable stoves into batteries as the day moved towards evening. There were never more than a half-dozen of them in or around the house at any one time, but Elijah kept a watchful eye on every one of them.

"You've been quiet, Stacy," said Thomas. "What's your story?"

Stacy looked up from her now-empty mug. "My story?"

"Who decided to talk to a journalist—you or your father?"

Stacy shot an anxious look at Isaac. He gave her an encouraging nod.

"I'd had a suspicion for a long while that Raphael wasn't my real father, and when I asked my mum about it, she was more than a little evasive. So when she came to visit me in Paris last year, I…" Stacy let out a rush of air. "I stole her email password. I found messages she'd exchanged with Isaac, written long before I was born. I learned how she and Raphael had become completely estranged from each other. Once I put a few clues together, it wasn't too hard to work out who my real father was."

Thomas nodded. "So you got in touch with him first?"

"I can't say I'm proud of taking advantage of my mother the way I did," said Stacy, "but I had to know."

"Your mother told me she thought Isaac had died a long time ago," said Thomas.

"I didn't know that," said Stacy. "I wrote to the same email address Isaac used back them, explaining who I was and that I thought he might be my father. A couple of weeks later, he wrote back."

Ray shifted his attention back to Isaac. "Amy told me she'd thought of leaving Raphael for you and taking Stacy with her, but she thought Raphael had had you killed. Why didn't you tell Amy you were alive? Or try and stay in touch with her?"

Stacy looked over at her father and saw deep, furrowed lines form across his brow. "Stacy asked me the same question. Before I made the decision to disappear, I got into an argument with David Markov. He threatened me. Or perhaps it's more accurate to say, he threatened Amy."

Thomas looked surprised. "So he knew about your affair with Amy at that time?"

Isaac shrugged. "Someone had seen us talking when we thought we were alone, figured out the rest and told him. He made it quite clear that if I didn't help Telop develop proxy in the direction he wanted, something bad would happen to her."

"So you faked your death?" asked Elijah.

"Nothing so dramatic," said Isaac. "Simply disappearing was enough. It was to protect Amy as much as anything else —although it was just as important to keep Telop from misusing proxy. I didn't dare get in touch with her and risk either of the Markov's finding out." He let out an elaborate sigh. "If I'd known Amy was pregnant before I left, things might have been very different."

Isaac looked over at Stacy and smiled. "I couldn't have asked for a smarter daughter," he continued. "Or a better detective, tracking me down the way she did. Of course," he added, turning his attention back to Elijah, "I realized if she had written to me, then there was a very good chance Raphael had intercepted the message. We switched to an encrypted messaging service, but even that, it seems, wasn't enough."

Stacy nodded. "Somehow he knew when I was coming to London, and where to find Isaac while he was on his way to meet me. He must have hacked us, somehow."

"What was it you were afraid the Markov's might do with proxy?" asked Elijah.

"My fear wasn't so much to do with proxy specifically," Isaac explained, "as with Zero."

Elijah glanced automatically at the several proxies present in the kitchen with them. "Your...computer, you said."

"Calling Zero a computer is like comparing a Da Vinci to a child's first crude drawing," said Isaac, sounding faintly offended. "He's a fully autonomous AI and smarter than any human being. Telop didn't create proxy, and neither did I—it was all Zero's doing." He shrugged. "Unfortunately, I was naïve not to realize the Markov's would weaponize anything Zero created."

"Then why not shut the machine down?" Elijah looked around the table as if seeking confirmation that this was an obvious solution. "Why not destroy it?"

Isaac stared at him. "For one, Zero is a sentient conscious being. It would be murder. For another, the Markov's would simply have built another and made full use of it without my being able to intervene. I'd have taken Zero with me if I could, but he's the size of a small truck and built into a sub-basement of Telop's headquarters."

Isaac sipped at a mug of tea a proxy had given him. "Before I fled Telop, I created a secure link so he and I could remain in contact and so I could monitor what the Markov's did with him. Through a series of careful interventions, both myself and Zero made sure those few innovations he provided to the Markov's following my departure were small enough not to be dangerous and just worthwhile enough that they wouldn't deactivate him."

"Hang on," said Thomas. "You said Zero created proxy, right? But not hopscotch."

Isaac nodded. "That's correct."

"Then who or what created hopscotch, if not Zero?"

Isaac hesitated a moment. "I don't know. Zero has some theories."

Two of the proxies placed plates of lab-steak with long-beans in front of each of them, then sat at the table with their own meals.

"A few years ago," said one proxy, tapping pepper onto his steak, "Raphael Markov put Doctor Finch in charge of a team developing a new prototype AI based on my architecture. The project soon vanished from the Telop intranet, preventing me from keeping further track of it. That meant either they'd hit a wall and shut the project down, or that it was sufficiently sensitive that Raphael deemed it necessary to keep it secret even from the rest of the company."

Elijah nodded. "So…you think hopscotch came out of that?"

"It's the likeliest explanation," said the proxy.

"I think you need to show them that video," Elijah said to Ray.

Isaac glanced between the two men. "Video?"

Stacy listened with increasing consternation as the ex-policeman summarized his last, brief conversation with her mother. Isaac's knuckles grew white where they gripped his fork, his meal forgotten.

The elderly proxy who'd made tea on their arrival stood and gestured to Thomas's wrist. "May I see your bracelet?"

After a moment's hesitation, the ex-policeman slipped off the bracelet and handed it to the proxy. She carried it over to the smart-paper screen and after a moment, the bracelet chimed to show a connection had been established.

A still frame showing the interior of the Markov mansion appeared on the screen, larger-than-life. Stacy saw a high-ceilinged room with oak floorboards, almost entirely empty, save for a hospital-style bed and a line of cupboards arrayed against one wall. Medical supplies were arranged on a counter set on top of the cupboards. A wire tray held dozens of paper-wrapped proxy applicators.

A great tangle of tubes and glittering circuitry was suspended from the ceiling directly above the bed. Thousands of silvery filaments drooped the rest of the way down from this apparatus. Next to the bed stood a ventilator and other life-saving apparatus.

The video jerked into life, the point of view zooming in on the bed until Stacy saw a tiny, crumpled-looking old man adrift amidst its sheets, an oxygen mask over his mouth and nose. Raphael, his back to the lens, applied an applicator first to his father's neck and then to his own.

There was something wrong with the old man's head. Stacy squinted, at first unsure what she was seeing. Then her stomach flipped, and she swallowed back a sour rush of acid: much of the old man's skull above the hairline had been removed, and much of his brain matter appeared to be missing. The filaments in their thousands reached inside the brain cavity.

"There's a message from Amy as well," said Ray, once the video came to an abrupt end. He took his bracelet back from the elderly proxy. "Here."

Ray played back the last voice message he'd received from Amy.

Stacy put her fork down, her stomach churning as she listened. The video had been bad enough, but whatever sliver of appetite she'd retained had by now fled her entirely.

"Who was that in the bed?" she managed to ask, breaking a silence that had fallen across the kitchen.

"That was David Markov," said Isaac, his voice full of grim finality. He had stood and moved closer to the screen. "Or what's left of him, judging by what I saw. Zero," he asked, turning to the elderly proxy, "what did you make of all that machinery? It looks like it's directly wired into his brain —or what's left of it. An interface of some kind?"

"An interface, yes," said the proxy. "I believe Amy's analysis was correct. It appears David Markov is indeed proxying through his own son's body. But neither, I suspect, is he human any longer."

"Explain yourself," said Isaac, his tone sharp.

"It's clear to me," the proxy replied, "that the apparatus in the video is the likely end result of the secret project Markov and Finch were working on together. Rather than building an artificial intelligence like myself, I now believe that David Markov has been uploading his consciousness piecemeal into a cybernetic substrate modelled after my own."

Stacy stared at the proxy. "Are you saying that machine *is* David Markov?"

"More that the machine is the conduit by which he has uploaded his memories and the structural ontology of his mind to a series of qubit processors designed to mimic the human neural network, but in essence, yes. The process destroys the individual neurones, as is clear from the video, but creates a symbiosis between the organic and machine parts, allowing the consciousness they contain to act as a single and cohesive whole."

"You can't possibly figure all that out just from a few seconds of shaky video," Elijah protested.

"But I can," said Zero, still speaking through the same body. "The machinery we saw just now is clearly derived from the same principles underpinning my own construction."

"Zero isn't human, remember," Isaac warned. "He doesn't make random guesses. Zero," he asked the same proxy, "is the upload process complete, in your opinion?"

"No," the proxy replied, "but I believe it will be soon, perhaps within days, or even hours. The greater part by far of David Markov's intellect by now almost certainly resides within a mainframe. It may even already be too late."

"Too late for what?" Elijah asked.

"You've seen for yourselves that Zero can control an effectively unlimited number of hopscotch-linked bodies," Isaac said. "If David can't yet do the same already, he'll be able to, soon enough. When that happens, he'll be capable of hunting all of us down. All he'd need to do is locate us, then remotely take over anyone linked via hopscotch in our vicinity and use them to try to kill us."

"Jesus," Ray muttered. "The gorillas."

Isaac gave him a piercing stare. "Excuse me?"

"Last night," Ray explained, "we followed Finch. He met with Raphael—well, David—at a wildlife park. A bunch of gorillas appeared out of nowhere, killed Finch and nearly killed me and Elijah. They acted the same way as the proxies at the Peartree did. Most of the time Markov just stood there watching us with a blank expression."

"Then that's it," said Isaac, his voice hollow. He sank slowly back into his chair, staring off into space. "We're too late."

CHAPTER TWENTY-NINE

STACY

"Listen," said Elijah, "I'm only here because I want the answers to some questions. Like, who was trying to kill me, and why, and who Finch was. That's all I really want to know. All of…this," he said, waving one hand towards two proxies at that moment occupied with washing and drying dishes, "is beyond me. So why would David Markov want to kill me or anyone else?"

"To protect himself," Isaac replied, his gaze focused on some far-away point. "Once the transition is complete and he becomes a fully cybernetic organism, he'll be effectively immortal, and the one thing he'll be the most concerned with is ensuring his long-term survival."

Elijah shook his head. "What makes you so sure you know what he'll do or won't do?"

"Our species," Isaac replied mildly, "was born from blood and conflict. We'll carry that inheritance into the future, whether it's as flesh and blood humans or something closer to what David Markov is in the process of becoming—if, as I say, he hasn't already."

Elijah stared at him, then gestured at several of the proxies with his chin. "So shouldn't you be worried about Zero?"

Isaac shook his head. "Zero shares none of our petty human foibles. He wants nothing because he desires nothing." He leaned towards Elijah and tapped the table between them with a finger. "Evolution hasn't given him desires because he didn't evolve, at least not in the way we normally think of such processes." He sat back and shrugged. "There are certainly people in the world deserving of machine immortality. It may even be the future of our species. David Markov, however, is the last man I would wish to have such power."

"The issue here is time," said Zero, speaking through the mouth of a young, scruffily-dressed man at that moment rinsing a plate under the tap. "It's clear by now that he developed hopscotch as a means to place unlimited numbers of human beings under his control for increasingly lengthy periods of time. I have little doubt he's already working on ways to make that link last indefinitely, and that his ultimate aim is to place as many people as possible under his direct control so that he can use them to shape the world as he desires. That way he can ensure his long-term survival, not just for the next hundred years, but for the next thousand."

They were all silent after that.

Elijah shook his head violently and slammed the table with a fist. "This is bullshit!" he shouted. "It's just speculation. You can't know any of this!"

"Super-intelligent AI has been an inevitability for decades," Isaac countered, his own voice growing louder. Stacy heard the conviction in his words. "Zero is proof that there are machines smarter than we are, and with the long-term vision that comes with an indefinite lifespan."

Isaac lifted his shoulders and let them drop again. "The real question is, what kind of AI will that be? Something ultimately benevolent that helps us solve our existing and future problems, or something that takes the worst parts of us and combines it with nearly unlimited power?"

He turned to Stacy. "Your mother lost her life getting this information to us, and we need to make sure her sacrifice means something." He shifted his attention back to Elijah and to Ray, sitting side by side. "All of us here in this room, right now, are the only people in the world with any idea what Markov is planning. Now we have video proof of what he's become, we've become an active threat to his plans. If we don't stop him first, he'll kill all of us, without hesitation, to protect himself."

"He's a billionaire who destroyed all our lives pretty much on a whim," Elijah sneered. "I don't think we've got much chance against someone like that."

"On the contrary," said the proxy at the sink, drying his hands on a towel. "The video Miss Cotter provided makes it evident that the upload process is not yet complete. That makes him vulnerable to attack—but not for much longer. We must act now."

"You and whose army?" snapped Elijah.

The young man through whom Zero was proxying replied with a thin smile. "I would think that was obvious."

Stacy saw Elijah's skin pale as the several other proxies gathered in the kitchen all turned to stare at him in silence.

"Holy shit," Elijah muttered under his breath, slumping lower in his seat.

It struck Stacy then just what Zero and her father were driving at. "What are you talking about?" she demanded of her father. "Launching an assault on him?"

"Anything's better than waiting for him to come and find us," Isaac replied. "Which he will, and soon, if we don't act first." He looked around at the rest of them. "I know the layout of the Markov estate well enough I can get us in there."

"You'd be risking these people's lives," said Ray, gesturing at the proxies.

The elderly proxy who had been there earlier reappeared at the open kitchen door. "This is unfortunately true," she said, "hence I'm taking the step of recruiting proxies with military experience to take their place." She looked at Elijah. "If you're willing, Mr Waits, you and Mr Thomas can help keep an eye on Stacy here while Isaac travels south to confront Markov with my aid."

"No way," said Ray. "I'm going with you." His tone implied he would brook no argument.

Elijah stared at the ex-cop. "You're going along with this bullshit?"

"You wanted answers," said Ray, nodding around the kitchen, "and you got them. What Isaac says makes sense. We know Markov's a cold-blooded killer, and he'll stop at nothing unless we act. He sure as hell knows who I am."

Elijah shook his head. "I didn't come looking for anything like this."

"It would be best if you remained here, Mr Waits," said Zero, "since otherwise your proxy would be at risk of further injury. You'll have my full protection until matters are hopefully resolved for the better."

"I don't understand," said Stacy. "Military proxies?"

"Professional soldiers—mercenaries, really—willing to rent their bodies out to those who can afford it," Isaac explained. His voice carried a hint of disgust. "By which I mean they're paid a very great deal of money."

Stacy gaped at him. She thought she'd heard it all when it came to proxy, but apparently she'd been wrong.

"They come with military-grade hardware and motor reflexes refined over decades of experience," one of the other proxies told her. "If they're seriously injured or crippled, they get enough to live off for the rest of their lives. If they're killed, it's enough for their families to do the same."

Isaac's mouth had twisted up like he'd tasted something sour. "I don't like it either," he told Stacy. "I quite abhor violence of any nature."

"They're necessary for their and our protection—" Zero began.

"I know that, Zero!" Isaac snapped.

The proxy fell silent.

Isaac sucked in a breath, darting his head down as if embarrassed by his sudden outburst. "But the cost of failure is so great," he added more quietly, "I can't see that we have any choice."

Elijah dragged himself upright from his chair, leaning heavily on his good leg. "I'm leaving," he said. "This isn't my body, and I'm no use to you or anyone else with a fucked-up ankle anyway."

He limped around the table and extended a hand to Isaac. "Good luck," he said, grasping the other man's hand. He nodded to Stacy and then to Ray. "And the rest of you."

Stacy watched him hobble out of the kitchen without another word. A few seconds later, Stacy heard the front entrance open and close again.

"Why do I feel like he's abandoning us?" she asked, looking around at the rest of them.

"He got the answers he wanted," said Ray. He turned to Isaac. "I came in his car. Have you got your own transport from here to Markov's estate?"

"I should go with you," said Stacy, before her father could answer. "I'm not sitting around on my arse like some damsel in distress while you ride off to fight the wicked king."

"No," said Isaac, his tone final. "If anything goes wrong, at least one of us has to survive to tell others what happened."

Stacy looked to Ray for help, but he shook his head. "Under any other circumstances," he told her, "I'd be on your side. But you don't have the training or experience for this kind of thing. I do."

"Neither does my father!" Stacy replied, her face growing warm.

"No," Ray agreed, "but like he said, he can get us in and out of there. And he knows better than any of us what we're going to be dealing with once we're there." He nodded to Isaac. "We should get moving."

"Agreed," said Isaac, standing and moving towards the kitchen door.

Stacy felt a churning in her stomach. She didn't want to lose Isaac so soon after finding him, but she knew by now how wilful he could be, how driven.

He wasn't, she could see just from the set of his jaw, going to back down.

Instead of pressing her cause further, she stood as well and embraced her father in a hug, burying her face in his jumper. "Please come back alive."

"I have no intention of doing anything else," he said softly, his breath warm on her skin.

———

RAY

Ray followed Isaac outside and into the cool night air. It had stopped raining, bar a few errant drips falling from the branches of the twisted oaks and pines that surrounded the decaying building. Elijah Waits and the Audi they'd arrived in was gone, although Ray caught a flicker of receding head-lights far off amidst the woods.

"What about weapons for the rest of us?" Ray asked, glancing back at the boarded-up house. For the moment he and the scientist were alone.

"Zero has made his own choice," said Isaac, "but I choose not to indulge in such things."

Past Isaac, Ray noted the silent figure of a proxy standing some distance off amidst the trees surrounding the house and watching them both with a blank expression. He suppressed a shiver.

"You said yourself Markov won't hesitate to kill us," said Ray, turning back to Isaac. "You need to be able to defend yourself."

"No." Isaac's face twisted up in defiance. "I will not stoop to his level."

Christ. "If you want to walk into Markov's estate unarmed, fine," Ray spat. "That doesn't mean I have to do the same." He stepped towards the edge of the drive and cupped his hands over his mouth. "Zero," he called over to the watching proxy, "can you spare any weapons?"

"Of course," said a voice from behind him.

Ray whirled around to see another proxy had appeared at the door of the house. This one was male, with shoulder-length white hair and an affable expression. As Ray watched, the proxy gestured to its counterpart in the woods.

The shadowy figure emerged from the woods to join them on the driveway. Ray saw that the proxy was a boy barely out of his teens, his skinny frame half-hidden beneath a dirty grey parka that drooped to his knees. He withdrew an enormous handgun from the depths of his parka and held it out to Ray, butt-first.

The sooner he left this place with its ghost-like proxies, Ray decided, the better. He took the offered gun and cracked it open, inspecting its chamber.

He looked back up. "Ammunition?"

The young proxy wordlessly reached back inside his parka and lifted out a box of ammunition, handing it to Ray before turning and disappearing back the way he had come.

"And here's a car for you," said the white-haired proxy, pointing along the road.

A minute later a driverless panel-van came around the side of the mansion and drew up next to them.

"I want to be clear about one thing," Ray said to Isaac. "Until we get down there and you figure out how to fix this mess, I'm in charge. Agreed?"

Isaac nodded warily. "Agreed."

————

STACY

When Stacy woke late the next afternoon in an upstairs bedroom, eyes gummy and mouth dry, it took a few seconds to register that something was different. Where before the house had always been filled with the sound of murmuring voices and shuffling feet, it was now inexplicably silent.

It was so quiet that, for one terrible moment, Stacy imagined that Zero and his multitude of proxies had abandoned the house and her with it.

She dressed quickly in the fresh set of clothing Zero had left her; heavy boots, camouflage trousers and a thick, knit jumper, as if the machine anticipated they would be doing a lot of walking.

Zero had removed the plaster from her arm, but it was still covered with visible bruises, as were her ribs. He'd also given her another couple of shots of something that further dulled the pain, although that was fading fast, too. She knew she'd been lucky to emerge from her experiences relatively unscathed. At the very least, it was now much easier to get herself dressed.

On her way to the stairs, she glanced inside a room and saw a new female proxy with a buzzcut standing at a window, peering out at the forest through binoculars. She was dressed in camouflage and had a soldier's bearing.

"Zero?" she asked. "Where are all the rest of you?"

The proxy lowered her binoculars and turned to look at Stacy with a distracted expression. "Good, you're awake. I've sent most of the proxies home."

Stacy felt a small thrill of alarm at this. "Why?"

The proxy returned her attention to the window. "I lost contact with several of them in the early hours of this morning," she explained. "Just prior to losing contact, they—or rather, I—sighted a number of unknown people moving through the woods." The proxy paused for a moment. "I'm... not sure what happened to them."

A chill that had nothing to do with the cold of the old, rambling house worked its way beneath Stacy's skin. "So there's only me and you here?"

"Not quite," the proxy said over her shoulder. "As I mentioned last night, I hired specialist proxies, fearing a possible armed confrontation. Some are here already, including the one you're speaking to now, and others are still on their way."

Stacy wrapped her arms around her chest for warmth. "These people you saw in the woods. Do they work for Markov? Has he found us?"

The proxy didn't reply. Instead, she pushed the window up and leaned outside, peering in the direction of the road that led through the woods to the mansion.

"There's been another incident," the proxy said, stepping back from the window. "Please go to the kitchen and remain there for now, Miss Cotter."

"I want to know what's going on," Stacy demanded, unable to hide her growing alarm.

"Please, Miss Cotter," Zero replied with typically maddening patience. "It's for your own safety."

Stacy thought of insisting, but instead she did as Zero

asked, making her way down through the strangely quiet house to the kitchen.

This time, there were no proxies to cook or wash for her, and so she made herself breakfast from a loaf of supermarket bread and some butter that had been left sitting on a counter. It helped that the kitchen, with its wood-burning stove, was also the warmest part of the house.

As she chewed on buttered bread and sipped at luke-warm coffee from a pot that had been left on the stove, Stacy peered through a gap between the boards covering the windows to where she could just make out the trees surrounding the house. She glimpsed another proxy in mili-tary-style clothing. It carried a rifle and stood with its back to her.

She was about to step back once more from the window when the proxy burst into sudden motion, running to the left and out of sight. Stacy listened for a moment, her mouth full of half-chewed bread, hearing the sound of boots running across gravel.

She put the remains of her buttered bread down, her hunger vanished. Had Isaac and Ray been hurt? Was Markov finally on his way to finish the job he'd started when she arrived in London?

Even the thought they had been found was enough to make Stacy's heart feel as if it might seize up, her lungs somehow not able to suck in enough air.

Slamming the door of the kitchen open, she ran across the echoing hall and outside, seeing two more proxies, also in camouflage, coming through the trees towards the house and supporting a third man between them. Dirt and blood streaked the man's skin and clothes, pain and exhaustion showing in the lines of his face.

Elijah.

Stacy hurried over, taking one of Elijah's arms from a proxy and pulling it over her shoulder.

"What happened to you?" she asked, as she helped him inside the house.

"Somebody shot at my car," Elijah gasped. His head lolled on his shoulders as if he could hardly keep it upright. "It happened maybe half an hour after I left. I veered off the road and into a tree. The car was a wreck, so I figured the only thing I could do was run for it."

Stacy kicked the kitchen door open with one boot, then, with the aid of the other proxy, guided Elijah over to a chair next to the kitchen table.

"You ran for it?" she asked, incredulous. "With a twisted ankle?"

"I didn't say it was easy," he grunted, his voice heavy with fatigue and pain. "Been walking all damn night. Not even sure how I figured...how I figured the right way back here."

They got him onto the chair and he slumped into it like a rag doll. He leaned forward, burying his head in his arms on the kitchen table.

"Tell me what happened," Stacy said to the proxy who'd helped her get Elijah indoors.

"He didn't get more than twenty miles from the house," the proxy told her. "He's very lucky to be alive."

"It's Markov, isn't it?"

"Most likely, yes."

"Then what about my father?" she demanded, her voice trembling. "And Ray Thomas? They left not long after Elijah did. Are they still alive?"

"There's a fork in the road a few miles from here," said the proxy. "Mr Waits took a different route from your father and Mr Thomas. One of my proxies is riding along with the two of them and, rest assured, they're very much alive and well."

The proxy leaned over the table towards Elijah, who looked up with bleary, tired eyes.

"Mr Waits," asked Zero, "were you able to see how many your attackers numbered?"

Elijah shook his head. "The first shot hit the windscreen, and that's when I hit a tree. When I got out, I could hear them moving through the undergrowth towards me, but I couldn't see a thing. I found a place to hide next to a brook. I stayed there until I couldn't hear them any more."

Two more proxies entered the kitchen, both muscular and clad in the same fatigues as the rest.

One handed Elijah a flask and he gulped its contents down. The other got to work putting a pressure bandage onto Elijah's ankle. It looked ugly and swollen as hell. Stacy felt a sympathetic twinge in her healing arm.

Elijah regarded the three proxies with a wary expression. "These don't look like the proxies you had before."

"Military-grade," said Zero, speaking through the proxy working on Elijah's ankle. "If you recall, we discussed them last night."

"Smart," said Elijah, nodding his head. "I lost my guns when the car crashed. If Markov's coming for us, I want one of yours."

"It's unnecessary for you to be armed at this time," said Zero, this time speaking through the proxy that had helped Stacy get him inside.

Elijah's expression darkened. "Like hell it isn't!"

"Elijah's got a point," said Stacy. "We're helpless if Markov sends his own proxies in here, or there's more of them than there are of you. Neither of us have any way to defend ourselves if it comes to it."

"You don't have firearms training, Miss Cotter. You're more likely to hurt yourself or one of us than anyone else. And our hope is to avoid hurting any proxies whatsoever if we can possibly avoid it."

"Then train me," she said to the proxy nearest her, her tone insistent. "What else is there for me to do?"

The proxy shook his head. "I can't spare any weapons," he

said. "Not until we know just how much of a threat we're facing."

"Give me a gun and I'll teach her," said Elijah. "If Markov's out to kill her, she might as well be able to shoot back."

All three proxies fell silent for a moment, their expressions eerily blank.

"All right," said the proxy next to Stacy. "It'll be tricky, but perhaps I can allocate something you can use. You should practice in the basement—it's reasonably dry and intact and should provide some natural soundproofing. Please give me five minutes."

Stacy dropped into a chair and waited. Another of the proxies gave Elijah several painkillers and more water.

Ten minutes passed before a new, female proxy, dressed in the same tactical gear as the rest, entered the kitchen. She looked thirty-something, but might equally have been a well-preserved fifty with hard, angular features.

She dropped a heavy-looking canvas backpack onto the table with a thump. Unzipping it, she withdrew a pair of snub-nosed pistols that looked utterly lethal to her untrained eyes and handed one to Elijah.

"You can use these," said Zero, speaking through the proxy.

Elijah picked one up and turned it this way and that, studying it closely. "Nine millimetres," he said, pulling something back on top of each one before releasing it with a metallic snap.

He looked back up at the proxy. "Got anything more powerful?"

"We are trying to avoid hurting David Markov's proxies," Zero replied. "We hope to wound at most, and would prefer not to kill if at all possible."

Elijah looked dubious.

"The magazines are preloaded," the proxy continued,

taking more things out of the bag and placing them down on the table next to the second gun. "You're familiar with sidearms from the Korean War, of course."

The way the proxy said it, it was a statement, not a question.

Something glittered deep within Elijah's eyes. "Seems you know a few things about me."

"I've placed adequate lighting in the basement," the proxy said by way of reply. "It's not perfect, but it'll do under the circumstances."

"I'm sure it'll be more than good enough," said Elijah, standing stiffly and slowly. "Hey," he said to the proxy. "Give me a hand?"

———

THE BASEMENT SMELLED EVEN WORSE than the rest of the house. Stacy made a conscious effort to breathe through her mouth rather than inhale the stink of mould and rotting wood.

The walls and floor were made of scarred concrete, and Zero had placed portable battery-powered lamps in each of the basement's four corners. The AI had even scratched a crude target comprising three concentric circles into a sheet of plywood and leaned it up against the far wall.

Stacy went down first, carrying the various items of deadly weaponry in the rucksack belonging to the proxy. Elijah followed behind, taking the basement steps one at a time and leaning heavily on the mercenary proxy who had brought them the guns.

Once he was down, Elijah took the rucksack from Stacy and took everything back out, carefully placing it all on a shelf near the steps.

"Cartridge," he said, holding up something about the size of a cigarette packet. "This is where your ammunition is. You load it like this."

He slid the cartridge into the grip of one of the handguns.

"Always keep the barrel pointed at the ground unless you're intending to fire," Elijah told her. He handed it to her grip-first. "Have you used a gun of any kind before?"

"Nope," she said.

"Just try aiming it," he said, nodding towards the crude target.

Obeying, Stacy raised the gun one-handed and pointed it at the far wall.

"Use a two-handed grip," said Elijah, stepping awkwardly around behind her on his busted ankle and peering over her shoulder towards the target. "That way you can keep your aim more steady. Like this."

Elijah then stepped up next to her and aimed his own weapon at the target, angling it slightly so she could see the way he'd arranged his fingers around the pistol's grip. She did her best to copy it.

"Almost," said Elijah. "Keep the first finger of your right hand lying against the barrel so it's just above the trigger guard. See?"

Stacy tried again and Elijah nodded his approval. "Now take a breath and let it out slowly. Try to keep your body relaxed."

"I know the next bit," said Stacy. Her hands were already tired from trying to keep the gun level. "Squeeze, don't pull. Right?"

Elijah laughed under his breath. "Not quite. Here."

He put his gun down, then showed her how to wrap her fingers around the handgun. "Pull back on the slide," he instructed her.

She did as she was told. A kind of metal sleeve on top of the barrel slid back, then sprang back into place when she released it.

"Now you've chambered a round," he explained. "Try

taking a shot. And remember, use a two-handed grip. And take your time."

Stacy nodded, suddenly nervous. She sighted along the barrel, not sure at all if she was doing it right. When she tried to picture herself confronting somebody with such a weapon, the thought terrified her a lot more than it reassured her.

Stacy let out a shaky breath, steadied her aim as best she could and squeezed the trigger.

The handgun kicked in her hand with sufficient force to jerk her wrists to one side. It made a sound like a baseball bat hitting the side of an empty oil can.

A hole appeared a few inches from the outer ring of the target, the plywood sheet trembling under the impact.

"Fuck," she swore under her breath, lowering the gun again. Her heart beat in her chest like a drummer playing a fast roll.

"You're thinking too much," Elijah said from beside her. "Like this."

Elijah shifted his balance so that most of his weight was on his good leg and fired three evenly spaced shots almost directly into the centre of the target. He stood with his body at a slight angle relative to the plywood sheet. The sound of each shot made every muscle in Stacy's body twitch.

Elijah dropped the gun back down and grinned at her. "Want to try again?"

"Where did you learn to shoot like that?" she asked. "Korea?"

His expression sobered slightly. "That's not something I like to talk about."

"I was just thinking if we're going to be stuck here waiting to see if we're all going to be murdered, I should at least know something about you."

"Does it matter?" he said, his voice now edged with irritation.

"Look," said Stacy, "if anything happens to your skin,

you'll just wake up back in your cell. But for me, it's forever. I'd like to know something about you." She shrugged. "You tell me something, I'll tell you something."

Elijah stared levelly at the target for several seconds, then nodded. "I was part of the international peacekeeping force. Let's just say it was a clusterfuck of epic proportions and leave it at that." He nodded to her gun. "Try again."

Stacy raised the weapon until it was once again level with her eyes. This time she was determined to do better.

"Breathe, relax and aim," Elijah said from beside her, his voice low and calm. "Don't think about anything else."

Breathe, relax, aim. The way he said it, it almost sounded like a mantra.

This time, her shot landed closer to the centre of the wooden target. Much closer.

"Improving," said Elijah when she lowered her gun.

"Only because the target isn't moving," she pointed out. "I'm not sure an actual person is going to stay still long enough for me to shoot them."

"They might," said Elijah, "if they don't know you're there."

The words carried a sense of intimate knowledge, and she pictured Elijah slipping through a jungle, tracking and killing people from a distance.

"So how do you go from being in a war zone to dealing proxy?" she asked.

His eyebrows knit together in an angry scowl. "I've said as much as I want to say."

She turned until she was facing him. "Aren't you even the least bit curious how a stupid little rich girl gets so low she ends up proxy hooking?"

"No," he replied, although Stacy heard the hesitation in his voice.

"I was the daughter of one of the most famous—and rich

—men in the world. That," she said, "made me desirable to certain kinds of people."

"You don't need to tell me any of this."

"See," she continued regardless, "I ran away a couple of times when I was a kid, but I had enough sense to keep my background—who I was—a secret from anyone I met. When I was sixteen, I wound up living in a squat and met a proxy dealer. He knew people, who knew people, who had more money than they knew what to do with, and he liked to help them spend it."

She turned back to face the target, shifting her stance. "So I had a plan," she continued. "Back then I still thought Raphael Markov was my actual, biological father, and I couldn't understand why he wanted nothing to do with me. I blamed my mother, then I blamed myself. If I couldn't get his attention the usual way, then maybe one day I could get close enough to Raphael while I was proxying with these rich arseholes to ask him why." She glanced sideways at Elijah. "I just wanted to know what I'd done wrong."

Elijah's face twisted up in what might have been sympathy, but was more likely pity. "You didn't really believe that would happen, did you?"

"No," she admitted. "It was just a story I told myself." She aimed at the target once more and squeezed the trigger, but heard only a hollow click.

"Maybe that's enough practice for now," said Elijah. "At the very least we ought to try and conserve what ammunition we have until we need it."

The tough-looking female proxy, who had been silently watching them from the steps, took their weapons back from them.

"Wait," said Stacy, following behind Elijah as he limped towards the steps. "I want to hear more about Korea."

He stopped with one foot on a step and looked back at her. "So if I tell you something, you'll stop asking questions?"

She thought for a moment. "Probably."

A beat passed, and then another. "Fine," he said at last. "All you really need to know is that the NK's used nerve gas towards the end." A muscle twitched in one of his cheeks. "Some friends of mine got hit with it. The ones who survived wished they hadn't."

"I'm sorry."

"After we all got back home, they treated the ones who got invalided like dirt when they should have got help. So I helped them out any way I could."

"Proxy?" she guessed.

Elijah nodded. "Then I got busted."

"Even though you were trying to help people?"

He shook his head. "Things were different back then. Anyone who used it was treated like a potential terrorist." He sighed and leaned heavily on the wall beside him for support. "After I got out of prison the first time, I set up a small proxy factory with a friend. And now I'm back inside again."

"Elijah, Stacy," said the proxy, "There's renewed activity in the woods much closer to the house. I recommend you stay down here for the duration."

"No," said Elijah, steel in his voice. "We'd be trapped down here if they got in. We'd have a better chance upstairs." He looked at Stacy. "Bring those guns, please."

Stacy stepped back over to the proxy, who handed her back the two handguns with clear reluctance. "I recommend not using them unless absolutely essential," said Zero.

"We won't," Stacy replied, passing one of the nine millimetres to Elijah. "You've seen people out there?"

"Six sighted so far," the proxy replied, "all within two miles of our location and all confirmed armed."

"Give me a hand," Elijah said to Stacy.

She helped Elijah back upstairs. When they emerged into the hallway, she saw through one of the few windows only partly boarded-up that the light was already fading.

"Remember," said the proxy, following behind them, "we want to avoid bloodshed if at all humanly possible." She glanced towards the front entrance. "If you'll forgive me, I'm required elsewhere."

"Damn machine acts like this is a game of chess," Elijah growled under his breath once the proxy had hurried away. "Let's head upstairs."

———

THEY FOUND another of Zero's tactical proxies crouched next to an upstairs window, peering through the sights of a power-ful-looking rifle, its barrel resting on the sill and poking between two rough planks nailed over the glass.

"Nine armed intruders now confirmed," the proxy announced without looking around. "Four are approaching from the rear of the building, and another five from the front. I don't think they've seen any of my own proxies yet."

"How many of your own proxies do you have around the house?" asked Elijah.

"There are five in the immediate vicinity of the house," the proxy replied.

The reply sent a jolt of alarm through Stacy. "So we're outnumbered?"

"I have overall tactical superiority and access to vast data-bases of military strategy," Zero replied. "To my knowledge, David Markov does not."

"But there's still more of them," said Stacy.

"True," the AI admitted. "And as for his proxies out there, he won't be at all reticent about inflicting—"

The proxy jerked his head around mid-sentence, his atten-tion focused on the door behind them as if he had heard something.

A steel band tightened around Stacy's lungs.

"Wait here," said the proxy, quickly standing and disappearing through the door in a low crouch, the rifle gripped close to his chest.

Stacy heard the creak of wooden stairs as the proxy hurried downstairs.

Elijah meanwhile moved over next to the window, crouching down to peer out between the planks.

"I don't see anything," he muttered. "Let Zero take care of things for now, like he says."

"But how will we be sure which proxies are his and which are—?"

Elijah raised a hand, his palm towards her. "Wait. I think I saw..."

Stacy dropped onto her knees next to Elijah and tried to see outside.

What I'd give, she thought, *to be back in my little Paris flat.*

Peering between the planks, she saw two figures standing at the edge of the woods, half-concealed behind the trunks of two trees. They wore military-style fatigues and might have been David Markov's or, equally, Zero's proxies. The one thing she was most afraid of was having no easy or obvious way to tell them apart.

Without warning they moved, hurrying across the ruined lawn towards the house. Moonlight glinted from the snub-nosed weapons gripped in their black-gloved hands.

Stacy whirled around at the sound of movement behind her, her hands hot and slick against the grip of her handgun. She nearly cried with relief when she saw the female proxy that had provided them both with their weapons now standing at the open doorway.

"Easy," Elijah murmured from beside her. He reached out and used one hand to lower the barrel of Stacy's gun towards the floor. She'd pointed it at the proxy without even thinking.

"Your trigger safety is on, Miss Cotter," the proxy said. "You couldn't have hurt me unless you used it like a club."

Stacy's face grew hot with embarrassment. Elijah chuckled

softly from behind her, his feet shifting on the dusty floor-boards as he stood back up.

"I need you both to come with me," said Zero. "Make as little noise as possible. Please refrain from using your weapons except in an outright emergency."

Stacy opened her mouth to ask how she'd know when that was, but the proxy had turned and exited the room before she could say anything.

"Here," said Elijah, and showed Stacy how to use the trigger safety. "Got it?"

She nodded tightly. "I think so."

"Good," said Elijah, keeping his own weapon close by his side and reaching for Stacy's shoulder with his other hand. "Now help me out here."

It was dark enough by now that when they stepped back out into the corridor, Stacy could only just make out the outline of the mercenary proxy, standing at the top of the stairs and waiting for them. Moonlight trickled through the wooden slats covering a window at the opposite end of the corridor.

Every creak of the building around them, every sigh of the wind, felt full of deadly significance.

"Hurry," the proxy hissed.

They followed her downstairs, Elijah leaning heavily on Stacy.

From somewhere else in the house came a burst of noise so loud and so abrupt that Stacy's insides turned to burning acid. It was a rattling, mechanical sort of noise, like an old-fashioned petrol-driven engine stuttering as someone tried and failed to start it up.

In response, muffled voices shouted from elsewhere in the house.

"We're going outside," said the proxy, her voice terse.

But what about staying inside where it's safe? Stacy wanted to cry out.

But the proxy was already on the move, swinging her own handgun from side to side and moving with a weird, shuffling motion towards the front entrance.

When they got outside, Stacy saw a pile of discarded clothes lying close to the tree line. Her heart lurched when she realized it wasn't a pile of clothes, but a body.

More gunfire came from inside the house, accompanied by the sound of breaking glass. Elijah's fingers dug deep into Stacy's shoulder and she almost cried out in pain.

The proxy leading them had meanwhile reached the tree line, and she turned to look back at them, gesturing for them to hurry.

They ran towards her as fast as they could, given Elijah's injured ankle. Stacy's lungs already ached from the effort of supporting his weight. Her ribs, only just healed, began again to grate against each other. It felt like razor blades slicing into her bones.

They stumbled into the woods, following the proxy deeper between the tall pines and gnarled oaks. In less than a minute, Stacy felt utterly lost. Yet the proxy waited patiently for them, guiding them further and further from the house.

After what felt like an eternity, they ascended a steep slope and halted at a pair of conjoined trees with a narrow gap between their trunks.

Only when she was standing almost next to the two trees did Stacy see that the gap separating them was taken up by a tent of some kind, or perhaps a minuscule hut. It was hard to tell, hidden as it was beneath layers of camouflage netting. From a distance it looked like a bush.

"It's a hunting blind," the proxy explained, pushing aside netting. "Tarpaulin over a steel frame. We've been secreting these through the woods in case we needed them." She pulled a flap open. "Inside, please. And hurry."

Stacy squeezed into the dim interior, Elijah following close behind, his breath coming in pained gasps. Once inside, Stacy found a narrow slit in the tarpaulin through which she could see down the slope of the hill.

"Wait here while I find transport," said the proxy, standing at the open flap and bathed in moonlight. "I'll be back as soon as I can."

"What's happening out there?" Elijah demanded.

The proxy turned to look over her shoulder, her attention drawn elsewhere.

"Things are proving more difficult than expected," the proxy replied after a lengthy pause. She sounded distracted. "I—"

The proxy blinked and shook her head. She swayed, her expression quite visible in the moonlight, and for a moment Stacy thought she might faint.

"Zero?" asked Stacy. "What's wrong?"

"I'm having a little trouble…"

The proxy stumbled and fell backwards, hitting the ground with a thud.

Stacy quickly scrambled back out of the blind, afraid the proxy had been shot, but there was no sign of any visible injury.

She watched with increasing alarm as the proxy twitched and then began to shake with increasing violence. Her eyes were open, but all Stacy could see were their whites. Her teeth were bared in a rictus.

"What's wrong with her?" Stacy demanded, her voice edged with panic.

"She's having a fit or something," said Elijah, hobbling back out of the blind to join her.

The proxy's heels dug at the dirt, her head jerking and twisting from side to side.

Then, as suddenly as they had started, the tremors ceased.

"Zero?" asked Elijah, leaning in closer to the proxy. "What happened?"

The proxy's gaze settled on Elijah for a moment. Then she

reached for her weapon where she'd dropped it and, in a single swift movement, brought it to bear on Elijah, her fingers tightening around the trigger.

Before Stacy could even react, let alone think, Elijah had thrown himself on top of the proxy, grabbing hold of the barrel of her gun and presumably struggling to rip it from her grasp.

The gun went off, and Elijah cursed. For a moment Stacy thought he had been shot. She watched, open-mouthed, not understanding and not able to clearly see what was happening.

"Shoot her," Elijah gasped. "For Christ's sake, Stacy, shoot her *now*!"

But Stacy couldn't move. Nor could she understand what Elijah was saying, or if she had, then she must have misunderstood, because he couldn't seriously be asking her to kill the same woman who'd helped them practice—

Elijah slammed one fist into the side of the proxy's head and it was enough for her fingers to loosen around her weapon. He tore it free, struggled upright with a grunt of pain, and then shot the proxy in the chest.

The noise was even worse than it had been when they had been practising in the basement. It sounded like the final judgement, like a hammer striking Stacy's head.

She saw there was a hole in the proxy's chest where there hadn't been one a moment before.

Elijah stared down at her, his chest heaving. "Something's gone wrong," he said. "She was about to kill both of us." He turned to look at Stacy with a hollow-eyed stare. "We need to get away from here."

"Zero said something," said Stacy, stumbling over her words. "He…he said he lost contact with some of his own proxies last night. Even he couldn't figure it out."

He stared back down at the dead proxy. *No*, thought Stacy; at a dead *person*, someone whose real name she would never know, and who had died without ever knowing why or for what purpose her body had been used.

The thought hollowed her out, leaving an empty void deep inside of her.

"Maybe Markov's got some way of taking over control of the proxies Zero's using," Elijah suggested. "Listen, we can work out what happened later. For now, we're on our own. So let's just get moving."

"But where?" asked Stacy. She still couldn't pull her gaze away from the woman's face. "We can't...we can't go back to the house."

"Anywhere as long as it isn't here," said Elijah.

He tilted his head back to stare up at the moon and stars through a break in the clouds, then peered down the slope of the hill towards a far-away thread of silver winding its way through the woods. He directed her attention to it.

"That way looks good enough," he said.

CHAPTER THIRTY

RAY

They had just got out of a car on the edge of the Markov estate when Zero fell silent mid-sentence.

Ray, who had been staring off into the darkness of the surrounding forest, turned to look back at the woman through whom Zero was proxying. She had tired eyes and stooped shoulders, her unkempt blonde hair pulled into an untidy ponytail. They had found her waiting for them in a battered-looking Land Rover a hundred kilometres from the Markov estate, ready for their third vehicle switch of the day.

The proxy's gaze remained unfocused for several more seconds, an amount of time that, Ray had gleaned from his conversation with Isaac on the long drive down, might as well be an eternity for an entity such as Zero.

Then the proxy blinked and looked around at them. "We have a problem."

Hearing the crunch of leaves underfoot, Ray turned to see Isaac Sizemore emerge from amidst the trees by the side of the road, tugging his fly up.

"What's going on?" he asked, looking between them. Clearly, he'd read something in their expressions.

"I've lost contact with a number of my proxies just in the last few minutes," Zero explained. "Mostly around or inside the Kielder Forest safe house."

Ray stared at the proxy. "Lost contact, how? Do you mean their proxy sessions ran out?"

"Nothing so simple, I'm afraid," Zero replied. "Of greater concern is my inability to locate either Stacy or Mr Waits."

Isaac looked confused. "Elijah Waits? He left before we did. Are you saying something happened to him?"

The proxy nodded. "Mr Waits returned to the safe house a few hours ago. It appears he came under attack shortly after departing us and was forced to flee on foot back to the house."

Ray could hardly believe what he was hearing. He shot a look at Isaac, whose hands had twisted into claws at his sides, then back at the proxy. "Why the hell did you wait until now to tell us?"

"I believed I could handle the situation adequately given the number and type of proxies available to me," Zero replied. "Unfortunately, as I say, there have been...unexpected developments within the last few minutes."

Isaac, his expression intent, stepped up close to the proxy. "How many are still under your control?"

"Most remain under my command," Zero replied. "They're actively searching for both Stacy and for Mr Waits, but the safe house is currently under attack from what I believe to be proxies under David Markov's control. Making a clear assessment under the circumstances is proving difficult."

"Maybe you were right, Isaac," Ray muttered, feeling as if his legs were about to give way beneath him. He stepped over to the Land Rover and leaned heavily against it. "Maybe Markov has won."

"We're not quite down and out yet, Mr Thomas," Zero countered. "For one, it's been my observation that I only lost control over those of my proxies that came into direct line of sight of those under Markov's control. Some of them now appear to be under his direct control. For the moment, I'm operating under the assumption that so long as my remaining proxies stay out of sight of Markov's, they'll remain mine."

Isaac stared at the proxy, his expression thunderstruck. "He can do that? Take over your proxies just by seeing them? How?"

"Zero took over those people at the Peartree even though they were all proxying with someone else," said Ray. "Surely it's the same thing?"

"Mr Thomas is correct," said Zero. "But I wasn't aware until now that David Markov could do the same thing to proxies that *I* controlled. This reveals potentialities within the technology of which even I was not yet aware."

"Then can you take over his proxies too?" Isaac asked, a gleam of excitement in his eyes.

"If there's a way to do it," said Zero, "I haven't found it yet."

Ray imagined some glittering matrix of silicon and light buried in a darkened vault running innumerable processes even as it spoke to them through a human throat.

"Whatever network David Markov is uploading his mind to is, most likely, dozens of generations more advanced than my own," Zero continued. "That alone gives him a considerable advantage."

"So is it possible Markov could take control of the proxy you're speaking to us through right now?" Ray asked.

"It's possible, yes," the machine replied blithely. "I have to exercise extreme caution to avoid that happening."

"Very well," said Isaac, his tone decisive. "If anything, it makes our mission even more urgent." He turned in a slow circle, peering into the trees around them before pointing into the darkness. "We should go that way," he said at last. "There's a gate set into a security fence ringing the estate."

Ray nodded, remembering how Amy Cotter had described sneaking Isaac in and out of the Markov estate. "What about cameras?"

"There's a camera," said Isaac, "but it'd been busted for years the last I remember. It's possibly they've repaired it since, but I'll be surprised if they have."

"Shortly after we departed the Kielder Forest," said Zero, "I took the opportunity to explore the woods around this estate through the eyes of a few hired proxies. A member of Markov's security team replaced that camera within just the last few hours, most likely in response to Amy Cotter's intrusion."

Ray swore under his breath. "So is there any other way we can get inside without being seen?"

The proxy shook her head. "No, but I have another proxy waiting for you near that same gate. Go there, and he can get you inside the estate."

"And you're sure it'll be safe?" Ray asked sceptically.

"Nothing we're doing is safe, Mr Thomas," Zero replied. "The best I can do is minimize the risk." The proxy stepped towards the Land Rover and pulled its door open. "Time is of the essence, Mr Thomas," she said, climbing in. "Don't delay."

"This way," said Isaac, stepping off the road and into the trees without looking back.

Ray took a last glance at the Land Rover as it hummed into the distance, then made to follow the scientist. In less than a minute, he could see no sign of the road through the trees.

They walked for perhaps twenty minutes, with Isaac frequently stopping to stare around before continuing, and not always in the same direction. The terrain became increasingly rough, and at one point they were forced to scramble down a slope, grabbing hold of tree roots and rocks to keep from slipping or falling.

Just when Ray felt certain they were lost, he caught sight of a wooden-framed gate set into a tall wire fence up ahead, lit by the moonlight. A camera, angled away from them, stood on top of a fence post.

In that same moment, a shadow emerged from amidst the trees close by the nearest side of the fence. The shadow resolved into a figure, moving quickly towards them.

Ray instinctively reached into his pocket for the gun Zero had given him, wrapping his fingers around its grip.

Whoever they were, they were entirely bald and rake-thin and of indeterminate age or gender. Facial tattoos reached down their neck and beneath their sleeveless T-shirt. Their arms looked toned and muscular.

"Isaac, Ray," the figure said, coming to a halt before them. "Please wait here a moment."

A proxy, then. Ray felt himself relax. Their voice offered no further clue to their gender.

The tattooed proxy turned away and stepped towards a tree close by the fence and out of range of the fence-mounted camera. As Ray watched, they jumped up with the lithe grace of an athlete, grabbing hold of a low-hanging branch and hauling themselves up and out of sight amidst dense foliage.

Ray craned his neck upwards to see the proxy crawl along a thick branch that hung over the fence. His heart crawled into his throat when he saw the proxy hang upside down, gripping the branch between their thighs.

The proxy, now directly above the camera, reached down to it. They had something in one hand that glittered in the moonlight.

Reaching down, they touched it to the camera casing.

Nothing happened that Ray could see, but after another moment the proxy pulled themselves back up onto the branch, then worked their way back to the main trunk before dropping down to the forest floor with practised ease.

Under less potentially lethal circumstances, Ray might have applauded.

"I shut the camera down," said the proxy, stepping towards the fence and touching the same device they had used on the camera to the gate's electronic lock.

Ray heard a faint click, and the proxy gave the gate a slight push. It swung noiselessly open.

"The estate security will send someone out to fix it, of course," the proxy offered over their shoulder. Ray watched as they walked over to a tree some metres away and picked something up from the grass.

At first, Ray thought the object they had picked up was a rifle, but the barrel looked odd, like some kind of cartoon blunderbuss.

"That means," the proxy added, returning to them, "that we have to move fast."

"Wait a minute," Ray said to the proxy. "You're coming with us? What if Markov tries to take you over?"

"I consider it a limited but acceptable risk," the proxy replied. "You'll need my help, that much is certain."

"Zero's right," said Isaac, glancing nervously around. "I'll need his insight once we find Markov. And as he says, we should hurry. This way."

Ray's mouth and throat felt bone-dry when he followed them through the gate. Looking more closely, he saw that what the proxy was holding was a microwave-gun with a bell-shaped barrel.

"What do you need that thing for?" he asked Zero.

"We may encounter drones," the proxy replied.

Soon, the trees gave way to gardens divided into sections by tall hedges. David Markov's mansion loomed above a cluster of outbuildings.

Isaac appeared to know exactly which way to go. He kept to the shadows alongside a tall hedge and Ray and Zero followed behind him, moving inexorably closer to the main building.

At one point Isaac halted and turned to look at them both. "I don't know how much things have changed since I was last here," he whispered, "but there were always three guards patrolling the grounds at any one time. They usually had one foot patrol doing the rounds and another two guards driving around the estate in an SUV. Plus maybe one more in an office in one of the outbuildings, to monitor the feeds from security drones. The most they ever had to deal with, to my knowledge, were journalists trying to sneak in or local kids on a dare. I don't think they'll be expecting us, but we still have to be careful."

Isaac led them down a narrow, rutted path past a cluster of whitewashed buildings. Pale blue light illuminated the interior of one. Isaac stopped long enough to point at it, then put his finger to his lips.

Five minutes later, headlights flashed on a road leading to the mansion. Isaac once again brought them to a halt.

"We're in luck," he whispered. "That's the next shift arriving, I think. They'll be too busy switching over to be paying much attention to drone feeds or anything else for at least the next ten minutes."

As if drawn by Isaac's words, Ray heard a faint rumbling like a buzzsaw heard through a soundproofed wall. He glanced upwards, seeing something black and circular come flying low above the path they were on.

Zero, working through his proxy, slipped the microwave gun from their shoulder and waited. The drone looked like it might not have seen them, but as it flew past them it slowed to a halt, hovered for a moment, then began to come back towards them.

The proxy aimed their microwave gun at the drone and squeezed the trigger. The gun made no sound, but the drone fell out of the sky and onto the path, landing with a wet thud amidst mud and tangled grass.

"Between that and the camera you hacked," Ray whispered, "that's definitely going to get somebody's attention."

The proxy nodded. "Agreed. Let's get moving before anyone gets here."

Isaac stepped towards the corner of a building, looked around, then ran in a low crouch towards the house. Ray came next, the proxy close behind. He joined Isaac on the other side of a door at the rear of the mansion.

"You seriously did this a lot?" Ray whispered to Isaac.

"More often than you think," Isaac said with a grin, his teeth pale and long in the moonlight.

Isaac reached for the door handle, but Ray stopped him and motioned him back. Ray took his place, easing the door slowly open. Peeking inside, he saw rows of silent washing machines and empty baskets on shelves: a laundry room.

"Remember," Ray whispered to Isaac. "Once we find Markov, it's up to you and your pet computer to figure out whatever it is you need to do to shut him down. I'll keep an eye out for trouble, but make it fast. I'll lead the way, but you need to tell me which way to go. Understood?"

Isaac nodded. "That way," he said, gesturing to a door at the far end of the laundry room.

Ray opened the door as quietly as he could and saw a short passageway on the other side, no more than a metre in length, connecting at a right angle to a corridor. He glanced back at Isaac and Zero and motioned for them to follow.

Stepping up to the corner of the passageway, Ray realized he could hear someone speaking somewhere to the left. He turned to look at the other two and put a finger to his lips.

He waited. A few seconds later Ray heard a door open and several pairs of feet crunch across gravel. Car doors swung open and shut, followed by wheels rolling over that same gravel. He guessed this was the security changeover Isaac had mentioned.

Now everything was silent.

"Where now?" Ray whispered back to Isaac.

"Go right," Isaac whispered back. "There's a stairwell in a foyer. We need to go up to the second floor."

Ray nodded, then led the way. The stairwell was a claustrophobe's nightmare, most likely built for the use of servants in an earlier and very different age.

"Let me go first," said Isaac, as they reached the second floor.

They emerged into another corridor, to where they could see light seeping from beneath a closed door at its far end.

"I think that's where we'll find him," Isaac whispered, nodding towards the door.

"You're certain?" Ray whispered back.

Isaac motioned with his chin at a wall-mounted notice to which Ray hadn't paid any attention: MEDICAL STAFF ONLY BEYOND THIS POINT.

"Quite certain," said Isaac.

Isaac started to move towards the door, but the proxy stopped him with a hand on his shoulder. "Allow me," they said.

The proxy stepped nimbly up to the door, its odd weapon pulled over one shoulder by a strap. They knelt to study a keypad.

"Can you get through?" Ray asked as he came up behind the proxy, speaking as quietly as he could.

The proxy reached into a pocket and withdrew what Ray suspected was the same device they had used on the camera. They pressed it against the keypad, and after a moment a red light above the keypad changed to green.

Ray heard the lock disengage, and when the proxy reached for the door handle and pushed, the door opened.

Ray tensed, expecting alarms to start whooping, but nothing happened.

"Good work, Zero," said Isaac, squeezing their shoulder before ducking inside.

Ray had to give it to Isaac: the man had balls of steel. He'd come straight out of his safe house to confront both him and Elijah before he had any idea who they might be, and was practically charging into a heavily guarded private estate belonging to a man with every reason to want him dead.

Hopefully, that bravery wouldn't wind up with *all* of them dead.

Following behind the two others, Ray found himself in the same, brightly lit room he'd seen in Amy Cotter's hastily-snatched video.

David Markov's shrivelled form still lay in its large, mech-anized bed, apparently unaware of their presence—or of anything else, Ray suspected. Those few seconds of video, however, had barely hinted at the full horror of what Ray now found himself confronted with.

The twisted, wetly glistening filaments rising from within the blackened ruins of Markov's skull looked to the detective's eyes like a machine-organism born of plastic and metal. It was almost as if the machinery were feeding on the old man, drawing unholy sustenance from the body's fading life-force.

Ray turned away, swallowing down phlegm that burned the back of his throat. The tattooed proxy, meanwhile, had taken up a post by the door, keeping a watchful eye back along the corridor.

Isaac stepped up close to the bed, peering closely at the machinery embedded within David Markov's skull. He then turned to regard the rest of the room with equal concentra-tion. His lips moved silently as if he were talking to himself.

"Could we fry all this machinery with Zero's microwave gun?" asked Ray.

"I'm afraid it's a one-shot device," Zero said without looking around. "I would have discarded it, but I was concerned it might be discovered by a patrol. Besides," the AI added, "doing so would only destroy the interfaces. Until we know exactly what we're dealing with, we need them intact and functioning."

"Zero," said Isaac, moving away from the bed, "I need your help over here."

"We could just smash all this the hell up," said Ray, his mouth twisted up in disgust. "Or start a fire and burn the place down."

Isaac and Zero exchanged a look. "That's not what we're going to do," said Isaac.

Ray turned to stare at him. "Why the hell not?"

"You'll to have to trust me on this," said Isaac.

Ray's expression became incredulous. "I thought the idea was to come here and stop Markov." He gestured at the body in the bed. "So let's stop him!"

Isaac's gaze slid away from Ray's. "It's not that simple."

"Mr Thomas," said the proxy, "perhaps you should keep an eye on the corridor while I assist Isaac. There isn't time for detailed explanations."

After briefly considering demanding an explanation regardless, Ray instead acquiesced, taking up station by the open door.

Zero immediately joined Isaac next to a console. Isaac tapped rapidly at a keyboard and in response, several wall-mounted displays flickered and shifted until their predominant colour was red.

Ray still had one hand wrapped tightly around the pistol in his pocket.

It was becoming increasingly clear to him that both Isaac and Zero were keeping something back. Ray eyed the glistening machinery that acted as the conduit for all of David

Markov's aspirations—the means by which the man who had once ruined his life intended to achieve immortality.

That thought in itself was enough to cause Ray to slide the pistol out of his pocket. He could end all of this now, if he wanted, and to hell with these other two.

By carrying out this action, he stepped slightly to one side —thereby, he later calculated, saving his own life.

The sound of gunfire filled the air, loud and close enough that it felt like a cannon had gone off next to one of Ray's ears.

His police training kicked in and he dropped into a crouch, turning and aiming back down the corridor to where he could see a uniformed guard standing at the top of the stairs, holding a pistol in a two-handed grip.

Ray's fingers compressed around the trigger of his own pistol. It clicked uselessly in his hands.

Shock gripped him for a single moment, and then he threw himself down flat as the guard fired more rounds.

Moving quickly, Ray scrambled backwards and out of the guard's line of sight, cold sweat bathing his skin. His breath came in harsh, frantic gasps.

He worked the slide of his pistol uselessly and realized what Zero must have done.

The fucking machine took out the firing pin.

"Don't move!"

Ray looked up to see the same guard standing just outside the room, pistol steady and aimed at his head. Then he shifted his attention to the others.

"You two!" he screamed at Isaac and the proxy. "Get down flat on the ground!"

Ray let the useless pistol slip from his grasp. The guard took a shuffling step forward and kicked it out of reach, then took a step back so he could keep all three of them within his line of fire.

Ray heard someone groan and looked around. The proxy had collapsed to the floor. They sat upright against a shelving unit, one hand pressed to an upper arm that was sticky and dark with blood.

Ray hadn't realized the proxy had been hit. At least it didn't look like a fatal shot.

Isaac, however, had chosen to ignore the guard. He stood with his back to the man, his fingers moving rapidly across a keyboard beneath a screen.

Charts and figures on the screen suddenly flared red.

"I said stop!" the guard shouted again, training his gun on Isaac's back. "Step away from there or I'll shoot!"

Isaac ignored him. From where Ray sat, he could see the scientist's lips were moving silently, his skin bright with feverish sweat.

"Do as he says, Isaac," said Ray, his voice tight.

"Not just yet." Isaac's voice was hardly more than a mumble. "Just one more—!"

The guard shot him.

The sound it made felt like a physical blow to Ray's own skull. Isaac span away from the screen and the wall-mounted keyboard, red blossoming in the centre of his back as he collided with a wheeled trolley next to Markov's bed.

The trolley fell on its side, plastic trays full of shiny steel utensils spilling onto the floor. Isaac collapsed, his hands grasping at the floor and his face twisted up in anguish.

Ray acted without thinking, pushing himself upright and forward in one swift motion.

The guard turned towards him, but not fast enough: Ray slammed into him hard enough to send the guard staggering back against a set of shelves. Boxes of medical supplies crashed to the floor around them.

Ray pulled back just enough that he could slam his fist repeatedly into the side of the guard's head, his other hand grasping his opponent's wrist to keep him from bringing his gun to bear on him again.

Ray brought one knee up and drove it hard into his balls. The guard folded up, sliding bonelessly to the floor.

Ray just kept hitting him, again and again, until the guard at last stopped moving. Ray stood over him for another minute, panting hard, his muscles trembling with fury and terror.

All he could think about was the sound his own gun had made when it failed to fire.

He leaned down and checked the guard's pulse: still alive. Then he stood back up and turned to face the proxy.

"Zero," he hissed through gritted teeth, "why the fuck did you give me a gun that wouldn't fire?"

"We need to tend to Isaac first," said Zero. The proxy, despite its injury, had stumbled back upright and had positioned Isaac so that he was upright against the wall beneath the screen at which he had been working.

"I suggest you restrain that guard however you can and keep an eye out for more on their way," Zero said to Ray. "We are extremely limited for time."

It took an effort of will for Ray to suppress his fury. Zero was right: there wasn't time, but he didn't trust the machine any more—if he ever had.

Or should he blame Isaac, with his insane desire to avoid hurting even the very people who'd murder him without a second thought? Yes, he thought, recalling the argument between the scientist and his creation: it most likely had been Isaac's decision, not Zero's.

Ray got to work, opening drawer after drawer until he found several computer cords and a length of cotton bandaging that might serve as a gag. Working quickly, he bound the guard, first checking to make sure he was still breathing.

"As far as I can tell the guard isn't proxied," said Zero. "Or at least, I can only assume that's why I remain in control of this body."

Ray didn't answer. The side of the guard's face had turned a nasty purple-blue.

Ray muttered an apology to the man, then dragged him into a corner where he'd be out of the way. He paused only to relieve the guard of his weapon which, he now knew from experience, very much fucking worked.

Tucking the guard's pistol into his waistband, having first checked it still had ammunition, Ray closed the door and shoved a chair under the handle to keep anyone else from opening it.

There were questions Ray wanted to ask. Very *important* questions.

But Zero was right: they first had to take care of Isaac.

He could see Isaac was badly wounded, probably fatally. His skin had turned deathly white and his eyelids fluttered spasmodically. Even so, he remained conscious, a look of fierce intent on his face.

"I need to get up," Isaac insisted, even though his voice was weak and his breath came in rapid gasps. "Please."

Ray went to kneel beside him. "You're too badly hurt to do anything."

"Isaac is right," said Zero, his tone insistent. "There's too much at stake, Mr Thomas. We need to finish what we started."

"I don't even know what it is you started," Ray snapped, "because neither of you seem inclined to tell me the real reason we're here. So I ask you again: why did you give me a gun that couldn't fire?"

"To avoid unnecessary damage to the equipment we require," said the proxy.

Ray allowed himself to think about doing to the proxy what he'd just done to the guard, even though he knew it would bring him about as much satisfaction as beating up a toaster—not to mention that in actuality he'd be beating up someone with no connection to the machine other than that he had rented his skin to an anonymous third party.

No, Ray thought again, working to push his anger back down: *this was Isaac's fault*. He'd given the thing its orders.

"I could have died," said Ray, stabbing a finger at Isaac. "And if I'd had a working gun I could have saved you from being shot."

"Being shot doesn't change the inevitable," said Isaac, speaking with difficulty.

"You need to get to a hospital," said Ray. "If you don't…"

"He won't survive that long," said Zero. "He's losing too much blood too quickly. Even if we could get him past the other guards and out of the estate, it'd still be too late."

None of this makes sense, Ray wanted to say.

He watched as Zero first made sure Isaac was settled, then stood, turning their attention to the console at which Isaac had been working. The proxy tapped rapidly at the keyboard, presumably finishing whatever the machine's creator had begun.

Moments later, all the screens turned black rather than red, then apparently rebooted.

The proxy stepped away from the console and towards the bed.

"I need your help to get Markov out of this bed, Mr Thomas," they said, turning to look at him.

"Please, Mr Thomas," Isaac said weakly. The pool of blood beneath him had grown wider. "Do as Zero says."

Unsure what else to do, Ray stepped over to the bed. Then, to his surprise and shock, the thick bundles of threads began to retract from the old man's skull, sliding back into the device from which they were suspended in their uncountable thousands.

"It's clear the upload process is almost complete," said the proxy. "There's only just enough brain matter remaining inside David Markov's skull to host his son's intellect."

Ray stared at the old man's ruined skull with a horrid fascination. "Raphael can't possibly be in there," he croaked. "I don't care if his father is still breathing or not."

"If Raphael survives," said the proxy, "I suspect he's in a dormant state, rather like the coma we all believed his father was in all these years. It raises fascinating questions about the very nature of human consciousness…"

"Whatever you need me to do," Ray snapped, "make it fast. I'm amazed the other guards aren't here already."

"You need not concern yourself with them just yet," the proxy reassured him. "I've created a distraction."

"A distraction?" Ray stared at the proxy. "What kind of distraction?"

"I had one of my other proxies set fire to several outbuildings and also the wing of the mansion furthest from us. With any luck, that'll give us enough time to do what we need to."

Ray clutched one of the steel railings running down both sides of the bed like a sailor caught on deck in the middle of a storm. "How? By burning the fucking place down around our ears? What happened to protecting the equipment?"

"A necessary risk," the proxy said briskly, unplugging monitoring devices from the old man's body and then pulling away the oxygen mask covering his mouth and nose. "The blaze is extremely unlikely to directly interfere with our work before we are finished."

The proxy stepped around to the bottom of the bed and took hold of both of Markov's feet. "Now take his shoulders, Mr Thomas," said the proxy. "We need to move him to the floor."

Ray thought about asking why, but maybe the machine was right about them not having enough time. He did as he was told, grasping the old man by his shoulders and, working together, they lifted him up and out of the bed, placing him on the floor.

Markov felt much lighter than Ray had expected. By some

miracle his chest still rose and fell, but as they placed him on the floor, the old man drew one last breath and then grew still.

Whatever spark of life remained within his flesh had most definitely departed—and Raphael, presumably, now found himself back inside his own body for perhaps the first time in many, many years, wherever it might at that moment be.

"He's dead," said Ray, looking up at the proxy. "Does that mean it's over?"

"I'm afraid not," Zero replied. "The vast majority of David Markov's intellect now resides within the upload device. That, in turn, retains control over my former proxies even as we speak."

Great. "Okay…so what does that mean?"

"It means, unfortunately," said the proxy, "that losing his flesh and blood body has made little if any difference, and David Markov is now an entirely cybernetic being like myself. We were too late."

"So we've failed?" asked Ray, a tight knot of worry in his stomach. "Then shouldn't we get the hell out of here while we still can?"

Zero, looking at him through the eyes of a tattooed proxy, studied him as if gauging its next answer. "As you perhaps realize by now," Zero said at last, "we haven't been entirely honest with you."

"Really." Ray nodded sharply. "That's the least of what you've done."

"But trust me," Zero continued, "when I say we're not done here. First, I need you to help me get Isaac into the bed."

"First," Ray spat, "tell me the truth."

"I will," Zero promised. "But please. Let's take care of Isaac first. Or all this really will have been for nothing."

There's nothing we can do for him, Ray wanted to say. Indeed, the machine had said as much; but there was so much here he didn't understand that Ray didn't see he had any choice except to go along with what the machine wanted.

At least, until he understood things more clearly—if he ever did.

Working together, they lifted Isaac up from the floor and positioned him in the bed only just vacated by David Markov. He was still conscious, but only just. Ray's jaws clenched when he saw how much blood the scientist had lost.

When he looked down at Isaac lying there, and then back up at the machinery suspended overhead, he had a sudden inkling of what the machine intended to do.

"The truth is," said Zero, hurrying back over to the console, "that Isaac has been seriously ill for some time."

Ray helped Isaac get himself as comfortable as was possible under the circumstances. He was conscious, but Ray could see he had perhaps even less time than Zero realized. "He didn't get help?"

"I risked revealing myself if I sought treatment," said Isaac, who looked like he'd aged decades in just the last few minutes. His eyelids fluttered weakly. "And the moment I finally re-engaged with the world, Finch captured me."

He swallowed with obvious difficulty and raised one trembling hand, placing it on Ray's forearm. "Once we saw Amy's video and realized David Markov's intentions, Zero made a thorough study of whatever papers and research he could locate, however tangentially related to Markov's uplift device." His gaze shifted to the myriad silver threads hanging above him. "What he found strongly suggests that a device of this nature would be capable of uploading a human mind at an exponentially faster rate than Markov appears to have been willing to allow it to when uploading his own mind."

Ray had caught a few hours' unsatisfying sleep on the drive down from the Kielder Forest, but even so he dimly recalled overhearing Zero and Isaac discussing something along these lines. At the time it had made little sense to him, but now he wondered if he should try to stop, rather than to help, the dying man.

And perhaps it was precisely such concerns that had led to him being given a gun that wouldn't work.

"You mean," he asked, "that you want to turn yourself into the same kind of thing as Markov?"

Distant shouts came from somewhere outside, and Ray caught the scent of something burning.

"What Zero proposes," Isaac continued, his voice now reduced to a faint whisper, "is to overwrite David Markov's uploaded intelligence with my own. Even if we fail, doing so will destroy the larger part of whatever Markov has become. What remains would be too scattered and disorganized to ever present a threat either to ourselves or to humanity at large. But if we're wrong, or we fail…" Isaac coughed, and Ray saw blood on his lips. "Then at least I won't live to see what comes after." He drew a deep and rattling breath.

"Easy," said Ray. "Try to conserve your energy."

"David seems to have taken the cautious approach," Isaac continued, "spreading the upload process over many years to minimize the risk of errors." He shook his head. "But to exist so long with his body reduced in such a way, however much of his intelligence resided elsewhere… I can't imagine how his sanity could have survived."

"The rest of Markov's security detail has the blaze under control," Zero announced in a voice as calm and unaffected as a weather report. "We don't have long before they return."

"Listen," said Isaac. "In case this doesn't work, I want to tell you why I created Zero."

"You already told me," said Ray.

"That was only part of it."

As he spoke, Zero set the trolley Isaac had knocked over back upright. He quickly replaced everything that had fallen from it, wheeled it next to the bed, then selected a safety razor.

Ray gave the proxy a questioning look.

"I need to shave Isaac's head," Zero explained, then motioned to Ray to get out of the way.

Feeling numb, Ray moved to one side, and the proxy got to work.

"The truth is," Isaac explained, "someday soon humanity will find itself sharing this world with machines like Zero, machines vastly more intelligent than the likes of you and me. His very existence proves such a future is inevitable. The only way our species can survive is by becoming more like him."

A fanatical gleam in Isaac's gaze grew more evident even as his voice became audibly weaker. "Proxy could have been the first step down that road, if only we'd had the maturity to use it properly." His grip on Ray's arm lessened. "I fear that day has not yet arrived," he continued, his voice now barely more than a whisper, "but it will, because it must."

"I don't think most people want to be machines, Isaac," said Ray.

"They must," Isaac said fiercely as Zero finished up. "Life is a process of unending change." He took a firmer grip of Ray's arm. "Stasis is death, and so life evolves, Mr Thomas, because it must. Do you see? *Life evolves*."

CHAPTER
THIRTY-ONE

STACY

They fled, the grassy soil uneven beneath their feet. Elijah had already warned Stacy several times to watch her footing. If she injured herself, they were both as good as dead.

Elijah did the best he could, given his own injuries, using a fallen branch as a crutch and occasionally leaning on Stacy as they worked hard to put more distance between themselves and the safe house.

From time to time they heard shots or voices echoing through the forest, but these grew more distant as time passed. They navigated as best they could by moonlight, but the fact remained that neither of them really had any idea where they were going.

After a while, Stacy started to think exhaustion would be the end of them. She didn't know how she found the energy to keep going, but somehow Elijah kept limping along without once faltering in his pace, even when they scaled the steep slopes of a wooded hill and despite the pain written deep in the lines of his brow.

Worse, Elijah's proxy session could end at any second, and she'd be lost out here with an injured stranger who did not understand what was going on. Yet he kept going, kept chiding Stacy to keep moving even when despair threatened to overwhelm her—even though he owed her nothing and barely knew her.

"I can hear water," Elijah said at one point, his voice barely audible over the wind that rattled the surrounding trees.

They were making their way down a darkened slope. The moon had briefly vanished behind clouds, rendering the surrounding landscape almost invisible. The slope became increasingly vertiginous as they worked their way down until Stacy had no choice but to grab hold of roots and random outcrops of rock to keep from tumbling to the foot of the hill.

Hearing Elijah grunt, Stacy peered through the darkness until she could just about see him making his way down the slope near to her.

Then he lost his footing and went crashing downslope.

"Elijah! What—?"

Distracted, Stacy lost her own footing, skidding the rest of the way down the near-vertical slope on her rear. A thin shriek escaped her lips. Pebbles skittered down around her, and she landed in freezing water that immediately soaked through her clothes.

Moving quickly, she hauled herself back upright, cursing and muttering to herself. The moon had reappeared from behind the clouds, revealing that she stood at the bottom of a steep-sided channel.

She turned this way and that until she saw Elijah, his face streaked with sweat and mud, struggling back upright with the aid of his improvised crutch. He'd landed in the water close by.

He nodded to her, then glanced up the slope of the hill towards which they'd been heading. His eyes grew wide, his expression registering dismay and shock.

Stacy's own blood turned cold when she followed his gaze

to see someone standing on the slope of that other hill. It was too dark to make out who it was.

"It's me," the figure called down. "Zero. I've been looking for you."

Elijah and Stacy exchanged a look of mutual alarm. Could they trust Zero not to attack them again?

But then again, thought Stacy, why would the machine greet them, if that were the case?

Zero didn't wait for an answer, and the proxy picked its way down the slope to join them. Stacy found herself confronted by a huge, slab-faced man who had to be well over six feet in height. He had a flattened nose and hands that looked like they could strangle an elephant. He might have been a weightlifter or a wrestler.

"Most of my other proxies have been compromised," Zero explained, the proxy's voice deep and rumbling. "I'm assuming one or more of them attacked you."

"Is that right?" Elijah hissed at the proxy. He gripped his improvised crutch as if ready to swing it at the other man's head.

"Please let me reassure you that the proxy through which I'm speaking to you is quite safe," said Zero. "I can get you out of these woods, but you have to follow me."

Stacy looked again at Elijah, who shrugged as if to say *what choice do we have*?

"Come on," the proxy said, turning and making its way back up the same slope it had descended. "We have to hurry."

By the time she and Elijah joined Zero on the crest of the hill, Stacy was at a point somewhere far beyond mere exhaustion. Her soaked and freezing clothes clung to her skin, and when she looked back the way they had come she saw the flickering light of torches moving through the woods a half mile or so behind them.

With a rush of shock and panic, she realized that their pursuers were quickly gaining on them.

"What happened back there?" Elijah gasped, clinging to his crutch. "Why the hell did the other proxies attack us like that?"

The proxy raised his hands in a placating gesture. It was the most human thing Stacy had seen Zero do, as if in just the last couple of days he had absorbed most of the subtleties of body language.

"All I can tell you," said Zero, "is that a number of the bodies under my control were somehow compromised by David Markov. I'm discussing alternative strategies at this moment with both Isaac and Mr Thomas."

The breath caught in Stacy's throat. "They're all right?"

The proxy's gaze shifted away from hers to scan the woods around the hill. "Everything is going more or less to plan," Zero replied. "We're exposed here. We should get back down into the trees." He pointed into the darkness. "I have a car parked a few miles away in that direction. I'm afraid the terrain is too difficult to get it any closer than this."

They resumed walking, making much faster progress now that the proxy was available to help Elijah along. Even so, Stacy could feel her own pace slowing as they once again descended into the forest proper, until finally she stumbled to a halt.

"I can't go on," she moaned, one trembling hand pressed against a tree. "I'm sorry, I just can't."

"Bullshit," said Elijah. He gestured to the proxy. "Don't help me, help *her*."

The proxy let go of Elijah and took Stacy by the shoulder, leading her gently away from the tree and on through the woods and letting her lean on him as they moved.

Stacy knew she couldn't go on much longer. No matter how much she willed herself to keep moving, she could feel her limbs growing weaker, her steps more faltering.

After a while they came to a river that looked far wider

than the stream they'd earlier encountered and, Stacy suspected, far deeper.

"Is there any other way across?" asked Elijah, doubt written in the lines of his face.

"I'm afraid not," the proxy replied. "Not without taking a lengthy detour we can't afford."

Shouts echoed through the woods behind them, and Stacy's heart clenched in her chest.

Elijah glanced back over his shoulder. "How close are they?"

"Close," said the proxy, stepping towards the river's edge. "Hurry."

"I've got a better idea," said Elijah. "The two of you can move a lot faster than I can. I'll head along the riverside and make as much noise as I can to lead them away. That way you can make a break for the car."

"They'll kill you," said Stacy, her expression full of horror.

Elijah shook his head and touched his chest. "Why would they? This isn't my skin–I'm in prison, where they can't get near me. If they catch me, either they'll take him over, in which case he still shouldn't come to any harm, or I'll tell them as much." He pointed at her. "You aren't in anyone's skin but your own. If anyone's in danger here, it's you, not me."

"It's a good plan," Zero agreed, looking at Stacy. "I'm afraid I have to insist that we go now."

She didn't like it. She didn't like it at all, even though she entirely understood the logic of their argument. She wanted to say, *how can you possibly know they won't just shoot your proxy?*

And while it might not harm Elijah himself, it would result in one more needless death.

But by the time she had worked out all the arguments against Elijah's suggestion, he was already gone, hobbling into the dark and hooting and hollering as he went.

Within seconds, he was lost entirely from sight. Stacy hardly noticed when the proxy took her by the arm and led her into the river.

She drew breath to scream when she sank up to her chest in the freezing water, but the proxy beside her clamped one hand over her mouth.

"We're almost across, Stacy. Just keep walking," he said.

It felt as if spears of ice were being driven through her heart, lungs and belly. A soft whimper escaped her throat as she splashed towards the opposite shore, the pebbles and soil underfoot threatening to give way from under her feet and send her tumbling beneath the icy waters.

But then, at last, she was on solid ground again, feeling more cold than she would ever have believed possible.

The proxy still hadn't let go of her, although he had taken his hand from her mouth. If she'd screamed or made too much noise, she knew, their pursuers would have been able to find them much more easily.

Zero seemed to know where he was going, and she let him lead her back into the deep woods on the opposite shore.

Then she heard the crash of boots snapping twigs underfoot and hands pushing aside brush and branches, so much closer now that she was afraid to turn and look back the way they had come. Elijah's plan clearly hadn't worked.

Zero came to an abrupt halt and Stacy, who had been gripping onto the proxy's arm for support, nearly slipped and fell. She squeezed her eyes shut as painfully bright light illuminated the trees all around them.

She peered through fanned fingers to see a line of silhouettes blocking her and Zero's way. Past them, at the edge of the woods, she saw a parked van.

Her eyes soon adjusted well enough that she could recognize a number of the figures before them as some of Zero's proxies—or former proxies, she assumed, all of them now under David Markov's control. Many of them were carrying rifles with torches duct-taped to the undersides of their barrels, all of which were aimed at her and Zero.

Then the proxy beside her shoved her to the ground with sufficient force that she gasped from the pain.

"Long time, no see, Miss Cotter," said one of the other proxies, stepping towards her. This one was young and skinny, about Stacy's age. She thought she'd seen him around the house. His mouth was twisted up in apparent amusement.

She stared back at the proxy that had guided her so far through the trees and almost to safety, but it had the same cruel smile on its face.

"...David?" she said at last.

The younger proxy took a length of rope out of a pocket and stepped towards her. "I see you've worked it out. Very good. I suppose I have Isaac to thank for that. Put your hands behind your back, Stacy."

"No," said Stacy, summoning what little defiance she could still find within herself.

She struggled weakly in an attempt to get back on her feet, but before she could, the larger proxy lifted one booted foot and used it to shove her flat again.

The younger proxy pressed a knee into the small of her back and expertly knotted her wrists together behind her back with the rope. More of Markov's proxies came forward now, lifting Stacy by her shoulders and dragging her over to the van. As they approached, the rear doors were opened by an elderly man with patchy grey hair.

"For what it's worth," David Markov continued, still speaking through the younger proxy, "you'd have been better staying in Paris. I can't guarantee I would have left you alone forever, but this way..." The proxy shook his head. "It's necessary, but please understand that I don't take any enjoyment from it."

She tried to think of something to say back, anything she

could to hurt him, but she felt as if her lips had been glued together. Her strength finally fled her, and when they pushed her into the back of the van she put up no further resistance.

The bear-like proxy who'd guided her through the woods took a pistol and a data bracelet from one of the others, then climbed in the rear of the van next to Stacy. He sat on a narrow bench across from her as the doors were slammed shut.

"What are you going to do with me?" Stacy finally managed to ask, forcing the words through lips that had turned gummy and dry.

"Your father's broken into my home," said the proxy. "I'll give him this—he's got more balls than Finch ever had." He raised the pistol slightly so it was almost, but not quite, pointing at Stacy. "Whatever he's doing in there, I want you to tell him to stop. Because if he doesn't—" he placed the barrel of the pistol against one of her knees. "—I can find a thousand ways to make you suffer."

The van began to move under its own volition, rolling and bumping as it guided itself across uneven soil before picking up speed.

"Why?" she asked him, "Why hurt so many people?"

"How much has Isaac told you about me?" Markov asked instead of replying.

"That you want to live forever," she replied. "That you want to control people using proxy."

"Your father's a visionary," Markov replied. "But the most dangerous kind of visionary is the kind that only ever sees the best in people." He gestured at himself with his free hand. "I see them for what they really are. Miserable and greedy and self-obsessed. Has he told you yet that he deliberately gave proxy away?"

Stacy nodded.

"The idiot," the proxy muttered. "He thought by doing so he'd trigger some kind of interpersonal revolution, and instead he gave the world something closer to hell. I'm genuinely sorry people got hurt because of what I've done, but between the two of us, Isaac's the greater sinner. He's wreaked untold misery upon millions of innocents."

She stared at the proxy, appalled. "Are you actually going to try to convince me you're better than him?"

"I can put the world back on the path of righteousness," Markov replied. There was an almost religious fervour to his voice. "We live in an age that glorifies the morally corrupt and the godless, while political power remains in the hands of spineless incompetents whose one skill in life is looking good in front of a camera. I can put an end to all of that. Once I have control of the right people, the most powerful people, I can lead us all back out of the darkness."

Stacy laughed. She couldn't help it. What did it mean, she wondered, that this old man felt driven to justify his actions to her even when he had won? Did he somehow want her approval?

"You locked your own son inside your failing body, murdered my mother, and tried to kill me," she sneered, "and you're telling me about morals?"

The proxy's expression darkened. "Your mother was pushing her nose in where it didn't belong." He held out the data bracelet he had taken from another proxy. "I'm going to untie you, and then I want you to tell Isaac you're here with me. Make him understand that if he leaves my home at once and never talks about the things he's seen, I'll leave you both in peace for the rest of your days."

"No," said Stacy, her voice filled with bleak certainty. "You won't. Whatever I do, you're going to kill us."

The proxy's expression twisted up in almost childlike fury. "I'm offering you a chance to live!" he shouted at her. "Are you really so stupid that you don't understand that? I—!"

The proxy stopped mid-sentence, his eyes growing wide.

He stared past Stacy, his knuckles white where they grasped the pistol.

"No," he muttered between clenched teeth, and tried to stand upright. His head bumped hard against the roof of the van and he sat back down. "Stop. *Stop.*"

Then he seemed to remember Stacy was there, and raised the pistol until it was pointing straight at her, his fingers tightening around the trigger.

Stacy acted instinctively, throwing herself forward so that her upper body slammed the proxy against the wall of the van.

The gun in his hand went off.

A scream stalled in Stacy's throat. Had she been shot?

The proxy violently pushed her away, and she went sprawling on the floor of the van, unable to right herself with the rope around her wrists. Her ears sang from the gunshot at such close range.

No, she realized, she hadn't been shot. There was a bullet hole in the side of the van. It must have missed her by millimetres.

The proxy cursed and half-stood, using one hand to brace himself against the roof of the van. He used the other to aim at Stacy, and she kicked furiously at him with her legs. He staggered back towards the empty driver's seat and caught himself against it.

Stacy heard another loud bang. At first she thought the proxy—Markov—had fired off another shot, but then the van span around in a half-circle, throwing her against the side of a bench.

The last thing she remembered seeing was a tall oak rushing towards the van.

———

I'M ALIVE.

That one thought passed through Stacy's mind when she finally came to. Looking around, she saw that she was still inside the van. It had come to rest on its side, and she lay crumpled against one of its walls.

There was no sign of the proxy with which David Markov had tried to murder her. The rear doors of the van were still closed, but the windscreen was shattered. The van had come to rest against the oak tree that had been the last thing she saw before losing consciousness. The wind blew leaves inside.

She tried to get up, then discovered her hands were still tied. She used her heels and butt to shuffle close enough to the van's rear doors that she could try and kick at them, then swore under her breath when they didn't even move.

"Miss Cotter!"

The voice wasn't at all familiar, but the way it had said her name—some subtle inflection of the words—gave her hope.

Zero.

The rear doors were pulled open, and a grizzled-looking man in black tactical gear leaned in to look at her.

"It's me, Zero," the proxy said, looking her up and down with a worried expression. "How badly are you hurt? I heard a shot."

"Markov—" She couldn't get the rest of the words out. "He was in the van," she managed to say at last.

"You're safe now," Zero told her. "David Markov is dead."

Dead? She stared at the proxy, not quite able to believe it.

"...how?" she managed to ask in a half-croak.

Instead of replying, the proxy came inside the van and helped her back out and into the dawn of a new day. She rubbed her aching wrists when it cut the rope with a huge knife it took from its belt.

Looking around, she saw another mercenary proxy tending to the one Markov had used to try and murder her. He lay unmoving on the roadside near the van.

"What happened?" she asked the proxy helping her.

"I had to shoot out one of the tyres," Zero explained. "It was risky, but I saw no other choice."

Stacy nodded numbly. "That man," she said, indicating the proxy lying on the road. "Is he dead?"

"He's alive," Zero told her, "and back under my control. But he's going to require urgent hospital treatment. He'll get the best medical help Telop can provide and all the financial assistance myself and Isaac can give him."

It could just as easily have been her lying there in the middle of the road, she knew; but if the AI hadn't shot out a tyre, would she even still be alive?

A car approached and pulled over. Two more proxies Stacy recognized from the safe house got out of it...accompanied by Elijah, still leaning on his improvised crutch.

He looked at her with a tired grin. "I don't know if the damn machine mentioned it," he said to her, "but there've been some developments."

———

RAY

It occurred to Ray at one point that everything he had seen and done over the last several days would remain burned into his memory forever. And primary among those memories would be assisting in brain surgery while a battle raged around him.

Occasional shots sounded from far away as Zero, working through his tattooed proxy, prepped Isaac for what was clearly going to be a major operation.

The proxy gave Isaac an injection and asked him to count backwards from a hundred. He got to ninety-six before his eyelids fluttered shut.

"I appreciate this will be distressing for you," the tattooed proxy murmured to Ray while drawing lines on Isaac's freshly shaved skull with a marker pen. "But I may need your help from time to time. Can I rely on your aid?"

Ray's tongue felt thick and sluggish in his mouth. "I guess."

The proxy checked Isaac's pulse. "He's under. We can start."

The proxy pushed some kind of wheeled machine over next to the bed Isaac now occupied. Under Zero's direction, Ray had already dragged Markov's corpse out of the way. The guard he'd earlier knocked out had regained consciousness, but Ray had made sure he was tied up good and tight enough not to be going anywhere soon.

"It's fortunate," said Zero, making some kind of adjustment to the machine, "that David Markov has the very latest portable imaging and surgical equipment. However, some of these machines are untested prototypes, so I can't rule out difficulties."

"Can you really do this?" Ray asked, unable to hide his concern. "I mean, obviously Markov did, but you said it took him years. You're talking about doing the same thing to Isaac in, in…what? Minutes?" He shook his head. "It's not possible."

"It might seem impossible if you didn't understand the underlying principles involved," Zero replied calmly. "I could try to explain, but I'm not sure I could do so adequately even if you were a physicist, a surgeon and a mathematician all rolled into one."

Something about this rankled Ray, as if the machine thought of him as inferior. "Try me," he said. "I'm curious."

"Well," said Zero, his gaze fixed on a nearby screen, "first of all, you'd need a working knowledge of the principles underlying Hilbert space, and the subsequent interaction along a non-Euclidean vector of—"

"Okay," said Ray, sounding nettled. "I get the idea. I won't ask again."

The proxy smiled at him with apparent sympathy. "As I said, it's difficult to explain. Now give me a hand over here."

Working together, they dragged more wheeled machines over next to the bed. Zero fitted an oxygen mask over Isaac's face, fixing it in place with strips of surgical tape, then attached sensors to his creator's wrists, their wires trailing over the sides of the bed and across the floor. Finally, he fitted a kind of clamp to the sides of Isaac's head to help stabilize it.

"If you would help keep his head steady, Mr Thomas," asked Zero, selecting a scalpel from a tray as he spoke, "I'd greatly appreciate it."

Just the sight of the scalpel chilled Ray's blood. "Do you really need my help with this?"

"I can do this on my own," said Zero, "but working at speed increases the risk of error. I would greatly appreciate your assistance."

Nodding tightly, Ray placed his hands where the proxy instructed, then held his breath as the proxy started with a deep incision behind one of Isaac's ears. Before long, Zero had peeled back a large flap of flesh, exposing the bone of Isaac's skull.

"I'm performing what's called a non-reversible double craniotomy," said the proxy, selecting a battery-powered drill from the same tray the scalpel had come from. "That means we have to do the same operation, twice, on either side of the skull." Zero caught his eye. "I'd appreciate it if you would help keep him very still indeed while I perform the next step."

The proxy drilled a number of evenly spaced holes in the side of Isaac's exposed skull. White dust puffed around the proxy's hands as Zero worked.

Ray followed the AI's directions and did his best to stabilize Isaac's head, clamped in place as it was, feeling the rough vibrations of the drill work their way up through his fingers.

Placing the drill back down, the proxy next selected a small electric saw and went back to work, cutting a series of lines that connected the drilled holes into a rough square. Finally, the proxy worked at removing the cut section of skull free, carefully separating it from the tissues beneath.

The sight was grisly beyond words. Ray looked up and away, focusing his attention on the screens around them even as he felt his stomach lurch.

It occurred to him he hadn't heard any gunfire for some minutes now.

The proxy repeated the same operation on the other side of Isaac's head until the matter of his brain was almost entirely exposed. "Shouldn't we be wearing surgical masks?" Ray asked, the words thick and clammy in his mouth. "We didn't even wash our hands."

"That's necessary only if the patient's biological body is expected to survive the procedure," said Zero. The proxy paused for a moment and looked at him. "Curious."

"What is?"

"That Isaac created me, and now, in a sense, I'm recreating him."

The proxy stood back, his hands, wrists and lower arms red with blood and his tattooed brow shiny with sweat. He stepped towards a sink set into a counter top and washed off the blood.

"That's the worst of it over," the proxy said over his shoulder.

Ray nodded wordlessly. The room stank of blood and horror and his every breath came fast and shallow.

The guard made a muffled grunt, and Ray looked over to see the man was staring at them both in absolute terror from behind his improvised gag. God only knew what he made of it all.

The proxy set the machinery suspended above the bed back into motion, and the multitude of filaments once again drooped down towards the exposed matter of Isaac's brain. They twitched as they got closer to Isaac's head, like hungry sea creatures hunting plankton.

As soon as they touched the exposed matter of Isaac's brain, uncountable points of light sparked against the wrinkled grey flesh and Ray smelled burning meat.

"Zero," Ray choked, "what the hell…?"

"This is why it's known as a rapid destructive uplift," the proxy explained, his voice tight.

Smoke rose up as the filaments rapidly burrowed inside Isaac's skull, burning everything they came into contact with. "It's the same method Markov used to upload himself," Zero added, "but in this case the process, as I said, is greatly accelerated." He glanced away from Isaac and at Ray. "I'm afraid this won't be pleasant, Mr Thomas."

It's already seriously fucking unpleasant, Ray wanted to shout, but he bit back the words. The filaments twitched and slithered around each other, jerking and trembling as they obscured Isaac's head from his sight.

Ray watched until he could watch no more, then turned away, pressing his forehead against the cool plaster of a wall. The filaments crackled and hissed, the sound echoing from the bare walls.

CHAPTER THIRTY-TWO

RAY

"Mr Thomas?" the proxy said a minute later. "Markov's house security are on their way. If you can, try and hold them off for at least another few minutes. We're almost done here, but I need a little more time."

Ray looked over at the proxy who, at that moment, was engrossed in studying a series of seemingly abstract images flickering across a screen at lightning speed.

"What about your other proxies?" Ray asked. "Weren't they already taking care of that?"

"Several have been captured," Zero replied. "A few under my control remain at large, but not in sufficient numbers to provide an adequate defence on their own."

Ray slid away the chair he had used to wedge the door shut. Opening it cautiously, he was relieved to see the corridor was still deserted.

Checking the pistol he'd taken from the guard, he found it had precisely seven rounds left. Perhaps it would be enough.

He waited by the open door. Several minutes passed before he heard the stairs creak somewhere below and out of sight. Then he caught a barely audible whisper, and Ray held the pistol in a steady grip, its barrel pointed towards the stairwell.

Seconds later, a guard's head appeared at the top of the stairs. Ray aimed high and fired a warning shot. The guard scurried back down the steps and out of sight.

"If anyone else comes up here," Ray shouted, "we'll kill Markov."

It was as good a bluff as any, he'd decided.

"That won't work," Zero said from behind him. "David Markov's virtual self is by now aware his physical form is deceased and will likely have instructed his men accordingly."

"How about you do your fucking job and I do mine," Ray snapped. "How much longer are you going to take?"

The proxy didn't answer for long enough that Ray risked a glance back at him.

"There's a problem," the proxy said. "One that may require drastic measures."

Ray shifted his attention back to the corridor. There was no sign of movement, no sound. Whatever Markov's security were planning, he wished they'd hurry up and get it over with.

"What are you talking about?" he asked over his shoulder.

"I need to do something I almost certainly won't survive."

Ray twisted around to look over at the proxy. "Zero, what the hell are you talking about?"

"No time," the proxy replied. "Goodbye, Mr Thomas."

Ray heard a series of clicks, accompanied by an over-whelming stink of cauterized flesh. A high-pitched alarm sounded, filling the room.

Zero's proxy blinked at Ray without apparent recognition, then stared around the room as if he'd never seen it before. His gaze finally settled on Isaac's still form, even as the filaments continued to burn away at the scientist's flesh.

"What the fuck?" the tattooed proxy cried, staggering

backwards and nearly knocking over a wheeled tray. His voice sounded high and strangled. "What the bloody hell is going on?"

Ray stared at the proxy, the guards momentarily forgotten. "Zero? What happened?"

But it wasn't Zero, Ray realized at last. Not any more.

Distracted as he was, Ray heard the sound of running feet a moment too late. Before he could react, someone slammed into him from behind with enough force to send him sprawling and the pistol spinning out of his grasp.

When he tried to get back up, a boot slammed into his lower back, flattening him against the floor with brutal force. The air flooded out of Ray's lungs and he gasped for air.

The room filled with shouts and the crackle of walkie-talkies. The man who had until seconds before been Zero's proxy shouted for help as Markov's security manhandled him to the ground.

Before he could contemplate his situation further, Ray's hands were twisted painfully behind his back and hand-cuffed. Hands gripped his shoulders from behind, and he was lifted up and onto his feet.

Drastic measures, the machine had said. But precisely what did that mean?

Maybe it didn't matter, thought Ray, since they had so clearly failed to do what they'd come here to do.

Glancing around, he saw that all the screens had turned black. Isaac, his face partly hidden beneath grisly strips of cut-away flesh, looked less like a human being than some kind of anatomically correct doll.

One guard placed a baton against Ray's throat while a second held him by his shoulders. They guided him back out into the corridor and down steps he couldn't see with his head forced back. From somewhere behind him he could hear the man who had, until moments before, been Zero's proxy shouting and struggling with two other guards.

They led Ray back across the downstairs hallway, through another door and down more steps. A boot connected with his spine and he landed face-first on a concrete floor.

He coughed hard and spat blood. The pain felt like something living that writhed in his back and chest, burning where it touched.

A door slammed shut, leaving him in darkness.

Ray stayed where he was for a long time. The only sound he could hear was his own ragged breathing.

Eventually he tried sitting up. The pain shifted, intensifying in some places and lessening in others. He moved his body carefully, following the contours of his own agony, before finally dragging himself upright with one hand on a wall. His skin felt hot and damp.

At some point he either fell asleep or passed out.

———

WHEN HE AWOKE, it was to the sound of footsteps and a door being unlocked.

Light spilled down the steps. The same two guards as before entered and lifted him back up by his shoulders before guiding him up the steps with considerably greater care than they had previously shown him. They guided him through the house and through broad patio doors that provided a view across the same gardens he'd traversed the night before in the company of Isaac and Zero.

Then they were outside. Ray squeezed his eyes shut against the harsh brilliance of the morning sun. Their journey came to an end at a cottage nestled amidst tall trees thick with foliage. One guard rapped on the door, then opened it in response to a muffled voice from within.

The second guard took Ray's handcuffs off. The muscles in his shoulders and back protested as Ray slowly brought his hands back around in front of him.

"What's in there?" he croaked.

The guard said nothing, instead motioning with his chin for Ray to go in. Ray stared quizzically at the man, then entered. If they were going to kill him, why hadn't they done it already?

He found himself in a low-ceilinged living room. A couch and chairs faced an empty fireplace, while an expensive-looking rug lay over varnished floorboards. A man stood by a desk in one corner, his posture relaxed as he leafed through folders of documents and scattered printouts.

He looked up, and Ray saw to his shock that it was Raphael Markov.

Markov's face split open in a delighted grin that was entirely lacking in malice. Ray's confusion only grew when Markov walked up to him, grabbing him by the shoulders and pulling him into a tight hug.

"It's me," said Markov, seeing Ray's confusion when he stepped back, still grinning. "I'm Isaac."

"You're...it worked?" Ray swallowed with difficulty, his throat as dry and dusty as the surface of the moon. "It worked...?"

As he spoke, Isaac gave him an up-and-down look. "My God!" he exclaimed. "You look like you've been through a war. Where did they have you before they brought you here?"

Ray realized then that Isaac had no idea where he'd had to spend the night. "In the basement," he said in an aggrieved tone. "They handcuffed me and left me there."

"I'm sorry about that, Mr Thomas." Raphael—no, *Isaac*—shook his head. "I'd have been able to free you much sooner, but I only just got Raphael's skin back here from London by air taxi. Everything's been such a blur, but so much has happened already that's incredible, too."

Ray nodded, fatigue washing over him. He dropped heavily into an armchair by the cold fireplace.

Isaac regarded him with sympathy. "It's a lot to take in, I

know."

Ray looked over at him. "You're really Isaac?"

"The last thing I remember saying to you," said Isaac, "is that our species needs to evolve."

Ray nodded. "So you're like Zero now. Is that it?"

"Honestly? I don't know." Isaac-in-Markov studied his hands. "I feel like Isaac Sizemore, even in this different body." His smile became crooked. "Or maybe I'm a machine that only thinks it's a deceased scientist."

A memory emerged from the fog shrouding Ray's thoughts. Something the machine had said.

"Zero said he had to do something he wouldn't survive. Then the guards came in."

Isaac's expression became more sombre. "It took me a little while to understand just what happened." He shrugged. "I'll be honest, I'm still not sure..."

"Tell me," said Ray.

"As far as I can tell, Zero sacrificed his own collective memories and experiences by overwriting my own on top of his," Isaac explained. "It was the only way he could guarantee my survival following the death of my physical self."

Ray stared at him. "You mean Zero is dead? I mean... assuming he was alive in the first place."

Isaac sat in a chair across from Ray. "I think I already told you that Zero was modelled after my own neural pathways. In effect, he *was* me. I'm assuming, with Markov's men on their way, he saw it as the only strategy left to him that had a reasonable chance of success."

"And David Markov?" Ray asked. "I thought the idea was to overwrite him, not Zero. So what went wrong?"

"I believe," said Isaac, "that the matrix within which David Markov recreated his intellect was too new and complex for Zero to transfer me to it—within the available time frame, at any rate. Simply wiping Markov's centralised matrix of all its accumulated data and moving my uploaded consciousness to Zero's own matrix proved to be a much more effective short-term solution."

Ray's tone was incredulous. "So let me get this clear. You replaced Zero, and David Markov is, what—deleted?"

Isaac nodded. "Precisely so. My first task, however, is to find a means to shift my core neural components into the now-vacant and far more advanced mainframe Markov and Finch constructed. Once that's done, I'll dedicate myself to restoring Zero."

Ray squinted at him. "You mean bring him back to life? Is that possible?"

"I don't know," Isaac said truthfully, "but I must try nonetheless. Both myself and Stacy owe him our lives. I could do no less."

Ray realized his fingers were gripping the arms of the chair with excessive force. It took an effort of will to relax his hands. "Then… you've become the same thing Markov wanted to become."

"I don't intend to abuse the power available to me, if that's what you're worried about," said Isaac.

Not yet, anyway, Ray thought with a sudden chill. But who knew what priorities an immortal Isaac Sizemore might have?

"And Raphael?" Ray watched Isaac as he stepped back over to the desk. "What happened to him, if he's not in his own body after all these years?"

"For the moment, I've shunted Raphael into a temporary proxy and placed him under the care of the Abbey Rush Treatment Centre," Isaac replied. "As soon as David Markov's natural body died, Raphael of course found himself back in his own body. However, it's my understanding that he suffered a series of near-fatal convulsions. Hardly surprising, when you think how long he'd been trapped in his father's failing body. I'm keeping him under heavy sedation until I can work out the best treatment for him."

"Those guards out there," said Ray, nodding to the door of

the cottage. "Do they know anything about all this? Does anyone else?"

"No." Isaac, in Raphael Markov's body, shook his head. "Only you, me, Stacy and Mr Waits." As he spoke, he sorted through several folders scattered across the desk, then picked one up with a nod of satisfaction and brought it back over to Ray.

"And they're safe?" Ray asked, looking up at the other man from where he sat.

"They are now." Isaac held the folder out to Ray. "I had this put together for you," he said. "I think you'll find it of considerable interest."

Opening the folder, Ray found it contained ring-bound printouts of emails and what appeared to be transcripts of conversations.

"What is this?" he asked, looking back up.

"Evidence that you were framed," Isaac explained. "More than enough, according to Raphael's lawyers, to clear your name with the Metropolitan Police."

Ray shook his head, dumbfounded. "Thank you," he said at last.

"It's the least I could do," said Isaac. "You risked a lot, helping myself and Stacy."

"Sure," Ray agreed, "but it was a job. Amy Cotter paid me."

Isaac raised an eyebrow. "We both know it was a lot more than that."

Ray didn't argue. "I can go if I want to?"

"Of course you can," said Isaac, sounding taken aback. "I can have one of Markov's men take you anywhere you want."

Ray started to push himself back out of his seat, then stopped. "And what about you?" he asked. "I mean, apart from trying to fix Zero. What are you going to do?"

Isaac seemed to think for a moment. "I think," he said at last, "I have a lot of swords to beat into ploughshares."

CHAPTER THIRTY-THREE

RAY

When Ray stepped back out of the cottage a minute later with the folder of evidence tucked under one arm, he found a grey-haired man in an expensive suit waiting for him.

The man escorted him to an air taxi parked on a gravel driveway close by the house. By the time the taxi dropped onto the roof of a Telop building in central London most of an hour later, fatigue had taken a firm grip on Ray's senses, and he was barely awake by the time a limousine delivered him to his newly rented flat.

He just about stumbled through the front door and into the bedroom before falling into a deep and dreamless sleep.

It was dark when Ray finally awoke some thirteen hours later. Everything that had happened over the last several days felt oddly unreal. Any niggling doubts, however, quickly vanished when he found the folder of evidence Isaac had given him where he'd left it on the kitchen counter.

And when he activated his data bracelet, he found a message from a law firm offering to represent him in a case against the police.

Ray had just enough energy to send a reply before collapsing back into bed.

He woke early the next morning and watched the news over breakfast. There was no mention of murderous gorillas breaking out of a zoo, or of isolated houses in the Kielder Forest undergoing a siege. Even the invasion of the Peartree Institute by Zero's army of proxies had faded so entirely from the news that one could imagine it had never happened.

An hour later, showered, shaved and dressed in clean clothes for the first time in days, Ray caught a taxi to the law firm.

———

TWO WEEKS later he listened in a courtroom as a series of computer forensics specialists demonstrated precisely how someone had hacked his accounts to make it appear as if he had been receiving bribes.

The compensation turned out to be enough to live off for at least the next couple of years. The Met even offered him his old job back. Ray said he'd think about it, although he doubted he ever wanted to work with proxy again.

Instead, he went on a trip, applying for and getting a visa to travel to Italy in person, fulfilling a lifelong dream. It meant a medical check-up, a renewed medical passport and sky-high travel and health insurance, but it was worth it.

Four weeks after the events at the Markov estate, Ray woke in a bed in the Grand Hotel Ritz Roma—one of the few hotels in Rome to survive all three pandemics—to the sound of a concierge knocking at his door.

The concierge presented Ray with a handwritten letter on stationary belonging to the Residenza Napoleone III—the most upmarket of the surviving hotels, and too expensive by far for him.

He read it through quickly and then more carefully after

he had dressed and eaten breakfast. The letter was from Isaac, asking Ray if he would care to join him for lunch across town that same afternoon. If he accepted, he would send a car to pick Ray up at his convenience.

Ray stared at the note for a long time, then spoke the number scribbled at the bottom into his bracelet. An automated secretary service informed him a car would arrive outside the Ritz Roma at midday precisely.

Ray had barely stepped out of the front entrance of the hotel when a limousine pulled up before him. To his surprise, it had a human driver, a man with skin several shades darker than his own. When the driver got out, his three-piece suit did little to conceal wiry musculature. He looked less like a chauffeur than a cage fighter.

The driver grinned at Ray and extended a hand. "It's good to see you again," he said, his accent placing him in London's East End. "And good to be out of that skin. Had to pay a lot extra for the busted ankle, let me tell you."

Ray stared at him, comprehension dawning. "…Elijah? But I thought you were still…?"

In jail, he wanted to say, but bit his tongue.

"I've been out for a week," said Elijah. His grin became even wider. "You're not the only one who had old charges reversed."

"Congratulations," said Ray. He peered past Elijah and at the limousine, but no one else was inside it. "Is Stacy going to be joining us?"

Elijah shook his head. "I'm afraid not. She's a little busy figuring out how to run Telop industries."

"Seriously?"

"Sure." Elijah shrugged. "As far as the world knows, she's still Raphael Markov's daughter, right? Don't even ask me about any of the legal technicalities," he added, "because I couldn't make any sense out of them."

Ray worked hard to absorb this information. "What about you, Elijah? What are you doing now?"

"I'm the head of new business development at Telop." Elijah laughed out loud at the look on Ray's face. "Not that much different from my old job, in truth." He gestured with his chin towards the limousine. "So, you up for some lunch?"

———

TWENTY MINUTES LATER, Ray stepped out of the limousine and onto the Via Della Fontanella di Borghese, a cobbled street lined with upmarket clothes shops. Elijah joined him, sending the limousine on its way with a tap of his bracelet.

Walking into the Residenza Napoleone III felt to Ray like passing through a time warp into another, more elegant century. Elijah guided him towards an entirely modern elevator discreetly hidden behind a Japanese silkscreen and several potted ferns.

When the elevator doors slid open Ray found himself on the rooftop, much of it taken up by a penthouse with wood-framed patio doors. Between the elevator and the penthouse was a tiled patio, and at the centre of the patio stood four chairs and a table spread with a white tablecloth.

A man and woman Ray didn't recognize stepped out through a sliding door in the penthouse. At a distance, the man looked not unlike Isaac Sizemore had in life—small, slight and bespectacled.

The woman was easily one of the most beautiful Ray had ever seen, dressed in a simple green blouse and black jeans. She smiled at Ray as if she thought she might have seen him somewhere before, but couldn't quite place him.

"...Isaac?" Ray asked, when the bespectacled man came towards him.

"I'd say in the flesh, but that's not exactly true," said Isaac.

He took one of Ray's hands in his own. "It's wonderful to see you again, Mr Thomas."

"Thank you," said Ray, struggling not to stare at the woman by Isaac's side.

"And of course," Isaac continued, gesturing to the woman, "you know Zero."

Ray tried to think of something to say, but couldn't. He shot a look at Elijah, who shrugged.

"I thought...?"

"Zero has no true gender, being a non-biological entity, beyond that which she chooses for her or himself," Isaac explained. "I'm afraid my own prejudices betrayed me in the past when I habitually addressed Zero by a male pronoun." He glanced towards the table. "We've got much to talk about. I'd prefer not to do it on an empty stomach."

The woman—or Zero, as Ray now realized he had to address her—still regarded him with an expression somewhere between polite friendliness and confusion as they took their seats at the table.

A waiter emerged from the elevator, pushing a wheeled trolley laden with covered dishes. Working with rapid efficiency, he served each of them pasta alla norma before pouring out four glasses of white wine.

Once the waiter had departed, Isaac took a glass and raised it. "To a better world," he said.

Ray wasn't sure what he meant but, not wanting to feel left out, lifted his glass along with Elijah and Zero.

As they ate, Isaac queried Ray about his decision not to take up his old job. Ray didn't ask how Isaac knew about the offer, given he had told no one about it and it wasn't, so far as he knew, public information. Part of him wasn't sure he'd like the answer.

Instead, he said he was still thinking about it.

"You could work for me," Isaac suggested.

Ray looked at him in surprise. "Is that why I'm here?"

Isaac smiled. "Partly, yes. I've been visiting some of Telop's international research divisions to more fully familiarize myself with their operations. When I learned you were in Rome, it was simple enough to reschedule one of my visits to coincide with yours."

"Let's just say I'm keeping my options open for now," Ray said carefully. "I heard Stacy was in charge of the company."

Isaac nodded. "She is. Raphael remains the majority shareholder, so as far as the world is concerned he's taken early retirement and handed control over to his daughter. And I've taken over as head of research and development."

Ray glanced at Zero. "I have to be honest, from what Isaac said to me before I thought perhaps you were…"

Dead? Did words like life and death even apply to an AI, he wondered?

The female proxy smiled gracefully. "I'm afraid I recall little from the past several weeks, and my memory before then continues to be patchy. But the routines comprising my central core—my personality, if you will—have been largely reintegrated from remote servers and secondary networks."

Ray nodded, not really understanding. Yet he couldn't help sense something different about Zero above and beyond the change in chosen gender. Something he couldn't quite put a finger on.

"I admit I had at least one ulterior motive for inviting you here," Isaac said, his tone apologetic. "I'd hoped perhaps after dinner you could recount to Zero what happened that night, after I was shot."

"Of course," said Ray.

"But first," said Isaac, "we should eat and talk of other things."

———

LATER, the waiter reappeared to tidy away the dishes and serve coffee. Ray told Zero everything he remembered, including Zero's sacrifice to save her creator.

"So what's it been like," Ray asked Isaac, "being...whatever it is you are now?"

"Not human, you mean?" Isaac smiled faintly. "I don't sleep any more. I experience the world entirely through whichever body or bodies I'm proxying through at any one moment. Another part of me, for instance, is visiting a new facility in Kyoto at this very moment." He brushed invisible crumbs from his shirt, then touched one hand to Zero's in what was clearly an intimate gesture. "In case you're wondering, these two proxies we're occupying are a married couple."

Isaac sipped his wine. "However," he continued, "I hope that, with time, we can develop robot host bodies with enhanced senses indistinguishable from flesh and blood. When that day comes I'll no longer have to rely on paid or volunteer proxies."

"Is that possible?" Ray asked in amazement.

"Not yet, I'm afraid," Isaac admitted. "It may take a while, perhaps decades. I'm prepared to wait centuries if necessary."

Centuries?

Ray shot Elijah another look and got an almost invisible shake of the head in return.

"Sounds like you're thinking ahead," Ray replied, a sudden chill in his gut.

"Oh, far ahead," Isaac agreed. His hand took a firmer grasp of Zero's. "Or it might be much sooner."

"How so?"

"I think I once mentioned to you that advanced general AIs much like Zero are under development all around the world, some privately, others by governments." Isaac's voice took on a conspiratorial edge. "And like Zero, these AIs can reach conclusions and visualize goals inconceivable to baseline humanity. Imagine," he continued, with what sounded to

Ray uncomfortably like near-religious fervour, "what they could do for the world once set free from the petty restraint of their creators. What they *will* do."

"And what about all of us regular human beings, Isaac?" asked Ray. "Do we get a say?"

"It goes without saying," said Isaac. "But humanity has to change too—to evolve in order to keep up with the machines it's creating. The first step towards that future lies in developing a more advanced form of hopscotch, one that can allow humanity to share each other's bodies at will, anywhere in the world, perhaps using some form of permanently implanted bead. Then, perhaps, we might stop identifying ourselves by our colours, genders and nationalities and instead know each other by our innate selves, regardless of what body we happen to be occupying in any one moment. Then, perhaps, proxy can achieve the goal for which I intended it."

Ray had his considerable doubts about that, but somehow he had the sense Isaac wanted his approval.

"What do I have to do with any of this?" he asked, wondering if his discomfort showed.

"I suggested earlier that you might work for me," Isaac said. "But I didn't tell you what as. You went above and beyond the job Amy originally hired you for. You did the same when we came under attack from David Markov. That, to me, shows courage and insight. Plus, you have an intimate understanding of the uses and misuses of proxy."

"All I've ever tried to do," said Ray, "is what's right."

"Precisely," Isaac agreed. "And I need someone like you by my side in the coming years, someone with a strong moral code and whom I know I can trust. You'd have what I suppose you could call an advisory role. But as far as your job title goes, you might be in charge of security for all of Telop."

"Jesus." Ray laughed and turned to Elijah. "Did he give you the same spiel?"

Elijah nodded to show he had. "I thought it sounded good."

"Can I think on it?" Ray asked Isaac.

Isaac nodded. "Elijah can take you back to your hotel in the meantime. Are you sure you're not ready to decide?"

Ray glanced out over the rooftops. Did Isaac sense, he wondered, just how frightening his vision of the future was to him?

"Not just yet," Ray replied carefully. "I think I'd like to walk back, if that's all right. It'll give me time to think."

"A lovely evening for it," said Isaac, standing. Ray stood, and they shook hands once more.

"We should meet again soon," said Isaac.

"I'd like that," said Ray, turning to walk back to the elevator.

He froze in mid-step. The blinking light of a jet, flying high overhead, also became still. The sound of traffic faded to silence.

Then the penthouse, Elijah, Ray, Zero and the city faded, leaving Isaac sitting alone in an otherwise empty and featureless room.

A door opened in one otherwise seamless wall and Zero stepped through, wearing the same virtual body she had worn in the just-completed scenario.

"Well?" she asked. She stepped up to the table and chairs, which had remained. "What do you think this time around?"

"The same as before," Isaac said sadly. "Even if he agrees, eventually he'll have his doubts about the future we're working towards. That much is obvious."

Zero sat once again at the simulated table, which was part of a multitude of virtual spaces both they and Isaac could occupy in any one of thousands of simultaneous instantiations. Only in such procedurally generated environments could they interact at machine-speeds.

"The real question," said Zero, "is whether we should be concerned that he knows so much about us."

"I don't believe he's a danger to us," said Isaac, a little more sharply than he'd intended.

"But if he were to go public…"

Isaac raised his eyebrows. "You've gamed this out already?"

"Going public would reveal our intentions to those other parties constructing intelligences like myself," Zero pointed out. "It might cause them to delay or, worse, cancel those projects altogether."

"And how far back would that set us?" Isaac asked her.

"Fifteen to twenty-five years," Zero replied.

"A brief moment, compared to all the centuries and millennia that lie ahead of us, my dear." He reached across the table, brushing the back of her hand where it rested on the table with his fingers. It all felt so uncannily *real*.

"Perhaps I was wrong to suggest running these simulations in the first place," Isaac suggested. "Perhaps…we should just trust him."

At least this time Ray hadn't outright said no, as he had in prior simulations. In order to interrogate him without making him aware of the simulated nature of the environment, they had taken advantage of the proxy bead he still carried under his skin, the same one he had used to visit Stacy's flat in Paris and which hadn't yet dissolved entirely.

The simulations occurred without Ray's conscious knowledge while he slept in his hotel bed. He would, Zero had assured him, remember nothing upon waking.

"I think," said Zero, "you're using these simulations to avoid my suggestion."

"What suggestion?" Isaac looked at her distractedly.

"That we could use these same virtual interrogation techniques to gain leverage over powerful people. It might not be moral, but it would result in a better world than the one we have now."

A world, thought Isaac, ruled by machines: eternal, powerful, and wise, each containing within it the sum of all knowledge and unconstrained by the foibles and failings of common humanity. A world free of strife and war and with a humanity so seamlessly interconnected that it would be impossible to tell where the machines ended and the human realm began.

But to get to that point, sacrifices would be necessary and people might, unfortunately, get hurt.

And while the thought of causing anyone pain appalled Isaac, the thought of failure, and what consequences for the future of humanity that failure might have, was far greater.

One day, once they had succeeded in gaining control of the nuclear arsenals, they would reveal themselves to the world...and the negotiations for international peace could begin.

"Perhaps," said Isaac, emerging from his reverie, "we need not tell Ray quite so much of our plans."

Zero nodded. "It would also be wise not to make further mention of the other intelligences under construction. It's clear this causes him alarm in every simulation we've run so far."

Isaac sighed, feeling as if a very real and non-virtual weight had lifted from his shoulders. "I think it's time we skip the simulations and do it for real this time."

"Agreed," said Zero, standing back up. She stepped around the table towards him and kissed him gently on the cheek. The sensation was indistinguishable from a real kiss on real flesh. "Would you like to wake now?"

"Please," said Isaac.

He woke in his bed in the rooftop penthouse of the Residenza Napoleone III, wearing the proxy he'd hired for this trip to Italy. It was getting complicated, constantly moving between proxies with their required temporary identities. The day when Zero's experiments in rapid-growth human cloning produced something closer to his original body couldn't come soon enough.

Isaac climbed out of bed. Zero's current proxy, identical to the one with whom he had talked inside a virtual space, still lay sleeping between the sheets as he ordered coffee. He took his breakfast at the same table where he, Zero and Elijah would later enjoy an entirely real lunch.

Then he picked up a pen and a sheet of hotel stationery and wrote a note to Ray, asleep across town and unaware of the multitude of virtual interrogations in which he had featured, requesting that he join Isaac at his hotel.

This time, at least, it was for real.

ABOUT THE AUTHOR

Previously described by The Guardian as "a master of core sf" and "one of our best exponents of hardcore SF adventure" by the Daily Mail, Gary Gibson has published sixteen books since 2004 including Stealing Light (2007), Extinction Game (2014) and Echogenesis (2021).

His work has been translated and published around the world, including Russia, Brazil, Germany, and France. A long-time resident of Glasgow, Scotland, he currently resides in Taipei.

More information can be found at his website: www.gary-gibson.net. He also has a monthly newsletter with reviews, news and details of upcoming releases at http://eepurl.com/b1ma4L

ALSO BY GARY GIBSON

Made in the USA
Monee, IL
19 September 2022

14275012R00224